CONTINUANCE

A NOVEL
by
j. Newcombe Hodges

CONTINUANCE

Copyright © 2009 by j. Newcombe Hodges

All rights reserved. No part of this book may be reproduced or transmitted in any form or by any means without written permission of the author.

This is a work of fiction based largely on technical facts and interviews. Names, characters and incidents are products of the author's imagination or are used fictitiously. Any resemblance to actual persons, living or dead is entirely coincidental – unless otherwise noted.

ISBN: 978-1-44868619-3

Redwood Press

ACKNOWLEDGMENTS

I am indebted to members of various organizations, agencies and private individuals within varied fields of expertise, for their valued input and support of this book.

I am especially thankful for the creative, philosophical and technical insights of Dr. Jack Leissring, Mr. Turner, Mr. Jones and Pedro. This manuscript delves into the covert operations of many Visibility scenarios, as well as the reckless minds of those whom possess this knowledge and the frightening technology at their disposal to change the course of human continuance.

Enormous gratitude goes to Nancy Gotwalt and E. J. Howe for their meticulous editorial and expressional efforts on this story.

I would like to thank those who can not be mentioned for bringing to my readers a layman's understanding of the varied technologies employed for obtaining information on every human occupant of this world. And the technology that awaits us.

The deepest of thanks go to Tribal Elder Ralph Burns, of the Kooyooe Tukaddu People, for his knowledge of the Paiute People's past and insight into the future of Mother Earth and *all* life forms which depend on her.

And finally, a nod and a wink; to those who know the truth.

CONTINUANCE
j. Newcombe Hodges

CONTINUANCE

BOOK ONE
THE MUSHROOM FARMS

"He also forced everyone, small and great, rich and poor, free and slave, to receive a mark on his right hand or on his forehead, so that no one could buy or sell unless he had the mark, which is the name of the beast or the number of his name. This calls for wisdom. If anyone has insight, let him calculate the number of the beast, for it is man's number. His number is 666."

Revelation 13:16-18

"The higher you climb, the farther you will see. If you can reach the stars, you will see tomorrow -- and yesterday will see you."

Attributed to the Nations by j. Newcombe Hodges

PROLOGUE

November 6, 2012

Old things have a menacing smell *about* them – ashtrays, uniforms and people. However; with Ancient things, the reek is retained *within* until opened. As with eggs, lies, legends and pyramids.

Such a pyramidal monument had risen from the Yucatan jungle, millenniums ago, and now loomed as a netherworld beacon for the nomadic spirits of its lost civilization.

On this waning moon evening, it would again guide the souls of the sudden dead.

Heavily armed soldiers, positioned at the edge of the denuded compound perimeter, were set for an assault upon the silent imposing giant. Their camouflaged fatigues displayed no identification of rank or country. Their weapons were state-of-the-art, as was their mission objective.

The only sounds were the low rumblings of power generators and an occasional jungle creature. The barren area around the Temple was illuminated with fixed stadium spotlights. Thousands of watts of glaring white light radiated down upon the no-mans land between the fence and the base of the temple. Three searchlights manually scanned the ten-foot high wire fence around the silent boundary, like burning fingers feeling for something to ignite.

A light breeze rustled the outermost reaching waxy leaves of antediluvian plants which were hugging the outside the fence. The angry vegetation constantly strained to engulf the uninvited human presence encroaching on the other side of the flimsy barrier.

A white flare ruptured the darkness above the building into searing brilliance; disclosing the 21st Century defenses that surrounded the uppermost tiers of the mammoth stone edifice. Stone and steel embattlements, built upon the ledges and steps of the ancient structure, erupted in automatic weapons fire. The anonymous attackers swarmed from the jungle; first destroying the defensive lighting, then blasting openings in the fence.

Grenades shook the ground. Concussions and shrapnel began taking agonizing tolls on both sides. The adequately armed but poorly trained rebel defenders struggled to hold their fortified positions against the swarming horde of professional mercenaries.

Four of the unidentified soldiers reached the main stone portal of the building and began placing explosive charges at the base of each enormous wooden door. One attached a radio-controlled detonator to each charge as the other three returned hundreds of rounds of tracer guided streams of lead into a group of defenders emerging from one of the three cave entrances.

The night sky continued to be filled with flares, creating surrealistic fluid shadows of the synchronized assault patterns upon the stone walls of the building. Greens and reds replaced the black and grey colors of the night. Stinging smells of burnt nitrates blurred the senses of the combatants along with anguished cries and numbing waves of noise and light.

For a split second all fighting ceased. The explosion destroying the wooden doors momentarily sucked the breath from every remaining living creature in the area, slamming many to the ground.

Three assault teams entered each one of the caves with precise execution, neutralizing any defensive barriers and personnel.

A specifically trained team of the attackers ran through the smoke and rubble of the Temple's massive burning doorway;

into the depths of the building, killing anyone who was before them. They reached a doorway that led to a stone staircase, dropping down twenty feet into a cavernous room. This was the mission objective. The attackers were to not use grenades inside the structure.

The two soldiers in the lead dove into the room and rolled, coming up with automatic handguns blazing, as the others on the staircase entered the fight with their weapon's laser sights slicing through the dust and smoke.

Within four minutes, all fighting had ceased above and below ground.

The main gate was opened as an unmarked 4x4 military-type vehicle pulled through; up to the shattered wooden doors. A tall man, wearing a black hat and carrying a briefcase, emerged from the front passenger seat of the vehicle. He opened the back door and helped out a frail, sickly man, who had a small lateral scar on his chin. They slowly walked into the Temple and down a stone staircase which led to a subterranean chamber.

As they entered the large room, one of the soldiers saluted the man in the broad-rimmed hat, "This structure is secure, Sir. We are clearing the outbuildings now."

The tall man walked to a table, put down his briefcase and looked around. There were five bodies, none in uniform, lying on the floor of the well-lit room. On the left, along the chiseled stone wall, were dozens of metal racks containing scores of computer servers. Upon the opposite wall were seven large monitors, all displaying satellite views of the earth and numerous scrolling lines of coded data. Placed down the center, for the full length of the room, were computer work stations. On the floor were cables running in every direction . . . as any hastily constructed command center might appear.

The man walked, to stand in front of one of the monitors; kicking aside the arm of one of the dead. He placed his hands on his hips. "Gentlemen . . . I want to see some Shadow People. Right now!"

So began the lies that became the legend.

Chapter 1

Friday, November 16, 2012.

There were no clocks striking thirteen, nor cause to nuzzle one's chin into the breast to escape vile winds blowing that brisk late fall morning. It was Sunnyvale, California, where one might stroll along the gleaming silicon pathways to hopefully stumble upon the next big thing. The aroma of mocha lattes wafted on the cool breezes and mixed with the noxious fumes of exotic automobiles, paid for with IPO dollars.

The importance of this November date, for the start of my chronicle, may be argued by some who will hold that the seeds of the events, which I am to relate, were actually planted millennia before. Sadly now, who really knows?

I have begun this story at the chosen time of 7:30 that Friday morning, when the threads of time began to display a weaving of foretold patterns, just as Mister Michael Fields unlocked the front door of his bleak, barely functional strip-mall office. He entered to find a mangled manila envelope, lying at his feet.

It had been forcibly shoved through the small mail slot in the door during the night, and not by any conventional mail service, for there were no postage marks, nor a printed delivery address on the outside. Only the bold black ink words, *M.S. Fields,* written in rough hand script across the front of the abused envelope.

Michael removed the contents. A small note, in the same deliberate handwriting scarring the front of the envelope, was the first item to catch his attention; a request to attend the funeral of Hugh Waterman. He sighed. Another body in a box; surrounded by flowers and crying relatives. Plus, the music was always so damn depressing that it inevitably brought on the sick realization of his own mortality. Soft and low tones, that if played backwards would cause one to start at the voice of the Grim Reaper calling, 'You're next'.

It was to him as uninviting as an appointment to have a tooth drilled by a blind dentist. Maybe there would be a wake and some food. He read on.

Mr. M. S. Fields,

Your presence is required at the funeral of Hugh Waterman. See attached itinerary and agenda.

The note plainly stated the reason for his mandatory attendance -- Hugh Waterman had died. What troubled Michael, as he turned the memo over, to perhaps discover some further details, was; who is/was Hugh Waterman?

Along with the short message demanding his attendance, was the aforementioned itinerary from Long Line Travel. It listed a pre-paid round trip flight, hotel information and a professionally printed agenda for the funeral.

Tuesday, November 20th, 2012 - Viewing 10 am, Church Service 11 am, Graveside Service at Arlington Cemetery 12:30 pm, Luncheon 1:30 pm.

However, the word Luncheon had a line through it with Meeting written under it.

'I guess the wake is off,' he thought.

Michael walked to his desk and turned on the computer, as he had done for far too many days before. He glanced at the answering machine to see if anyone had left a desperate communication -- perhaps pleading for his vast consulting expertise to save some troubled cutting-edge technology project. There were no messages in his digital bottle.

In the world of technology, Michael Fields could only be described as so outside the box that they nailed the lid on so he could not climb back in. However, in the various scientific, investment and consulting factions that make up the Silicon Valley community, there is a fine line between cutting-edge and down right whacky. He had not crossed that line into being a mad scientist, yet. Perhaps just *a little pissed off* scientist.

Michael was known as one of the 'go-to-guys' when two technologies needed to be joined together to get a third, which was greater than the sum. Whether it be developing software, intelligent hardware or just coming up with a whole new way of getting companies and organizations to their future faster. It was his expertise. And it was his passion, his gift. However; he often referred to his skills as being a curse. But it paid the bills and kept him in the mild surroundings of Northern California.

He hated snow and the Mid-West; both meant restriction.

There was nothing physically or socially that would set him apart from any other tech-head in the area, except that he was nearing *over the hill* when it came to being viewed as a 'whiz-kid' by the younger bottom-line managers of the new technology companies. He was thirty-six with a slight 5' 10" build, waning physical endurance and a slowly eroding hairline. He loved baseball, complicated films and late-night horror movie hosts.

Married once, divorced once, no children; he lived in an apartment complex just off Mary Avenue. He subsisted in a life-style befitting a pedestrian.

On the outside Michael was a pretty ordinary citizen, except for his work; that addiction which had shaped his life, up to now. And he had a recent history of strange dreams and headaches. He had self-prescribed a regiment of aspirin and English Ale to counteract the episodes. Although, he began to wonder if the ale might have caused the dreams . . . or even the headaches. He continued to research the cause and effect vigorously.

Since his mutually agreed departure from the technology giant NexTrÉ Corporation, over three years before, he had been on his own path redesigning others' futures. *'Michael Fields, Emerging Technology Consultant'* was what he had printed on his business cards.

Turning the manila envelope over, he read what appeared to be a phone number with a circle around it and the word *Call* written beside it.

Times being what they were, for the off-course Wizard, he picked up the phone and proceeded to dial the number. He stopped after the first four digits. There were just seven numbers with no area code and he noticed that the prefix was not one that was designated for his 408 area. Apparently there had been a mistake in the author's transcription of the number or it was left over from the last time the envelope was crammed through an undersized mail slot. He continued to dial the last three digits out of curiosity.

"Please state your full name," the digitally enhanced voice commanded -- through the small speaker of the telephone handset.

"Michael Scott Fields."

After a swift sequence of binary tones and a noise that resembled a submarine radar blip, the monotone voice returned, "Confirmed. Do you have any questions on your travel itinerary, Mister Fields?"

"Not on the travel, but I do have a few things that . . ."

"All of your questions will be addressed when you arrive in Washington, DC. We realize that your time is valuable Mister Fields, and we appreciate your willingness to provide consulting services on this project on such short notice."

I haven't agreed to anything, thought Michael.

The voice droned on with its mechanical dialog, sounding like a human trying to imitate a computer or a computer that didn't give a damn. But it was a real person; so real and dark, Michael could almost smell the words. "Time is of the essence, Mister Fields. The Program Office has determined that your past employment history and knowledge base will prove invaluable in meeting a number of critical deadlines."

"OK . . ." Michael slowly responded as the tedious voice spoke over his and continued its message, "A retainer of five-thousand dollars has been electronically deposited into your checking account to show our good faith and to cover any initial billings that you may be submitting for your services on this project."

"How did they get access to my bank account?" Michael was beginning to feel tightening in his chest.

"And just for a matter of record, due to the nature of the Program, discussions of your involvement in this operation are strictly prohibited. I am sure you understand the need for secrecy in the world of intellectual properties, Mister Fields.

Also, our records indicate that your Secret DoD clearance is still active, is this accurate?"

"I believe so."

"It is," confirmed the voice without patience. Breaking the millisecond of silence, a quick series of emotionless instructions began jabbing at his eardrum. "A driver will pick you up at the baggage claim area at Dulles Airport and take you to your hotel. The same driver will pick you up the next morning. The Program Director expects to see you at 10 am on Tuesday the 20th at the Funeral Service. Have a nice day."

The voice was replaced by a dial tone.

It was obvious the person on the other end of the call had never had a nice day in their life.

Michael looked at the handset, as he slowly hung up.

The mysterious voice, on the secure phone line, was his first step into the underworld of Black Projects. Actually, he did not know it at the time. In truth, he did not know anything at the time; *especially* the truth.

Michael turned to his desktop computer. He accessed his bank account via the web. There is was, as the voice had indicated, $5,000 deposited at 10 pm, the night before. The transaction originated from UPipe Holdings.

"*What's going on here?*" Michael asked the screen.

He searched for UPipe Holdings within the vapor bowels of his search engine. There was nothing out there that even came close to matching his query. But apparently UPipe was a real company, as the deposit proved to be a great testimonial to that fact.

The voice had mentioned his past employment history was a key element in The Program's need for his assistance; whatever the Program was supposed to mean. If this UPipe could access his private checking account, he was sure they had the means to dig into every virtual aspect of his data-accessible life. The whole situation was clawing at his emotional security screen and it did not feel very comfortable. Privacy invasion was difficult to defend against and the luxury of an offense was only available to the other side. He knew one could never win a defensive battle, especially in a digital world.

Throughout the rest of the morning he worked at his desk writing a system design document for putting Radio Frequency Identification tags on some local company's circuit boards coupled with a network of devices that would read them at each of the company's assembly stations.

Not only was it an outdated implementation using stagnant technology, it was a waste of time. It was a waste of Michael Fields.

His work now was focused on putting others' ideas of 'someday' technology solutions into documents that would be pushed from one corporate department to another. When viewed closely, the proposals had nothing to do with the real world or could actually be accomplished within ones' lifetime. He had been reduced to a clerk, by his own means of misguided self importance, thinking he could build his name into a commodity the Valley desperately needed.

He had missed the Bus to Success and perhaps there was not another one due. He was hoping that the best day of his life had not already occurred.

He left at noon to get his only dark suit cleaned and sit under a tree to wait for a falling apple.

II

Sunday, November 18, 2012

It had not been a comfortable weekend due to the events of Friday; the envelope, the deposit in his account and the anxiety of the upcoming trip to attend a funeral of someone he had never known.

In the transient world of bleeding-edge technology, there is a constant stream of associates, but few on a level that could be labeled a friend. Michael had one. He picked up the phone and called Parker.

As expected in the wonderful world of instant communications, an answering machine came on, "This is Parker, leave a message."

"Hey, it's me. It's Sunday, around 4 pm; just wanted to see if you knew of a company called UPipe Holdings. I got a consulting job with them Friday, but don't know too much about their line of work. Actually, I don't know anything.

"I need to fly to DC tomorrow morning, back Wednesday night. And this is the weird part; I'm going there to attend a funeral for some guy named Waterman. Give me a call when you can. You've got my cell phone num . . ." The machine cut him off.

Michael may have been outside the box, but Ian Thomas Parker didn't even know there was a box to be outside of. He was employed full time by some kind of think tank entity nestled in the Santa Cruz Mountains.

Parker had the classic bad-boy look; shaggy hair, an ear-to-ear smile and he only shaved when he had to conduct a presentation to some big shots. He lived on the computer, typing elaborate algorithms and always trying to get a page of code down to a few lines. He had to wear fingerless wrist supports on both hands for his self-induced carpal tunnel syndrome.

Parker rode a motorcycle, wore urban-assault clothing and had some kind of New York accent, which was odd since he was born and grew up in San Diego. He was the second son of a six-member Navy family that had migrated from New Orleans.

He held a Master's Degree from Stanford University in computer science and lived in a pastel colored bungalow on the Santa Cruz beachfront.

What fascinated Michael the most about his thirty-two year old side kick, who only went by his last name, was that Parker was convinced that there was a conspiracy around every government action, and *They* controlled everything and covered up even more. He had always said that he had proof and *someday* he would let it out. He would even figure out who *They* were. Michael was patient.

Parker's major claim to fame was his notoriety as one of the world's best software hackers. He was actually arrested a couple times for breaking into a few corporate systems. No damage was done, that was not Parker's way. He just wanted to see what kind of junk programs the amateurs were writing for the world's biggest companies. That is one reason why Michael had hired him at NexTrÉ; to make their product, GMCS, as unbreakable as possible. And the main reason he was now up in the think tank; breaking others' code.

Michael turned on the TV to catch the national weather forecast; it was going to be cold with occasional crappiness in DC as usual. He packed his suitcase accordingly and placed his aging dark suit into a garment bag.

He looked out the window of his apartment to check on the black SUV that had been sitting across the street since he returned home from work on Friday. As he opened the blinds, the window of the vehicle quickly closed. But not before Michael was able to see a man in a black suit jacket, white shirt and black tie pointing a small parabolic antenna at his front door.

Chapter 2

Monday, November 19, 2012

The flight to Washington, DC from San Francisco was uneventful. A sunglass adorned driver was waiting at the baggage claim area, as arranged, holding a sign; *Mr. M. Fields.*

It was a quiet, disquieting half-hour trip in the blacked-out SUV to an older, but clean hotel in Arlington.

After opening the rear passenger door and taking out the luggage, the driver stood to the top of his six-foot plus height and looked down at Michael. "Someone will meet you in the lobby at 0900 hours to take you to the funeral." With the efficiency and personality of a robot, he climbed back into the driver's seat and pulled away.

Michael checked in and went up to his room on the 11th floor. After tossing his suitcase, garment bag, computer case and overcoat on the bed, he opened the sliding glass door to the balcony and walked out. Georgetown University was visible from his room on the other side of the Potomac and a single sculling crew was out on the river. They were either learning the fine art of synchronized rowing around icebergs or being punished for something; in either case they were paddling fast just to keep warm. Michael imagined the training difficulties involved with getting an ancient Trireme underway. Although whips and chains quickly aided in straightening out the learning curve back then.

The trip was scheduled to last until 6 pm the following day with the scheduled departure of his flight back to San Francisco. Michael had packed all of the necessary items required for a one-night visit.

As he walked back into the room and unpacked, he began to delve deeper into his present information-deprived situation. Maybe this Hugh Waterman was some long-lost rich uncle who was going to pass on his millions to him. No more working for the rich man. No more writing System Design Documents for corporate cube-dudes to pore over, in order to justify their existence. He would have the resources to achieve a level of success that would rival anything he could imagine. Perhaps an estate in Nice with vineyards as far as the eye could see . . .

The ringing phone broke his jet-lagged induced fantasy.

"Mister Fields! Welcome to DC," a loud baritone male voice greeted, resonating in a very distinctive western twang. Michael held the phone off his ear as the booming voice continued, "Like to thank ya' for coming on such short notice."

"And you are?" Michael queried slowly.

"Wagerhaffen, Gus Wagerhaffen. I'll be your Point of Contact during your stay here. Actually right now, I'm down in the lobby. Would ya' like to come on down to the lounge, for a drink? Say, in five minutes?"

"Sure, I will be right down. I will be wearing a blue shirt with . . ."

"I know what you look like, Mister Fields. See ya in a couple minutes."

Michael hung up the phone and repeated the strange name; *"Gus Wagerhaffen?"*

Michael entered the dimly lit hotel lounge within the prescribed five minutes. An instrumental version of an 80's pop song from a one-hit wonder artist was softly playing on the wall-mounted speakers; the smell of decades-old carpeting filled his head. As his eyes adjusted to the lack of illumination, a slight smile of vintage recollection reformed his lips. He spotted a nicotine coated mirror ball still hanging over the parquet dance floor. It was a remnant of disco days; back when this place must have been the spot to party on Saturday nights -- over thirty years ago. A large out-dated video monitor now resided on the stage, no doubt installed for another chapter in the lounge's history of entertainment attempts, Karaoke. The establishment was now attempting to be just another sports bar, and not a very lively one. The place was void of sports fans. Perhaps the gloomy ambience would give rise to a reemergence of the bohemian coffee shop era. That should be considered for the next business attempt in the room, Michael thought.

Apart from three customers: two 30ish looking men in suits sitting at either end of the bar and a commanding-looking gentleman at a corner table, there was no one else in the establishment. Not even a bartender.

The older patron at the table, with his black Stetson occupying a quarter of the simulated wood surface, raised his hand to Michael in a gesture to join him. He was dressed in a dark sports coat, white shirt, blue suspenders and a green string tie. He wore a strong weathered face that could have only been earned by years of working the high desert. Michael's host had already set up two drinks on the table. And as no surprise, it was exactly what he always drank on special occasions; single-malt scotch with three ice cubes.

"Michael! Damn glad you could make it." The cowboy slapped Michael on the side of his upper arm. "Here sit down, take a load off. You just flew across the whole damn country. Your arms tired?" A big laugh erupted from the western relic.

Michael took up his position across the table and put on his best smile while he rubbed his upper arm.

"Well, Mister Wagerhaffen . . ."

"Gus . . . just call me Gus."

"Alright and you can -- keep calling me Michael. So Gus, who is, was, this Hugh Waterman?"

"A real fine gentleman, who will be greatly missed by a whole shit-load of people," Gus replied, smiling and holding up his glass to salute the memories of this Hugh someone. He began drinking the entire contents of the glass.

Michael picked up his own glass, "What did he do? Did he know me?" He took a small drink and put the glass back precisely onto the water ring that had formed on the table top.

"Why was I brought out here to attend this . . . event?"

Gus repositioned himself in his chair and leaned forward. "We thought you could use a break. Take a couple days off. See the sites." He leaned back and straightened his string tie, "Help save the human race."

Michael's forced smile was becoming more strained as he tried to determine if this was small talk or the man across from him was a lunatic, "That seems a bit over the top. Save the human race?"

Gus smiled as he removed his fixin's bag from inside his coat to roll a cigarette. "Ya' know, sometimes I say the damndest things." He looked to his left, "I kind of like this place, know why? Hardly any people in here, it's quiet. Lots of elbow room." He held up the bag, containing rolling papers and tobacco. "You don't mind if I smoke, do ya'?"

Michael slowly shook his head, "No. Go ahead."

Gus laughed out load, "Good, 'cause I was going to, anyway." He held one of the thin papers in his left hand and slowly poured some finely-chopped tobacco along its center. He put the bag down and began to roll the bulk into a cylinder. "This is one on my only vices. But, it's a free country . . . you can be legally addicted to anything you want – as long as it's taxable."

Studying Gus' face closer; the square jaw, deep-set dark eyes, chiseled cheek bones -- Michael could envision him as being hired by a Hollywood casting agency to portray a Minor League baseball coach in some sports Comeback Movie . . . or a cop.

Gus paused in his cigarette manufacturing activity and squinted at Michael, "You know what the biggest manifestation of parasites on this planet is, Slim? Humans!" He motioned with his right hand over the table top, "Just a coverin' the earth; using up all the resources. Every damn square inch of dirt has someone's butt sittin' on it. Do you know that every measly grain of sand on this planet of ours is owned by someone or some group or some government? It's just amazing." Gus licked the paper to seal it and put it in his mouth. He began patting his coat looking for a light.

Michael struggled to initiate another subject, besides the results of the human presence on earth. Looking around and seeing no ashtrays, "Is smoking in bars still allowed in the DC area?"

"I don't have time to read the papers, son." The loosely-rolled cigarette was bobbing up and down as he talked with flakes of tobacco floating like confetti, "Who knows what's been outlawed these days. Hell, *I* might not even be allowed in bars in DC." Gus had a laugh that could be heard over the next ridge.

He finally lit the dangling cigarette in a dazzling display of fire, smoke and falling flakes of ignited tobacco and took a deep drag. He blew the smoke straight up over his head.

"They tell me that you're a whiz at developing remote code formulation stuff that can generate satellite authorization codes to control and activate service devices."

Did that come out of this grizzled cow puncher? And who are They that keeps cropping up? Michael was taken a bit back by the level of techno-speak Gus was delivering and had to re-evaluate his initial profile of the man. Things certainly were not what they first appeared to be.

Michael took another drink and collected his thoughts, "That's right. I was involved in that technology a few years back. It was a software application called GMCS, an acronym for Global Monitoring and Control Systems. I worked with it up through Version Two. It was mainly designed for point-of-sale stuff; satellite radio service activation, cell phones and the like. That was over three years ago. The company delivered the final product a year after I left. I'm not sure what the final version was, that the client actually received."

The blue cigarette smoke was beginning to hover over Gus like a thundercloud. "That was when you were some kind of software manager for the NexTrÉ Corporation, I believe."

Again, Michael was surprised by the amount of his personal information Gus possessed, "Yes. I headed up the project in my department."

"Have you ever met that CEO of NexTrÉ?"

"Brandon Bancroft? No. He was way too high up in the cor-poration to ever come down to meet the worker bees. No, wait. I did conduct a presentation once where he sat way in the back. He gave me a thumbs-up at the end of it, and walked out. I guess you can say he knew who I was, but not the other way around."

"He still lives in that huge spread he has up in Napa?"

"I think he moved to Maine, or Singapore or someplace else when he shut down the company in late 2010. He's got his billions, he could live anywhere."

"It must be nice. You know, if I could live anywhere, it would be up around Tahoe. Sure is a beautiful area, up there in the Sierras. You must have been there, living so close in the Bay Area. You know what the original name of Lake Tahoe was in the Washoe Native language? Ha! Me neither." Gus dropped some ashes into his glass of ice. "People should know these things. Wonder how you spell it? Why don't you look that up, when you get a minute or two, *this evening*?"

Michael was nearing the end of his own drink, waiting for lightning to emerge from the cloud overhead and was sure this conversation was just alcohol induced. Why was this Texan rambling on about Lake Tahoe and Washoe Natives?

Gus' weathered face appeared to soften in a fatherly manner, "Tell me this Michael, are you happy? I mean with your work, where you live, where you're headed in this life."

Was this guy a career counselor? Michael wondered.

"You enjoy being a consultant, or whatever the hell you do, or would you rather have the best full-time job in the world? And working for the best damn employer in the world?"

Michael sat back and wondered what kind of answer Gus was looking for, as if he was in some kind of game show.

"I really don't know. I work for myself now, sort of a consultant. I do what I feel like doing and don't really have any set hours. I suppose if the right situation came up, I would seriously think about going back into a full-time thing. But only if, as you say, it was best full-time job in the world and working for the best employer in the world."

"Best *damn* employer," Gus corrected him, as he leaned forward, with his elbows on the table, "I may have some leads for you, see'ns how, there aren't too many of *you people* out there."

Michael's sudden facial expression of total confusion was not enough to prompt Gus to explain his last statement.

Gus dropped the yellow-stained cigarette butt in his glass of melted ice and took out a pack of chewing gum from his shirt pocket. He removed a single stick and began to meticulously remove the paper, then the foil.

He held the naked gum in front of him, examining the thin grey strip as he slowly rotated in the air, "Here's an interesting fact; on June 26th, 1974, in a supermarket in Troy, Ohio, the first product with a Barcode was scanned at a check-out counter. Know what it was? It was a 10-pack of chewing gum. Imagine that. A little stick of gum was the beginning of electronic scanning and tracking items with an embedded code."

Michael nodded, "I'm imagining. Think of what Caesar or Hitler could have done with that."

The Texans' eyes closed to slits as he put the gum in his mouth and took out another stick from the small package. He tossed it in front of Michael. "Here, put this in your pocket and when you get to your room, chew on it for awhile."

Gus fixed his gaze on the gum as Michael picked it up and put it in his pocket. The big man moved his chair back and stood up, "Alright Michael, I've got to be heading out. This was a great meeting and I learned a lot. I'll pick you up tomorrow morning, in the lobby, at 9 am. Oh, almost forgot, does 3938 mean anything to you?"

Michael stood slowly and thought about the numbers, "No, not really."

Gus' eyes squinted, "How about The Foundation?"

"Again, that doesn't mean anything to me," Michael replied, very confused.

A smile wrinkled the leathery face of the six-foot wrangler as he picked up his hat, lifted his hand in a short wave and disappeared out the lounge entrance, with some remnants of the blue cloud following him. One of the business suits at the bar immediately rose and left behind Gus. The other one looked over his right shoulder, at Michael, then turned back to the bar. Michael sat back down staring at the exit, with Gus's big voice still in his ears.

Two people, a man and woman, entered the room. They were dressed in hotel employee uniforms. The man went behind the bar and the female walked to Michael's table.

"Would you like another drink?" She asked. "It's on the house."

"No, thank you. I've got to be getting up to my room. It's been a long day."

"We don't get too many, like *you people*, in here," she said, wiping off the table and picking up the glasses.

"Like *what* people?" Michael asked quickly, still looking for an explanation for the phrase.

"You know – 'hush hush' and all that."

"Oh." Michael looked at the nervous man sitting at the bar. The worrisome figure looked down at his cell phone and began typing some email.

"Oh, I understand, can't talk about it," the waitress whispered. "But those three guys that came in before you were sure pushy. They made Carl and me take a break. I don't make any tips on my breaks, you know."

Michael reached into his pocket and pulled out a couple dollars and put them on the table. "Here ya go. Sorry about . . . my associates. They don't get out much." He looked over to the bar. The man was gone.

Michael stood and made his way back up to the 11th floor.

When he arrived at his room, he shut the door and quickly removed the stick of gum from his pocket. It was either very old or something else was in the wrapping, for it did not bend. He peeled off the paper and foil, revealing a flash memory device. Michael immediately set up his laptop and plugged it into the appropriate port. After a few moments, a panel appeared stating *Memory Device Locked - Password Required*. The cursor continued to blink on the input field, impatiently waiting for the correct string of letters and numbers.

"*Great. Now what?*" Michael flopped back in his chair in frustration.

Maybe Gus had thrown down that particular stick of gum by mistake and the memory stick was in Michael's possession by accident. No -- Gus had paid too much attention to making sure it was in his pocket before he left.

He began entering the usual combinations of letters and numbers that people normally use when they begin thinking they are clever; dates, his own name, a variety of combinations and cases. Nothing cleared the security panel. Maybe Gus' name was the code. But he had only heard it once.

"Wagerhaffen, *I wonder how you spell it?*"

Gus had said the same thing; *I wonder how you spell it* . . .

He activated the wireless Internet connection to the hotel network, brought up his search engine and typed in 'Washoe Indian Lake Tahoe'. Back it came, *Daowaga*. He entered the word into the security field of the panel.

The file opened in an amazing explosion of a hundred pages of text and tables onto his screen with links to scores of other files embedded in the memory stick. For Michael it was as if all his old love letters had come back to haunt him.

There it was, his NexTrÉ project; GMCS. And the date of the software version, listed as a Build, indicated it was Version Five, three iterations past where he had left it. He quickly scanned key areas of the code looking for the remote activation algorithms he had written, the plurality of different deactivation digital codes and those bizarre frequency shifting tables. The program had been extensively modified, but the base structure was still there. And, as he expected, many new features had been added. As well as a whole series of files he could not open, written in an extension that he had never encountered before . . . *XZX*.

Three years of his life; junk food, no sleep and a marriage; right there in glorious black and white on his laptop monitor. He had never actually seen the finished product; probably only a few people at the top of NexTrÉ and the customer actually ever saw it. The program itself was developed in a modular architecture in four separate departments.

He put his hands down in his lap. *How did Gus get this? All of this?*

CONTINUANCE

That must be why they brought him out to DC, he reasoned; to work on some upgrades or something for the finished product he was viewing.

This was amazing, for he now had the complete software code for the application, plus all of the architectural diagrams and hardware interface design documents for what must be the final version of GMCS, right in front of him.

He kicked off his shoes, took his laptop offline and ordered room service. Settling in for a long night of digesting the contents of the memory device, he felt like things were looking up.

The 'hush hush' man, who had remained at the bar after Gus left, walked softly to the door located next to Michael's. He noticed the 'Do Not Disturb' sign on Michael Fields' door and nodded. As he entered his own room, he pulled out his cell phone to join a scheduled conference call with the Program 3938 Security Office about the Gen Zero in the next room.

Chapter 3

Tuesday, November 20, 2012

Michael had packed his suitcase and laptop, checked out of his room and was sitting in the lobby at 8:45 am. He lost count of the number of cups of coffee he had consumed in the last ten hours. And there was that half-hour of half-sleep that came over him at 3 am. He was both tired and wired; each condition fighting for control of his consciousness.

His mind was reeling with the amount of information he had received on the flash drive, which was now buried deep in his suit coat pocket. Since he had left NexTrÉ, it was obvious that GMCS had developed into something way beyond simple device activation. It appeared that the scope had changed from a utility program for authorizing consumers to activate their cell phones and cable TV to something that was controlling a multitude of systems and mesh networks. More than once, during the night, he had thrown up his hands in frustration as he encountered countless dead-ends in the flow. It was as if chunks of a whole new programming language had been written and the timing and export functions were just plain nonsensical.

The lobby doors slid open and in walked Gus, dressed in nearly the same clothes he had been attired in the night before.

"'Morning Michael!" he bellowed from across the room.

Michael waited a few moments for Gus to get closer before returning the greeting so as to not get involved in a shouting contest. He would lose.

"Good morning, Gus."

"Have an interesting evening?" Gus asked, without really asking about the flash drive.

"I just did some reading. Old work documents and such."

Gus smiled and motioned to the door.

"Well, let's get rolling. Got everything you came with?"

"That and more," Michael responded, picking up his gear and following Gus out to the waiting car.

The man, who had sat alone at the bar after Gus had left, was standing just outside the lobby door with a small overnight black bag. He nodded to Gus as they passed.

The same driver, whom had picked him up from the airport, placed Michael's bag and laptop case into the trunk as Michael and Gus settled in the back seat. The doors shut and off they rode to a small church in a quiet residential area in Arlington.

II

10 am – The Viewing

The street was lined on both sides with high-end automobiles, and the church parking lot was filled with black limousines and even blacker SUVs. Scores of people, in sunglasses and dark clothing, stood in small groups in front of the church. The majority of the assemblage appeared to be over 50, with smatterings of 30ish couples and their rambunctious children.

As they pulled up to the curb, two of the dark-suited men in the crowd moved to each side of the car and opened the doors to allow the passengers to exit. Michael could see himself in the sunglasses of the attendant as he climbed out of the backseat. The clear plastic earpiece, with the white coiled wire running down into the back of the shirt collar, was easily visible from the short distance.

Gus led the way, making a path through the throng, occasionally acknowledging an acquaintance or two. They walked up the steps of the church and entered the sacred house of salvation and hope. The morbid organ music and choking incense were not aiding Michael in either of these goals.

To the left of the entrance a small line of attendees were signing a guest book. Gus kept moving to place them in another line of mourners in the center aisle.

Michael stood ahead of Gus in the viewing line, which was moving slowly forward, past the open casket that rested on a movable platform placed directly in front of the alter.

This is the damnedest consulting gig I've ever been on, thought Michael.

The large lady in front of him paused for moment, shook her head slowly and moved to the left, allowing Michael a full view of the late Hugh Waterman.

The Universe took a hard turn to the right -- nearly sending him to his knees as his legs turned to gelatin. A thousand packets of short-lived images and clips of past events in his life erupted in his brain, sending billions of bits of once true data into the falsehood regions of his skull. This was not Hugh Waterman.

He grasped the side of the casket with his right hand to steady himself and unconsciously spoke aloud, "This is Howard Linn." Time stopped as he recalled the six months of twelve-hour days working with Howard on the GMCS project. There was no mistaking this was the same man who was the Program Manager, sent from the client to oversee the hardware and software migration testing. Even down to the small lateral scar on his chin, there was no doubt the body in the box was Howard.

A hand on his shoulder and the voice of the old cowboy behind him brought Michael back to the present.

"You OK, son?"

"Yes, I'm fine. Just . . . just some things are a bit . . ."

He continued to mutter as he walked to his left towards an usher who was directing the congregation to their seats.

Michael sat between Gus, on one side, and some Army Lieutenant Colonel on the other as remembrances of the late Hugh Waterman were being read off by a steady stream of acquaintances and associates. No relatives were visibly present, or anyone that he could determine to be a relative; as none appeared to be willing to divulge such an association. Each member of the audience was drawn by the same morbid artist; in stark black and white, without emotion or expression.

Each Speaker executed animated eulogies, choreographed to the conveyance of their prepared texts, all performed within their time allotted.

He tried to match the accolades being delivered with the person *he* remembered, who was now in the casket. The presenters were talking about two different men. They did not know this man. Or, perhaps Michael did not know this man.

But, he *did* know Howard Linn. It could not have been *all* an act. Howard was just a regular guy; loved to play darts down at Q's, drink a beer, discuss UFOs with Parker and learn everything there was to know about the restoration of '43 Jeeps from Rickman.

For the next half hour Michael conducted in his mind, his own silent memorial service to a friend that, it seems, he never really met.

The church service ended with little hope and the assemblage reassembled at the bottom of the steps in front of the old colonial house of worship. The gloom was enhanced by low grey skies, promising a cold shower to further dampen the proceedings. Portions of the somber crowd moved to the cars parked along the street, while others formed in small required groups; waiting for the hearse to be loaded with its morbid cargo before continuing the agenda at the cemetery.

Gus guided Michael to a waiting SUV. "We won't be going to the graveside service."

The same driver whom had picked him up from the airport and drove them to the church service was now holding the passenger door open as Gus moved inside.

"Once around the park," Michael greeted the driver as he slid into the enveloping back seat beside Gus. The driver closed the door without a response or expression, as if he was thinking about the donut shop he should have opened instead of being a chauffeur to this wise ass.

The car slowly pulled away from the somber gathering, waiting for another black SUV to get in front of them; they both sped away; heading west, back the way Michael had first arrived. Turning around, Michael could also see the same type of vehicle pulling into position behind him. Both of the escort vehicles had activated blue blinking lights, which were embedded in their grills and taillights.

Michael looked forward and spoke to Gus, "Well, this whole thing is/was interesting. And I do have some questions about the late Mister Waterman. . ."

"All of your questions will be answered in a bit. This is not the time or place," Gus said slowly, also looking ahead and behind.

Michael saw the sign for the Dulles Airport. "Are we heading back to the airport? A bit early for my flight, I don't leave 'till 6 pm."

"Not exactly. We're going to take 495 North up here in a while, then up to 270." Gus appeared anxious as rested his chin on the back of his folded right hand, elbow on the door arm rest, and looked out the right side passenger window. He was drumming his fingers on the seat beside him, with his left hand.

"There are some meetings we have to get to, up by Thurmont, Maryland. You'll be staying there for a few days."

It took a second for the words to sink into Michael's already waning reality. *A few days?* He didn't want to sound like he was whining. "OK. But, my return ticket will have to be changed. I was scheduled to leave today. Actually, I don't have clothes enough for a couple more days on the road."

Gus did not turn his head, "Did they get that itinerary wrong again? That damned travel agency. Someone should get over there and kick their butts."

Michael felt like he was sinking deeper into the plush leather seat. Well, they had paid for his time and there really wasn't much back home that was pressing. Actually, there was nothing back home that required his presence. He sighed softly and watched the Virginia commuters fight for position in the opposite lanes, as he remembered a time when there *was* something back home that required his presence.

Virginia turned into Maryland as a light rain began to fall on the oil slicked roadway. Very little conversation took place between Gus and himself, as Gus was being very talkative to someone on the phone; speaking in low tones and ambiguous phrases, often mentioning Michael's name. Wind driven streaks of water slithered across his window, fighting their way to the rear of the vehicle.

His own phone buzzed. The display identified the caller as Area 52. It was Parker.

Michael answered, "Hey. What's up?"

"Can you talk?" Parker sounded concerned.

"I can hear you."

"How was Waterman's funeral?"

"I need to talk to you about that one." Michael wanted to blurt out the whole story of Waterman being Linn, or vice versa, without Gus sitting next to him.

Parker continued, "I went to some places in cyber-space where mere mortals are banned, with credentials I don't have, to get you some info on your client. You owe me big time."

"As long as you had fun," Michael calmly replied, trying to give the impression that it was just a normal social call.

Parker began his briefing.

"OK, in a nutshell, UPipe Holdings, actually pronounced UP Pipe, is an organization set up to channel money to a variety of covert black projects. They get *their* bucks from both the Public and Private Sector. They were formed back in the Nixon era to distribute these funds to projects that provided support for Executive Order 11490; projects that the Spooks have to develop scenarios for, under the guise of Continuation of Government."

"What did you call them?"

"Call who? Oh, you mean the Spooks? They're covert employees of various three and four letter government agencies."

Michael could see Gus eyeing him.

"Well, that's great news . . . Carol. If you find out anything more on that real estate deal, let me know. I'm always interested." It was as close as he could come to letting Parker know it was time to hang up.

Parker wrapped it up, "I've got to talk to you about some other things, too. We'll get together as soon as you get back. Don't forget anything you learn."

"OK, thanks for calling." Michael closed his phone and put it in his lap.

"They just won't leave you alone, will they?" Gus asked with a glint in his eye.

"Who?"

"Women! Don't matter if it's important or not, they just gotta call ya and talk about it. Everything's a damn drama."

"Oh, yeah. Right. That was Carol. My real estate agent. She wants me to look at some property."

Michael turned in the seat to face Gus.

"Can you tell me something Gus?"

"As much as I can . . . seein' that I'm just a simple country boy."

In a pig's eye, thought Michael, looking back to the official chase vehicle.

"Do you work for UPipe? They're the ones who hired me."

Gus laughed. "UPipe? Those bean-counters? They just push around our budget money from column A to column B. Never really met any of them; probably nice folk, but they are always on my butt about expense reports."

At least he was not hiding his involvement with UPipe, Michael thought.

Gus brought out a bag of caramels from a black canvas tote on the floor. "Want one? I have to eat these 'cause Johnson, our driver, won't let me smoke in his fancy auto-mo-beels." He leaned forward, "Will ya Johnson?"

As expected, no expression or reply from Johnson. Gus leaned back, "You'd think he was making the payments on these things himself. A real fun guy." He put a caramel in his mouth.

"Speaking of fungi, you know how they grow mushrooms?"

Gus has a knack for some real strange small talk, thought Michael. "There are a couple places near Monterey where they grow them, but never been there to see what goes on inside."

"They lock 'em in dark, cool places and feed 'em bullshit."

Gus did not laugh at his own joke as he dug in the bag for more caramels. Michael smiled, nervously.

"If not for UPipe, then who do you work for?"

"Ya know, Slim, I often ask myself the same question. And most of the time I get different answers. Oh, as you can probably see, it's with the good ol' United States government. But I must be honest and say I work for every single one of our fine citizens."

It was obvious that Mister G was a pretty good dancer, for he wasn't stepping on any toes and just going in circles.

Gus pushed a button on his door console and a glass dividing window rose up between himself and Johnson.

"I assume you were able to get into that memory stick and look at some of the files."

"Yes, no problem. I spent quite awhile looking at some documents and the GMCS code."

"See anything that ground your gears? Was there anything that appeared strange or out of the ordinary? Any weird symbols show up?"

"The code appeared to look pretty straight forward. I did notice that a lot of new stuff had been added since I left NexTrÉ, but didn't get that deep in the functionality of those lines. And I didn't really have a chance to get into the hardware modules; not enough time."

"But you could figure them all out if you had more time?"

"Well, yes. I suppose so. Just have to run some of the modules and determine what it is that they're supposed to do or process. Find out what the commands are asking for and what the modules eventually do with the data; just some systematic investigation."

"Think you can tell who wrote the new stuff?"

"The entire thing is really a compilation of a number of programs written at different times; perhaps by dozens of software engineers. It looks like all of the new code, that was written after I had left, was done by two or three key individuals. You can tell the work of specific engineer. They all have their little quirks in writing notations."

"Think you could track them down, these key individuals?"

"I'll look for Easter Eggs."

Gus looked at him like he had just put on a pair of fuzzy rabbit ears.

"Easter Eggs?"

"Programmers are a unique bunch, sometimes working 48 hours straight or sometimes not showing up for days. During those marathon sessions, when they're going non-stop for days, they tend to get sidetracked or bored or just wackier than normal and place things into the code, mainly for the benefit of amusing other programmers. It's kind of like graffiti or Cheat Codes in a video game."

"What kind of things do they put in there?" Gus popped another caramel into his mouth.

"Oh, pictures of their cars or girlfriends. Or quotes from their favorite movie, like; "We'll always have Paris' or 'It's in the hole!'"

Gus stopped chewing, "It's in the hole?"

"Anyway, these are called Easter Eggs and can be accessed by a series of keystrokes. Maybe I can find one that would give more info on the programmer."

"What is the world coming to? All these new-fangled things just amaze me. Where is this all gonna lead?"

Michael had a pretty good idea that if anyone on earth already knew the answer to that question, it would be Gus.

Gus dropped a caramel wrapper on the floor. He glanced up to the rear view mirror and saw Johnson looking at him. He sighed and reached down to pick it up and put it in back in the bag. Turning to Michael, "You said something about Firmware? What in the world is that?"

Michael tried to put his response into words that Gus might understand, "A small computer program that works inside a device, like an ATM or RFID reader, which gathers all the information the device has read and sends it to a main computer database someplace by a cable or wireless connection. The main computer is called a server. In many cases the Firmware will let the server talk back to the device."

"Now isn't *that* something; two computer-things talking back and forth to each other?" Gus sounded genuinely awed.

"Actually it's very simple. Just need a connection between the two; phone line, satellite or optical cable."

Gus was nodding, while looking past Michael. There were gears turning in his mind.

Michael wrinkled his forehead, "When NexTrÉ delivered this to the government, didn't they provide the complete source code? "

Gus did not look pleased, "Oh, we got the source code. Everything that was contracted for -- was delivered. You have the whole program on that stick I gave you."

"Then you want me to upgrade it or something?"

Gus smiled, "I want you to memorize it, Bucko."

Michael eased out a stranded smile of his own, "OK."

There was one more thing that he needed to ask Gus, "There were some notations on something named LiquiCode. I'm not familiar with it. Don't know if it is some programming code or what. I may have to dig deeper into that if I'm to really get into the program."

Gus looked out his window as the convoy passed the backed up traffic in the right lanes. "There they are; the little people . . . the sheep. Every one of them is feeling safe and secure in their private little worlds. They're all thinking that they are under the protection of some divine sheep dog that keeps them from killing each other."

Gus pushed the button to lower the window behind Johnson. "I wouldn't spend too much time thinking about LiquiCode at this time. OK?"

It sounded like an order.

Gus put his hands in his pants pockets and leaned back, "I just got off the phone with my admin people. Your flight back to San Francisco has been put on hold until after some meetings we're going to attend over the next couple days. You'll probably get out of here on Friday. Don't worry, you're in good hands and everything's being taking care of. Enjoy the ride."

The conversation was at an end.

Michael looked out his window into space. There were too many questions he wanted to ask and it made his brain ache with the weight of them, as they piled up. He will do as Gus suggested and just wait for the time and place.

After another half-hour, the three-car convoy turned off the highway. It was the Thurmont exit. After a quick left turn they began climbing into the surrounding sun-drenched covered hills. The evergreens supplied a much needed touch of life to the previously passed landscapes of dried corn fields and brown grasses.

"You won't be a needin' that phone for a bit, Michael. Why don't you turn it off and save the battery?" Gus sort of smiled and began straightening himself in the seat. Michael turned off the phone as a sign appeared on his left, *Catoctin Mountain Park*.

"This is a great Resort. You'll like staying here for a couple days. Already got a cabin for you and some comfy clothes hanging in the closet. A great place for a meeting, don't ya think?" Gus was acting like a kid on his way to an amusement park.

Another sign flashed by the car on the right . . . *Camp David*.

Chapter 4

There were a couple of camps on the mountain, mainly used by federal employees and their families for vacationing. As the caravan drove up to the entrance of one of the more remote ones, they were waved in by a guard at the gate.

The place was pretty deserted, as most sensible people do not visit resorts in November; unless they had been 'ordered' to be there.

The three vehicles pulled up to a two-story cabin that sat at the far end of the complex. A metal plaque, stamped and painted with the number 17, was nailed onto the porch support column. The drivers jumped out of their seats and opened all of the passenger doors. Four dark suited individuals emerged from the front vehicle and five from the one behind Michael's car. All eleven of the passengers gathered at the foot of the stairs, leading up to the porch of the cabin. The somber drivers removed computer bags and luggage from the SUVs. When every trunk was empty and every door was shut, the convoy vehicles drove away. No one had spoken a word throughout the entire process. The only sounds were idling engines, metal doors closing and the brisk evening wind passing numbing ears.

Two of the earpiece wearing 'suits', walked up the stairs. They opened the cabin door and held it wide for the travelers. They remained standing there, on either side of the portal, like Gargoyles protecting a most sacred den of angels.

The cabin was furnished in an unsurprising rustic wood motif; a living room, a dining area, a fireplace, a bathroom and what appeared to be two bedrooms. There was a staircase leading to the second floor, directly in front of the entrance. However; a rope was placed between the banisters and a sign hung from the middle, stating: *No Admittance*.

A large dining table, with six chairs positioned around it, filled the dining area. Michael looked to the far end and saw a demure woman dressed in khaki slacks and a forest green jacket adorned with the camp's logo. She was standing erect, holding some papers to her chest with crossed arms. She moved forward to meet the group, "Welcome to Cabin 17. I am Marcia Smullen, Assistant Director of the resort facilities. I see there are not enough chairs for all of you, but those that wish, please be seated."

Gus rushed to the nearest seat, as if he was in a musical chair game and beamed as he took possession of it; beating out a tall, skinny guy who had almost dived for it.

"It's all in the wrist, Proctor."

Miss Smullen, who had stepped back during the seating melee, came forward again and held up the papers, "I am handing out maps of the resort and special event schedules. I know some of you will not be staying in the cabins during your stay, but I am sure that some of the events will be something you will enjoy attending."

Michael had to think about her 'will not be staying in the cabins' statement. Eleven people just arrived, with luggage, for a three to four day stay. Where *would* they stay?

Miss Smullen went on for a bit longer, handing out the papers and then turned the gathering over to Gus. He stood up and addressed the small, somber faced assembly.

"I know most of you flew in late last night or early this morning and you might be a bit bushed, but I just want to say thanks for showing up. I have been told a few of you, including myself, need to break out into groups to go over some pressing matters. You all know where the meeting rooms are and where your quarters are located, so I won't keep you. I just want everyone to assemble here at 0800 hours tomorrow morning. We have a lot to go over."

The group began dispersing; some leaving the cabin to claim their luggage and find their own cabins, while others moving to the living room to apparently continue with some discussions.

Gus noticed the group heading to the living room and quickly turned to Michael, "Let's go see your place."

CONTINUANCE

Michael went down the steps, picked up his gear and walked with Gus over to the cabin assigned to him for the duration of his stay: number 12.

The place was comfortable, if not overly rustic. He was not there to pretend to be some pioneer roughing it for the weekend, with a microwave and wall embedded TV. He just wanted to sit and rest and think.

"Why don't you get settled in? Those comfy clothes I told you about should be in the closet in the bedroom. They have wireless LAN here, so you can get online if you need to check email or do some work. As I told the group, I need to get to another meeting, but I'll be back here at 5:30 and we can go into town for some steak and beer. Sound good?"

Michael nodded his head, "Sure, that would be great."

Gus turned and started out the door, "Alright, see ya in a couple hours, son." The door shut behind him.

Michael took his luggage into the bedroom to unpack.

The place smelled as any cabin in November smells; musty -- mixed with a permanent wood smoke odor. And it felt cold, not just temperature, but it seemed like the place did not want to be inhabited. It wanted to be alone for the winter. It was not inviting. Or maybe it just did not want *him* there.

He walked out on the porch and sat in a rough hewn chair and looked out over the hills and down to Cabin 17.

He thought of the men that traveled up from the funeral with him; *this was their world*. Michael could see something in their faces that demanded dark places and whispered exchanges of limited words. They were some very powerful individuals. Add to that the high-speed convoy with lights flashing . . . he was involved in some pretty serious business at a very dangerous level.

The fact was; he felt he didn't belong in any way. This place was where *those* people gathered for brief periods of head counting. Who still was and who wasn't.

Perhaps it was some sort of fraternity or one of those exclusive lodge societies with their goofy hats, cumbersome rituals and secret handshakes. He thought back on the events of the day for a moment. He has not seen even one of these people shake hands.

He slowly rose and went back inside where he took out his laptop and continued looking at the material on the memory stick. It was something to do for a couple hours to take his mind off the uncomfortable surroundings and his returning headache. His eyes had been bothering him more than usual. Not itching or tired, it was something else. Bright lights were becoming more bothersome.

The time passed as all time passes; linear and lost.

When he finally decided to take a break, he checked the cypress-wood clock over the sink in the kitchen. It was nearly 5:30 pm.

A knock on the screen door casing confirmed that the clock was correct. Michael could see the remnants of a by-gone era of Western Americana, standing just outside his door. Gus had arrived to pick him up for dinner.

"Come on in!"

As if walking into a saloon, the door swung open and Gus erupted into the room. "Well, shut that computer thing down. You can do that later -- let's get goin'. Johnson's got a stand-up comedian gig later," he joked.

Michael closed the lid on the computer and put it back in the case.

"Why don't you bring that contraption along, just to be safe," Gus suggested.

As they walked out to the waiting SUV, Johnston stood in the cold mountain air, holding the car door open for them. "Put his case in the back, will ya?"

The case was placed in the trunk and they pulled away in the waning November evening light.

Ten minutes later, they pulled into parking lot of a local 'family-style dinner' restaurant which was built at the base of the mountain. Johnson parked, just as the ever present SUV shadow, containing two 'suits' from the complex, drove up to a space a few yards away. As the 'tails' emerged from their vehicle, Michael recognized one of them as part of the party that had traveled up from the funeral earlier.

Michael turned in his seat to exit, but Gus touched his arm, "Just a second." He reached into his pocket and pulled out an empty pack of matches and gave it to Michael. "You'll be a needin' this in a few days. Put it in your wallet."

Gus watched to make sure that the matchbook cover was secure in Michael's wallet. "OK, let's go get some grub."

They were seated in a room off to the side of the main dining area; the booth sat against the wall facing the entrance to the little enclave. Apparently steak dinners and beer for both of them had been preordered, for it began arriving at the table within moments of their seating.

Gus looked around the empty small room, "This is great, don't 'cha think? Not crowded, peaceful; just regular folks sitting around and enjoying themselves."

Michael wondered just how many *regular* folks were actually in the place.

Gus began to cut into his steak and stopped. He lifted his fork and began using it to emphasize his speech. "Just too many damn people on this rock, that's the whole problem. Where ever you are, someone else wants to be there too. Just stand in some obscure corner aisle of any grocery store for more than three minutes and someone will want to get at what you're standing in front of. It could be the nastiest, smelliest thing in the whole place, but someone will want it and ask you to move. And if you refuse to let them get what they want, all hell could break out."

He put down the fork and took another swig of beer. He looked over at Michael, who was slowing eating, not sure of what Gus was leading up to.

Gus continued with his views on overpopulation, "Wish I could have a portable trap door. Just put it down in front of me and when they want to be where I am -- I can send them to where I'm not." He began to cut his steak again. "Yep, that would be just great. Maybe put one right at the entrance of the store, so when I get there, I'll be the only one in the place." He filled his mouth and looked to the other room, "Just too many damn people," he mumbled.

They sat and ate quietly for a few more minutes, only exchanging comments on the food and the service. After they had finished, the waiter cleared the table and coffee was brought back to them.

Gus put a pack of sweetener into his cup and began to stir it with a spoon.

"The next few days are really going to be something, Michael. Life changing, I would say." Gus paused from fixing his coffee.

Michael picked up his napkin, "Gus, who were all those people we saw in Cabin 17?"

Gus waved his hand, "Just some associates that showed up for tomorrow's meeting. You will meet most of them over the next couple days."

Michael had to ask, "Is this some kind of club or something?"

Gus tilted his head back and let out a long belly laugh, "Club?" He had to pause to breath. "I never thought of our little organization as a club. But, I guess it is, in some respects. It's damn hard to get in and the dues are insane. Yet, the benefits are out of this world."

Gus wiped his hands on the tablecloth and reached into his coat pocket. "Let's get you up to speed."

He took out a crumbled envelope. Looking to the other room, he handed it to Michael.

"I want you to read this, might shed some light on a few things for ya."

Michael opened the multi-creased envelope and took out a paper. He unfolded it and leaned closer to the candle on the table. It was a handwritten letter from Hugh Waterman to Gus, dated October 19, 2012.

Gus,

CONTINUANCE

No access to a secure computer network. Paranoia may be setting in. I'm forced to send you this through trusted curriers.

SC lives: 20°19'59.77N – 89°49'56.36W

He will be home on 11/6. Meet you there.

Need Michael Fields, ASAP.

Going downhill. George says maybe a few weeks.

God! Bless America.

Hugh

There were a series of unrecognizable symbols at the bottom of the letter.

Michael slowly lowered the paper to the table, but he could not take his eyes off it.

"I got this on October 23rd. Hugh hung in there for a few more weeks, and died on November 11th. We flew the body back from the Yucatan on the 13th."

"I don't understand most of this or those symbols at the bottom. And what did he mean, 'need Michael Fields, ASAP?'"

Gus took back the letter and looked it over again, "So, you've never see these crazy doodad symbols before? That's interesting."

He began to drum the fingers of his left hand on the table as he looked at the letter then at Michael. He stopped suddenly, as if he had come to a decision.

"The skinny on this is that Hugh was after Bancroft, your old boss. It became an obsession after Hugh found out that GMCS was modified and he wanted to get a copy of the revised source code 'cause he was sure that it was being changed for some weird purpose only known to Bancroft. Hugh thought the world of your skills, Michael, and knowing that you could find the changes in the new GMCS programs, you could tell us what their purposes were. That is why Hugh wanted us to bring you into . . . our confidence."

Gus looked around the room, then back at Michael.

"Hugh had Bancroft followed for months and reports were that he had tracked him down to the Yucatan. That note confirmed his efforts."

"So, Hugh must have got the code."

"What I gave you was a copy of the original GMCS and some added files that we discovered in the Bunker. I knew you would need those. Maybe when you put them all together it will show us what Bancroft was up to."

"Is Bancroft helping?" Michael assumed that he was not.

"I really can't tell you too much more about that situation . . . at this time. It probably wouldn't make any sense to you anyway. After tomorrow's meetings you might be ready. We'll see how it goes." Gus placed the letter back in the envelope, then into his coat pocket.

Michael thought back to the letter, "And who is this George, that Hugh mentioned?"

"Just someone Hugh knew." Gus put both hands on the table and smiled, "You're probably plum tuckered out. We should get you back to your cabin. You're gonna have a real long day tomorrow."

There was no bill.

They arrived back at Michael's cabin, a few minutes after 8:30 pm. Johnson retrieved the laptop case from the trunk and handed it back to Michael at the foot of the steps. It appeared that the case had been opened, as the top zipper was not closed as it had been earlier. Johnson remained standing in the cold, looking around the area as Gus leaned out the open door of the vehicle.

"You have a good night, son. Why don't you look at the file named *SC Letter*? Alright, see you at 8:30 in the morning, in Cabin 17." He moved back inside as Johnson closed the door.

Michael continued to stand in the biting cold as the departing black vehicle quickly floated into the night, as if being ferried across the River Styx. Only the bobbing tail lights were visible as delicate, blood-red tinted snowflakes danced after them.

Chapter 5

7:45 am Wednesday, November 21, 2012

Michael walked over to Cabin 17 in the cold morning mountain air. He dressed in a flannel shirt, a heavy jacket with the resort's name on it and a pair of dark denim slacks; which were all hanging in the closet of his cabin. How they got there, how *he* got there were some serious questions which he needed to find some answers. There were even underwear and socks in the dresser drawer; nothing was missed for his visit and it appeared enough extra clothing had been supplied to last a week.

As he entered the cabin, it appeared that most of the individuals from yesterday's initial meeting in the cabin were already there and dressed in similar lumberjack clothing. Gus was not visible but was somewhere at the rear of the group as Michael could hear his booming voice over the entire assemblage.

A middle-aged woman walked out from the small kitchen to the right of the dining room. She had on thin rubber gloves, a baseball cap turned backwards on her softly graying head and a bottle of window cleaner in her right hand. She was headed for Michael.

Gus intercepted her and they both walked over to Michael together, "Good morning, Michael. Glad you showed up a bit early." He pointed to his left, "This is Nancy. Nancy, this is Michael Fields; he will be joining our meeting today. We spoke of his 'background' earlier."

She stepped closer to Michael and looked into his eyes. He moved his head back slightly as her 'inspection' was immediately uncomfortable. "Glad to have you with us today, Michael. Please excuse the way I look, just doing some cleaning. Hope everything goes well for you in the next few days. Oh, let me fix that collar." She had a sense of compassion in her voice and a warm grandmotherly smile, with intelligent eyes and something on her mind as she fixed the collar of his shirt.

"Thank you." Michael smiled back, wondering if her duties were actually more than cleaning up cabins, making visitors presentable and conducting intense eye examinations.

There were the two 'suits' standing next to the front door, as Gus walked over to stand between them. "Looks like everyone's here, let's go down." Michael began to walk towards the exit, but stopped as Gus moved towards the fireplace. The rest of the group held their positions.

When Gus was within four feet of the hearth, the wall to the left of the mantle slid open; revealing a stainless steel elevator door.

Michael stood motionless, staring at the opening.

The metal doors of the elevator slid apart and Gus motioned for Michael to enter. Three more of the group moved in with them as the rest of the cluster moved closer. They would wait for the next ride; to wherever the thing went.

There were only two buttons on the panel in the car, apparently one for up and the other down. But from everything Michael had been exposed to over the last forty hours, they could have been for left and right. Gus selected the bottom one. It lit up, the doors closed and they began to descend. Soft music filled the cabinet so as to cover up the moaning of the straining cables, which were being unrolled from the second floor of Cabin 17.

Michael had no reference to how far they traveled, but it was more than three stories, he was sure of that. After a gentle stop the doors opened to an area that resembled a spacious Corporation lobby with two more Suits seated on a couch to the far right side. A uniformed armed guard, wearing shaded glasses, black SWAT clothing and calf-high black boots, was standing ten feet to the left of the elevator door opening. Gus waved to the seated men, they waved back. A green light, located on the wall near the armed guard, responded positively to their arrival. He motioned, with his automatic weapon, for them to enter.

A receptionist, seated at a polished counter directly in front of them, smiled and motioned for the group to enter a hallway behind and to her left.

"If I find out who pinched my ass on the way down, he's a dead man," Gus bellowed, laughing.

Following Gus, the group proceeded down the hallway, which was perhaps twelve feet wide with scores of people moving in both directions along its cavernous length. Gus' group continued down the passage to a room marked Conference Room 1C. Outside the door, three small vehicles resembling golf carts were parked. One was a two-seater, while the other two looked as if four to five people could ride in them. The door glided open as Gus stopped in front of it.

Inside the room, resting upon the plush blue carpeting was a long dark mahogany table with no less than ten chairs positioned around it and five more along the opposite wall and to the left. A huge video screen, dark curtained walls, coffee, donuts . . . and two inhabitants completed the room's contents. The two residents, who were sitting at the back of the conference table, stood up as the elevator riders entered.

As each person entered the room, they picked up folders from a stack that was on a small roll-away counter, just to the right of the door. After everyone had a folder in hand, they went straight for the free pastries laid out on a table at the back of the room.

"Gus, we are very pleased to have you come and visit our humble hideaway, once again," the male of the two already in the room, groveled.

"Yo', Burt. Hey, Sandy," Gus replied as he dug through the donuts. Finding the perfect Long John, he turned to face them.

"Listen; want you two to meet Michael. He came in from Silicon Valley to help us out on the code thing."

Michael moved forward to be introduced.

He held out his hand. "Michael Fields. Glad to meet you."

"Burt Murphy, welcome to our burrow." Burt did not shake his hand, but only raised his in a small acknowledgement. Michael half-smiled and then returned a half-wave.

CONTINUANCE

"I'm Sandy Ayers," the smartly dressed woman identified herself as she moved to the front of the room. His outstretched hand followed her as she passed. "Please, have some coffee. This meeting may get boring. Don't want you nodding off," she called back over her shoulder.

The rest of the group entered the room from their ride down in the elevator. They picked up folders joined the others in taking up positions at the long table.

"So, did they give Hugh a good sendoff?" Burt asked concernedly as he walked to the front of the room. He took up a chair to the right side of Sandy'.

"It was very nice," Gus mumbled with his mouth full of pastry, "They really went all out for ol' Hugh. Saw a lot of familiar faces. No press. No GenZs that I recognized. Well, except for Michael here." He lowered himself into a chair at right-center of the table, holding a very large bowl of roasted peanuts that he had somehow latched onto. He placed it on the table in front of him. He signaled to Michael to sit next to him by pointing to the adjacent chair.

'No others? It seemed liked Gus knew everyone who was at the funeral,' Michael thought. 'Did he say Gen Zee?'

Sandy stood at the head of the table, holding a white folder with a large purple band printed along the bottom. Michael looked around the room and saw that all of the folders, now placed on the table in front of each attendee, had the same cover. She put on a pair of thin reading glasses that rested on the end of her nose. You could tell who was in charge of this portion of the meeting.

"All right, let's get started. I am Sandra Ayers, Senior Mission Manager within the Program Office of 3938 and this is Burt Murphy, my Assistant Mission Manager. We would like to thank you all for coming as this is quite an occasion having you all in the same room at once. It was unfortunate that Mister Waterman's passing allowed us to accomplish this without causing suspicion, but it will provide us the opportunities for some real hardball discussions over the next couple of days."

She turned to face Michael, with her hand outstretched.

"I would like to welcome our guest, Mister Michael Fields. I know you all received his profile and GenZ qualifications and have approved his attendance."

All nodded as Michael's eyes passed from one to another. He occasionally nodded back to those who had made the effort to look up from their folders.

"You are all familiar with most of the upcoming presentations, but please be tolerant as we need to get Mister Fields up to speed as he is 'joining' the Program. I know this is highly irregular, but the situation demands it."

The room lights dimmed, except for small spotlights which illuminated each position on the table where the members had placed their folders. The diminished illumination exposed a tiny red light within the small black plastic dome over the screen. A camera was on. There were more than the occupants of the room, watching the proceedings.

As Michael looked around the dim area he felt cautiously impressed with the men around the table, the mysterious folders and Sandy. It was obvious that she was all business and everyone knew and respected it.

And who said he was joining anything?

Miss Ayers began the presentations, with a touch to her remote, which she held in her left hand.

The screen lit up with a graphic or something Michael had never seen before. Sort of a purple ink spot, like one would see when a fountain pen leaks and had been rubbed to one side; it looked smeared. It must have been a logo of sorts, but there was no lettering to indicate the name or designation of the organization it represented.

In big red letters, across the bottom of the screen was printed: EYES ONLY.

The slide changed and a block diagram, that only a government employee would understand, appeared.

"As you all know, the second annual system-wide alert of all military, civilian and jointly run underground installations is coming up in December. In preparation, a facilities inspection of *our* MF was conducted last week and we were only cited on two items. The voltage fluctuation on Fuel Cell Bank 4 was .43% off for a 24 hour period, and air quality was 1.3% below Code 821 for the testing period. It was only a couple dirty collector plates that should have been cleaned per SOP. Overall, I would say that we passed with flying colors as the corrections took only hours to rectify."

Everyone nodded their heads and lifted eyebrows in pride. Michael didn't have a clue what they were talking about. Actually, he didn't care.

"We will see how the December alert transpires. Hopefully it will be as successful as last June's." She had trailed off the last of the sentence and appeared disturbed at the thought.

Sandy brought up the next slide. The title read Program 3938, with a satellite map of the United States.

"Time is running out Gentlemen. I am confident you all appreciate the intense gravity of the situation. I hate to say it, but it appears that our recruiting of Mister Fields may almost be too late. 3938 and the whole December Pact are at stake, if the *SC Letter* is to be believed."

Gus broke in, "Sandy, I think your people may be looking too hard at them charts and timelines of yours. The reality of the situation is that Michael here has the entire source code and reads it like a book. Right, Michael?"

Michael slowly nodded. *Maybe he should start caring*, he thought.

"This is like falling off a cow to him. I wouldn't start heading back to the barn, yet. The Santa Claws situation is being dealt with even as we speak."

Sandy pointed at the large bowl in front of Gus, with the edge of the folder she was holding.

"Those things are filled with fat. They're gonna kill you."

"Hate to die of nothing," Gus retorted, smiling.

A hand rose from the other side of the table.

"I think all resources should be placed at Mister Fields' disposal to expedite this work, as well as putting him in contact with our field intelligence personnel and any others that would be available."

All mumbled in acceptance.

"Already have that lined up, Morgan. He will be ready to hit the ground running by Monday with Field Intelligence support."

Michael spoke up, as the voice of the unknowing, "This may not be the time or place, but I really don't know why I am here; wherever here is."

The fan of the ceiling-mounted projector was all that could be heard.

Sandy slowly looked around the room. "This may be redundant for the rest of you, but it is essential that Mister Fields be briefed on the following information."

She pressed the advance button allowing the slide to change to a side view diagram of what appeared to be a multi-storied, many fingered mall.

"Hey, I always enjoy looking at these," Gus spoke up, leaning back in the chair.

Sandy picked up her laser pointer and faced the screen.

"This is the MF complex, which we are in at the moment. As you can see from the slide, it is a self-sufficient complex capable of maintaining a working residential community of 7,000 people. It contains waste disposal, water purification, medical facilities, power generation stations, permanent housing areas and so on. We are presently here." She pointed at an area located on the first floor, titled Level 1, in a single wing on the west side. It looked like a hallway leading into, or out of, the complex. He could see the elevator they rode in, down from Cabin 17.

"Make it do that 'turning-around' stuff," Gus said, making circles in the air with his finger.

The graphic, on the screen, began rotating in a 360 degree movement. Michael marveled at the image. Not only was the structure massive in height, but the width seemed to be the size of many football fields.

"The complex is six stories in height, or *depth* in this case. If the structure was built on the surface, it would span out over an area of one-hundred and sixty-two acres. There are over four-thousand rooms designed for permanent occupancy of DP personnel and three-thousand areas for offices, labs and operation departments. In addition, there are over three-hundred shops and centers for providing various services to our employees."

"Why hasn't this been on the news or on some documentary program? This is really marvelous," Michael asked Gus.

"Because it doesn't actually exist," Sandy answered as she turned to face him with a slight smile.

"Kind of like us," Gus broke in, nudging Michael. The gathering, at the table, all mumbled in humorous agreement.

"Well how long has this underground thing been going on?" Michael asked.

Gus chimed in, after popping another peanut in his mouth, "Here's the poop on that. In 1951, construction began on a facility called Site R up near Waynesboro, Pennsylvania. It was to be the disaster recovery site for all communications. They got the whole thing fully operational in 1953 when Eisenhower got in."

"How many people live there?"

"It's not really designed as a habitat for a large contingency to have a permanent occupation; it just runs 24/7 with shift changes. Although, it has been modified to house around a thousand if needed. Not like our MF," he boasted. "Oh, the Russians have one that can hold a reported 50,000 in Yamantau Mountain. But, that's just asinine."

He looked over at one of the gentlemen sitting directly across the table. "The Russians are still gonna put 50,000 in one location? Where are their heads?" The man shrugged and looked down at his open folder.

Burt stood up, "I would like to point out that an MF facility is designed to house a distribution of key government, infrastructure, medical and communication personnel within a self-sustained living and working environment for three months.

55

The MF is directly connected to all of the other underground facilities in a number of areas through a network of hardened buried optical fiber cable routes and satellites. If any or all of the other underground facilities become inoperative, an individual complex will still be able to facilitate all governmental duties."

Michael tilted his head and spoke up, "I think I'm getting the idea here, but what if only one underground place survives, from whatever it is that it's supposed to survive from and the President and all those government guys were in another one? Who would be President?"

"Guess we would have to draw straws," Gus laughed. "The loser gets to be President." The others at the table exhibited dubious smiles.

"What does MF stand for?" Michael tried to appear professional, although he was tapping his feet fast enough to ignite the carpeting.

Gus was still getting over his last joke as he turned to Michael, "Mushroom Farm."

"I see . . . the *mushroom* thing." He looked at Gus who winked back.

Michael felt this was the time and place.

"Now, may I ask; why am I here? You are showing me all this stuff, which I know must be beyond Top Secret, and bringing me to Howard Linn's, I mean Hugh Waterman's, funeral . . ."

"Think of it as indoctrination son." Gus slapped him on the back. "I'm sure this next presentation will answer a truck-load of your questions."

The screen turned black. Then another title slide appeared: *Global Monitoring and Control Systems (GMCS)*.

The same strange purple ink blot appeared; which was on the last title slide.

A gentleman, in his late 50's, rose from the end of the table and walked to the front of the room. He had the appearance of a Business Development guy; dark suit (and not just worn for funerals), white silk shirt, power tie, suspenders and perfect hair. That is always a giveaway of a BD guy, the hair. And maybe the cuff links.

Sandy sat down as the BD guy stepped to the right of the screen and flashed a cheesy game show host smile.

"For those of you who do not know me, I am Mark Bryant, the new Division Manager of the GMCS Program or as we call it – *Global Visibility*. I have replaced the late Hugh Waterman and will try to live up to his standards, dedication and success."

Hugh Waterman was the Division Manager of the entire GMCS Program? Michael was stunned. No wonder he was able to get the source code; he was NexTrÉ's customer. And all the crap he had told him, over beer at Q's, about the lame-brained, demanding customer . . . oh, boy.

And now all of Hugh's work was being turned over to this guy, up there, showing pre-prepared slides and strutting around like a clueless peacock. Hugh had been a hands-on guy; this Slickster had never touched anything but a golf club and a martini glass in his whole career. He must be a real pro at shaking hands and doing his "Damn glad to meet you," routine.

Perhaps the Program might have had enough of independent thinkers and doers, based on the past actions of Hugh. They certainly found the perfect replacement for their new breed of managers; a jellyfish who only knew what to say and do by following the directions of a superior. Was Gus that superior?

Bryant continued as the next slide appeared, showing a flat graphic of the entire world.

He went into a scripted narrative, probably prepared by a marketing slave; "GMCS is exactly what it stands for, Global Monitoring and Control. A software program that will allow anyone, who is authorized, to log onto the system and see data on any item that has been electronically tagged, anywhere the Department of Defense has remote devices to read them; anywhere on earth. We call that Visibility. We can obtain the current condition the item is in, where it has been and where it is supposed to be. The amount of information we can obtain from the tag and interfaced sensors is almost limitless. That is *truly* Global Visibility."

Michael knew that part of GMCS was originally designed for Radio Frequency Identification technology tracking through satellite and terrestrial networks. But it looked like the software had grown to include the reporting of data received from every type of electronic tagging technology on the market and monitoring the tagged items by satellite imagery. It had become a very effective tool for implementing the technology that the Department of Defense currently had out there.

Bryant read aloud the text that was showing on the screen – it was apparent that he was not that familiar with the origin of GMCS. It may have been the first time he had actually seen the slide.

"GMCS was contracted to NexTrÉ Corporation for development, testing and sustainment in 2005. The deliverables included a global asset management software application, firmware that is placed into hardware for its operation and reporting, various client/server modules and a robust Universal Data Capture edgeware component. The initial package was delivered in late 2009 and became fully operational in 2010. The expansion of the system has been going on ever since, as new tracking technologies and global areas of visibility are added."

He activated the slide animation and yellow dots began to be superimposed all over the graphic.

"These are the server locations of the GMCS network; as you can see every operational area is covered: CENTCOM, PACOM, and etcetera. Each server receives item data from millions of data capture points or readers. The information received is from RFID -- both active and passive, barcodes, biometrics and our own taggant sources."

Again he advanced the presentation and blue lines started to appear, connecting the dots.

"As the graphic depicts, all servers are connected to the fallback systems at Site R and the other COM Centers."

Another slide appeared, showing the Earth with a number of small red stars around it.

"This is the current satellite population that Program 3938 utilizes, in their stable geosynchronous positions. I must point out; at this moment *none* of our birds have been compromised." Pleased mumblings emitted from the assembled audience.

"However, to limit any possible degradation of service due to the situation that occurred in January, all data exports have been switched from satellite to physical terrestrial optical fiber feeds. Except the data coming from ships in the open oceans -- that is still satellite fed. This precautionary measure will continue until the source of the event can be isolated and resolved. However, this brings up a possible cascade situation, for at the current 32 terabytes per second of data being sent through only one media, it is straining our capacity and visibility may need to be reduced, again."

He turned to face Michael and put on his best fake smile.

"With the addition of Mister Fields to the Deep Purple team, we are confident that this situation can be alleviated so that we may bring all systems up and continue with our Prime Mission." He was such a bullshitter.

'What the hell was a Deep Purple?' Michael thought he was working for UPipe Holdings.

Turning back to the audience, Bryant went on with his briefing, "We are trying to get access to all of the December Pact satellites through the usual diplomatic channels to determine if any anomalies are detected or if there are any renegade command lines present. It has been difficult; not with the Surviving Nation's systems, but the others."

Michael raised his hand, "Surviving Nations?"

Gus looked around the room and then up to Bryant, "We can save that for tomorrow."

Bryant nodded and continued, appearing to be somewhat annoyed at Michael's interruption, "As we know, all Automatic Identification Technology enabled items may be tracked for supply chain and logistic purposes; however, during the last situation all of our resources had to be reallocated to maintain just DoD and other governmental visibility. As the situation cleared, we at the GMCS Network Operations Center have been concentrating our efforts on damage control at this point.

"If the situation occurs again, we will be forced to limit bandwidth and focus on absolute minimum visibility. We will filter for only Deep Purple assets."

Gus broke in, "Well, Bryant, that shouldn't happen again, 'cause we got Michael here to see that it doesn't."

Bryant looked down his nose at Michael, "That is very comforting, Gus." He did not mean it.

Bryant walked back to his seat, smiling at the rest of the attendees while straightening his cuffs as if he had just won The Masters. As the room lights grew brighter, Michael could see a disgusted look on Gus' face, as he watched Bryant strut across the room.

Sandy stood and introduced the next presentation . . . and the next.

Briefings were conducted throughout the morning with lunch being brought in while the talks progressed into the late afternoon. Everyone in the room took their turn at bringing the rest up to speed on their vital issues; talking about new waste treatment equipment, budgets, Diversity Training requirements from the HR people and a new policy on procurement. One of the presenters had mentioned something about a Foundation, followed by Gus slapping the table and yelling, "Not here!"

Michael had drained the coffee pot and was at the point of requesting a biological break when Gus stood up.

"That will conclude today's session, as Michael has not been cleared to be exposed to any more of this stuff. However, shortly after we leave here, he will be one of us. So tomorrow we can dump the whole enchilada on him and the two other new people. I must add, the two new people are not GenZ."

All present applauded softly, but it was difficult to determine if the response was attributed to the news that the meeting was finally over or that no other GenZ would be present.

"Well, I want to thank you all for showing up. I know you all have pressing issues involving your own areas that need to be attended to, so I won't keep you any longer. Everyone be back here tomorrow morning, 0900 hours. We will be covering some of the more serious situations in more detail and hopefully by then Mister Fields will be able to provide some enlightening developments. I would like those of you who are involved with the Yucatan situation to come with me."

He turned to address the man at the far right end of the table who had rambled on about the importance of Diversity Training. "Barney, could you get Mister Fields processed after this?"

"Sure thing, Gus."

"OK, see you all tomorrow."

The room began to empty. As the group left the room, they slid their folders into a slot on the roll-around counter where they were originally piled. As each folder went into the slot, a small green light illuminated.

Gus turned to Michael. "I'm going to turn you over to Barney here, for a bit."

Gus forgot about the folder slot and walked through the doorway with his folder in hand. A red light appeared over the door.

"Gus, your folder!" Sandy called to him.

"Damn, sorry." Gus placed his folder into the slot, clearing the red light. He left the room with three gentlemen who were in the meeting and walked down the hallway towards the elevator.

Barney led Michael into the hall, where they climbed into a two-seater cart. One of the multi-passenger units had already departed. The motor whined softly as they traveled down the corridor, away from the direction Gus' group had departed. They passed more smiling people, statuesque security guards and scores of administrative offices, as they progressed deeper -- into the enigma.

Chapter 6

Michael and Barney rode down the long corridor as sounds of birds softly chirping flowed from the ceiling speakers. The walls were adorned with large flat monitors displaying outdoor settings from around the world; trees, mountains, oceans and waterfalls. They turned a corner to traverse down another hallway. Murals of lush foothills covered both sides of the corridor. The speakers above Michael emitted sounds that matched the visual impressions around them. Every couple of minutes the monitors would show the purple splotch and the word, Continuance.

There was a hint of ozone in the air. *It must be the purification system,* thought Michael. Probably using ion purifiers -- yeah that was it, because Sandy mentioned 'cleaning the collectors' in her briefing.

"So Michael, Gus tells us that you were one of the original architects of GMCS."

"That's right, started putting it together back in '05. It was actually a spin-off of another smaller program we had developed for strictly Radio Frequency Identification tracking. Things like inventory control and supply chain applications."

"Exciting stuff I suppose, but it's really over my head. I'm just a simple administrator, Human Resources and the like."

Two other carts had moaned passed them, each moving casually-dressed, happy people to a more important place.

Barney slowed as they approached a door marked Human Resources. "And we are here." He stopped the cart along the wall and plugged the vehicle's charger into an electrical outlet. He pointed to the door. "Right in there, if you please."

Michael exited the vehicle and the door to the room slid open automatically as Barney neared the portal. They were immediately greeted by a bubbly blond with teeth right out of a tooth paste commercial. "Hi there, you must be Michael. I'm

Michelle. Say . . . that's a coincidence, Michael and Michelle." She giggled and shook his hand.

Michael was now convinced that the ideal job for someone who had made it through college on a cheerleading scholarship was in Human Resources.

Barney took the file that Miss Prom Organizer was holding, touched her arm and leaned in, "We need to get Michael processed into Deep Purple as soon as possible, Michelle. I assume all is ready for his identification procedure?"

"Yes Sir. Right this way Michael."

All three walked to the door of a windowless side office marked 'Catacombs'. Michael stopped and looked at the out-of-place placard.

Barney spoke over Michael's shoulder, "Just some inside humor from the Human Resources gang. We are also in charge of morale in this place. The staff wanted a lighter side to our environment so they gave 'interesting' names to all of our offices." They entered the office and Barney moved behind a massive desk. Michael entered behind him and stood in front of Barney. Michelle moved to the left side of Michael, after shutting the door.

The room resembled a CEO's office with a couch, leather chairs and some real house plants. The walls were adorned with plaques, awards and a picture of Barney with the President. The desk Barney sat behind was solid hardwood, buffed to a shine that eliminated the need for any mirrors in the room. A lamp on a small table at the end of the couch provided illumination for half the room. The lamp on the desk supplied the other half.

"How did they get that desk in here? It certainly didn't come through that door," Michael mused.

With a half-smile, Barney opened the folder, which had the familiar printed purple band across the bottom.

"Please, both of you sit down."

Michael sat in one of two leather chairs, facing the front of the desk. Michelle settled into the other one, opening her notebook.

Barney removed more than too many papers from the folder and laid the stack in front of Michael.

"Here are a couple forms that you will need to sign. And as you can see, they have already been filled out for you."

The ink blot that had appeared on the title slides of the presentations was also on the upper right corner of each document.

"I'm not familiar with this purple mark. I saw it a couple times today, already. It doesn't have any text on it. Is it UPipe or something?"

"No, not UPipe, it's our logo. We use it for official business and identification purposes."

Michael leaned forward, "And who are *we*, specifically?"

Barney leaned back to maintain a comfortable presence zone, "We are an agency of the United States Government, but not officially established as such. In other words, we don't exist, but still get funding. We accommodate and manage various projects and support Executive Order 11490 through the 3938 Program, as Sandy spoke of in the meeting."

"Then what is Deep Purple?"

"That is the human component of 3938."

"OK, fair enough -- I guess." Michael looked down at the paperwork in his hand. The first page read, *Michael, please sign these. It is the best job in the world, working for the best damn boss in the world; Me.* It was signed *Gus*.

Michael quickly glanced at some of the forms that were under Gus' note. "So, according to these forms this is essentially my first day of work as I become a full-time employee in the 3938 Program?"

"Actually, if you notice on Form 1131A, Field 17, you will become a 'life-time' employee in the 3938 Program -- as a member of Deep Purple."

Michael found Form 1131A and sure enough, Field 17 confirmed Barney's bizarre statement.

"Are you a life-time member?" Michael asked, looking to both of them.

"Actually I am. Michelle is not."

Michelle looked down, obviously hiding some inner response that she did not want to be let known.

Michael turned to Barney, "Who said I wanted to join 3938 or be a 'human component' in Deep Purple?"

"Gus."

"Gus? What say does Gus have in all this? It's my decision, I should think."

"Who Gus wants on the DP rolls, Gus gets. And by the way, only the best are asked, if that helps."

Michael leaned back in the chair holding the stack of papers and forms in front of him. He began reading the first one, which was on first glance, an offer letter.

"If you would like to be alone for awhile to go through those, we can come back. But, we are under some time constraints."

"No, this shouldn't take too long."

He continued reading the letter, which nearly resembled a notification of being adopted by a Royal Family. Apparently, this Deep Purple thing was *very* deep and beyond exclusive.

However, the words were impressive but the wording was somehow dark; as if written by fingers driven by a small remembrance of hope in a hopeless situation. They almost appeared as some soul pleading for help from a lifeboat, rather than a large agency dictating what your miniscule niche will be in a bureaucratic pyramid.

Trying to ignore the feeling of the document, he concentrated on the purpose of the letter, which was a summary of his expected duties, work location and salary.

It was pretty straight forward in the work requirements; supervise a team to bring the current and future versions of all visibility software applications up to robust departmental standards and specifications. Right up his ally, so no concerns there.

The location was a bit vague, as it seemed to be indicating that the work was to be performed at both his home office and the MF.

The salary was the clincher; almost three times what he had ever made anywhere.

"Does this number include a sign-up bonus or something?"

"No, that is your first year rate. It will, no doubt, go up as time passes. As far as a bonus, a number of things are planned." Barney smiled.

Michael knew that this was one of those offers you could not refuse. He took mental stock of his present life situation. His worldly possessions could be assessed on a bar napkin; a small assortment of permanent-press clothing, some worn 90's-styled furniture (divorce leftovers), a five-year old car and a miniature mountain of computer related equipment -- with cables. And there was his struggling business; actually it could only be weeks before rigormortia would begin setting in.

He looked for an exit clause, just in case this Purple thing didn't work out.

"This life-time employment statement, can I walk away if I see the need?"

"At any time you wish. There is just a gag agreement that you must sign that prevents you from talking about the Program for one year. It's standard procedure for a project like this. But, in the entire length of the program, not one person has left. It is a great place to work." Barney was definitely a Human Resource Pro and probably a great used car salesman on the weekends. This prompted Michael to bring up another question.

"Do I get weekends off?"

"Set your own schedule. We just require everyone to meet their project milestones. You can enter and leave the MF anytime you wish, just not during the alerts. As you heard earlier, the next one is coming up in a few weeks."

Michael knew that he would never get a better offer than this, and if he did, he could always leave this one. It was time to see what was on the other side of the fence.

"Alright, give me a pen. I hope I don't get writer's cramp from signing all these forms."

Michael began scribbling his name on the documents. Health insurance, tax withholdings, Diversity and Sexual Harassment understandings; all of the normal administration paperwork one would be subjected to in any job.

Then the last form appeared from the bottom of the stack. It stated that he would allow the embedding of a traceable taggant to provide employee identification and to meet all security requirements of the program.

"You want to explain this one to me, Barney?"

There was a pause as Barney and Michelle exchanged glances.

"In order for all Deep Purple employees to access required work areas, handle Program sensitive material and be tracked within the system, they need to have the required causation e-signature."

"You mean that you are going to implant a Radio Frequency Identification chip in me?" Michael sat back, feeling like a head of livestock.

Barney leaning back slowly with claps hands under his chin. "Not as such. RFID is just used for tracking cases, cartons and containers. It's pretty limited in range and too expensive."

He slightly raised his right hand and turned it, palm out, to Michael. His left hand pointed at a small purple dot at the base of his little finger.

"It is more like a tattoo. A little, deep purple tattoo."

"Ah, I get it -- Deep Purple." Michael nodded with a small sense of enlightenment to the name and a huge enlightenment to the sickening implications.

"It is made from a programmable powder called LiquiCode that is mixed in the ink. The compound is a natural shade of purple, actually violet."

He put his hand on the desk, palm up, so that Michael could inspect it closer. Then he put down his other hand, palm up. They both had the small tattoo in the same spot under the little finger. The image was that of the purple ink blot logo that appeared at the top of every form he had just signed.

"And I get those?" Michael was not sure on signing the last form.

"They can be removed if you decide to leave. But, you need them to work for the Program at your required security level."

"Will it hurt?" He hated needles.

Barney chuckled as he leaned back in the overstuffed chair, "You will get a topical, local anesthetic. Don't worry. You are too valuable an asset to the Program for us to want to have you experience any pain."

"Pain comes in many forms, Barney."

Michelle moved uneasily in her chair, head still down. Her smile had left from the moment he had asked about her being a DP. Yes, there were many forms of pain.

"Alright, Barney, here ya go." Michael signed the last document and picked it up to hand over to Barney. It weighed more than anything he had ever held in his life.

Barney placed all of the papers into the folder, except the last one, and handed the file to Michelle.

She stood up and held out her hand, "It was so nice to meet, Michael. Congratulations on being chosen for Deep Purple." Her enthusiastic demeanor had faded completely as she finished the sentence. They shook hands. She opened the door, glanced back at Barney and went out. Michael could hear the door being locked automatically behind her.

Barney stood up with the single sheet of paper he had kept in his left hand and turned around. He placed his right hand on a small plaque that rested face up at the left end of the credenza. Half of the wall slid open to the right, taking the picture of the President and Barney with it.

"Well, that answers my question on how you got the desk in here," Michael marveled.

"Let's get your identification into the system, shall we? This way, please."

They walked into the newly exposed room, which resembled a large elf workshop. There were ten people in the room, some sitting at lab tables while others moved about the area.

They proceeded to a lab table, which was laden with some serious electronic equipment that was being monitored by a bearded man in his 30's wearing a traditional white lab coat. There was a sewn-on name label over the top left pocket; Larry

"Larry, this is Michael Fields. He is here to get his ID."

Larry turned to his computer and typed a few strokes. "Yes, have you right here Michael. Please be seated. This won't take long."

Michael sat on a pre-propositioned stool that was facing the table, while a young woman walked across the room with a tray of plastic bottles and cotton swabs and placed it on the table top.

Larry handed Michael a paper mask to put over his nose and mouth, as he put one on himself.

"Is this going to be some kind of surgery?" Michael asked as he put on his mask.

"Not really, the masks are mainly used so we don't breathe any of the LiquiCode powder. If it gets in your lungs, you can be tracked forever, and you will have a chronic cough," Larry informed his patient while adjusting his own mask. "I've heard that they actually do that for tracking terrorists and other 'bad guys'. Spray the stuff around their camps and places they hang out."

The female assistant touched Michael's arm, "Hands on the table, please -- palms up."

She took a cotton swab and cleaned the target areas with alcohol and applied the topical anesthetic Barney had mentioned with another ball of cotton.

Larry pickup up a gun-looking device and held it in position, under the little finger of Michael's right hand.

"Will I feel this?"

"It will be excruciating. But, don't worry . . . we only lose five percent of the people that come in here." Larry responded in a matter-of-fact tone.

Michael quickly pulled his hand back.

"Relax," Larry laughed. "Just a joke – you won't feel anything. It's just some of our departmental humor."

"Funny." Michael cautiously returning his hand to the table as the device was returned to position; at the base of the little finger. Larry pulled the trigger and a dull sound, resembling an air gun, was heard. Michael only felt a quick pushing sensation. Larry lifted the gun and performed the same procedure on the left hand.

Michael looked down. There they were, two small purple logos and no blood, yet.

"OK, the raw code is in there, now let's program them." Larry took off his mask and reached for another device that looked like a powerful flashlight with a cord leading to the computer.

"I like to tell my clients what it is that I'm doing. Makes them feel more at ease."

"That works for me, Larry," Michael said through his still-attached mask, eyeing the strange contraption that Larry was now aiming at his hand.

"When the tattoo is first applied, the LiquiCode contains nothing but binary Ones. Ninety-six of them, see?" Larry turned on the device and the computer screen showed a string of ninety-six number 1's when the light passed over each of Michael's new tattoos.

"I will now 'burn' the code to your number. Oh, burn just means that we program the LiquiCode nanotubes to align to your ID number and it can never be changed. It turns off the Ones that are not needed in your number and makes them Zeros. It won't actually burn you." He chuckled at his victim's wide-eyed anxiety and looked over at Barney.

"Will you verify the number, please, Barney?"

Barney and Larry looked at the computer monitor.

Larry pointed at the screen, "It's a GZ code." They looked at each other. "A GenZ . . . with The Foundation," Barney whispered, confirming the code. They then slowly turned and looked at Michael.

Barney began to nervously write Michael's LiquiCode Identification number on the piece of paper he had brought with him. He read off the numbers slowly so Larry could confirm that it corresponded with the ID number on the screen. They both signed the paper.

"Where do you get these numbers? Who issues them?" Michael asked.

Larry's attitude had changed to that of an employee, rather than a wise-guy co-worker, "They're generated by the computer system. It just makes them up, I suppose. Unless it knows something we don't, Sir."

Larry looked at the computer monitor, "Barney, I am also reading a Visitor Smear. Does Mister Fields still have his on?"

Barney moved in front of Michael. "Oh, my. Let's get that off." He motioned to the female assistant and looked back at Michael. "You met Nancy in the cabin, topside. Remember where she touched you?"

"Let me think; she did straighten my collar. Right here," he pointed to the area Nancy had fondled.

Larry spoke between them, "You were, what we call, Smeared. A small amount of LiquiCode is covertly smeared on your clothes with a special number that is just for temporary use. It acts as a visitor tag so they can track you and let you enter authorized areas with an escort."

The female aid wiped Michael's collar with a wet sponge, "And keep you from going into places you aren't supposed to." She put the sponge into a metal container and shut the lid. She nodded to Larry who conducted another read.

"OK, only getting the Ones." Larry pointed at Michael's collar, "Without that Visitor smear, no doors would have opened and there would have been armed Security personnel on you within seconds. The Visitor smear was the LiquiCode powder mixed with corn syrup, so it washes right out with water on a sponge. But when it is mixed with other types of substrates, it is rather permanent." He sounded like a commercial for the stuff.

Barney pointed up to one of the ceiling lighting panels. "One of the tubes, in most of the lighting fixtures in the complex, is also a transceiver. Larry can read you anywhere in the building. Well, not just Larry. The 3938 system can detect your location anywhere they have readers."

Larry looked at Barney then his watch, indicating that is was time to go home.

"Sorry, Larry, I get carried away. Please continue."

Larry picked up the light device, "All right, Mister Fields, here we go."

The light was placed onto the right hand tattoo and a quick flash followed. Then the left hand was flashed in the same manner.

"OK. Time to check the code out," Larry said, turning back to the computer. He clicked on a square that said READ. Data immediately appeared; a long sting of numbers that, no doubt, meant Michael Fields -- life-time employee of Deep Purple.

Michael wondered aloud, to Larry, "Why did you have to hold the light right over my hand to read the numbers?"

"Well, Sir, once the code has been activated, we can read those numbers up to a hundred feet or more. It depends on the power of the reader. This one is set very low so I make sure I just get only *your* hand's code. It just makes it easier during this process, as there are so many other tags in the area that I didn't want to spend time scrolling down the list to isolate yours.

"We could probably read from longer ranges than a hundred feet, but we would need some pretty powerful readers to do it. Who knows what Security already has in its toolboxes of goodies? I'm just a lab tech." Larry shrugged. Michael noticed that Larry had no tattoos.

The young lady put small adhesive bandages on each tattoo as Michael removed his mask.

Barney leaned over, close to Michael, "Now don't shake hands with anyone."

"I couldn't do that with these bandages. Plus, my hands are numb." Michael smiled.

"No, I mean *never* shake hands with anyone. We wouldn't want your code to get on someone else's hand, would we?" This was not just idle talk, this was a serious directive. Michael quit smiling.

Larry clarified the statement, "Some particles of the powder can come to the surface over a period of time and rub off. It is just a natural result of the body's rejection system. But the powder is biologically safe and the code will never degenerate to a point that we cannot read it as it is duplicated hundreds of times in the tattoo. The reason for not shaking hands is that there is a slim chance that enough of the code can come off in one instance to leave an entire ID number on someone else. It is highly unlikely, but just be careful."

Barney stood upright and reached for the paper that he and Larry had signed.

"Very well, Mister Fields, that's it for the ID process. Let's go see what stuff the Program is assigning to you." Barney had become Mister Human Resources again. Michael was becoming a bit confused at the personality changes of Larry and Barney. *'What's up with this Sir and Mister Fields formality and a GenZ with The Foundation?'* He asked himself.

They left the lab through another door in the back of the room and headed down a less decorative hallway then when he had rode in the cart. The passage must have been an employee corridor, not used by visitors.

As they reached the end of the hallway Michael stopped cold. In front of him was a round room, no not just a room; another world. He was looking at the tops of trees -- lots of trees and they were real. He stepped out onto an overhanging walkway that circled above the entire room. He looked down to see a small waterfall surrounded by flowering plants, gardeners and people sitting at benches. The place must have been thirty feet high and a hundred feet across and he was about fifteen feet up off the floor of the room. Stone pathways below were laid around the outside of the whole room's floor, with some leading into the garden area.

"Are we still underground?" Michael asked in wonderment.

"About sixty feet or more, I should think."

"This is absolutely amazing! What's all this for?"

"It's a break area for the employees, plus it helps out the CO_2 filters. Actually there are four atriums in this complex. This is the West one. All part of the basic self-sustaining design."

"How can they keep all this growing down here?"

Barney pointed to the ceiling, "All of the overhead light panels contain, what you could call, grow lights. Something to do with the spectrum they emit. All of the lighting in the whole complex emulates the sun's cycle, matching the time of day on the surface. When the sun goes down, so do most of the lights. At night around here it resembles twilight. That really helps with all our internal clocks."

Michael began to think aloud. "You know, one of these MFs would really be great on the Moon. Instant colonization, just dig a hole and put in an MF. Think it will ever happen?"

"The Moon . . . or Mars; all it takes is water and money," Barney said, while looking forward, deliberately not making eye contact. "I'm sure *you* know more about that than I."

Michael could hear a bit of disdain in Barney's voice. Or was it what the color green would sound like; as in some form of jealousy? Whatever the cause, it was becoming increasingly more uncomfortable for Michael.

"Let's keep moving . . . we have one more appointment."

They walked around the garden rim, on the protruding balcony, to another hallway where Barney proceeded down at a faster pace.

As they neared a door labeled Classroom 7, Barney stopped.

"Let's try out your ID tag, Mister Fields. You go in first."

Michael moved towards the door. When he was within a two foot range of the sensors, the door slid open.

"Great, everything seems to be fine with your implants."

They both entered the room as a small green light above the door casing illuminated, indicating that both of them were authorized to enter.

The room was a typical classroom setting with four rows of tables and four computer consoles in each row. An Instructor's desk was positioned at the front of the room with a projection screen and a white board. Metal cabinets covered the wall in the rear.

There was one other person in the room; a man in his early 60's who walked with a cane and wore eyebrows so bushy they extended out and over the rims of his glasses, giving the appearance of scraggly-grey vegetation cascading down an ancient ceramic wall.

"We finally made it, Mister Rininger. Sorry you had to wait." Barney apologized.

"No problem. Just straightening things up after today's training session," the Instructor replied in a very thick Germanic accent.

"This is Michael Fields. He is a GZ . . . with The Foundation. I believe you have some things for him."

The old man clearly displayed a startled pause, then smiled, "Ya, right over here. All is in order, Mister Fields."

Rininger motioned for them to follow him to the wall cabinets where he stopped and opened the one hugging the corner of the back wall. He removed two locked metal boxes and a laptop computer case. He then carried the items to the last row of student positions. Leaning his cane against the edge of the table, he pulled a keychain from his pocket that held ten or more keys of various sizes, shapes and colors. Searching through them, he found the key for the first metal box. After two attempts at guiding the key to the lock, with head held back to get a focused image through his bifocals, he opened the small chest and removed an envelope marked M. Fields. He dumped the contents of the package onto the table.

"Mister Fields, this is your new ATM card. It is set up with your new bank account with our own credit union. All of the information about the account, such as: the initial balance, pin number and such, are on this paper. Please make sure the spelling of your name, address and social security number are correct. All of your payroll checks will be directly deposited into it. It is advised that you close out all other accounts you have and only use this one."

He handed the paper to Michael and held up the card, continuing with his instructions.

"This ATM card is enabled with a LiquiCode child/parent security link. That means that only *your* hand can insert or present the card to a reader for verified transactions."

He passed the card to Michael and unzipped the computer case.

"This is your Program-issued laptop, again linked for only your authorized use. It is smeared so we know where it is at all times. The tattoo reader is under the lid so it knows when you are near it." He lowered his voice, as if speaking to himself, "Actually, millions of readers know when you are near them."

Barney looked a bit annoyed with the last statement, but said nothing. The scholarly gentleman continued, "All of the association rules, that enable you as the only user who can operate it or carry it in and out of here, have been entered into the Management System."

He stopped and looked up.

"Look who I'm talking to; I understand you are the man who helped develop the GMCS. Plus, there is all of your other 'attributes', being a Gen Z. Sorry, I have to do this with everyone new." He shifted his weight and continued with the session.

Michael decided that he would not show any sign of surprise to what people were saying and reacting to him. Maybe the GZ code meant that he was hired as a Vice President or something. And what was with this Foundation thing? He would need to talk with Gus.

Rininger tapped the laptop cover with his finger, "Barney has made sure that all of your New Employee documentation is on the machine, as well as, all of the information that you will need to get up to speed on the program."

He placed the computer back in the case.

"The hard drive is smeared and encrypted, but there is a tutorial on that when you first turn it on. I know you won't have any trouble getting this up and running, with all of your skills."

Barney closed the metal box as Rininger opened the second one.

"You can go through all that computer stuff tonight in your cabin. We have a secure LAN installed in there also."

"And here is your Grape." Rininger held up a cell phone with mobile computing capabilities.

"This unit has all of the usual phone features, web access, GPS, secure e-mail and some additional operations that we have had installed. We call it a Grape, because DP employees began calling it their Purple Berry. The phone is multi-band to work anywhere in the world. And there are additional keys, as you can see, that allow scanning of all AIT devices; RFID, barcode, LiquiCode and the like. It is very helpful in verification checks of other DP personnel and assets. And, to comply with our security mandates, the reader will only allow you to operate it by holding it in either tattooed hand."

Barney put everything into the computer case and handed it to Michael. Mister Rininger pulled a 'receipt of goods' from the box and had both Michael and Barney sign it.

Barney smiled, as if he just unloaded a used car that had the odometer turned back, "OK, that's it, Mister Fields. You are now officially on the Deep Purple team."

They thanked Mister Rininger and left the room, heading towards the lobby to catch a ride up to Cabin 17.

Michael walked out of the elevator while Barney remained inside. "Well, Mister Fields. I don't have to tell you how lucky you are, to be brought into the DP family," his voice echoing from within the metal box.

Michael had been waiting for this 'welcome speech'.

"Thank you Barney. Yes, I really am one lucky guy." Michael almost laughed at his own obvious lack of sincerity during the exchange.

"Well, hope to see you again. Stop by if you ever get back here at ol' MF-1." Barney pushed the down button and the doors closed.

Michael headed back to his cabin, looking down at his bandaged hands. *"What have I got myself into now?"*

As he opened the door to his temporary housing, he could smell pizza. There, on the dining room table, was a box containing a giant thick-crust, with everything, and a six pack of beer. On the box was a note: *'Welcome to DP. Gus.'*

He opened the box and took out a big slice and opened a beer. He moved to the living room where a fire had been started in the fireplace and sat in one of the two chairs facing the hearth.

He finally had some time to sit back and think about everything that had happened since he had arrived in DC. As he set the can down on a side table he glanced at the small bandage on his hand.

The HR girl, Michelle, was visibly upset about not being a member of Deep Purple. *What the hell did it all mean?*

He looked back down at both hands. Once again, others had put him into a slot. But, this time it would for the rest of his life. Maybe it was all for his own good. Perhaps now all his work and struggling would amount to something. The uneasy feeling, that the mere mention of his GZ ID causes everyone to treat him like royalty, would not go away.

Maybe tomorrow the pieces of the puzzle will come together.

As he finished the beer his relaxed brain recalled what Barney had said when they parted: *Ever get back to MF-1?*

Chapter 7

8:30 am Thursday, November 22, 2012

Michael, once again, entered Cabin 17. Two plain-clothed guards were sitting in the living room. One of them recognized Michael and actually smiled and waved. He told him to go right down where he would be met by a 'guide' and shown to the meeting room.

As arranged, an armed guard (wearing the now familiar calf-high 'Storm Trooper' boots) was waiting for him in the lobby after the elevator door opened on Level 1. The two walked past the receptionist and down the hallway to the same room that was used for the meeting the day before. Michael's new tattoo allowed him to enter without incident. The guard nodded and returned to his position in the lobby.

The room was fully lit and unoccupied. The table that had held the two-dozen donuts and coffee jugs, during the meeting the day before, now looked like a Vegas buffet. There was a full complement breakfast in five heated chafers containing scrambled eggs, bacon, home fries – the offerings were beyond plentiful. Two stainless steel urns containing coffee and four carafes of various juices sat at the far end of the table. *There must be enough food here for twenty-five people*, Michael thought.

The door slid open and Sandy walked in, accompanied by Burt Murphy, her Assistant Mission Manager, whom he had met the day before. Burt walked over to Michael by the food table; Sandy went to the front of the room to set up the projection system.

"When Gus is involved in a formal meeting, it's always an all-out affair," Burt said to Michael, looking at the buffet. "Good to see you again, Mister Fields. Did Barney get everything taken care of for you?"

"Good morning, Burt. Oh, yes, Barney is quite efficient. It's obvious that he's processed more than a few new employees."

"Well, none as important as you, I can tell you."

As Michael stood, puzzling over Burt's last statement, the sliding door announced another arrival. There was no mistaking who was entering the room. "Woo-e. I smell bacon!" It was Gus. He went straight to the buffet table and began filling his plate. Michael and Burt followed his lead. Sandy remained at the front of the room typing on the podium keyboard, like a monkey possessed.

The feeding frenzy went on for another fifteen minutes as the remaining attendees joined the meeting. There were ten people total in the room, three women and seven men, when Sandy tapped on the table with her pen.

"It is now 0900 so let's lower the lights and begin." She was, once again, running the show. Everyone took a seat at the conference table. Gus sat in the same chair as the day before, tossing his hat to his left and placing his plate in front of him. Michael sat next to him, as Gus directed by slapping the chair with his hand.

"You will notice there are no folders for this meeting. Now that Mister Fields has been processed into the organization, everyone in this room, and *only* those in this room, is cleared to view the material that will be shown here today. I will be accessing the required presentations directly from the 3938 Zeus Hard Drive."

Gus straighten up in his chair and broke in, "If you're walking around in the Zeus Drive, you better be *damn* sure that the right file comes up on that screen, or some heads are gonna roll."

Sandy was taken back, "The customary security procedures were followed, Gus. We are not touching anything else in there."

Gus leaned forward, "Remember when that virus got in there? It took us ten days to track down the jerk that wrote it. And when his body finally got back here, there were only two bullet holes in it, instead of the ten I ordered!"

He leaned to his right and whispered to Michael, "You know what the funny part was? Some Chinese software company actually wanted to hire that piece of crap. So . . . I sent them the remains." He leaned forward and laughed. "Sometimes I crack myself up."

Michael attempted a smile. It wasn't convincing.

Gus sat upright and gave Sandy a side look, "And you *really* don't want Mister Field's people to start coming down on you if something is screwed up on the Zeus Drive." He leaned back and waved for her to continue.

Sandy straightened her jacket and looked around the room. "As you all should already know, per program security guidelines, none of the following presentations may be downloaded or duplicated in any media or fashion." She glanced at Gus, who nodded in approval of her statement.

Michael was still looking at Gus, *'Mister Field's people?'*

She advanced the presentation; seven dots were slowly super-imposed over the map of the United States. Under each dot was a designation, MF-1 through MF-7, numbered from east to west.

"This is Program 3938." She stood for a moment to look at the map.

Michael's eyes could not widen any further.

"There are *seven* MF installations within CONUS, the Continental United States. Each of these facilities is located on the Northern Ley Line of 39 degrees, 38 minutes North Latitude. All spaced evenly, every 7 degrees West Longitude from the spot I am now standing, Camp David."

Michael had forgotten to breathe. He began again slowly so as to not show his wonderment.

"I thought there was only one." Michael spoke to no one in particular.

To the right of the map appeared a panel listing all of the MF locations:

- MF-1: 3.45 miles NW Thurmont, Maryland
- MF-2: 17 miles SW Dayton, Ohio
- MF-3: 9 miles SW Hannibal, Missouri
- MF-4: 53 miles N-NW Salina, Kansas

- MF-5: 32 miles W-SW Denver, Colorado
- MF-6: 7.58 miles SW Nephi, Utah
- MF-7: 7.75 miles NW Fernley, Nevada

Sandy pointed to the panel, "These are the Mushroom Farms. Three of these facilities' true functionalities are not revealed in any governmental documentation, below Top Secret. The published operations are listed as Remote Communication Support Sites, contained within a sparely manned structure. The other four . . . we shall not discuss here." She moved to the next slide. It was an aerial view of a farm; a house, two barns and three silos. The text at the bottom of the slide read; 98 degrees, 14 minutes west.

"This is MF-4; fifty-three miles North-North West of Salina, Kansas. As you can see, there is nothing very extraordinary on the surface because each MF is a self-sufficient underground facility." Her enthusiasm seemed -- indifferent. Michael could tell that she was obliviously bored at giving the presentation. He wondered how many times she had stood in front of the same slides and delivered the same words to other new inductees and government officials?

"Each member of the December Pact is authorized to build similar facilities. Obviously some have less. But, most say they have met or will meet their quotas, one way or another."

Michael thought, *What the hell is a December Pact?*

He spoke up, "And each of these facilities can support 7,000 people?" He was trying hard to convince himself that this was real. "For how long?"

Gus responded, "As Burt mentioned yesterday, they can stay down there for a little over three months. Hopefully that's all that will be required."

"You mean a total of 49,000 people can be put in these seven things and all live for three months? Underground? Without coming out for anything?" Michael was speaking to the room, but only using his eyes to move around the table, as his body had frozen.

"Actually, we can accommodate over 84,000 by combining all of the other existing sites; Austin, Oklahoma City, Cheyenne Mountain, Huntsville and The Area," Burt responded.

"Nine Federal departments are also replicated within Mount Weather." He showed a listing of the Departments on the screen;

Agriculture

Commerce

Health, Education & Welfare

Housing & Urban Development

Interior

Labor

State

He turned back to the audience, "The Transportation and Treasury Departments have offices in there, too. As well as at least five Federal agencies; Federal Communications Commission, Selective Service, Federal Power Commission, Civil Service Commission, and the Veterans Administration. The Federal Reserve and the U.S. Post Office, even though they are private corporations, are in there somewhere, also. We only provide communications and defense support in our main three MFs."

The impact of the slide was also affecting the other two new employees, as their faces were stuck in a look as if they had just seen the Loch Ness Monster walk across the table.

As Michael seemed to be the only one of the new inductees able to speak at the moment, he directed his next question at Gus, "And what do you mean by 'all that will be required'?"

Sandy stood erect as if taking an oath, "Our national security is dependent upon our ability to assure continuity of government, at every level, in any national emergency situation that might conceivably confront the nation." *She must know the Executive Order by heart*, Michael thought. *What a shame*.

She again touched a key on the laptop and the entire screen under the camera dome came to life with the now recognizable logo at the top center with the words, December Pact, across the middle.

"The reason I am going to show you all this presentation is not just to introduce the Pact to our three new employees, Mister Montrose, Miss Siebert and Mister Fields, but also to provide new developments and updates most of you are not aware of, or have access to. There will be no note taking throughout the length of today's meeting."

The slide changed to a graphic of the world with many countries filled in with two different colors, along with a number under each country's printed name.

"This is a graphic, which shows the current population of the Earth, based on each country's 'contribution'. The countries in yellow are December Pact Nations. The ones in blue are Alliance members to those in yellow, and the ones in white . . . ," she paused. "The ones in white will not be relevant to today's discussions."

The next screen was titled *Executive Summary - The Lorgronson White Paper*. Sandy began to walk around the table, telling the story of Dr. Phillip Lorgronson as slide after slide lit up the room.

In 1998, Dr. Lorgronson published a paper in an obscure New Age publication called The New Arc. It was based on the results of a highly elaborate software program he and his team had developed that would enable simulation models to be run on the minimum number of humans that would be required to maintain the entire current world infrastructures. He had filtered these infrastructures down to what he considered to be the absolute bare necessities to maintain a continuance of the Human Race upon this planet at the present level of technology. The final number was 8,000,000 or .001% of the estimated population of the earth in 2010.

The historians and analysts began running the numbers and calculated Lorgronson's final minimum population figure was approximately the world population at or around 3100 BC, within the same time period of the building of the Great Pyramids and the Bronze Age. They also determined a third of the inhabitants were living in Asia, while the rest scattered around the globe in nomadic tribes and small agricultural villages.

His model included data from every essential source, including:

• Amounts of agricultural effort verses output levels to maintain eight million.

• Locations and population requirements to maintain key communication and logistical services for essential geographical and demographic areas.

• Consolidation of energy requirements, usage areas and demand cycles.

He had concluded in the paper thirty-three percent of all present occupations would not be required; as he made the analogy of the Butcher, Baker and Candlestick maker. The later skill-set would not be needed as technology long ago solved the problem of illumination within our shelters. One good electrician was now worth more than 10,000 candlestick makers.

Dr. Lorgronson had finely tuned the daily operational requirements of the human presence on Earth to a point where it was viewed as a Guide for the Repopulation of the Planet in the event of a world-wide catastrophe.

This initiated a surge in studies, simulations and controversies around the globe. Most backed by world leaders who found this to be a perfect opportunity to begin compiling lists of prominent individuals in their fields as listed in Lorgronson's paper. Within a year, governments of nations around the globe had completed their lists of the chosen eight million.

Lorgronson's occupational breakdown of what was considered to be required to 'start over' was used as the blueprint for compiling the lists.

Farming, forestry, fishing   3.76%

Operators, fabricators, laborers   18.33%

Precision production, craft and repair   12.69%

Service occupations   21.14%

Technical, sales and admin. support   20.64%

Managerial and professional specialty   23.44%

The ratio of male to female, according to the simulation, dictated that 67.62% were to be male, 37.38% female. That calculated out to be 5,409,600 males and 2,990,400 females of the total 8,000,000. He had based that on a maximum birthrate of one child per female every nine months to provide a population increase of nearly the present projections of 35% by 2020. He claimed that the occupational skill projections would more than support this growth.

Many had to rethink this last claim, as there would be other factors to consider, such as; infant mortalities, women who were unable to become pregnant, and others who just did not want to become pregnant. Input from women around the world, could only be described as hostile; "Yeah - like I want to give birth every nine months – for how many years?" Many were convinced that Lorgronson never had a girlfriend in his life.

And there also appeared to be more leaders than actual worker bees in the listings. Still, it was becoming the baseline for some serious thinking on 'what if'.

However, the model had precisely calculated that the eight million had to be distributed in key geographically locations around the globe in order for success. This was a safeguard against plague and natural catastrophes that could decimate an entire population, which had been established within a particular region. It was obvious that one nation would not be able to overtly accomplish this, as all governments were now knowledgeable of the scenario and would not allow such a thing to transpire on their soil.

A series of meetings were held with 150 nations. After the discussions, only 95 remained, as some pulled out from internal pressures, while others were asked to leave. In the end, all endorsed a covenant affirming that the Lorgronson's model of a total, amounting to only eight million people, would be divided evenly among the participating countries; resulting in a regulated number of 84,210 per nation. This became known as the December Pact and was regulated and enforced as aggressively as any nuclear weapons treaty.

However, the larger world powers began negotiating deals with Alliance countries on adding to the total of the greater nation's numbers by absorption of a smaller country's allocation, in exchange for a variety of aid, thus increasing the number of their ideologies, without breaking the accord. It eventually came down to geopolitical sectors, resulting in ten regions. Even though each nation was allowed 84,000, the number within certain regions showed huge power blocks, not unlike the existing patterns of military presence. The final numbers were ten major powers with an average of 800,000 each.

Sandy had circled the room and was now standing to the left of the screen.

"As many took Lorgronson's whole premise as folly and actually no more than a numbers game, it did give rise to the realization that if only a few humans were left on Earth to start over, someone would still have to be in charge and be supported by a population with similar ideals, goals and beliefs. However, not unlike being the first to claim a plot of land and plant a flag, a multitude of political, economic and culture mandates must be issued and met for that plot of land and all its inhabitants to become successful."

Michael wondered what kind of civilization would have risen if a military dictatorship had been the first to land on Mars. For that matter; what kind of Earth, if the same factions were the only ones remaining after a world-wide catastrophe?

Sandy took off her glasses, signaling the end of her portion of the briefing and directed the group's attention to another woman, at the end of the table.

"I would like to now turn over this presentation to Miss Rosen."

The lady at the end of the table, now identified only as Miss Rosen, walked to the front of the room in a manner resembling someone who wanted to get something off her chest. As Sandy sat down, another slide filled the screen, titled *Occupational Skills- 3000 B.C.*

Miss Rosen, who reminded Michael of his old English Teacher, Miss Goodman, definitely demanded attention, "I would like to expand upon Lorgronson's occupational breakdown of what was considered to be required to 'start over' with only eight million individuals. As you can see, if the human race was to begin a repopulation effort with the numbers and skill sets that Lorgronson had outlined, it would not work. The reason being, the requirements must be based on an agricultural effort and not on today's industrial and service platforms. It would mirror the world, as it was for human survival in 3,000 B.C."

She turned to the screen which now displayed a slide entitled, *3000 B.C. Skills and Percentages*:

Farming, forestry, fishing, etc.: 37.94%

Fabricators, laborers: 11.8%

Precision production, craftsmen and repair: 22.19%

Service occupations; cooks, etc.: 13.23%

Technical, sales and administration support: 4.64%

Managerial and professional specialty: 10.2%

"Our MFs are staffed according to this 3,000 B.C. model. It is more realistic and our chances of a successful continuance are greatly enhanced. We believe that this is our Ace in the Hole, which will provide a competitive advantage in the end; actually, in the beginning. This is one reason why approximately only fifteen percent of our DP personnel are managers and admin support. I know what you are thinking -- very rare for a government operation."

Miss Rosen showed another graphic of the world with sparsely placed stars.

"The cities of the ancient world were generally small and had to be supported by much larger rural populations. Urbanized societies will not work with only eight million people in the world."

She quickly turned to face the audience -- Michael was ready to duck a flying eraser.

"In following the 'new beginning' scenario, with only eight million emerging into a world void of other humans; canned and freeze-dried goods, most roads, underground gasoline supplies and various forms of housing will most likely still exist. There needs to be a shift in the thinking of existing repopulation scenarios. We will not be starting from scratch, as was the case of our Bronze Age ancestors. We will have the knowledge of the entire human experience within our databases; medicine, science, agriculture, civil and industrial engineering – means to bring the surface to life again."

She put both hands on the table and leaned forward.

"And I must remind everyone that this in no way should be associated with the mission statement of the Polar Moon Base project, which relies on oxygenation processes. I know a number of you have been involved with this program and your cross-project intelligence has been of great value to us."

Michael sat through the December Pact briefing with stunned bewilderment and had remained in his chair as the lights came up and the rest of the group headed for the toilets and coffee urns. The bottom line of the Pact was only .001% of all humans on Earth are qualified to be 'saved'. What type of logic would need to be demanded of a mind to make a ruling on who shall be spared to continue the species and who . . . dies?

The big voice of Gus broke his delirium, "I need to fly over to MF-4 later tonight for some meetings early in the morning, so I won't be able to see you off tomorrow; Johnson will get you to the airport by 0900 tomorrow morning to make your flight back to San Francisco at 1030. He'll pick you up at 0600. Your flight information is on the table in your cabin."

"I'll be ready," Michael murmured, trying to digest the timetable that had just been jabbed into his ear.

"A couple more things; do not use any other cell phone, just your Grape. And only use the Program issued laptop as it has all the security bells and whistles. And you can keep them spiffy clothes. A Field Intelligent person will be contacting you in California to offer any help you may need."

Michael blinked, for the first time since the lights came up. He stood up with Gus, "Thanks for everything."

"Alright, Partner. We'll see you in MF-7 on the 26th. I expect you to have all of the GMCS files assembled by then. We need Bancroft's final version of the application. Oh, by the way, there's going to be some Mexican food in your cabin tonight. I love that stuff. I know a place where they still make it the original way. Think it's time to go get some."

He leaned close to Michael, "All those slides you saw on the screen? They're all bullshit; including that lunatic Lorgronson."

Gus turned and left the room.

Chapter 8

Randolph "Gus" Stoddard was brought into this world amidst the lightning strikes of a hot Texas evening storm on June 23, 1955, in San Antonio. He was to be the oldest son of Raymond Stoddard, a Medical Supply salesman and his wife Diane, an Oklahoma-born registered nurse.

Gus, as he was to be known by his high school classmates, was named after Randolph Scott, whom his mother adored. Perhaps adored was too light a sentiment as was evident on March 2, 1987, when Diane draped the entire house in black and wore widow weeds for a week after Mister Scott died in his Beverly Hills home.

As Gus neared graduation from college, he was approached by the CIA and was immediately hired, after receiving a BA in Intelligence Studies and Analysis.

He rose through the ranks quickly, becoming a Project Manger for a number of covert operations. His approach to his work, as well as his personal life, became more shadow than light; as many were hearing more of his reputation, while most were seeing less of physical appearance. He was becoming known as the ghost who walked around things.

By the time Gus had reached forty he had crossed over into the realm of an untouchable. He was brought into an organization, only known as The Foundation, to coordinate operations with the government. So vast were his resources in protecting the country from the 'bad guys' that a call to his personal secure cell phone, from the President, was not uncommon. It was said that he could organize and supervise the overthrow of a third-world nation in a weekend. He thrived on the dark underbelly of the 'government with the government' like a virus. Many considered The Foundation a Shadow Government.

In 1998, The Lorgronson White Paper was published. Within two months, forty-three year old 'Gus' Stoddard received a call to put together a team to provide a list of 50,000 'required' individuals and a comprehensive program on how to keep them around after the 'big one'. He was given a blank check to devise and direct what was to become Program 3938; a monumental joint venture between the government and The Foundation.

For the next fourteen years; Gus staffed, directed and built the massive project. It had consumed every moment of his life and drained every ounce of compassion he might have had left for his fellow humans. For he was cutting the herd, taking out the best stock for populating a new world, to replace the one which the existing civilizations were to enviably destroy. That was the original mandate . . . that was his belief. He had found his role in life, where every action and word was for effect.

Gus had never married, his work was his life. He had never known any other devotion but to lead others according to his own mandates and ideology of what is good and bad. He had written his own commandments and in his mind, the end justified all means. Perhaps it was due to his early submergence into the darker side of the human condition. Sawdust left over from his years of sawing the log of intelligence gathering and second-guessing the echelons of terrorists and power brokers. Each indistinguishable from the other; all intertwined and lying in a septic bottom layer within the cradle of human decency. And the saddest aspect of his entire career was that the 'bad guys' were on all sides of the game board. He had only encountered a few good people in his life.

He had often sat alone and pondered his own question, 'Why should I be a part of saving the world?' His answers were varied, but always carried a common meaning, 'It will just be repopulated with the same scum that exists now, ruled by the same Committees.' He knew that it would just be an endless cycle of political deceit, religious fanaticism, destruction and rebuilding.

He had lost his only sister, perhaps the closest person in his life, in 2008 to cancer. His father had died only a year before his sister's passing. With his ailing mother still living in the family home in San Antonio and being taken care of by his younger brother and his wife, Gus had turned more bitter towards his fleeting existence and the meaning of it all.

Moving into the fifteenth year of the Program, he wanted out. Not just out of the Program, but out of the pecking order he was in on the human food chain. He wanted a life. No, it had become larger than that, he wanted it all. He wanted The Foundation.

Over the previous decade he had formulated a perfect world, in his mind, which would be comprised of a few million good people. People that would possess inner strengths and skills which will allow them to be dropped anywhere in the Universe and survive. Not just survive -- but thrive. He had staffed his MFs with such people, only to discover that the ones willing to be part of the Program were not the kind of people that could actually start a new world. They were sheep. They needed daily schedules and had to be 'taken care of.' The real Doers and Pioneers he needed would not subject themselves to be 'shrooms. Unfortunately, those are the ones who would not be around after the end. They would be the lone figures standing at the edge of an oncoming nuclear shock wave, shouting, "That's all you got?" They all would be just like him.

The self-portrait of his life was painted in dark shades of isolated grays and hung in a bare gallery, alone. No one was allowed to get close enough to examine the harsh brushstrokes or search for the missing open skies of Texas. There were no spaces left for adding color. He wanted to start over with a blank canvas.

The note from Hugh Waterman, one of the few good people he had known, stating that Bancroft was within reach, provided Gus with the exit he was searching for to make the final move toward his chosen goal.

He had not left the meeting to go to MF-4. He had left the 3938 Program and The Foundation. He was heading to the Yucatan, to Bancroft's Bunker. He would then be able to guide the remnants of the human race into a new beginning -- his way.

Chapter 9

Friday, November 23, 2012

Michael slept on the plane most of the way back to San Francisco. He opened the door to his apartment in Sunnyvale at around 4 pm, with the phone ringing in the living room.

He dropped his gear on the couch and picked up the handset. "This is Michael."

"Hey, Parker here, I'll meet you down at Q's, at six. Need to talk. Important." His voice had a two-fold tone, one of concern and another of a stronger evil twin demanding Michael's attention.

"Alright, see ya there," Michael responded to Parker's unfamiliar insistence.

Parker hung up without the usual parting warning of some conspiracy out to get us all.

Michael responded in kind, looking at the phone in his hand, "Well, that was short and not so sweet."

He made a quick sandwich, went through his junk mail and headed out to meet Parker at their usual hangout, only a half-mile away.

Michael pulled into the one of the few remaining parking spots outside the sanctuary from nonsensical community rules. As he climbed out of his car, he noticed Parker's vintage English motorcycle parked in his usual space facing the front door, over the customary oil spots.

The neon signs in the window lit the way as a lighthouse providing a safe harbor away from the hidden shards lying just below the surface of cold reality and into an era of far ago; jukebox music, dartboards, pinball machines and beer. It was a lodge house where the members of the Valley's high-tech clan could mingle amongst their own kind. He spotted the clansman he was to meet at the far table on the left.

"Parker!" Michael called out and lifted his chin for an acknowledgement. Parker looked up and motioned to him to take up the chair across from where he was sitting. A pitcher of local brew and two glasses were already on the graffiti-adorned small wooden table.

Parker began pouring from the pitcher into the glass placed at his guest's position, as Michael walked across the stained linoleum to the table. "Mister Fields. Glad you could make it." Michael did not shake hands, although it did not make any difference if he did offer to; Parker never did do the handshake thing. Said it was too barbaric.

"So, how was your visit to DC? Anything interesting that would truly astound me?"

Michael sat down and picked up the glass, "Man, I've been on the most bizarre trip of my life." He took a drink. "Actually, I'm still on it . . . for the rest of my life."

"Hopefully that will be for a long time," Parker responded, turning to observe a new high score being reached on the pinball machine by a very intense, black-haired young lady in full Goth attire. When her gyrations subsided, he turned back to Michael and picked up his glass. "So you went to a funeral for someone you didn't even know. He left you something in his will, or something?"

Michael's face showed his pent up frustration with wanting to tell all, "I didn't know who he was, but I knew who he wasn't."

"So, Waterman wasn't Waterman?" questioned Parker in an odd tone of voice.

"Yes and no. I really want to talk to you about this DC trip, but I can't . . . 'cause of security crap."

"Well, maybe I can help you with that." Parker pointed at Michael's hand. "Did your ink pen spring a leak?"

Michael felt as if a ghost had just passed through him; a cold, clammy tightening of every cell in his chest. He had been careful not to show his palms, from the time he had walked in the door. In one of those moments, which resided within the second that his friend had asked about his hand, his entire friendship with Parker began spinning into a very dark abyss.

Michael put his hands into his lap. He had to be sure that he wasn't just becoming paranoid, "Maybe. Could you describe the color?"

Parker leaned forward and looked right into Michael's eyes, "Purple." He leaned back, "A Deep Purple."

Michael wanted to run, hide under the table, anything that would remove him from the moment. He felt like an underworld fugitive who had just been discovered and he did not know why he should be having such feelings.

Parker loosened the two wide straps on his left wrist support and slid it off, over his fingers. He laid his hand on the table, palm up. There were LiquiCode tattoos on both hands. He was a DP. "I'm your Field Intelligence contact."

Michael didn't know if he should hug him or hit him.

"How long have you had those?" Michael demanded.

"Over a year or so, Waterman got me in to track changes in GMCS that Bancroft was screwing around with from remote locations. Did Gus fill you in on that whole mess?"

Michael could not respond.

Parker was looking down, shaking his head as he put his wrist supports back on. "Sorry about not letting you know the truth."

Michael turned to look at the overhead fan slowly spinning above the four dart players at the other end of the room. There were no words coming to him that would allow him to verbally accept Parker's apology. He felt betrayed, used and abused -- but not angry. Somehow it all seemed like everything leading up to the present moment had been preprogrammed, like some kind of bizarre chess game. The one person on earth who would have devoted every waking moment to expose the whole DP and Program 3938 was actually in the middle of it all. The question of Parker's depth of involvement finally formed into rambling words and emotions.

"Just what does a Field Intelligence person do when they are doing intelligence stuff and not telling their friends and getting them tattooed and signing up for . . .whatever?" Michael asked, still looking at the fan and sounding like some 15 year-old kid who wasn't invited to a party the night before.

"OK, calm down. We're both in this and we have a job to do, together. Waterman wasn't just a Program flunky doing Gus' bidding and kissing the Program's ass. He got me in to help him uncover the real story behind the Program, Bancroft and the zealots at the top. Hugh knew it was essential that you be a part of it, also. The world is in a real bind here. It took some doing, but here you are, you're in," He faded his voice out, "with your tattoos and your Grape . . ."

"Just like a nice little mushroom, huh? Thanks for nothing." Michael turned to Parker and leaned forward with sarcasm coloring his face, "And you and I are off on some adventure to save the world. Save it from what? You better get back to researching coffee shop franchises run by extra-terrestrials or something."

Parker turned the glass around to read the imprint, "Listen. There are some major things that you don't know about yet. This thing goes a lot deeper than what you've been told."

"I thought you were the champion of exposing conspiracies and here you are with *your* tattoos and Grape . . ."

Parker slapped the table, "I'm in this to do exactly that! Waterman knew I needed to be on the inside to get the dope on this thing. And, for the record, I didn't know they were actually going to bring you into the Program. Hugh had suggested it a few times, but the first time I heard something was actually being done to make that happen was when you called me asking about UPipe. I don't know what sealed the deal."

"It was a note from Hugh to Gus, just before he died. Waterman wanted me in to figure out what Bancroft was doing with GMCS."

Parker nodded, "The note Hugh wrote that had Bancroft's bunker coordinates in it."

"You knew about the note? Holly cow, what else?" Michael now eyed Parker with even more suspicion. "What do you know about the bunker?"

Parker looked down to his right at the layers of yellow wax on the linoleum floor, paused for a moment, then looked Michael in the eye with a veil of fear one only finds buried within a frightened soul. "I was there."

He sighed and turned his head to the left with arms folded on the table. He tried to focus his hearing and thoughts on the jukebox song and the din of voices in the room, anything to bring back a sense of comfort in his own existence.

Michael sat back in the chair. He watched Parker stare into nothingness for a moment then raised his eyes to the wooden beam above his head, adorned with emblems of a variety of sports teams.

Michael had to accept the reality that everything he once believed his life was based on, was just a flimsy excuse to go another day without committing to anything. Well, he was now committed; to something that was larger than any one person is allowed to experience in a lifetime. Whether it was a blessing or a curse, the direction was now the fixed course that his life and that of his long-time friend sitting across from him in this small hideout from tomorrow, were set upon. They were bonded by the wishes of a dead man and the hopes of those yet unborn - for the rest of their lives. It was now time for Michael to reach into his pack-rat collection of experiences and knowledge and provide any support he could to his tormented companion.

"Why were you in the bunker?"

Parker turned his attention back to his own table and filled his glass.

"I got the call to be on the plane to a secret airstrip called UX7, near Uxmal, on November 7th. I guess the raid went down the day before on the 6th, as Hugh had directed in his note. They needed me and the rest of the team to dig into the system Bancroft had set up in the bunker."

"How many were on the team you went with?"

"There were five of us, Red and I from here and three others from the east coast." He continued his story with more animation. "Anyway, we were taken to this stone building that looked like it was built a couple thousand years ago." He began drawing on the table with his finger, using the water that had collected in small pools and rings, from the glasses. "It was almost square with about twenty stone steps leading up to the entrance. The place was crawling with military-type personnel; setting up fences around the perimeter and directing trucks of supplies to various locations around the area and marching around like militia love to do."

He drew a box and some lines.

"A big generator was cranking out electricity near the main entrance and massive power cables were attached to it, running up the steps and into the building. We were escorted inside by uniformed guards who were speaking in both English and Spanish; three walked ahead of us as if expecting trouble and two behind, all with automatic weapons. When we got inside, there were a few passages, all opening to stairs leading underground."

He moved the pitcher aside and expanded his drawing on the table.

"We were guided to the passage on the left and took the stone staircase winding down about fifty feet or so. After going through what was left of a massive stone door at the bottom, there was this huge room with computer server racks set up all along the walls." He added depth to his painting by raising his hands and panning around him. He stopped for a moment to take another drink.

"Lights, set up on tripods, were in every corner and a row of workstations were in the middle with keyboards. There were a ton of wall monitors."

He lowered his voice and slowly nodded his head, "Two of the monitors had bullet holes in them and there were dark swatches on the floor, in different parts of the room, which we figured must have been blood stains."

"Any idea how many were in the bunker or the final casualty count?"

"No idea. Things were pretty cleaned up by the time we got there and no one was allowed to talk about it -- to us anyway."

He wiped his wet hands on his pants and picked up his glass.

"We set up our equipment and each took a server rack and began doing our thing . . . trying to figure out what the previous occupants were up to. There were a total of eighty-six servers in there, so we were stuck in that place until Tuesday. Almost twelve days in that dungeon. That's when I got your voice-mail and called you."

"So, *that's* why you weren't around."

Parker looked to his right at a neon beer sign that could have changed the course of civilization if it had been hanging in a church during the middle ages.

"Hugh was there, too."

Michael was beyond bewildered.

Parker put both hands on the table and gestured in a question, "So, did you get GMCS?"

"Gus gave me a copy, I put it on my computer - but it won't run."

Parker leaned back, shaking his head, "You must have put some strange language in there that really screwed up things."

"Me? I looked at the code and it's almost unrecognizable. The programs I got from Gus were way beyond what was delivered to Hugh as the so-called 'final product'. There are some files in there that have extensions which aren't recognized by any application on the computer. I'm going to start digging into it to look for Easter Eggs, I might find a lead there."

"No, don't need to do that; you just need to get a hold of Neal Foster."

"Neal Foster?"

"He came into NexTrÉ a couple months after you left and three months before I did. I'm sure I talked about him before to you."

"I can't remember. You probably did."

"He can write some amazing code, just can't spell worth a damn. He took over where you left off; well, Neal and a guy they called VJ. Neal supervised all of the heavy lifting and VJ supervised the migration stuff. There were about fifteen all together, but those two were the only ones who had access to all of the modules. They made all the pieces fit to Bancroft's specifications."

"Can we get them here?"

"Last I heard, VJ was teaching in Cambridge, lost forever in the bowels of an MIT artificial intelligence lab, but Neal is still in town. He's writing code over at Green Sand Biometrics, across from the Hangars at Moffitt Field. I think Neal is the only one we need to talk with."

Parker signaled to Peter for another pitcher then turned back to Michael, "Let's meet tomorrow, up at the park, about noon. Bring your laptop, I'll bring mine. We'll compare notes and I can show you some of the stuff I got off the servers in the bunker and fill you in on some of the other things I found out."

Michael got a sudden sense of paranoia, "Should we be talking about this in here?"

Parker erupted with his patented smile, when you knew he had beaten the system again. "There are no readers, cameras, microphones or any of that other AIT crap in here. We took care of that a year ago. This place is nothing but a black hole in the world of surveillance. It's great that the people who invent and implement that surveillance junk also hang out here. It's probably the most secure place, outside of the White House, in the country."

He turned in his chair to face the bar, "It's cash only here, a manual register behind the bar, no streetlights with sensors outside the front or back door and an old fashioned burglar alarm. No transducer light tubes, the pinball machines are the old relay types and the windows are gel-filled so lasers can't read back any audio off them. Rickman set up one of his super-duper jammers so RF can't get in or out. Ever notice your cell phone won't work in here? The place is a Faraday Cage. And we all know each other."

Parker paused and lifted his glass. Michael lifted his in the toast, "Well, we do now."

Parker stood up, raised his glass and called out, "To the Spooks!"

The whole bar responded in kind and reveled in their cleverness.

Is it not ironic that those who had authored the present doctrine, penned the correct ideology within the false textbooks, and had developed the technology to maintain control over the dissidents; are those which the leaders fear most?

Chapter 10

Saturday, November 24, 2012

"You think you should be sitting this close to my laptop? The reader will detect you here and they might think that we're up to something." Michael moved the computer off his lap and held it in the air.

Michael and Parker were sitting on a patch of brown grass overlooking the salt evaporators on the south end of San Francisco Bay. The morning sun was reflecting off the salt in an unworldly diachronic spectacle.

"We *are* up to something. Don't worry, I'm not here." Parker smiled holding up his gloved hands.

Michael placed the computer on the grass between them. He went to his files and pulled up the *SC Letter*.

"Well, to start off, Gus got this letter from Bancroft in January." He began to read it aloud.

"We are nearing the new beginning at the end of the Long Count; where the earth shall begin to renew and Human Beings will assume their intended roles in the Universe. MU is the answer. Beware of ESA and the Righteous. This cycle's knowledge will be gathered to aid in the next."

Parker sat upright and it appeared that he was going to say something, but relaxed and waved his hand for Michael to continue.

"The Mushroom Farms hide the truth. GenZs will take their place."

Parker nodded his head and picked up a small stone and threw it towards a pool of rancid brine. "Wow, Bancroft was farther out there then I thought. I've heard the Long Count stories before, but 'getting this cycle's knowledge' and the MFs actually growing mushrooms; he must have been on mushrooms when he wrote this thing."

"Gus was insistent that I read this and try to come up with my own version of a translation."

"Well, what have you come up with, Sherlock?"

"I think he's talking about some kind of catastrophe that is supposed to happen, and humans will be thrown back to . . . hell, I don't know."

"The file says SC Letter. What is SC?"

"It stands for Santa Claws. That's the code name that the Program has given to Bancroft."

Parker watched a seagull circle over his head, "I get intelligence reports sent to me by my team leader, once a week. Last Tuesday there were confirmed sightings of Bancroft in North Africa. This morning I get one that says he is now in the Middle East. It seems like he is really making the rounds for support."

Michael looked up to see who Parker was talking to, "So, you think he has another facility someplace that could act as his backup network operations center?"

Parker looked back at Michael, who was still watching the bird, "He's got the money . . . and apparently the support of a few other psychotics out there."

He waved his hand to get Michael's attention, "OK, show me what you've found in the last GMCS build."

Michael opened the source code for the main application. Parker looked to the screen and began reading the initial notations.

"Yep, that's Neal's work on the top. He never could spell maintenance or restaurant correctly." He took out his personal cell phone and pulled up a number, dialed and waited.

"Neal, Parker here. Hey, I really need to talk to you about this girl who wants to meet you. Call me ASAP. Bye." He closed the phone cover, put it back in his jacket pocket and looked at Michael.

"Got his voice mail, but he should be calling back any time."

"Can we talk to Neal about this stuff?" Michael asked with a worried look on his face.

Parker leaned back on his right elbow, "It's been rumored that a few DP personnel had disclosed the Program to some friends and another to family members. None of them were ever seen or heard from again. I know it sounds like a story you tell around a campfire; they could be just rumors started by the Program strong arms. But, then again, it would not surprise me if they were true. A whole bunch of strange crap is happening here."

Michael tried to ease his anxiety, "Well, *we* should be OK, I mean, we both are DP. And this is information we both need to know. But bringing Neal in on this might get dangerous." He paused, looking at the code. "What choice do we have? As you spotted right off, there are too many holes in this that we need to fill."

Parker brought both his knees up and wrapped his arms around them, "I think the less we divulge to anyone, the better. At least until we figure out what the hell is going on here. Honestly, we can't divulge what we don't know, at least until we find what it is that we can't divulge. We need Neal, period," he deduced in some form of pretzel logic.

Michael was scrolling through the firmware files, "I have to report to MF-7 on Monday morning for orientation and other stuff. I'm supposed to stay a couple days. Learn the ropes and so on. Maybe I can get into the system there and find out more."

Parker watched the lines of code roll by, "I'll get you directions. Nice drive through the Sierras. Shouldn't have too much trouble with snow, but take chains just in case. It'll take about five hours from here."

He leaned back and rubbed his eyes, "Maybe you should give me all of the stuff that Gus passed to you. I'll go over it while you're at the farm."

Michael took out the memory stick that Gus had given to him, "Everything's in here. You might as well have it, the more eyes the better."

Parker took out some aluminum foil and wrapped the memory device and put it in his coat pocket. "It's smeared, no doubt."

"You always carry aluminum foil?"

"Never know when them-thar Aliens will be a tryin' to zap your brain – makes a good hat to bounce off those beams. And . . . when I know that I'll be needing it to wrap up a smeared memory stick," he replied, smiling.

They continued to walk through the new code and assigned tasks to each other for dissecting various sections of the programs. After a couple hours of keyboard pressing, Michael returned to his apartment to pack for his first week in a Mushroom Farm.

He waved to the headphone adorned Spook in the SUV, still parked across the street, as he slowly closed his front door.

Chapter 11

9:10 am Monday, November 26, 2012

Michael was driving east, nearing his exit to MF-7. He had left his apartment at around 4:30 and still had to deal with the commuter traffic all the way from Sunnyvale to the Nevada border. Gus was correct in one aspect of his philosophy; there were just too many people.

Michael had packed for the week he was to spend at MF-7 for his on-site briefings, orientation and room assignment. He was scheduled to leave and return to Sunnyvale on Friday, the 30th.

He glanced down one more time at the printed directions Parker had emailed him, just before turning off the interstate at exit 46, marked Fernley West.

He was to turn left off the exit ramp, go down to the gas station, make another left turn and continue to a dirt parking area on the right.

He drove the route and found the parking lot with a sign reading "Casino Parking Only." There were over a hundred cars parked on the dirt lot in a loosely organized fashion.

A once-white van was parked near the entrance as he turned into the lot. The desert sun and sand had claimed the first layers of paint and the fight to keep it clean must have been over years ago.

He slowly pulled forward to where the van was sitting and stopped along side. To Michael's surprise, written on the side of the driver's door, was the name J&K Mushrooms. *'Wasn't this place supposed to be a secret?'*

He lowered his window and called out to the only inhabitant of the decaying mini-bus; the driver.

"I am supposed to catch a ride to MF-7. Is this the right place?"

The unshaved, bulbous-nosed man in the driver's seat called to Michael through the permanently half-opened window, while picking up a clipboard. "Name?"

"Fields, Michael Fields."

The driver adjusted his clear plastic framed glasses, scanned the paper on the clipboard and made a writing motion with his pencil. "OK." He threw the paperwork in the seat next to him, "Get in. No others are scheduled for a while."

Michael grabbed his computer case, his travel bag, locked the car and climbed into the back seat of the grime-covered vehicle. The driver picked up his radio, "Fields -- The Farm's front door." Michael shut the door and the van sped out of the parking lot leaving a cloud of brown desert dust that settled on the assemblage of parked vehicles.

The course was easy as there were few roads to get lost on in the middle of nowhere. They went around a bend to the left, passed over the Truckee River, then turned right onto the paved two-lane road designated as 447 and continued north.

The noise of the engine and the unhealthy metal-on-metal grinding of the undercarriage filled Michael's ears with little confidence of reaching the MF. He sat next to the sand-blasted window looking at the leftovers of a dried-up prehistoric ocean bed. Just brown desert with mounds of sagebrush and blackened rocks; charred by centuries of sporadic wild fires.

A large warehouse interrupted the vast desolation of the landscape. Over fifty cars were in the parking lot and a weathered sign announced that they were passing *J&K Mushrooms, Farm #7*. Michael turned his head to follow the sign, *'This must be the worst kept secret in history'*, he thought, as the van kept moving north.

They traveled another half mile then slowed and veered left onto. . . there was no name for the road. All around him were brownish sand mounds with primeval shrubs and dried vegetation. Abandoned mobile homes and crumbling shacks occasionally appeared; all possessing a portion of the side yard which was designated as a permanent storage area for old cars, water heaters and various unrecognizable metal forms.

"It's pretty isolated out here!" Michael called to the grayed-hair driver, who looked like he could have been a castaway from the gold rush days of 1849.

"Desolate *here*? You should see where they put MF-6. It's out in the middle of nowhere in Utah. It's like going to the moon. Now, as far as this place, it's just pretty much stuck in another time," the old desert-rat replied over the interior noise. "But from the 1840's to around 1950 or so, this was a real growin' area . . . really growin'. The main East to West railroad line and the original Lincoln Highway used to pass right through that small town we drove through back there; Wadsworth. But the railroad changed their route, the whole town burned down and Highway 80 now runs south of here, so everything just quit growin'."

That was a fitting statement, for there was nothing growing there now. But that may have been a good thing, for the foothills were painted in multiple shades of stunning browns and stripes of pastel clays. Patches of grey tumbleweeds dotted the slopes as shadow-protected scraps of snow highlighted the small gullies. There were no cookie-cutter housing complexes covering the wilderness that were now infesting the rest of the country. All around the two travelers, time had slowed and was barely marching in place somewhere within the folds of the 19th century.

The van bounced and swerved to miss ruts in the depressed hard clay road for another half mile, then entered a well-used lane on their left. Michael looked out the right side of the van and saw a street sign. In the middle of nowhere, a street sign. He caught his breath as he read Hooterville Road.

His mind flashed back to his days working with Hugh Waterman at NexTrÉ. Hugh had often said that he was going up over the hill to Hooterville to try his luck. No, come to think of it, he had said, "*Do his thing.*" Michael had always thought that he was talking about Reno and the blackjack tables.

Another bump and the van pulled over to the right side of the dirt way and stopped.

"OK, everyone out." The driver called to all of his passengers.

"Out? Out to where?" Michael responded, looking around and observing only an old, depression-era clapboard house, which had six uncoordinated upgrades of colored wood sections and metal siding. Not a single piece of window glass was intact.

The old desert rat climbed out of the driver's seat and opened the sliding door. "I'm going to the outhouse; you need to go into the main house."

Michael picked up his gear and climbed out of the van, *The Main House?* He saw a red placard nailed to the side of the dwelling: Condemned.

The driver reached inside of his coat pocket, pulled out a card and handed it to Michael, "Here's my card. When you need a ride back, just call me."

Michael looked down at the homemade business card, "OK, thanks . . . Vern. I'll be doing that, I'm sure."

"Well, talk to ya soon." The old-timer turned and walked towards a dilapidated structure that must have been the outhouse. It was in worse shape than the Main House.

Michael put the card in his wallet and walked in the chilled desert air to the door of the decaying dwelling. He paused for a moment to gaze at the cloudless blue sky and surrounding hills. The van window did not allow such a pristine view of the small valley, nor did the rumbling interior even hint at the smothering silence that accompanied the landscape. He opened the door to the ramshackle building.

As was expected, the door creaked on its rusted hinges as he entered the obviously abandoned structure. What he wasn't expecting was a small foyer with a contemporary door in front of him. He slowly opened it and stepped inside.

He was standing at the head of a carpeted staircase, which descended in a smooth left turn to a gleaming reception area that resembled a hotel lobby in some Vegas casino; marble floor, well lit, air conditioned -- but windowless. There must be some regional thinking behind each MFs entrance, as was demonstrated by the rustic entrance to MF-1 through Cabin 17.

At the bottom of the staircase was a pretty Native American receptionist sitting at a desk console wearing a headset and typing on a computer. An artistic chrome logo representing the characters MF-7 was mounted to the front of her counter. She paused and looked up, "Mister Fields?"

"Yes. I'm Michael Fields," he responded, still awestruck by the portal he just crossed from the early 1920's outside - to the 21st century inside.

"I am Katherine. MF-7 welcomes you. Please have a seat while I let Mister Dobbs know of your arrival."

He sat in one of the leather chairs and listened to the soft instrumental playing from the overhead speakers. On the coffee table in front of the couch next to him were publications of local real estate and Nevada tourism. Across the room in another small waiting area was the familiar armed SWAT security guard in the all too familiar boots. He was not wearing sunglasses, which seemed logical, as there was no sun.

Over the reception counter, at the intersection of the wall to the ceiling, was a thin line of mirrors. No doubt he was being watched.

Another female office worker entered the lobby from a door located to the far left of the receptionist. Her footsteps echoed as she walked on the mosaic floor to Katherine's console. She placed a folder on the desk, talked a moment to the girl and returned back through the door she had entered from, quickly smiling at Michael.

The receptionist answered a call then looked up to Michael, "Mister Dobbs will meet you downstairs, Mister Fields. You are DP staff and not operations personnel, is that correct?"

"Yes."

"Well then I will not need to have you sign in or smear you, just walk to the elevator. The system will log you in. Have a good day."

He stood up and began walking to the elevator door located at the south end of the lobby. He paused at a glass case covering two porcelain Native American figurines; one was a warrior in full battle regalia and the other, a beautiful young girl in a deerskin dress.

He turned back to Katherine, "What tribe do these represent?"

"Those are Paiute, the same as me. A large number of us work here. This facility is surrounded by the Pyramid Lake Paiute Reservation," she replied, smiling proudly.

"Oh, I didn't know that. Thank you," he replied, walking towards the elevator. As he neared, the door opened. It had read his hands from five feet away. *"Impressive - I think,"* Michael thought softly aloud. *What or who else was reading his code and from how far away?*

When Michael emerged from the elevators' decent, a man nearly his same age was waiting to welcome him. He was wearing a Hawaiian shirt, flip-flops and a pair of sunglasses on the top of his head.

"We are glad to have you with us, Mister Fields," His arms were down at his side, holding a familiar purple banded folder.

"Please, just Michael."

Something was wrong with this picture; a beach-bum with sunglasses, standing in a stark hallway – perhaps fifty or more feet *under* the sand, where the sun will never shine.

"I'm Marco Dobbs, in charge of MF-7's IT operations. Actually, I'm the guy everyone yells at when their computers lock up or the printers are out of ink."

"Oh, I am sure your duties go deeper than that."

"I was *nominated* to get you settled in and make sure your office network and communications are configured correctly. Judy Benson normally does this, but she's out on maternity leave. So, let's get you someplace to live, shall we?"

Marco led the way to a two-seater cart and off they went into the depths of Farm #7.

"You may get lost a couple times in this maze at first, but I'll give you a map so you can, at least, find the elevators and mess halls."

They continued on and parked at the entrance to one of the atriums. "We need to take the elevator from here. We're going down to Level Five. This is Level One. The elevator you just got off of only goes from topside to this level. And you need to have your DP tattoo to take the ride down from here."

The elevator had six buttons, one for each level. Marco pressed number five and down they went.

Level 5 did not appear to be much different from the level they had just left. As he exited the elevator car, Michael noticed a laminated map of the 5th floor on the wall. It occurred to him that the floors were numbered from top down, not bottom up as on the surface. Did that mean that the big-shots were on the bottom floors?

He asked Marco as they walked.

"Well, I suppose that's true. Level One is mainly administration, accounting, the telephone exchange and the two underground warehouses where all of our supplies are kept. There is also a chapel and some stores – like a mall. There're some recreation areas on the North Side of Level One also."

They turned a corner and Michael noticed a hallway sign indicating Rooms 501 – 550.

"All of the regular hourly personnel work on Level One. You know the nine-to-five employees who get to go home every night, like normal people."

"Level Two and below are for DP personnel only, as I mentioned before. Level Two has water treatment, air condition, air quality and waste disposal. Level Three contains living quarters for permanent support personnel and a very well equipped hospital and crematorium. The radio and television studios are just off the West atrium circle on Level Three. There are living quarters on all floors, except One."

Michael was getting confused with all of the floor numbers and what was located on them. He hoped the map that Marco promised him would be highly detailed. Marco continued his verbose narrative as they moved down the hallway.

"Levels Five and Six are for the managers. They call them the Executive Floors. Our tattoos will not allow us to go down to Six; that's where the big wheels live and all of the vaults are located. Like, if you live on Level Four, you can only go down to Level Four, no farther."

They stopped halfway down the hallway.

"And here were are; Room 521 -- your new home office."

The door opened as Michael moved towards it. They both entered. The room was a suite containing an office area furnished with a desk and two chairs, a phone, printer and floor lamp. Connected to the office was a sitting room with a couch and two lounge chairs, an entertainment center with TV, a coffee table, two side tables and a bar/counter separating the area from a small, completely furnished kitchen.

Through a double folding door was a bedroom with a huge king bed, armoire, another entertainment center and a very spacious bathroom.

He looked around half expecting to see windows. There were curtains that covered the wall where windows should have been located. Perhaps to make the place look more like a hotel room then a steel-reinforced concrete hole in the ground.

"This is my office?" Michael stood in the middle of the suite.

"All yours," Marco said, panning the room with his hand. He placed his folder on the counter. "Why don't you hook up to the LAN and see if you can log on to the MF Network and get your email. We'll try the printer, also."

Michael unpacked his computer case on the desk and sat in the chair. He plugged the power cord into the wall and connected the LAN cable into his Program-issued laptop. He began booting up the machine.

Marco picked up a paper that was lying next to his folder and walked over to the desk. He handed it to Michael. "Here are some rules for housekeeping they want me to go over with you."

He stood as if he was giving an oral book report in fifth grade.

"There is no maid service due to the level of security that is maintained on levels four through six, so you need to do your own cleaning. You can put your towels and bedding in the hallway on Mondays, Wednesdays and Fridays and it will be picked up and swapped with clean replacements. Toiletries are also dropped off on Wednesdays, in a plastic bag. Enough for a week, unless you need more, then dial "0" and ask to speak with Housekeeping."

He relaxed and sighed, "There, got that done. Judy has this whole 'Welcome to MF-7' speech down to a science. Hope she comes back soon."

He walked to the fridge and grabbed a can of soda, but kept his head inside, still looking for something to snack on.

"Because it's a government facility, there are inspections every so often. Nothing to get excited about, just making sure no one is a complete hog," The voice echoed from inside the cold box. Michael was hoping Marco was not getting frostbite.

Marco pulled back from the refrigerator and stood up. "Can you log on?"

Michael turned back to his laptop. An MF-7 login screen filled the display. He typed in his screen name and password that was on the paper that Rininger had given him. The screen showed an animated graphic of a code reader scanning his hand. An encryption screen flashed then the MF-7 home page appeared on his screen, with the greeting, "Welcome Mister Fields."

Marco sat at the counter and pulled out a check-list from the folder he had carried.

Michael was still looking at the Welcome screen, "Yep. No problem."

"Emails?"

Michael clicked on the email icon and a single message appeared, welcoming him to the organization.

"Everything seems fine." He began checking on everything the website offered.

Marco made a check mark on his paper. "Great. Let's print out a test page of the email to see if your printer is working."

Michael performed the task with no difficulties. Marco sat at the counter, continuing to check off those things that needed to be checked off, which applied to Michael's move-in.

"About the email service, you can get emails for anywhere, but you can only send to those who are within the approved 3938 network. That would be 3938.gov."

"Let me guess, in the spirit of security."

"They watch us like a hawk. Don't want us sending anything to the 'outside' and getting ourselves into trouble."

"How comforting that someone is watching out for us." Michael's world closed in a bit tighter.

"Were you ever in the Navy, Michael?"

"Is that on your check-list?"

"No, just wondering. If you were ever ship-board in the Navy, it would just make adjusting to this place a bit easier."

"No, I never was in any branch of the Service."

"Well, this place is run like a ship. Actually, more like an enormously long, six story tall submarine."

"Really, then who would be the Captain?" Michael smiled.

"That's Edwards, our MF Unit Manager. You'll meet him. Great guy. keeps us on course."

"Well, there must be an admiral for this fleet of buried submarines," Michael joked.

"That would be a guy named Gus something. Never met him and probably never will. Really up there I hear. Only reports to the President and people like that."

Michael went limp in his chair as Marco closed the folder, completing his orientation tasks.

"Say, if you ever want to get out and do something, I'm down the hallway across from this one, in good ol' Five Eighty-Two. I've moved in there permanently. Don't need to pay rent. Oh, I do have an IT department, up on Level Three, where all the servers and switches are located, so I spend most of my time up there. I couldn't be shut in a small place like this all day, every day."

Michael was still a bit numb from hearing of the level of authority Gus commanded. "Do I have a place to go to do to some work outside of this room?" he asked, worried about the possibility of getting cabin fever and very concerned with the possibility of being restricted to his room.

"Yep. The Software Engineering Lab is up on Three also. I'm sure you'll spend a lot of time there. And for just getting away for a bit, we have two movie theaters, a nightclub of sorts, and a bowling alley over in Old Town."

"Old Town?"

"That's the older District of the complex, over on the southeast side of Level One, about a half-mile from here . . . after navigating all the elevators and hallways. It was the first part of the complex to be built and occupied back in '08. It was where the excavation crews and contractors stayed during the building of the rest of the place."

"I need to know something Marco. On the way here I saw a warehouse that was labeled J&K Mushrooms. The van I rode here in had the same name on the side of it. What's that all about?"

Marco sat down and smiled. "That building is our supply receiving warehouse for the stuff we keep in the East and North Stores; the food warehouses. Almost everyone who works at J&K are hourly contract employees, as are most the staff who work up there on Level One. They enter the complex from that building. We call it the Back Door. All of our supplies are delivered there and sent down in the freight elevator. It was the first structure built topside as they dug this place out."

"Doesn't anyone question the sign? Not very secret if you have a twenty-foot sign."

"Not at all, J&K Mushrooms is a real company. It's the civilian contracting arm of 3938; handling things like warehousing, construction and staffing."

Michael sat in the chair slowly shaking his head. *Parker must love this stuff.*

"Building this place must have been quite an effort. How did they pull that off without the press getting a hold of it?" Michael wondered.

"It was just another mining operation. Nevada is filled with mining operations."

"But they must have taken a lot of dirt out of this hole."

"Well, I wondered about that myself a while back, so I looked it up. There are around five billion cubic yards of dirt that are dug out of a one cubic mile hole. I figured they took out about a third of that to put in this complex."

Michael began to wonder more, "I know there is a lot of sand and dirt out there in the desert, but it might have been pretty obvious that something big was being dug, if tons more dirt were just dumped around the area. I mean a pile of dirt, maybe a mile long, half mile wide and one hundred and fifty feet high is something that might draw attention. Maybe they dug another hole and put it in there." Michael joked and they both laughed.

"Actually, that may not be too far from the truth. There are some old mines and hundreds of gullies and ravines out here that needed filling in. And Fernley, the town just down the road, was doing some major expansion during that period. Tons of new businesses, warehouses, housing complexes and roads were being built. They surely would have used up any new dirt that came along. It was perfect."

"Interesting," Michael nodded. But he knew something was not right. Spy satellites would have picked up on the scale of activity that was going on here. Apparently, the construction of the MF did not matter to those watching.

"You said the J&K building was where the supplies came into the complex. I thought this place was self-sufficient?"

"It is. We have enough stuff in our own food warehouses to keep us going for three or four months. But, why use it up as long as we can get fresh stuff delivered? Our foods stores just have freeze-dried stuffs and anything you can imagine in a can."

Marco looked down at his paper, "Well, that completes the check-in list -- just need you to sign here." Michael signed on the line over his printed name.

Marco stood up and placed the paper in the folder and took out a pamphlet, "Before I forget, here is a booklet that tells all about MF-7. Actually, all of the MFs are pretty much the same. The map of the place, that I promised you, is in there too. The booklet is smeared so you will not be able to take it out of the complex. If it's scanned near the exit doors from Level Two to One in the stairwells they won't open or if it's detected in the elevator, it will stop at Level Two and not go any higher. Great technology, I love it." He handed the pamphlet to Michael and headed towards the door. "I've got to get back upstairs and deal with secretaries who can't get their emails. If you need anything or just want to get away, call me. I'm in the book - Dial 7582."

"Will do, thanks for everything."

Marco stopped and pointed at the room's portal, "Oh, about your door. It will only open automatically for you outside in the hallway and of course for Security with their master code cards. You need to use the door knob here to get out from inside. Nothing automatic on this side, 'cause you wouldn't want it opening when you walk by, after getting out of the shower. Talk to ya in a bit." He opened the door and went out. Silence set in around Michael.

He picked up the booklet Marco had left.

It was filled with maps of every floor, locations of barber shops, laundry facilities, the garage and the hospital. The garage on Level One fascinated him, as the published inventory listed; four All-Terrain Vehicles, ten four-wheel drive SUVs and two helicopters. The picture looked like the inside of an aircraft carrier. The access to the surface was through a tunnel to the main South warehouse and up the huge freight elevator, into the J&K Warehouse. There were only two entrances to Level 1, the freight elevator and the lobby elevator from the Front Door.

Level 4 contained the singles' dormitories. The men were located to the North end and the women to the South. '*I won-*

der if there is a barbed-wire fence between the two?' Michael mused, thinking that three months underground, may create some security problems in the biological-urge department.

The section describing the four mess halls stated that they can serve over 20,000 meals a day, around the clock, during the alerts. And the power-generating system can supply enough electricity to sufficiently maintain a town of 3,000,000 inhabitants. As well as, over 400,000 gallons of fresh water are processed from Pyramid Lake every day.

The facts went on for five pages.

"Someone must be really proud of this place," Michael thought aloud. He closed the booklet and looked at the cover's graphic depicting well groomed, dressed for business corporate-types, sitting in meetings, walking down carpeted hallways and looking out large boardroom windows to the western sunsets. Not one Hawaiian shirt. And where was this window? The only thing missing was some big lettering across the whole graphic; *Welcome to Utopia*.

He tossed the reference guide onto the desk and turned back to the computer screen. "OK, let's get to work."

He opened the GMCS source code he had transferred from the memory stick to his Program-issued laptop and began his search for clues to the author.

Michael harbored an inner demon, which constantly reminded him that for the past couple decades of his working existence he had not achieved anything he personally considered note-worthy. Perhaps he had set his expectations too high. It might be today, on this project, in this place, that the value of his worth would rise-- or maybe tomorrow.

As he worked, it was difficult to forget the fact that he was nearly one hundred and fifty feet underground, sitting in a land-locked submerged submarine with two ID tags embedded into his hands that could be detected by anyone with a Liqui-Code reader, from any location -- at any time.

Chapter 12

There was no perception of time in Room 521. The lighting was adequate, the silence was thick and the overall feeling was constant; luxurious imprisonment.

Michael had accepted it, knowing that is was only for a few days as he kept fully focused on the pixels in front of him. Line after line, page after scrolling page of code was telling him a startling story. It was almost a horror story of a software program, which was born into servitude to powerful management applications, then was remolded into an entity that fed off data from world-wide networks to empower anyone with the authorized access to monitor every individual and control all major data activity on the planet.

There were new subroutines, backdoor algorithms to scan and jimmy open ports, such as 116, 9995, and 9996 into firewalls and routers. Scores of device drivers and changes to the network management protocol were all added after he had left NexTrÉ.

He followed the attached installation instructions to load the program into his machine. He needed to actually run the application to test it fully.

He activated the run-agent and waited for all the modules to begin running. He then clicked on the GMCS icon that was placed on his desktop.

His computer froze up

He rebooted and tried to run the program again with the same results. He either did not have enough of the program to allow it to start up or the code was written to run on a specific machine. Or . . . he was just losing his touch.

His phone clicked and a music box chime was followed by woman's voice. She began an announcement, which must have been sent to every phone and public address speaker in the complex. "At 1630, from the MFTV studios, Mister Edwards, our Division Manager, will be broadcasting an important message to all MF-7 employees. Please tune in to Channel 97 for this special announcement. Thank you."

He looked at his watch, it was 4 pm or 1600 hours in the world he now resided within.

He fixed a cup of coffee, cleaned himself up and walked over to the entertainment center and found the TV remote on one of the shelves. Upon pressing the power-on button, a field of blue appeared on the screen with an MFTV logo in the center. A soft female voice filled the room from the surrounding speakers embedded in the walls, "Welcome to MFTV." Music rose and subsided. "Your 24-hour entertainment and information source for the entire MF network." Music again, up, then down. "The Menu button on your remote will allow you to scroll through the entire offering of channels and services we provide."

He used the prescribed Menu button and directed the set to switch to Channel 97.

He waited a few minutes, looking at some self-promo 'commercials' of MF-7. Which was odd, for no one knew of the place, except those already inside it and they were already sold – or bought.

The screen changed to a smartly-dressed man around fifty, with a red mustache and glasses. He was wearing the customary dark suit, white shirt and blue tie and holding a fountain pen. An American flag was behind him, on his left, and a Nevada state flag on his right. Some pictures, probably of his family, were on a lowboy behind the flags.

He looked personable and calm.

"Good afternoon. For those of you whom I have not met personally, I am Thomas Edwards, the Division Manager for MF-7. I wanted to take this opportunity to discuss the upcoming Alert.

"As you all know, this year's first semi-annual system-wide alert was conducted from 2400 hours on June 10th through 2400 on the 22nd. And I must congratulate all of you on a very successful operation. We are still receiving kudos from every agency involved and our Lessons Learned documentation was distributed throughout the MF network to be incorporated into the next alert at a number of other MFs.

"And you should know if you read your emails, that the next alert is scheduled from 2400 hours on December 9th through 2400 on the 21st. For all of you who still have not figured out military time; 2400 is midnight . . . Bob McAlister." He smiled as he verbally nudged, apparently, one of his managers.

"This means that all DP personnel will be required to move in on the 7th and 8th of December. No more of this moving in a couple hours before and after lock-down. This time no one will be allowed in or out during the duration of the alert. No excuses. The system will not allow an override from now on.

"I really need to emphasize the need for all of you to comply with the customary twelve-hour shift schedule for the duration of the exercise. There were a number of times during the last alert that shift turn-over meetings, beginning a half-hour before shift change, were often neglected, resulting in some systems problems and some very upset people who wanted to go home. Your managers are instructed to conduct shift rule briefings this year and they will be mandatory. I assume that all of you have received, or will shortly, your duty assignments.

"All hourly and non-DP personnel will be on leave for the alert period and extending to Wednesday, Jan 3.

"As in the past, I know a lot of you will be taking your leaves after the alerts, but please have all of your travel arrangements completed before you get here. The lock-down will be total this year with no outside communications allowed, except to the other MFs and official Grape calls.

"I need to read this from Special Services; during this year's alerts, all of the Special Services will be operating on twelve-hour shifts also. This means that the bowling alley, theaters, food courts and shops will be open around the clock for both shifts. This will allow all DP personnel to participate in the bowling and video game tournaments. The Auditorium will be open for basketball, volleyball and a few concerts by our various employee musical groups.

"First run movies will also be playing, from our studio, on channels 87 and 88, around the clock. I am sure a number of other activities are being planned by your individual departments, as well."

He reached to his left and picked up a piece of paper.

"And, here's one near and dear to my heart, the Waste Management Department's Poker Championship will be broadcast live on Channel 84. I will get past Round Four this year." He smiled again, laying the paper on the desk.

"For those of you who work from remote locations, you all should have your ticketing completed by now, thanks to the great work of Long Line Travel. The airport shuttle fleet will be operating from the Reno airport both Saturday and the Sunday, before and after the alert. Try to get here early as the coordination of getting seven thousand faces in their places is a major part of the alert. I would really appreciate it if that phase went smoothly.

"And, as always, do not drive your own vehicle here for the exercise. We do not want hundreds of cars sitting in the Casino Only parking lot for two weeks, for obvious reasons.

"I expect all of you will perform your assigned duties with the utmost efficiency and professionalism, and make the December alert the best we have ever had and shine above the other MFs. Thank you for your time."

An MFTV logo appeared on the screen with some unidentifiable elevator music playing in the background. Michael turned off the TV and moved to the bedroom.

II

Tuesday, November 27, 2012

Michael slept until 8 am, that first night in his new 'home'. Although, he did not feel that he actually slept too soundly or anything resembling peaceful. He would occasional wake up as his subconscious began shaking him hard; reminding him that he was a hundred feet underground. That wasn't natural.

He was surprisingly satisfied with the water pressure and constant temperature of the shower; he quickly mastered the coffee maker in the small kitchen and the water tasted pretty good. He was even able to tolerate the somewhat biased morning news program on MFTV channel 31.

For the rest of the morning he explored the subterranean world where Fate had now placed him. By following the map in the booklet, he found the Level 4 East Mess Hall, had a big breakfast and made his way up to the Software Engineering Lab on Level 3.

He walked up to the door of the Lab and it opened without hesitation, allowing him access. As he entered, ten sets of eyes stopped looking at what they were doing and fixed on him. But only for a moment; he must have not been that interesting to look at; no Hawaiian shirt or SWAT uniform.

This was not a lab that he was used to working in, as there were no lab coats, no piles of cables, stray monitors or keyboards sitting on shelves along a painted white block wall.

To his left was a glassed-in room with five wide-screen monitors on the wall, each showing different views of the world from a few miles up. The one in the middle was larger than the others with PACOM labeled across the bottom of the screen.

Superimposed on the multiple views were hundreds, maybe thousands, of red, green and yellow dots. In front of each monitor was a console with one and sometimes two technicians, wearing headphones and typing on keyboards. An even larger monitor took up the wall at the front end of the room, which displayed pie charts and graphs showing readiness and status of the entire system. Along the glass wall he was looking through, were four Help Desk stations with personnel handling calls. An office at the far end of the room was labeled, 'Daily Operations Manager.'

He turned to his right to see an office with a closed door that read, 'Earl Draper – Network Manager.'

Michael had walked into, what appeared to be, a Network Operations Center.

He walked forward on the very thick carpet into a large area that was filled with cubicles; names and titles on small plaques described the occupants' roles; Data Analysis, Database Administrator, System Architects, Configuration Manager and Software Development. He looked in the two-person

Software Development cube and saw the back of someone sitting at a desk wearing a green and yellow 50's-style bowling shirt adorned with a *Sputnik Drive-In Restaurant* logo. He was staring at the computer monitor and using his index finger to scan along a line of object code.

Michael knocked on the metal lining of the cubicle, 'Hi there."

The man in his early 30's rotated around in his chair and looked up at Michael. "Hey. What can I do for ya?" He had a sucker stick protruding from one side of his mouth, was wearing Bermuda shorts and untied black and white vintage sneakers.

"I'm the new guy, Michael Fields. They said that I could work up here. I'm a system developer; software and hardware design guy."

"Yep, they told us that you might be showing up; got a space all ready for you." He pointed at the work station next to him. "Earl said that when you arrived, I should take you in to meet him."

"I see that this is more than a lab, looks like a Network Operations Center."

"Sure is. Our NOC monitors the entire GMCS PACOM network, and a bunch of other things, from here. I'm Bernie, the resident 'bug killer'. And believe me this software has its share of critters." He stood up, turned off his monitor and moved past Michael. "Come on, let's go see Earl and then I'll show you around."

Michael turned and followed.

As they walked to the front of the area, Bernie pointed to cubicles as they passed, "The database dweebs sit in there, Mister 'I know everything' sits in there, an untouchable cute girl sits over there . . ." He wasn't that informative.

They stopped at Earl's door and Bernie knocked. An unwilling voice from the other side half-heartedly responded, "Come on in!"

The room was broken ino two areas; to the left was a conference table with six chairs around it, a small couch, video screen and a white board – the usual furnishings for a meeting room. On the right was an office that resembled a science fiction museum.

There was a shoeless, thin man, standing on the office couch, placing a framed movie poster of some spaceship zapping crowds of running humans, onto the wall.

"It's me, Earl."

"No, I'm Earl," the man joked back, doing a final alignment of the frame. An unlit cigarette dangled from his lips.

The pale man on the couch, wearing dark green wrinkled slacks and a brown sport shirt, talked to the wall, "Bernie, did you email back to Joan on the second shift Help Desk about the error she was getting when she entered data into the Disposition field for the Alaskan Field Service page?"

"Yeah, I told her not to do it again."

Earl nodded his head, "OK. I'll check that one off the list."

He slowly turned and stepped down from the couch while adjusting his horn rim glasses. "So, you must be Michael Fields. Welcome aboard. Did Bernie show you around?"

"We were going to do that after we came in here," Bernie answered, while bending over to look at a studio prop laser gun mounted in a glass case on the meticulously arranged desk.

The Manager stood in front of Michael with his hands in his pockets. "What do they have you working on, Michael?"

"I'm to assist in any upgrades to GMCS at the moment."

"Fun stuff, I'm sure. Well, all we do here is just monitor the implemented system and try to keep it running." He turned and picked up a bundle of lovingly stacked papers, "And churn out reports. That includes the hardware out there too. You know; the RFID and other reading devices."

"How many Field Service Technicians do you have out there?"

"What do you think, Bernie, maybe thirty-five?"

"Close to that now, maybe forty, depends on if you're talking new installations or just repair. I think forty is a good number, as they have grown again, after the problems we had a couple months ago went away. Harris would know for sure."

Earl looked at Michael with a suspicious smile and crossed his arms, "You know, I received an email directly from the 3938 Program Office saying that you were joining MF-7 and working in our office and I should support you in any way that I can. And you were to have full administrative privileges and permissions for accessing any part of the system." Earl nervously unfolded his arms and put his hands back into his pockets, "I only get emails from those people if the President is visiting or war has broken out. Somehow I think that your mission is more than just upgrading GMCS."

Michael held up both hands and smiled nervously, "Honestly, I'm just doing upgrades. I'm assigned to MF-7 because I live in Sunnyvale."

Earl fidgeted with his red bow tie, "Well, I'm not going to stand in your way. Just do your thing and anything you need, just tell Bernie. He knows the ropes here. As far as any help I can offer, I am up to my ears in keeping this place running like a finely-tuned watch, so I can't offer too much. And I don't need to get distracted by anything that the Program geniuses are fooling around with that would upset our reporting system here."

He put his left hand behind his ear and rubbed his head, "Just don't do anything that would bring the system down or get Security busting in here." The little man waved to the door, "OK, you guys go on your tour. I've got a report to get out. Nice to meet you, Michael, I'm sure you will fit right in." He pointed down, "Tie your shoes Bernie."

"Put yours on, Earl," Bernie responded, also pointing down.

Earl looked down at his blue socks, turned and walked back to his desk as Michael and Bernie left the suite and shut the door with the sneakers still untied.

Bernie began moving towards the back of the area. "Let's go into the Network Operations Center and see how things are going."

They entered through the glassed doorway and stood within the dimly lit room which was twice as large as the office area they just left. Bernie looked at the large monitor mounted on the wall at the other end of the room. It was now presenting a view of the entire Pacific coast of the United States from two hundred miles up.

A woman, looking to be a young forty, walked out of the Operations Manager's office.

"Holly, this is Michael Fields, the guy that Program sent down here. I thought that you should meet him. He's the brains behind GMCS and all around nice guy, I've been told." Bernie was acting like he was showing off a prized hog.

"Welcome to the PACOM Network Operations Center, Michael. I'm Holly Harris, Daily Ops Manager. I heard some good things about you from Hugh. He'll be really missed; spent a lot of time in this room. Glad you could join DP."

"Well thanks, but I don't know what all he could have said about me that would get you guys excited."

"Oh, you would be surprised. We wanted you on the roles for over a year now, but the Program Office kept saying, 'not yet.'"

He felt a little embarrassed at her praise, but chilled by the fact that the Program had known about him for a long time before now. He wondered how much information had been gathered on him in that year.

He stood in front of the nearest monitor and looked up at the information it was displaying; a satellite view of the Eastern Seaboard, from Maine down to the southern tip of New Jersey with an overlay of all of the major roadways. Five small blinking icons, in different colors, were shown on the roads. Harris walked up next to Michael. "On this monitor, we are tracking some very important containers being transported via different routes, from upper New York State, to the port of New Jersey."

Next to each of the icons was a small panel showing an identification number, speed of the truck and a timestamp – counting down to some zero reference time.

"Why is the time ticking off on those?" asked Michael.

"That's a time track showing when the shipment is to pass the next checkpoint. If you notice, Truck Number Three is in the minus. If they don't pass the next ground scanner in four minutes and twenty-three seconds the icon will turn red and the Security car, following it, will be contacted. If there is no response, the electrical coil on the truck will be remotely pulsed for twenty seconds and then turned off. Reactionary Teams will be notified and armed helicopters will be swarming around the stopped vehicle in minutes," she explained.

"Hope the driver is well paid," he joked.

"If it isn't the right driver," she looked at the name of the driver being displayed in the panel, ". . . a Mister Louis Mahoney, he won't have any more need for money . . . or air," Harris informed him without a compassionate wrinkle on her face.

She led Michael down to the center monitor.

"There was a reason that Hugh wanted you here. I want to see this." She pointed at the satellite image of Tokyo and the surrounding area, down past Yokohama, from one hundred miles up.

There were a large number of green, very few red and only a couple of yellow dots superimposed all over the image. "Go to Device Type," she asked the technician. The dots were replaced by thousands of small squares of the same colors.

She turned to Michael, "The original dots you just saw are RFID readers; showing their status. Green means they are operational, red are the ones that are down and yellow are being upgraded or undergoing an install."

She looked up to the screen, "The squares you are seeing now are *all* the Automatic Identification devices in the area we are viewing; Biometrics, LiquiCode, voice recognition, optical character recognition, etcetera." She looked back down at the technician. "Would you bring up this same area; showing February 10th of this year?"

A few clicks on the keyboard and more than half of the dots turned yellow or red.

"What we see now was a situation we had, beginning in late January and lasting up until the middle of March. On a daily basis, we were intermitting losing data feeds and connections to and from all AIT devices, not only in Tokyo, but all over the world. Then around March 16th everything went back to the stable condition that you first saw. Because NexTrÉ no longer existed, it was almost impossible to find anyone who could dig into the source code and find what was wrong."

Bernie stepped up, "That is when they brought me in. But to be honest, it beat the hell out of me. Then it all went back to normal, as Holly said. And I had nothing to do with the change. I'm still looking for the bugs or the cause, as we can't have that happen again. I'm finding some small glitches, but nothing that would cause the outages."

Holly turned to Michael, "We lost a lot of data during that period and the security of the free world was at stake because we could not effectively track containers entering ports or monitor the movement of some 'individuals' we have covertly tagged and need to know their whereabouts on almost an hourly basis."

Michael turned around to see the monitor on the wall behind him. A sign above it read: Monitoring, Analysis and Maintenance. There were pie charts in three corners of the screen with continuously changing percentages. In the lower left corner was a column of categories, which were links to other areas of the monitoring program.

A large green dot was located at the top of the screen, indicating that the system was meeting readiness status.

He turned back to Holly, "Could you do something for me?"

"Sure."

"I would like to see this MF, including the surrounding area to about fifteen miles, and all AIT devices."

She smiled and turned back to the technician at the console, "Could you bring that up on Monitor Two, Janet?"

Within moments, a satellite image of Fernley, the desert, the J&K Warehouse, the Front Door shack; all appeared on the display with hundreds of AIT devices in their customary colors.

There were none displayed within a two-mile perimeter of MF-7.

"As you can see, nothing is able to penetrate our security shields. We are invisible to the digital world," Holly proudly stated.

Michael nodded, "Very interesting. This is some amazing technology you have here." He would have said the same thing after a new kind of mouse trap demonstration, just to be cordial to the presenter. The whole intrusion capability of the system was not sitting well in his mind.

"Can I see all of this on the computer in Bernie's cube?" Michael asked.

"Sure, you have access. We set that all up when the Program Office told us that you were going to be with us." Holly looked at Bernie, "He does have Administrative permissions, doesn't he?" Bernie nodded.

Michael anxiously took a step forward, "I would like to get started on this now, if that is OK?"

"Sure thing; well it was nice to meet you. I am sure we will be seeing a lot of each other." Holly turned and walked back to her office as Michael and Bernie exited the NOC and took the nine steps to Bernie's cube.

"You can just move into here, that machine is all yours." He pointed at a desktop computer workstation in the corner of the cube.

"Thanks, you won't even know I'm here. I don't snore," Michael said as he settled into the imaginary seclusion of the small office and turned on the large monitor. He reached down and powered up the computer tower to the left of the chair. The display bloomed into the MF-7 login screen that he had always seen when he logged into the system from his room.

"In order to get to the GMCS Administration menu you need to use an asterisk after your password," Bernie informed him.

He logged in as Bernie instructed. The GMCS login screen appeared.

"Say, Bernie. I was just given this program and I loaded on my laptop. I try to open it and the computer freezes up."

"One more security thing that was added; you need to run it on a computer that has a LiquiCode reader so that it can scan you first."

"What if I need to use an ordinary laptop for some reason?"

"Oh, I see what you mean." Bernie went to a file on his computer. "I'm going to email you this little program. You should have this, being an Administrator of the system. Just click on the install icon and it will load a patch into your laptop's registry; you know where the passwords and registry things reside, I'm sure. It will ignore the lack of a reader in your machine and it has a Super user Program 3938 authorization code that will let you on the network. The final program we got from NexTrÉ had a field for the code to be entered; this will do that automatically. Our guys added the LiquiCode reader bypass thing later 'cause our field service guys were not issued a Program laptop. They're not DPs. Without this patch, if GMCS is not put into a Program-issued laptop the whole computer freezes up, as you must have found out." He finished typing. "OK, you should have the email when you get back to your own computer."

Michael looked at the computer he was using, "Then this machine doesn't have a reader?"

"Oh it's got a reader. It's in the keyboard. It read your tattoos. They're watching you." Bernie turned back to his monitor. "Have fun".

Michael looked at his screen. There was an icon labeled GMCS ADMIN at the right lower corner. He clicked on it.

The monitor flowered into the Main Menu screen for the finished, delivered program he had worked on for so long with Hugh at NexTrÉ. It looked very impressive in the flesh. He had just dealt with the code and he often found it difficult to imagine what the whole beast looked like from the inside out.

He performed the same steps that he had asked Holly to show him on the large monitors in the NOC. The satellite view of the area around MF-7 was pretty boring and it was true that nothing indicating the presence of a digital device within a mile of the facility.

For the next three hours he ran through screens and functions, comparing them with what he had been reading in the new code.

Bernie had left for the day and Michael had not even noticed.

He tested a LiquiCode reader in Hawaii by clicking on a green dot, which indicated that it was an ATM in the airport. The device reported its real-time status showing that a Mio Yakamoto was withdrawing three-hundred US dollars; her passport number appeared with a link to the Japanese passport database, the serial numbers of the three one hundred dollar notes were displayed and a video feed from the ATM camera was showing her face on a panel in the upper right of the computer monitor.

The impact of this global tracking system on individual privacy was going against the grain in his mind. He had to back away from the monster. He shut down the computer and made his way back down to the mess hall for a quick bite and then continued down on to room 521.

However, the systems' power of intrusion was addictive. He had the apparatus to know where nearly every mass-produced object, government-created document and licensed person on earth was located. He could view down to the most secure and guarded information that was ever compiled on a single individual or item. Michael had access to a tool that any totalitarian regime could only dream of possessing. But what frightened him the most was that anyone in the government, with proper access permissions, was using it.

He went to his email and opened the message from Bernie. He transferred the new bypass codes into his personal computer where the patch installed with no problems. He then effortlessly connected to the network with his own laptop and brought up GMCS. He was in.

Michael marveled at the visibility available with the program. It was now able to make anyone using it the ultimate voyeur. Any person carrying any form of his or her government issued identification, was a bucket of information that could be dipped into at any time and from nearly any location on earth.

Michael dove deeper into the capabilities of the system; viewing the early morning wet streets of London and accessing information on the people walking by a common vending machine at an Illinois rest stop on US 40. He checked the contents of containers aboard ships in the mid-Atlantic. He was able to read the serial number off a dollar bill being put into a soda machine in Topeka, Kansas. He even received a listing of contents within a household refrigerator that was connected to the Internet, in Pretoria, South Africa.

Invasion of the world population's personal activities was not only possible, it was happening – hourly.

He had to try one more thing. He accessed a door access card reader in El Paso, Texas. On the screen appeared the entire configuration file of the reader. He found what he was looking for . . . the access code for the device. He retyped the code and sent the new configuration file to the unit. He had just reprogrammed the thing from a thousand miles away. This meant that he could program an access door with a code that only he could use. Unfortunately, the reader would now not let anyone else in. He went back in and changed the configuration back to what it was before he changed it.

He was overwhelmed with the magnitude of total control over the everyday movement and activities of the worlds supply chains and inhabitants, which the system provided its users.

Michael slumped back in his chair and put himself on record, to whoever was listening, "Thank you for protecting us from ourselves, you Bastards!"

Chapter 13

Michael looked at his watch; it was 10:45 pm. He had been reading code, spying on the world, studying hardware interface schematics and running the government's version of GMCS for over eight hours.

His laptop emitted a soft tone alerting him to an incoming email. He opened the message; it was from Gus with a subject line reading: Channel 121. There was nothing else in the email.

He sat for a moment staring at the screen. The only thing he could think of was the television. He pickup up the remote control and turned on the TV; switching the channel to 121.

A small red light flashed on just above the screen, behind a small black plastic strip. On the screen appeared a young woman with a headset, looking right into the camera.

"Good evening, Mister Fields. I am confirming through scan data, that you are the only one present in the room. Is this correct?"

Michael slowly sat down in the leather chair that faced the screen, eyes glued to the female face that was staring back, with his mouth agape. He quickly snapped back to the moment, "Yes. I'm the only one in here."

"That is what the scan of your room indicates. Please stand by."

The image of the woman switched to . . . Gus. He was sitting in what appeared to be a large office. No tie, coat or hat.

"Michael! Great to see your smiling face again. Come on son, smile."

"Hello Gus," Michael pushed out the words with the stale air he had in his lungs, as he had forgotten to breath every since the TV started talking to him.

"No one told you about channel 121?"

"No."

"Good. It's our secure teleconference link. How's your accommodations, got everything you need out there?"

"Everything is fine, Gus. What do you need to . . . see me about?"

Gus pushed a button on a panel on his desk and the image of Brandon Bancroft appeared in the top right of the screen.

"Remember this guy?"

"That's Mister Bancroft. We talked about him a while back."

Gus pushed the buttons again and the image of Bancroft filled the screen as the image of Gus went up to the right hand corner of the screen.

"Let me tell you a bit more about him."

The image turned into a video of Bancroft at a number of gatherings, accepting awards, meeting dignitaries, talk show appearances and so on.

Gus began reading from a paper in front of him.

"Brandon James Bancroft. Born September 13, 1950 in North Platte, Nebraska. Only child, parents now deceased. Went through an average educational process and went on to receive a PhD in Computer Science and Artificial Intelligence from the University of Nebraska in 1980.

"Went to work, blah, blah, blah and became Vice President of Artificial Intelligent Systems at Zapof and Green in 1995. Quit there after getting everything he wanted out of the place and started his privately held NexTrÉ Corporation in 1998. He subsequently made a bazillion bucks, shut down NexTrÉ in late 2010 - and then disappeared. There it is; what the world knows." Gus put down the paper.

The video finished with Bancroft boarding a jet to someplace and the image fading to black. The whole screen returned back to just an image of Gus at the desk.

Michael shrugged, "That's about all *I* really knew of him, until you told me about Hugh chasing him."

"Well, that's what the world was told. In truth, Bancroft was a nut. Everything he did, everyplace he went; anything that involved making a decision, was guided by his obsession to first consult with some ancient hoodoo of some sort or another. Horoscope is one thing, but calling on the spirits of ancient priests and Mayan Winged Serpent Gods about a stock tip is another."

Gus reached across the desk and picked up a book.

"It got to a point where he believed that his success was preordained and he was some kind of 'chosen one'."

Michael was leaning closer with every new revelation of Brandon Bancroft passed to him.

"When the 3938 program contracted NexTrÉ to develop GMCS, naturally Bancroft became privileged to a lot of information about the MFs and Deep Purple. Hugh used to say Bancroft was constantly bugging him about getting on the DP list. He claimed that he had to be the one in charge of all the databases in the MFs, which contain the accumulated published knowledge of the entire span of the human race. Think of it as our version of the Library of Alexandria."

Gus leaned forward into the camera so that you could almost see his breath on the lens. "Like, we were going to let that loco ride herd over our data."

Gus closed the book. "I would get emails from him saying the Long Count is almost at its end and it's time to prepare for the new awaking or he had been chosen to be the caretaker of the knowledge. I finally had to confront him about three months after GMCS was delivered, and I let him know we no longer had any ties with him. I told him, flat out, there was no way in hell that we would risk having him associated with the program, especially as a DP."

"Then, about a year ago I received that note, which I asked you to look at; the one titled SC Letter.

"I read it, but nothing really connected."

Gus picked up a sheet of paper and began to read it aloud.

"We are nearing the new beginning at the end of the Long Count; where the earth shall begin to renew and Human Beings will assume their intended roles in the Universe. MU is the answer. Beware of ESA and the Righteous. This cycle's knowledge will be gathered to aid in the next."

He held the paper closer and squinted, as his eyes were visibly tired.

"The Mushroom Farms hide the truth. GenZs will take their place."

He looked back at the camera.

"Well, this note confirmed it for me, Bancroft was insane."

He dropped the paper on the desk, shaking his head.

"Then I started getting reports that were very disturbing. My sources were intercepting communications between a Santa Claws and a number of terrorist cells, which we had been monitoring around the world. The emails and other transmissions were originating from hundreds of transient points, which we tried to trace back but every one was just a dry well when we got there.

"As our people began assembling the puzzle from all of the pieces of information, a very serious picture was forming.

"As you have probably guessed, Brandon Bancroft was Santa Claws and he was out to get revenge or set things straight; he was thinking in his warped mind. The key to most of the puzzle was his constant references to the Long Count before he disappeared."

He reached over to pick up another piece of paper.

"Let me read you this. 'The Mayan calendar began on Julian date 584283, which equals August 11th, 3114 B.C. in our Gregorian calendar. This means that the end date of the Long Count, 13.0.0.0.0, some 5125 years later, will be at 11:11 am GMT, December 21st, 2012 A.D.'"

Gus put down the paper. "Bancroft believed the Earth was going to get renewed in some way on that date. And he was not going to be part of the renewal 'cause he was not going to be down in an MF and be saved, from what he thought to be, the end of the world." He shook his head and went back to the Brandon note.

"This cycle's knowledge will be gathered to aid in the next."

He looked up at the camera and sort of twisted his face into a hard think. "We believe this is referring to some kind of 5125 year cycle, and another one is about to begin. Bancroft was on this Itzamna kick about being the keeper of the knowledge and he was planning to access all other MFs databases and transfer the data to some database clusters he had somewhere. That's what Hugh found out and that is why he chased him all over this planet. GMCS was remolded to accomplish this and Hugh was pissed."

"Hugh's people were able to finally track down where the data was being dumped from the devices he had hijacked with his firmware 'updates'."

"It seems that Bancroft had built a complex, inside an old Mayan temple, in the middle of the jungle near Uxmal in the Yucatan. For us to finally locate it was a piece of cake, thanks to Hugh's exact coordinates he had put in his note."

"The raid took place on November 6th, as Hugh had directed. Brandon Bancroft was there, but somehow managed to escape. However, scores of his people were rounded up and we were able to take over his communications and datacenters."

"Did you manage to shut down his operation?"

"Within hours of the raid, The Shadow People were on the plane to Uxmal."

"The Shadow People?"

"Our software hacker team. They can get into any system and make it spill its guts. A real eccentric group of Banditos, but they managed to get some of the information we needed."

So that was the name of Parker's team. That figured.

Gus straightened himself in the chair and took a drink of water from a glass sitting just off camera.

"Here is the last thing I need to talk about tonight. This must not be discussed with anyone, at anytime."

Gus took a breath and looked down at the SC Letter and began to read the last line, in a subdued voice. *"The Mushroom Farms hide the truth. GenZs will take their place."*

He looked up to the camera.

"From what we found in some documents and files at the bunker, was Bancroft was planning on guiding the new Human Race to greatness again after the Long Count was up."

Gus put his elbows on the desk and raised both hands, palms up.

"And if there was no competition, he would have it all."

Michael felt something he really didn't want to hear was about to come his way, "Competition?"

"The 3938 Program and the December Pact nations. We are positive Bancroft had his terrorist-buddies plant nuclear devices around every MF."

Michael froze in time, as the seconds of silence crawled by like hours, with millions of nightmarish images filling his mind. The walls were closing in and everything in his being was clawing to get to the surface and run into the desert. As his soul cried out to whatever was listening, he nearly threw up. Reality sucked.

Gus' voice slapped him across the ears and Michael, once again, focused on the screen.

"We've had teams scouring the areas over the MFs with deep scanners, for a few weeks," Gus sighed. "Haven't found anything, yet."

"Have you told everyone in the MFs? You . . . someone should get them out of there . . . here," Michael stammered, as the realization of where he was sitting crawled up and down his spine.

"We can't evacuate because the operations going on, inside the MFs, need to continue to maintain national security. Everyone in charge knows about the situation and we are all confident that the nukes will be found soon and moved to a safe location for deactivation."

The words had no effect in calming Michael's stomach.

"That now brings us to you, Michael."

Gus held up his hand and began folding his fingers, one by one, as he talked, "We have a good idea where the devices are buried. We are fairly confident on what the devices look like and are contained in. What we don't know is if they are set to go off at a predetermined time or if a command is sent from the satellites. And we do not know if the MFs are the only targets or if every facility in the December Pact has had devices planted around them. Bancroft may have made alliances with other countries or he may have decided to just get rid of every human being on earth, except for his people. If those devices explode, there will be retaliatory strikes all over the globe with one nation claiming that another country planted the nukes."

He put his hand down on the desk as if totally exhausted, "Michael, somewhere in that source code or masked in those other documents I passed on to you, there has to be something that will provide us with the procedures and codes that will allow us to turn off the nukes after we move them to the safe areas. We know GMCS has something to do with their deactivation. Maybe Bancroft added code to it, but we need to know where he could have done the modifications. We need a clue on where to look in his system."

Gus leaned forward and pointed at the camera as if he had better make the next words the most important part of the conversation, "And if you find anything, contact me immediately. And make sure I am the only one you contact."

This was more than an order; it was a command from nearly the highest authority in the government.

It was obvious that the strain was wearing Gus down. He leaned back in his chair with a groan, lifting his arms up.

"That's enough for tonight, Michael. Get some sleep, if you can. Just keep plugging away at it."

"Good night, Gus. I'll do my best."

"Do better than that."

Gus pushed a button and the screen immediately switched back to the lady with the headset. "That concludes your conference, Mister Fields. Is there anything else I can help you with?"

Michael thought for a moment.

"I was just wondering," his voice was still a bit shaky, "Where are you located?"

"We are in MF-1, in the Level Two communications center."

"You control all of the conference calls from there?"

"Yes, there are five of us in this room. For your own information, if you would like to set up a video conference, just request a time and participants via email to us at VCO@3938.gov. Your application will be reviewed per your security level and your call may be granted. You are invited to visit our site at 3938.gov/VCO."

"Thank you. This session has been most informative." Michael wondered if she was some kind of windup doll.

"Good bye, Mister Fields."

The image turned blue and the little red light over the screen went out. As if that actually meant anything.

Chapter 14

Wednesday, November 28, 2012

Michael had not slept at all after Gus had divulged the fact that nukes were probably planted in the dirt right over his head. Michael had acquired a sense that his eyes were closed and someone had thrown a large rock in the air. He was just waiting for it to come down on top of him at any moment.

At 9 am he packed his bags and took the elevator to Level 1, then up to the lobby. Surrounded by marble, chrome and shimmering chandlers, he took out the homemade business card in his wallet. He dialed Vern's number, on his Grape, for a ride back to the parking lot in the J&K van.

"OK, Mister Fields. You just wander outside and wait for me. It shouldn't be too long," the dusty voice instructed.

"Thanks, Vern. I'll be out by the road." Michael hung up the phone and quickly proceeded up the lobby staircase to get to the exit.

He opened the decrepit door of the clapboard house that encased the MF entrance and stepped into the cool desert air and brilliant morning sunlight.

Parked on the dirt road was a beige pickup truck; dented and sand-blasted, with an old black dog sitting in the bed.

Leaning against the front fender was a leather-faced man wearing faded jeans, worn cowboy boots and a weather-beaten hat which Michael had often seen in old westerns. Two long, almost white braids flowed from under the hat and draped down over the shoulders of the stocky man.

Michael looked down and nonchalantly walked towards a spot twenty yards behind the truck to wait for Vern and the van. Being the only other person visible within a hundred square miles, it was hard to create a low profile.

"You are the one called Fields?" the man called out.

Michael stopped and slowly turned around. "Yes, I'm Michael Fields. What can I do for you?"

The man stood away from the truck with his hands in the pockets of the un-buttoned, heavy tanned-hide coat, "We need to talk."

Oh, God. Now what? Michael thought, dropping his shoulders.

The stranger walked heavily towards him, kicking up the powder-fine desert dust into a small cloud that followed his boots. His large belt buckle flashed in the morning sun as he stopped within inches of Michael's face and looked into his eyes; first one, then the other. "Yes, you are Fields. The change has not happened, but I can see it in your soul."

Security is really getting weird. Michael backed up a couple steps to gather some sense of comfort with the situation.

"And you are?" Michael asked glancing at the ceramic eagle feather earring hanging from the man's left lobe.

"Call me George. You couldn't pronounce my real name. Not yet." He was eyeing Michael up and down, taking stock of his appearance and what he was carrying.

"OK George. Again, what can I do for . . . ?"

"Looks like you've got all your gear. Come with me." George turned and walked towards the truck.

Michael called to his back, "But I'm expecting a ride . . ."

"Vern won't be coming." George took out his right hand from the pocket and lifted it into the air, then pointed at the other side of the aged vehicle as he opened the driver's side door, "Get in the truck."

Michael walked cautiously around the right rear of the truck, passing the dog. It only gave him a passing glance and laid down in anticipation of the bumpy ride to follow.

"Put your gear in the back, Martin won't bother it," George said as Michael was opening the passenger door.

He did as he was instructed and stepped up into the passenger seat. After a quick grinding of gears, the truck began lurching forward as he shut the door.

Making a U-turn in the desert dirt, George drove them out to the main road and made a left; going north.

"Aren't we going to my car?"

"Not for a bit. Gonna' head up here a ways."

Michael could not find any seat belt and was not sure of the speed limit, but he knew it was not over seventy miles per hour; which they had exceeded a few miles back. Martin was hanging off the left side of the bed; ears and tongue flapping like ripped sails, with his watery nose to the wind. It appeared that he was smiling.

Michael took a guess and spoke over the country music playing on the radio, "Are you a member of this Paiute Tribe?"

"Yep, been a 'member' for nearly sixty-six years."

Michael felt embarrassed after his last comment. He thought he should move into something lighter, not only to change the mood but to make his self a little more comfortable with the present situation; kidnapped by some lunatic driver, "So George, why did you name your dog Martin?"

"When he was six weeks old, he pissed on my new Martin guitar and ruined the finish. After fourteen years I keep reminding him of that day -- by calling him Martin. Paybacks are hell."

Michael was sure the dog didn't have a clue, but apparently it made George feel better.

The truck slowed and made a jolting left turn off the pavement and onto another desert clay road. There were white patches along the edges of the trail; not snow -- alkaline.

A small, single-level house came into view as they cleared the crest of a recent fire-blackened hill; probably due to a dry-lightning strike. George slowed and turned into the gravel drive. As they parked next to the tired little dwelling, George turned off the truck engine and turned to Michael, "I need to talk with you about Hugh Waterman and what's coming. Let's go inside."

He opened the driver's door and climbed out to drop the tailgate for his old companion, Martin. He raised his head and looked down the road to see if anyone had followed. Michael picked up his bags and followed George into the rough-cut lumber structure. *This guy knew Hugh?*

George stomped his boots on the throw rug leading into the small kitchen, "Set your stuff down anywhere." He pointed to his left, to the living room area, "Have a seat in that big ol' brown chair, it's the most comfortable. I'll get some coffee going." Martin passed them both and walked in the direction George had indicated. He rotated in two small circles over a well-worn rug in front of a propane heater in the living room before flopping down. With his chin resting on his paws, his tired old eyes became fixed on Michael.

Michael sat in the deep leather chair and looked around the wallpapered room. A rock-faced fireplace dominated one wall. An original water-color painting hung over the mantel. It depicted a lone, blanket-draped Warrior, his dog and horse, clustered by an open winter campfire. The painting represented an era George could have stepped out of; it could have been him and Martin, huddled in the picture. Two dust-covered windows provided filtered light through the openings below the lowered shades.

Upon the mantel rested a pair of wedding rings, in a hand-decorated clay plate.

The house had seen decades of use as the wood floors attested to; with worn paths of feet moving from one room to another -- from one owner to another. It was comfortable. A single bedroom was through a door on Michael's left with a corner of a deep burgundy braded rug visible from his chair. The small, yellow and white kitchen was to his right. A window above the sink funneled sunlight onto the wood counter top and across the faded and chipped enameled face of the refrigerator. When they had entered he had noticed an outhouse, a propane tank and cistern outside.

"Do you have electricity out here?"

"I got a generator out back. Gives me enough power to run the stuff I got and keep the well pump going. The Utility Company won't run any lines here 'cause it's a Squatter's place. Not officially recognized by the State. I moved in here about twelve years ago, after old man Kantor died. It's worked out for me and Martin."

George brought out two mismatched mugs and gave the one with a San Francisco 49ers logo on it to Michael. George sat on the over-stuffed couch, in front of a heavy wood coffee table. "It's kind of like your MF, it doesn't exist," he gave out a short laugh and took a drink of his coffee.

"You said you knew Hugh Waterman? How did that come about?" Michael was warming his hands on the coffee mug, recovering from the lack of heat in the truck cab and feeling more relaxed with George. But he still needed some answers to his abduction.

George sat back and took off his hat. Michael was taken back by the image of the stately man sitting across from him. His etched face demanded respect and his mannerisms reflected that he had been well educated. This was not some desert-rat.

"Hugh Waterman knocked at that door, late one night – almost a year ago. Hugh was a very sick man. And chasing that Bancroft nut, all over the world, sure wasn't helping any."

"You know about Bancroft? Can I ask you to do something for me?"

George eyed him, "What?"

"Hold up your hands."

"Is this a stickup? Don't make me sic Martin on you. Oh, hell. He wouldn't get up for anything but dinner. OK, you can steal the mug."

Michael smiled, knowing George might already know what he was looking for, "Are you a DP?"

"No, I was just Hugh's friend . . . and doctor," he quietly replied.

"His doctor? I don't understand."

"I'm what you would call a Ritual Leader. You know, one of those Medicine Man characters you White Guys have tried to show in the movies. But I'm for real -- natural healing techniques; organics, fresh air, exercise – the whole regiment. It took me years of studying from my grandfather. He was a Shaman, too. No, he was beyond that – the man was amazing; a walking encyclopedia of herbs and plants and their healing properties. And a whole lot more, of which I will tell you . . . some day.

"Actually, my education was a hell of a lot longer than going through medical school. And he was on my ass every day. I had to learn every song, all the body movements, how to hold the rattle just right. And all those prescriptions I had to remember almost made me run away from home. Well, actually I did . . . but that's another story."

He smiled and looked down, as strong memories of his beloved grandfather flooded his soul. "And of course he had never written anything down -- had a mind like a trap."

He looked up at Michael and winked, "I cheated and took copious notes. You should see my notebooks, thicker than most medical journals."

"Then you must be passing the knowledge on to the next generation, like your grandfather did . . . your son or grandson?"

George looked to the fireplace mantel for a long moment then back at Michael. In a low, slow voice, "No. There is no one. It appears that the ancient knowledge will return to the ages. The *Strategos* will fall upon another. He bowed his head and rotated his coffee cup to watch the thick liquid form a counterclockwise whirlpool.

Michael could feel anguish in George's voice. The old man looked up, "Well, I suppose it was bound to happen. No one cares about tradition anymore. But, let me tell you, there are some things I have seen and experienced that modern science would have trouble talking their way out of. When you cross over into spiritual activities, you just go along for the ride.

He leaned back into the couch, "There was a man, an old man. Lived down by town in a little house; smaller than this, actually. He was totally blind. But, everyday he would walk around town – different routes, stopping at different houses . . . just to pay his respects. He had the ancient way, the third eye . . . way beyond what modern science can explain."

He leaned forward and sat on the end of the cushion, looking Michael in the eyes, "One day my grandmother was washing dishes and looked out the window, 'Oh, they are so anxious today. I better get them something to eat.' She says. I go over and look out . . . nothing or no one there."

"So?" Michael said, wanting to know the point of the story.

"She could see the old man's Familiars. His invisible animal guides. They were otters. They led him around the town, and all of the Elders could see them. Those ancient ways and abilities are now being lost. Just as the way the salmon are losing their past, since humans have changed the routes of their rivers and put up dams, they don't know where to spawn anymore."

"Is that why you brought me here? You think I can help with these lost . . . ancient ways, or something?" Michael was very confused.

George waved his hand, "No, I just get off on tangents sometimes. Nobody to talk with around here; except Martin over there. And he's tired of hearing about it."

Martin, with eyes still closed, wagged his tail twice after hearing his name. Or maybe he was agreeing with the old man.

Michael smiled at the gift of friendship he was receiving, then leaned forward, "What did Hugh die of?"

"He had prostate cancer. Those fancy doctors, The Program sent him to, didn't do anything but prescribe drugs and kept pushing him to get chemotherapy treatments. He knew if he started those he wouldn't be able to keep chasing Bancroft. So, he turned to me; just to buy himself a few more months. I gave him that."

Michael could see George's genuine feelings for Hugh as his eyes and voice drifted with a mellowing pain.

"Our last meeting was a month before he went to the Yucatan. I told him he only had a few weeks left."

Michael remembered Hugh's note to Gus, which he read in the restaurant, *'Going downhill. George says maybe a few weeks'.*

"You don't have secure internet access out here, do you?" Michael had a suspicion.

"I know what you're getting at . . . Hugh never brought his computer out here. He knew they could track his location. This place was a sanctuary for him."

"Then Hugh wrote a note to Gus, before he went to the Yucatan, while he was here?"

"Yep. I took the note and passed it to one of my people, to get to *Gus* in MF-1." He didn't look pleased. There was something about the way he referred to Gus that soured the words.

"Your people were able to get that to Gus, at MF-1?"

"The CIA, Secret Service and most Ninja got nothing on my guy's abilities," he beamed.

"Then you know about the bunker and Hugh dying down there?"

"I'm aware of the whole situation. I'm well informed on . . . things. Most of my training was focused on methods of tapping into the *puha* or power."

Michael leaned forward in his chair, "Is that how you knew I was leaving the MF and Vern was not coming to pick me up?"

"Naw, he called me on my cell phone. I had told him I needed to talk with you. When you called him -- he called me. I get a pretty strong phone signal out here. There's a cell tower just down the road."

Michael felt really foolish. "Oh, I thought you meant that you can do some mind things. You know; magical stuff. Sorry."

"Now don't write me off that easy. Technology is one thing, but my people have been tapping into some pretty interesting energy stuff for a couple millennia. Remember the old blind man?" George put down his mug on the floor and stood up. He began to walk to the bedroom but stopped and turned around. "Oh, I forgot to mention that the old blind man would walk into the lake and stay submerged for hours."

He turned and went into the bedroom. He returned with a long wooden box -- highly decorated with radiant blue diamond shapes and white triangle symbols. He set it on the coffee table and gently opened it. "This is *my* 'doctor's little-black-bag.' I inherited it from my grandfather and all that ancient knowledge which goes with it."

Inside were a pipe, a gourd rattle, a dozen small cloth bags and a thick envelope. He removed the sealed packet and handed it to Michael.

"Hugh told me to give you this in person when you got here."

Michael took the envelope and read the writing on the outside, *'Michael Fields – Important'*. He opened it and removed some folded papers and two compact disks from inside, dated October 17, 2012.

Michael,

When you read this I will be dead and you will be sitting in the brown chair, holding a 49ers mug. Did I get that right? Of course I did.

And how did I know this would happen? I knew I was dying and I arranged with George to make the rest happen. It's pretty simple.

How did the Mayans know that December 21st, 2012 was going to be the date for a 'new beginning', as Bancroft had stated? It was pretty much the same as what George and I planned to get you this letter. It is not prophesying, they just followed a timeline that was planned a millennium before.

I don't want to get too deep into this; that is George's department.

As you know by now, we tracked down Bancroft and will attempt to take over his operations on November 6th. I managed to get the coordinates of the bunker where he set up his headquarters, from the same sources who provided the information in this envelope. You don't know them, yet.

On the enclosed disk labeled Number 1, is the final version of GMCS -- Bancroft's version. It is <u>not</u> what was delivered to the government. As you will see, significant changes have been added.

There are two components and related files that stand out as the most foreign; the time synchronizing algorithms and the XZX files. Pay attention to those, I am at a loss to what they mean. But, you will . . . soon.

I'm out of my league on this one. I am not a GenZ.

Two things: Do not use your Program-issued laptop to test this program and do not tell Gus that you have this information.

Good luck and tell George 'hi' for me.

Hugh

Michael lowered the letter and looked at George, "Hugh says hi."

George looked up to the low ceiling, "Hi Hugh. See ya soon." He walked back to the kitchen talking over his shoulder, "Want a refill on the coffee?"

"Yes, thanks." Michael stood up and went into the linoleum-floored kitchen with his mug. He sat down in one of the two chairs tucked against a small yellow table. Martin had followed them and took up a prone position at the opening between the kitchen and living room, as if he didn't want to miss anything said.

George finished filling Michael's mug and put the coffee pot back on the gas stove.

"Thanks, George. Tell me about Hugh -- the real Hugh. I only knew him as Howard Linn. I listened to quite a few of his acquaintances giving eulogies at the funeral, but the remarks all seemed very superficial. I guess you knew him pretty well. It sounded like you two had become real friends."

George leaned against the counter, "Tell you about Hugh . . . Got a minute?"

Michael smiled and nodded at George's humorous summation of his captive situation.

"Well, as you already know, he was sixty-one when he died. He smoked like a chimney, worked his ass off and would have never retired.

"Hugh was married for nineteen years, to a lady named Annie. She died about thirteen years ago -- he wouldn't say how. But after that he sold his house, pulled up roots and just poured himself in his work. For the next three years he was on the move and never kept a permanent address; just went where the government sent him on never-ending covert assignments."

George moved over to the other chair at the small table and sat down.

"Then ten years ago, he was recruited by . . . some people. That is where he ran into Gus. I guess his professionalism, drive and knowledge of computer systems really impressed Gus. He brought him in to his operation as the Division Manager of the entire GMCS Program for 3938. Let's just call it a Level 4 position.

"Did I mention that Hugh helped develop the operating system that almost every computer uses today? He worked at that big software company – well, it wasn't big when he started there in '79. That's where he met Annie."

Michael thought back to the Hugh he knew, "I've seen his work on directing the software architects at NexTrÉ."

George shook his head, "I couldn't get him to slow down. He wouldn't hesitate in jumping into any situation with both feet, no matter the odds. Fate just broke his stride"

"What did he tell you about Bancroft?"

George shifted his weight and pointed at Michael, "When he started to tell me about the things that were going on with Bancroft, it really knocked me for a loop. Not in what he was doing so much as the fact that he was doing it now. I wish I could explain further, but Bancroft was pushing a time-line forward that was not to be for years.

He lowered his hand and leaned back in the chair. "The path that Bancroft was on, whether he was conscious of it or not, coincided with a number of ancient cultural prophecies. Many of which had been floating around the Nations for a few hundred years."

"You mean about December 21st, 2012?"

"I suppose the date could mean something, with the Mayan calendar and sun spots coinciding; I mean about the new beginning thing. Just like with the Ghost Dance, someone got the meaning all screwed up and think it's some kind of threat; although, this 2012 prophecy has gotten elevated up to an 'end of the world' deadline. Well, I suppose it could be the end of a lot of things, but not the world. Not the earth."

"What *lots of things*?" It was difficult for Michael not to shake at George's confirmation of the prophecy, so he put down his coffee mug.

"This whole crazy world has gone into a linear way of thinking; innovative growth, creative financial structures, centralized and decentralized government. It seems that everything has shifted away from looking at things in a circular state. I suppose I mean traditional patterns and beliefs have been abandoned because they do not allow for expansion – and profit."

He held up his hand and put his head down. "I'm getting a little off base here. Let me get right to the point."

He turned and looked Michael in the eye, "Do you know about the nukes?"

"Yes, Gus told me about them last night. That is the main reason I was getting out of there this morning."

George was relieved that he did not have to break *that* news to Michael.

"What do *you* know about them?" Michael asked, hoping for some sane answer.

"Supporting insanity is a great tool for terrorist nations. They can fund it and promote the results as divine payback.

I'm not really sure that the crates have nukes in them or not. But, until I hear different, I don't think we should take any chances."

George lowered his voice, as if he didn't want the world to hear what he had to say next . . . only Michael. "I'm going to tell you, what I told Hugh."

"OK." Michael said slowly, preparing himself for something he knew he didn't want to hear.

"The Hopi have a prophecy, which is a list of nine signs that must be fulfilled before the earth is reborn into its Fifth World. Unfortunately, six of them have already been met. Stuff like concrete highways and spider-web cables all over the land. The ninth one says that some big blue inhabited thing will fall on the earth. The ancients really could connect the dots by building on the 'as-is' with logical 'to-be' layers. Now I don't see any blue thing falling on my head for quite a while yet, but the Hopi never put dates on their predictions. Based on their track record, I'm going to keep looking up.

"But, the Maya were fanatical about dates. They had calculated that the poles of the earth will shift and something associated with radiation or divine intelligence will take the earth into a new beginning. One door will close and another will open. Scientists have figured out their calendar and think this rebirth will begin on December 21st."

Michael was afraid that he may have a front row seat to this Mayan prediction.

George squinted and lifted his finger, "Let's assume that Bancroft was *totally* immersed in the Mayan thought process, not just playing the part. He would have adopted a circular way of thinking. The shifting of the poles will not be an astronomical occurrence -- it will be a catastrophic event involving superior control and ideologies. Specifically: The shifting of the world's superpowers, bringing a new order to mankind – perhaps from east to west or north to south. It could be based on their own Prime Meridian and not the magnetic poles. The Maya took the East as being the origin of the world."

George's face grew more intense and his voice lowered to almost a whisper and Michael had to move closer to hear.

"And how will this be accomplished? Through the *threat* of total nuclear annihilation. Sure, the weapons will be used -- they just won't be detonated."

Michael's head was swimming as he leaned away, "So, what you're saying is that Bancroft planted the nukes to possibly blackmail the December Pact nations? To bring them down by getting enough payment to set up his 'buddies' as the new world superpowers?"

George nodded, "That might be the first step, followed by a show of strength. Some dramatic demonstrations of control -- something that would send us back a hundred years, or so."

"Fear is a terrible weapon, Michael. It either turns people into warriors or slaves. In today's world, there are few heroes left to protect the rest." George clenched his fist and sighed.

He stood up, "But, I could be wrong. I'm waiting for word from the top. I've got to go start up the generator. Back in minute." He went out the door to the back of the house.

Michael sat in the chair and looked down at Martin, "Well, you heard everything. What's your take on it?"

The dog only looked up, without moving his head. He too sighed and closed his eyes.

Michael had to stand up and walk around on his weakened knees. He stepped around Martin and went into the living room. On the wall, behind the big chair he had first sat in, was a wooden frame . . . thick glass covered the face. Inside the box hung a Silver Star and a picture of a twenty-four year old George, in a Viet Nam era Marine Corps uniform. The medal was being presented to him by some general.

Michael heard the generator start. Within a few moments George entered the door to find Michael standing in front of the case holding the medal.

"Ah, looking at my mementos. Another time . . . another me."

"George, this is amazing. Why were you awarded this?" Michael was beyond impressed.

"Got into a fight . . . got lucky . . . got out." George calmly replied as he walked over and opened the wooden box.

He picked up a small, oblong object and motioned to Michael, "Come over here, I've got something I want you to have."

Michael walked to where George was standing. The warrior placed the item into his hand. "This is an ancient artifact that has been taking up room in my magic box for too many years . . . I want you to take it. It will provide safe passage in a time of great peril."

Michael looked at the small clay object. There were diamond shapes and lines resembling lightening bolts, painted on the grey, aged surface.

"It has served me well in many lost times. You must take it. No more talk about it." George closed the box. "OK, let's get you back to your car."

The three took up their positions in the truck and George drove them safely back to the Casino Only parking lot, where Michael climbed into his own vehicle and headed west . . . away from MF-7.

Chapter 15

Michael's drive back to Sunnyvale was difficult. He couldn't concentrate on the road. His mind was filled with George's hypothesis on Bancroft's real plan. Was he actually going to detonate the devices or just planning on using them to initiate a shift in the world's political hierarchy? Could he still do it, being on the run?

Upon his arrival back to his apartment, Michael called Parker and told him to come over ASAP; to drop everything that whatever it was Field Intelligence people do.

Within twenty minutes, there was a knock on his apartment door.

Michael opened the door to see Parker standing there with his finger to his lips. He motioned for Michael to follow him.

Michael picked up Hugh's envelope and they walked to the sidewalk in front of the apartment complex.

Parker began to speak, but Michael cut him off, "Let's take a walk. I need some exercise." Parker looked confused until Michael motioned with his eyes towards the eavesdropper in the SUV.

They turned the corner and stopped. Michael looked back to the parked vehicle and whispered, "There's a guy in that car across the street from my apartment, with a parabolic antenna. I know he's watching me."

"Not surprising. Your apartment is probably bugged too. By whom -- I have a few ideas. Could be the Program, could be the *other* guys. Really makes no difference, they all want the same information. So, why are you back?"

"I had to get out of the MF."

"Claustrophobia?"

"No, the fear of being blown into little-bitty, microscopic pieces. There are some serious things going on, Parker."

"Before I forget, Neal called me back. He's anxious to meet us. He thinks your name is Rhonda."

"Funny. You should get together with Johnson."

Parker was in the dark on the joke, "Get with who?"

"Never mind, can you get Neal to meet us tomorrow?"

"No problem. So, you want to tell me about being blown up? You look like you're in one piece to me."

"Bancroft is going to blow up all of the MFs with nuclear devices already buried on top of them . . . I think."

Parker just stood on the sidewalk staring at Michael. It was evident that wheels were turning in his head as his eyes were not focusing on Michael's face.

"Hello? Did you hear what I said?"

Parker turned and began walking faster down the sidewalk, "Let's go over to the coffee shop." He was still in some haze as Michael caught up with him and matched his pace.

Parker began talking fast and gesturing with his hands, more than usual. "I found a file in the bunker. It was named 'Righteous'. When you read that SC Letter to me, last Saturday, the word kind of clicked but it didn't mean anything to me -- until now."

They crossed the street and turned right, towards the small café.

Michael moved into their path, turned around to Parker and began walking backwards, "And? What about the file?"

"I've got it on my memory stick at home." He stopped, "Damn, I should have never left that thing there. No matter, they think I'm there." He began walking again, passing Michael who was stopped and still facing backwards.

"And why would they think you are still in your apartment?" Michael asked, speeding up to keep alongside.

Parker held up his wrist supports, "I left a decoy." Michael couldn't figure that one out, but didn't want to put too much effort into it with apocalyptic horsemen charging around in his head.

Michael looked back in the direction of his apartment, to see if they were being followed by the SUV. There was no sign of it.

They got two coffees. Parker paid with cash and they walked outside to sit at one of the sidewalk tables, next to a small tree. There were two metal chairs and an umbrella impaled in the table's paint-chipped center. Michael put his paper cup down on the wobbly table's top and sat across from his friend. He moved the chair back to get a clear view of Parker, without the umbrella pole getting in the way. He held Hugh's envelope in his lap.

Parker raked his chair across the cement and seated himself, with legs crossed, facing the street. "OK. Who told you there were nukes planted at the MFs?"

"Gus. He said there were bombs planted around every MF and probably the December Pact complexes. Bancroft could be targeting all world governments, too. Gus told me Bancroft doesn't want any competition."

"Oh." Parker was becoming uneasy, hearing so much about Gus' involvement and the information he had been passing to Michael. He returned to Michael's last statement, "The December what?" Parker was in the dark again and it was chipping away at his 'expertise' in the realm of conspiracy theories.

"I'll explain that one later; just think of it as ten major world powers with their own versions of Mushroom Farms."

"Well, then just tell me about the nukes at MF-7," Parker asked.

"The Program is sure that they are controlled by satellite link. You know, turned off and on and reprogrammed remotely . . . Gus said they have almost discovered them all -- at all the Farms. He told me that they will be moved to safe areas to be deactivated, as soon as someone can figure out how to 'talk' to them. He thinks GMCS is the key to turning them off. That's what I am supposed to be doing, finding those satellite command codes."

Parker looked around, seeing no one else was near them, "I found a file, as I said, in one of the servers I was digging into at the bunker. It stood out because it was so large. When I opened it, there was this whole document on how Bancroft was going to guide the new Human Race to greatness again after the Long Count was up. He planned on recruiting a million or two of the ultra-rich scattered around the world; with himself as the leader -- acting as some kind of god. He had developed his own Continuance of the Species program. It was called *Righteous*. I thought it was just another one of his whacky lists."

"Did you get a list of names?"

"They were in the file; that is why the thing was so big. It was like the 'who's-who' of the worlds most *commanding* people -- and a lot of nut-cases that I have read about. Names, addresses, income; it's really comprehensive. I spent a whole afternoon going down the list wishing I was that rich." He took a drink of his coffee and waited for a lady walking some kind of mutant lap dog to pass.

He leaned onto the table, "Bancroft was going to set up a whole upper echelon of political, business and military leaders in some kind of new world order. And the real amazing thing about it was that he had sold memberships in this 'after the apocalypse' club. There is even brochure text in the file that he had sent these people . . . like he was selling condos."

Michael cracked a small smile as this part was sounding almost funny. "What did he promise them?"

"First of all; existence after whatever was going to wipe out all human life on earth and second, the chance to rule their very own new nation of survivors. It was like a 'be the first on your block to run your own county' thing. He claimed that all human life would not be destroyed in the 'big one', just major populations. There would be millions left, coming out of mines, caves and various shelters without any leadership or directions. It was perfect for the types of people on the list. But the main thing that was understood, when they signed up for this club, was that Bancroft was to be the supreme leader."

"Did it get into how he was going to accomplish this 'world rule?"

"No, just the list of names and that other stuff I told you. He demanded payment of half a million US dollars in gold. And for that he would set them up in a number of plush underground locations from December 20th to December 26th; complete with maid, Holiday parties and butler services. Bancroft stated that the whole thing would be over in a week so very little provisions were needed."

"Underground for only a week -- after a world-wide nuclear holocaust? Do you have the feeling that he really didn't want those people to survive?" Michael smirked.

"It sure looks that way. I think it was a way for him to get the rest of the 'unwanted' into concentrated areas where he could do away with them. That is what he meant by '*Beware the Righteous*" in his SC note. He took it upon himself to get rid of them. He sure didn't like them . . . that's for sure."

Michael smiled, "Wonder if he got 'em all?"

Michael watched a pizza delivery car take a corner at 40 miles per hour, assuming the same rights to the road as an emergency vehicle.

He lifted the envelope from his lap. "This is from Hugh."

Parker looked around, then at the envelope, "Did you just get it? How? What's in it?"

"It's kind of a strange story."

"It can't be any stranger than Bancroft's whacko tale."

"A friend of Hugh's, a Medicine Man of sorts named George, gave it to me at his house in the desert."

Parker just stared at Michael, wondering what he was on and why he was wandering around the desert. "I was wrong – it is stranger."

Michael tapped on the envelope, "I have Bancroft's revised version of GMCS on disk."

Parker blinked back to reality and put out his arm to grab the envelope. Michael pulled it back and looked around, "Not here. There's more inside then just the disk."

"Like what? Beads and rattles?"

"Another disk that has the firmware codes, authorization codes and the entire network diagrams of what Bancroft had set up. Everything his system touches is in here"

"Let's go load it up." Parker pushed his chair back and was standing up.

"It won't run."

Parker slowly sat back down. "Well, ain't that just great. What good is it?"

"According to Hugh, there is a component missing and some radical code files. He was sure that I could find out what it was and get the programs to run. He also told me to run this on my own laptop, not the Program's."

"How can you do that on a civilian computer? There must be some security things in there that tie into the LiquiCode reader. And what about authorization codes to let you on the 3938 network?"

Michael smiled, "Sometimes, things just go your way. I got the registry patch that overrides those little problems. I've already put them in my personal laptop."

Parker put his elbow on the table and rested his chin on his hand, still pondering the Medicine Man and Hugh connection, "Do any of those magic files tell us how Bancroft could get control of the world's digital systems."

"According to a note from Hugh; yes. I haven't gone through the whole package. You'll need to help me there. But from a quick read of the network diagrams I could see that he might have been able to pull it off. He could duplicate all of the MF databases, actually hundreds of different databases; like plugging in a hose to a clone of the real computers."

Parker squinted as his brain tried to envision such a feat.

Michael leaned forward and tapped on the table with his finger for added emphasis, "He could gain control of every digital device on the Global Grid by uploading his own updated firmware changes to them. I found dual data export and import parameter settings in the new Device Manager Module document. Essentially, anything that gathers and sends information to a central computer can be reprogrammed to also send its data to Bancroft's network at the same time."

He slumped back in his chair, "Bancroft would be able to monitor and control any device that had the GMCS firmware installed in it from his bunker in the Yucatan."

Parker ran his fingers through his hair, "From what you are saying, I think he could upload a type of virus to any device that had a microprocessor in it and was hooked up to a network. You realize how many of those things are out there? ATM's, RFID readers, passport scanners, power grids . . ."

Michael cut him short, "From what I have seen at the Network Operations Center in MF-7, there seems to be a thousand bazillion. That includes camera controllers and biometric scanners. And I know when the uploading of the firmware took place; between January and March of this year. Every device on the main GMCS system went down for a period during that time. It almost crashed the whole system. And, as you said, microprocessors are everywhere; everything from vending machines to refrigerators to satellite interfaces."

Michael remembered the large quantity of red and yellow dots on the February monitor, "When you were in the bunker, how close was he to taking over the systems, any idea?"

"Well, thinking back on what we found at his headquarters, I'm sure he was at a point where he could turn off and on a power grid or a sanitation system anywhere in the world. From what you've told me, I'm sure he could also control satellite configurations with a touch of a button from that underground control station."

Michael was thinking almost faster than the words could form, "He couldn't do this alone. He was brilliant, but not a system implementer. It would take some major migration skills."

They both looked at each other and almost at the same instance, "VJ!"

Parker got out his personal phone and quickly made a call.

"Red, it's me. A guy named VJ was with NexTrÉ . . . until a while back. He supposedly moved on to MIT to run the Artificial

Intelligence Lab. He doesn't have a tattoo, but I really need to know where is now. Make it top priority. Thanks."

He hung up and put the phone back in his jacket pocket. "OK, we need to find someplace safe and go over everything in that envelope."

"I suppose Q's is the safest, from what you've told me."

Parker stood up, "Let's get back to your place. We'll pick up your laptop with that patch you told me about. I want you to load it into my computer, too. Then we can run over to Q's. It's 6:30 -- Peter will be there and let us use the back room."

They picked up their cups and began walking back to Michael's apartment.

Michael thought it was time to throw a wrench into the soup, "George told me that Bancroft may *not* have intended to detonate the nukes. Just use them as blackmail."

Parker stopped and put his hands in the air, "Well, let's just call ol' Bancroft and see what his plans were, shall we? You think he was just going to tell everyone that he had planted nuclear weapons and hoped the world believed him?"

"Gus said they are there. He said that the Program has a good idea where the devices are buried and they're fairly sure on what the devices look like and what they are contained in." Michael was trying his best to convince Parker that everything he was saying was true, although he was now having a hard time believing it himself.

Parker's phone began ringing. He took it out of his pocked and opened the cover, "It's Red."

He put it to his ear, "Hey. Find anything?"

Michael watched as Parker listened to the report, occasionally nodding. "OK, thanks. I'll need to talk to you about some other things later. Talk in a bit." He folded the phone and returned it to his jacket.

"It was as we expected, VJ didn't go to MIT at all. When he left NexTrÉ he moved down to Mexico. Wann'a guess where? Uxmal. Wann'a hear something else?"

"Of course," Michael responded to the no-brainer.

"Red intercepted a causality list from the raid. VJ, real name Vijay Bakshi, was on the list among the dead."

There was a long pause. "Great. Now we have to go on our own resources." Michael was feeling more exasperated by the moment.

They continued their trek to the apartment as Michael tried to put the situation in some kind of order.

"OK, so we think we know how Bancroft was going to get into the MF databases and how he planned to control the world's digital networks and power grids. And the 'why' of it all just amazes me. He wanted to either; blow up of all of our MFs and December Pact complexes to eliminate any competition for ruling the survivors. Maybe he just wanted to blackmail the world's superpowers -- to set up his own empire. All based on an ancient Mayan prediction."

Michael stopped and turned to Parker, "You don't think he could go somewhere else and still pull it all off, do you? Think he has another complex somewhere?"

Parker spoke with some hesitation, "If you were sitting down this next bit of info would be easier to take."

"Now what?"

"Red told me that Bancroft's name was on the list also. He didn't escape, like Gus told you. He's dead."

Michael felt the big hand of the universe punch him along side of his head.

He just blurted out the first thing that came to him, "Then how are we going to find out if the nukes are armed or just planted to scare us?"

"Well, if they *are* really there, that's enough to scare me." Parker picked up the pace to get Michael's laptop.

Michael kept up beside him, "We need to get back to MF-7 and search for it."

Parker stopped, "We? Listen, Captain America -- I'm packing a snowmobile suit, grabbing a copy of 'Igloo Building for Morons' and heading to the farthest northern reaches of Canada."

"You can do that tomorrow. I need your help right now."

Parker nervously patted his hands together, "Go back to your place. I'll meet you at 6:30, at Q's. I don't want your SUV spy-guy to see me again. They think I'm still someplace else."

Parker walked away, leaving Michael standing with his empty paper cup and an envelope that could either cost him his life or save the lives of millions of people.

As planned, Parker met Michael, right at 6:30. They spent most of the night configuring both of their laptops with the new registry patch and loading the late Brandon Bancroft's revised GMCS. The program did not work.

Chapter 16

Thursday, November 29, 2012

The meeting with Neal was set up for 8 pm in a localized Mexican cantina. He was already sitting at a table with a Margarita and a basket of chips as Parker and Michael walked in the front door. He had combed back shoulder-length black hair that touched the edge of a black leather vest, which covered the front of a long-sleeved denim shirt. He was stroking a thick, salt and pepper mustache that rode down each side of his mouth. Parker walked ahead and pulled out a chair, "Hey, Neal, great to see you again. How are things going over at Green Sand?"

"They're going . . . something to do. How are things in your world of Freedom of Information Acts? Find them pesky aliens, yet?"

Parker sat down, motioning for Michael to join them. "You're funny. Hey, here's something funnier; there's no one named Rhonda. I just needed to get you here."

"I knew something was up. I don't think you even know any girls. Who's your friend?" he asked, suspiciously looking at Michael with a stare that could have stunned a small animal.

"This is Michael. Michael Fields. We're working on a project and could really use your input." Michael nodded, with his hands in his lap. Neal's eyes softened and a smile began to spread his mustache like eagle wings, "So, you're the great Michael Fields that I took over from at NexTrÉ. I've heard a lot of good things about you." Michael smiled back, thankful that the 250 pound biker was not going to pull his heart out through his butt.

Neal looked back at Parker, "You still riding that Vincent?"

"It's out front, staying downwind from that hog of yours." They both laughed . . . Michael had no clue on what was so funny.

"OK, what's up? How can I help you two on this project?"

"Well, first of all, tell me what you know about Bancroft."

"Talk about funny people, and I don't mean ha-ha funny. After you left he started having meetings with the software architects on adding all kinds of new modules to the GMCS that was already delivered to the government. We all thought that they were additional task orders that the customer wanted in order to give the program more capabilities. But, the screens were changed to resemble some stone-age video game. The whole device management module was redone to accept anything that even resembled a stream of ones and zeroes. It looked like the government was asking for super data capture and artificial intelligent processing capabilities out of GMCS."

He finished his Margarita and ordered another one. Parker and Michael only ordered beers.

"But, as I was developing some of this stuff, the requirements were calling for strange things like; for example, put in ways to access private company, bank and other governmental databases. And upload firmware changes to remote microprocessors without Field Service notification. He needed the program to change satellite authorization codes and time frames . . . It didn't feel right."

"Did you meet with Bancroft during this development?" asked Michael.

"There was no talking with him. You could talk to him, but I don't think anything got through. He just waved his arms around and said stuff like, 'Our work will guarantee continuance.'" He just shook his head.

Neal leaned on the table, "I don't know what having billions of dollars does to ya, but I can tell you that it screwed that guy up, 'cause he would walk around wearing something that looked like a garage sale rug; telling us that he had this mission of continuing Itzamna's work."

Parker and Michael exchanged looks, knowing that they may be on the right track.

Neal's new drink arrived. He picked it up, took a drink and looked at Parker, "I had to look up this Itzamna person. It turns out that he was a chief deity of the Maya. They believed that he was the inventor of writing and books and keeper of all knowledge." He grabbed another handful of chips. "He also was credited with creating the calendar and chronology."

There was a sudden silence at the table as Neal and Parker watched Michael's whole body go limp as if a heavy load was just lifted off his shoulders. He slowly lifted his head, "Neal, did Bancroft ever have your team work on some time-syncing programs?"

"We did write some strange metric-time stuff for him, but VJ would have been the one to test it out. Don't think anything ever came of it." Neal responded with a questioning look.

"Oh, I think a lot came of it. Think you could dig up those sync programs?"

"That's an easy one. When Bancroft got the final version of GMCS, he closed the company doors and everyone grabbed whatever wasn't nailed down. I snagged the Test Server and share drives. Thought I could set up my own server farm; but never got around to it. I had to do some work on the bike and a bunch of other projects that I had been putting off first. I've got all the hardware I took stashed in my garage. I'll hook it up to my system and dig around for the sync stuff."

Michael thought about the nuke activation process, "And look for anything that has the phrase 'satellite codes' in it too."

"If I find anything I'll email it to you."

"Are you able to encrypt the emails?"

"No problem. It will be in a 256 bit format. There's a program I'm going to email to you first, called Chicken Wire that will convert it back. Just copy whatever is in the stuff I send you and paste it in the text field."

"Chicken Wire?"

"It was late one night when I created it, couldn't think of anything creative."

"Send it to my private email address, it still works - I hope." Michael wrote down his old email address that he used for his business, back before he was transformed into a mushroom.

Neal stood up and walked to the bathroom.

Parker turned to Michael, "I want you to come over to Q's tomorrow night, about 8 pm. We're going to take care of your visibility situation."

"And how are we going to do that?"

"There's a guy named Ron, an intern over at the hospital, who is gonna fix you up, like he did me. I called him earlier and he gets off his shift at 7 pm. Don't worry, just a quick localized surgical procedure."

"What? You're gonna cut these things out?"

"No, don't be silly . . . just a piece of them." Parker smiled, knowing that the anticipation of the operation would be worse than the actual procedure.

"You're loving this whole thing, aren't you?"

Parker leaned back in the chair with his beer held high, "Oh, yeah."

Chapter 17

Friday, November 30, 2012

Parker sat in a chair, leaning against the wall, drinking a beer and smiling like a Cheshire cat at Michael, who was sitting at a table in the back room of Q's with his hands in his lap. There was the intern Parker swore 'knew what he was doing' rummaging through his bag, as if he was stalling for time before someone found out he was only a convenience store clerk. The young doctor began spreading a towel on the table and in a very professional tone, asked, "Are you left or right handed, Michael?"

"Right."

"Very good, please put your left hand on this towel, palm up." He removed a magnifier with an encased light from his bag and had Parker hold it over the tattoo. He cleaned the tattoo and surrounding area with an antiseptic swab and applied a topical anesthetic. "We'll just wait a minute or two for the area to become numb. There will be some bleeding, so if it bothers you, just look away."

"Are you sure that this works, Parker?" Michael asked his grinning friend, who was holding a small metal tube in his left hand.

"It has so far. Just don't forget to cover the tube when you take your gloves off. If they read you in two different places at once, they'll go after and bring down the one that's moving."

"Comforting words."

Doctor Ron removed another antiseptic swab from its sealed package and cleaned the area once again. He next picked up some kind of stainless instrument with a tiny blade slightly protruding from its circular end and proceeded to cut out a small solid purple divot, on the edge of the tattoo. He cautiously placed the item into the tube Parker was holding, which was filled with some liquid.

"That will do it." Parker screwed on the lead cap and slid the tube into a lead sleeve.

"That wasn't too bad, was it?" Ron asked.

Michael inspected the small hole in his hand. "Will I need stitches?"

Ron smiled, "No. This is just a small puncture wound. Looks like a hamster bit you. I'll put this bandage on to keep it clean. You should be fine in a day or two."

Michael leaned to Parker and spoke in almost a whisper, "Does Ron know what these tattoos are for?"

Parker leaned back, but did not whisper his answer, "I told him we're mass murders and this is how they track us."

Ron laughed, "Parker told me some stuff about what you guys do, working for the government on some Area 51 projects; Alien technology and back engineering. That's all I really want to know." He held up his palms, feigning a push back.

"Area 51? Oh, yeah . . . *Those* projects," Michael responded, looking at Parker with a 'you're so full of it' expression. The mass murderer story was better.

Parker picked up the gloves and handed them to Michael, "These are like mine with a piece of malleable lead covering the tattoo area. Whenever you want to leave and go somewhere that you don't want *them* to know about, put on the wrist supports and take the 'decoy' tube out of the lead sheath. The Spooks will only be able to detect the decoy in the tube. They will think you have never left . . . wherever you leave the tube. That's what I am doing, right now. They think I'm still at home."

Parker patted his back pocket, "You have to make sure that you leave your wallet beside the tube also. They can track your driver's license and credit cards because they've been printed with LiquiCode. And when you go out, only carry cash that you got from a teller at the bank, not from an ATM. The ATM associates your card to the serial numbers on the currency. Again, the bills are printed with the stuff."

"You mean that you've been driving that two-wheeled Brit antique all over town without a driver's license?"

Parker put his hand on Michael's shoulder, "This whole world has gone counterproductive with its over-reliance on technology and cookie cutter mass-produced products. Both are so easy to break."

He opened the door.

"And I don't go *all* over town. OK, let's clean it up in here and get a pitcher. Michael's buying."

Michael looked down at the bandage on his hand that was turning a pale crimson, "And tell me, one more time, why did I do this?"

"There are going to be times when you will need to be in two places at once," Parker replied as he walked out the door and back into the bar area.

Chapter 18

Saturday, December 8, 2012

Michael caught the taxi to the airport at 5 am, took the short shuttle flight to Reno, jumped on Vern's J&K van and arrived in his Level 5 room at around 9:45 am. He had packed nearly every piece of casual clothing he owned, along with his one suit, in case there was something special he had to attend. Like his own funeral.

During the morning's flight and van ride, he was haunted by the fact that a nuclear device was buried in the dry desert sand over his room in the MF, just waiting to be activated. A sane man would have not made this trip. But, in similar pretzel logic thinking that Parker often used, he concluded that the same insanity, which created the present situation, could only be solved by someone in the same frame of mind.

He had also packed his lead-lined 'decoy', as well as his wrist supports, as Parker had instructed.

In his subterranean room, he waited to unpack, choosing instead to set up his own modified personal computer which should allow him to log onto the 3938 network.

The computer emitted a soft ephemeral tone indicating that he had mail. There were ten emails, mostly from HR on Alert Procedures, conduct and other instructions to the sheep on how to play nice in the flock.

Two of the messages, marked urgent, were requests for timecards from all hourly personnel and a new procedure for writing new procedures.

He logged out of the Program email and went to the browser. He typed in his own personal website control panel address and password. When the site let him in, he went to his mail manager and scanned for new messages.

There was a message from 'Base 20'. *It must be Neal*, he thought. The subject line read, 'What's on your side?'

He opened the email and a number of pages of unintelligible text scrolled up the screen. He could see that it had been encrypted. No doubt with Chicken Wire, which he had loaded on the laptop earlier.

He copied the text and pasted it into the program and hit descramble. There it was; a subroutine that would change his laptop's clock to some bizarre form of time base that a Mayan priest would use if he had a laptop a couple thousand years ago. The idea made Michael stop for a moment; as the notion of converting his 21st Century digital technology device to keep time with the daily activities of a civilization that was cutting out hearts in 3110 B.C. If he thought about it too much he would have to go lie down. He had lots of work to do.

He followed the tedious, but easy loading instructions at the beginning of Neal's email and placed the required portions of the program into the various locations where the time-sync files resided on his computer. When he finally finished, he rebooted the machine to set its internal clock to the program. He expected the confused machine to never operate again.

To his surprise, it *did* reboot and everything seemed to be loading as normal; nothing, at first glance, appeared to be any different. He looked at the time at the bottom right of his screen. He checked his watch to see that the actual date and time was December 8, 2012 - 10:43:18, but the computer clock read; 4 Manik 10 Mac - 12.19.19.17.7 – 44:6967 and the last two digits were advancing two numbers for every second.

He tried to run the agent program that would start GMCS. He clicked on the icon on his main screen and the command panel scrolled through the lines, activating the necessary components that would allow the application to run.

He started the browser and entered the locahost port.

A security panel appeared, demanding a name and Administrative Password.

Michael only had to think a moment before he pulled out his wallet and removed the matchbook that Gus had handed to him that night in the car, on the way to dinner. He opened it and saw the name SantaClaws was spelled out on the inside of the top cover, while an additional fourteen numbers and letters, some in upper case, were carefully written across the bottom section.

He entered the information into the two fields on the security screen.

It would not allow him in. Then he remembered what Bernie had said about the asterisk. He retyped: *SantaClaws** and entered as an Administrator. That was the key.

The main Menu Screen looked nothing like the version he had worked on earlier in the NOC. As Neal had told them, it resembled a bizarre video game. But it did have the same number of navigation buttons that mirrored the original content. He clicked on the button that was titled; Device Management.

His laptop screen proudly displayed the Device Management Module page with an impressive set of links to choose from. He chose the Configuration icon and the graphic was replaced with an array of buttons, each representing a specific type of data capture device. There was one in the middle of the selection named: LiquiCode Readers. He had never even heard of LiquiCode until his visit to Camp David and the icon was not on the version that Bancroft had originally delivered to Hugh. He clicked on the button.

A satellite view of the earth over North America appeared on the monitor with a small panel asking for him to select a region. He placed his cursor over the general area of MF-7 and clicked.

His computer began accessing the web through the secure 3938 network. Within moments the aerial map magnified to an area that appeared to cover one hundred miles.

The map began to fill in with small blue dots. There were so many the screen was nearly covered in blue. He zoomed in to the image again to where he was viewing an area that covered only a few miles across. There were not as many dots, which allowed him to move his cursor over a single one and click the 'Retrieve' key.

A new screen was displayed, which showed a detailed report on the dot he chose, which was listed as a LiquiCode

Reader. The name of the reader, IP address, location, power settings, and host address – everything necessary to remotely activate and monitor a single reader was on the screen. The one he had chosen was a soda vending machine located at the entrance to a local grocery store in Fernley. The configuration fields showed that it was monitoring every dollar bill put into it, what product was purchased, what day and time – and the person who bought it; if any of their identification cards, in their possession, were smeared.

Michael looked at the addresses of where the vending machines were sending their information on customers. There were two database addresses; one in standard black-colored text, the other was in blue. He accessed other readers on the map. They were all sending their data to two locations. Apparently one host was the soda machine distributor that used the data for sales and replenishment of that particular machine. The other – that was what he needed to find out.

He switched back to the source code for the Configuration Management module. There is was; the host IP database address, where the black-text address was sending the machine number, day and time and product sold. It was as he had speculated; this limited data packet was for the vending machine distributor.

The blue colored text was the database address where, not only the data which went to the distributor was being sent, but currency and purchaser ID numbers were also being exported. There were other fields for additional information to be extracted also. Sensor information; temperature, humidity, radiation level, accelerometer – the listing covered every sensor one could monitor.

He brought up the map again and picked blue dots from all over the world. Each was sending a second, more detailed, stream of data to the same database address as the first soda vending machine was commanded to do.

Michael could only stare at the screen as the impact of what he was seeing sunk into his mind. He kept selecting blue dots until he was convinced that every appliance, automobile, vending machine and electronic device in the world could be manufactured with an embedded LiquiCode Reader and GMCS edgeware to report its use to a central covert database. There must have been millions of readers reporting on the users and methods of operation, including any machines with products inside and the debit card or currency being used to buy them.

He remembered what Parker had said about all currencies being printed somewhere with the violet power. He pulled out a five and ten dollar bill from his wallet and held them up to the light. *"How can you tell?"* he wondered aloud.

He looked for anything printed in purple or violet. He was certain that debit cards were, just by looking at the number of readers listed as an ATM.

He remembered what Rininger had told him about the LiquiCode reader on his Grape. He pulled it out of his bag and turned it on. A few beeps and a couple screen refreshes and the words 'Good Evening, Mister Fields' appeared on the panel. He found the menu key and searched the displayed icons. There it was, AIT Reader. He highlighted the tiny graphic and a new graphic appeared, showing a collection of read devices from which he could choose from. He chose LiquiCode. When he activated the icon, a band of bluish light appeared across the top of the device. He pointed it at his left palm and pushed the Read button.

Ninety-six single-digit numbers appeared on the display, preceded by the characters GZ. It was his tattoo emitting his number to any device within range. He pointed at his computer and two lines of numbers appeared. It was what Rininger had told him, the computer was tagged, as well as the hard drive.

He pointed the Grape at the paper money he had taken from his wallet and laid on the desk. A series of lines, each with ninety-six single-digit numbers, filled the panel. There was a line for every bill.

He walked around the room scanning. Nearly everything in the suite had LiquiCode tagging.

He took everything out of his wallet and placed each item on the desk, separated by a couple inches. As he scanned his driver's license, credit cards, every denomination of bills and new debit card; each displayed an individual ninety-six digit number.

Looking at the configuration screen, it appeared that if any LiquiCode smear was detected by a reader for a period of three consecutive seconds, it would report. So, slowly walking or just pausing by one of these things would generate a report of a LiquiCode presence and all the information related to the ID. And when the device reported, the GMCS application program would be able to obtain the data for some, yet unknown, reason; by only a select group of individuals.

The last revelation put the icing on the cake; each device could be activated, configured and polled from anywhere in the world with just a laptop and the program he was using.

He tried an experiment. He went to the map and chose a slot machine in a local casino. He chose the option; Poll Reader.

Data appeared on the screen showing more information than he had ever expected, including the name, driver's license number and debit card account of the lady playing it at the moment. And he confirmed his suspicion on the currency, as the report listed the serial numbers and denomination, of every bill she had in her purse, as well as, her prescription medication bottle.

He began asking himself an endless stream of unanswerable questions. Who else had this program and where were the databases and main application located? How many items in the world have been printed with LiquiCode? Who is providing all these readers and GMCS firmware to the manufacturers?

This had gone way beyond the simple asset visibility of supply chains he had known when he was with NexTrÉ Corporation.

He had to check one more thing. He went back to the satellite view and zeroed in on MF-7. It showed the shack on Hooterville Road, the surrounding desert, the main road and the J&K warehouse. It also displayed hundreds of blue dots.

He went back to the main screen and asked for all readers of any AIT group; barcode, biometric, iris scan, RFID – all of them. The map showed a solid mass of dots in and around MF-7, including the surrounding towns. They were littered with red dots for barcode readers, yellow dots for RFID readers, and so on.

He zoomed in and chose a specific green dot.

All of the information related to the device appeared in a panel; the type of device, the power settings, the IP address and the Host IP address. It was all there, RFID readers, biometrics and LiquiCode. Bancroft was able to see who was in each MF at all times. In truth, *anyone* with this program could see who was in every MF and monitor every sensor. They could drill down to actually take an inventory of all supplies and conditions of security.

He needed to step away from the screen. He took a break to make some hot water in the microwave for some coffee. He wondered if the microwave knew that he was the one pushing the buttons and was now reporting it to someone up the pipe.

That gave him an idea - *up the pipe.* Every dot that he had seen on the map was a reader reporting to the databases by either a hard-wired LAN or a wireless network. What about satellites? Were there central hubs sending the data up and receiving commands back down by satellite links? That would not be anything too difficult, but how would configuration of readers in the middle of the most remote areas of earth; deserts, jungles and oceans, be accomplished? Certainly not in real time as the system would have to account for the time delays. That would cost a fortune to maintain continuous links with all the readers by satellite. They would need to only come on during predetermined intervals.

He went back to the computer and looked for his original algorithms that generated activation code patterns which he had put in the first two versions of the software to bring cell phones on-line. He knew where they were supposed to be in the code, so he jumped to the general section.

They were there, but they had been modified and expanded so much that it took him several minutes to figure out what had been changed. His original code allowed a different activation code for every day of the year for each phone that the original program was to activate and provide remote service. The code was now modified to every minute of the year;

that would be 525,600 separate frequencies, which had to be stored in the device memory and he could see that was for only a specific type of device that he could not identify. There were no annotations to help him.

He looked back down at the clock. How many hours were *now* in a year? The computer's new day was now twenty hours long; ten from midnight until noon and ten from noon until midnight. That made only 7,300 hours in a year compared to the normal 8,760. But, there were now 100 minutes in every hour within the Bancroft world; that would make 730,000 frequencies that needed to be synchronized.

Bancroft's security system for protecting the nuke's deactivation code was coming into focus. First: The bombs would have to be located, which the original GMCS could not accomplish. Second: A lock could never be made between the nuke and the deactivating source. These were packets of information that relied on precise time synchronization of the device, the command and the host.

And it appeared now that every data capture device in the world was loaded with Bancroft's new firmware. Only *he* could control the data and turn them off and on.

Michael went back to the Menu page and chose Asset Status. A panel appeared asking for an asset ID or name.

He typed in Michael Scott Fields and hit Search. The search came back with 417 names with a string of information for each, including: age, address, cell and home phone numbers and so on.

He scrolled down to his name, the only one in Sunnyvale, California. The last piece of information listed his present location; in x, y and z coordinates and associated text. They were the coordinates of Room 521, Level 5, within the blackest hole in Nevada -- MF-7.

This system knew where he was, right now. Which meant *anyone* with access to the Bancroft system also knew where he was right now. And they would be able to follow him, and every other member of Deep Purple, for the rest of their lives.

Chapter 19

Sunday, December 9, 2012

It was 11:30 am when a knocking erupted from Michael's door, interrupting a Three Stooges marathon on Channel 103. He cautiously opened it, as this was his first visitor; not counting that first day when Marco initially brought him down.

There stood Parker. And there stood Michael -- frozen in place with the door half-way open.

Parker was shaved, had a haircut and was wearing a golfing sweater over a sport shirt. He even pressed his slacks and wore casual dress shoes. He was not wearing his wrist supports.

"You gonna invite me in?"

Michael could only provide a hand motion to enter to the 'familiar stranger' standing at his threshold.

Parker entered the room and looked around as Michael looked both ways down the hallway before closing the door.

Parker leaned against the counter top, "Yep, all the same. Except for the original prints on the wall, the sitting area, king size bed, 42" TV and the fact it is a suite – otherwise these rooms *all* look the same." He looked back at the TV, "Ah, Curly's the best." He turned to the desk where the laptop was sitting. "You do have more crap on your desk than mine, but otherwise, all the same. Think I'll call Human Resources in the morning to see if I can get an upgrade for my frequent flyer miles. I'm assuming they won't be honored after Armageddon."

Michael turned off the TV and walked to the kitchen, "Is your room down the hall someplace?"

"No, it's up on Level Four, room 432. All of the rooms on Level Four are like a dormitory. It's got a great view of the beach and the room service is superb. French Maids and champagne every morning," Parker sarcastically answered as he sat down on the couch and ran his hands over the leather. "You know, this used to be Hugh Waterman's room. I never came down here, though. Level Five is for the bourgeois. It looks like you have some friends in high places."

Michael sat at the counter, "How . . .how did you get here?"

"Red and I took an early shuttle flight from San Francisco."

"No, I mean down here? I was told that if you lived above this floor, you couldn't go down any farther."

"Shadow People, my Dear Fields. Red and I can go anywhere in this place. Most of the normal restrictions were lifted for us. I haven't tried, but I'm sure we can get into just about any restricted area in the entire complex. Well, except the vault area, down in Level Six. Each MF has around fifty million dollars in gold in their vaults for use after whatever conflagration awaits us. Now *that* would be a fine sight."

Michael smiled a genuine smile, for misery does love company, "It's good to see you, although I wish it wasn't down here, in the catacombs, waiting for our 'big one'." He crossed his legs and arms, "That's a new look for you. You clean up pretty good."

Parker leaned back and put his arm out along the top of the couch, "All part of the game, my friend. I don't want to stand out in a place where everyone is a suspect. Most of the security systems here were put in just to watch those who were meticulously investigated to be allowed in here."

That triggered a question that Michael had wanted to ask, ever since Parker revealed his DP involvement, "So, who do you report to? You have an office?"

"I'm with the Leone team. I'm not sure who he reports up to, but it has something to do with Homeland Security and that whole multi-armed beast. His office is in MF-6, near Denver and mine is wherever my laptop is sitting. Red and I asked to be here for the alert 'cause it's near our homes. No sense wasting taxpayer dollars to fly us over to Denver and back."

"Well, aren't you the conscientious one."

"I'm here to serve my nation -- anyway I can," Parker replied, slapping the arm of the couch.

Michael got that *I don't understand* look on his face. Parker waited for the question.

"OK, Mister America. See if you can answer this for me; when I get on GMCS, I can read LiquiCode on just about everything that is printed or painted. How come I never heard of it before now? It must have been around for quite a while to get into the everyday world so extensively."

Parker took a deep breath and proceeded to fill Michael in on the covert implementation of LiquiCode.

"The powder was invented about nine years ago. Because it could be programmed to hold and emit a specific identification number, it was perfect for mixing into inks, paints – any liquid substrate. It made RFID chip technology look like Morse code. Before long, anything that had to be tracked for reasons of security had the stuff mixed into it someplace. It started out with the government requiring all manufacturers to print their existing product's barcodes with a secret black ink, which was provided to them. The ink had the powder already mixed into it, but the manufacturers didn't know that. The cover-up story was that the ink could be detected by a UV light and help with anti-counterfeiting. The general public didn't know that every single item with the ink on it could be remotely tracked by a covert network of readers; along with who bought it, and so on."

"So, only the government controls the distribution of the stuff, along with the identification number database?" Michael asked.

"Well, it's *governments* now."

Michael shook his head, "So, I can read tagged items from anywhere on earth with GMCS?"

"Just about everywhere. The readers, which can pick up the code from the powder, were manufactured in some plant in Utah and distributed to specific companies for integration into their machines. It was a government mandate. ATM machines, vending machines, slot machines . . . the list was huge. Japan, Singapore and the UE were next to get on the bandwagon after that. Before long, every government on the planet was licensing the stuff from us. It was a great way to keep tabs on the masses. They're even putting readers into florescent light tubes now."

"I've heard that one, but didn't understand what it meant . . . until now. And the public doesn't know?"

"Why should they? It's just another way to maintain security. All government issued identifications, currencies . . . even food packaging have the stuff in them. Here's a good one, even the primer paint on new cars have it now. The junk is everywhere."

"So I have found out," Michael said, looking down at his marks. He quickly looked up to see if the red light above the TV was off and moved over to the desk.

"I got Neal's time-sync program yesterday."

Parker rose quickly and went over to the desk bringing one of the chairs with him. "Get it to install?"

He sat down next to Michael as the screen of the laptop faded into the Login Screen of GMCS.

"Oh yeah, and everything in the program works," Michael pointed at the time and date indicator at the bottom right of the screen, "Check that out."

The date panel showed 5 Lamat, 11 Mac, 12.19.19.17.8, as the time read 48:8125.

Parker could only stare as the seconds jumped by in two's, "What is *that*?"

"The whole machine is running on Mayan time, a Base 20 system. The clock appears to be a form of metric timekeeping. It allows GMCS to run, but very few of my other programs on the computer will. I keep getting alerts that certain licenses and certificates are out of date."

"Oh man. I'm such a dunce!" Parker exclaimed. "There was this big digital readout on one of the walls in the server farm in Bancroft's bunker, and it showed a five segment number, just like that one. I should have realized that it was some kind of time stamp."

Parker was beside himself with not suspecting that such a thing could be done. "All of the indicators were there; that the computer's time had something to do with running GMCS, but I just didn't get it. I'm really slipping."

"Hey don't worry, we got it running. Let me get into it," Michael said, trying to calm down Parker from his self-condemnation. He typed in the *Santa Claws* admin name and password.

Nothing happened.

Parker eyed Michael, "Impressive."

"I forgot the asterisk." He entered *Santa Claws**. The main GMCS screen instantly appeared. He clicked on the ADMIN icon.

The graphics on the Menu page made the screen look like it was designed by a Mayan Priest; maybe it was because Bancroft believed he was Itzamna.

"Oh, this is some crazy crap," Parker quietly responded to the modifications made to the original program.

"Watch this." Michael clicked on the Device Status icon. The satellite view of the earth came up on the screen with massive blotches of color scattered around the land masses.

"I'll zoom in on MF-2 in Ohio." He chose the area and pulled the image into a view of thirty miles. The blotches turned to individual areas of sensors and readers. Each device showed its type and status in color.

"Well, that looks like what the current GMCS does," Parker commented.

"OK, now a little closer." Michael zoomed into the MF itself. Every reader around and within the complex was visible.

"Damn. This shows every device inside the MF. I didn't think that was possible with all of the security shields that are in place." Parker was both excited and very worried. "What about here?"

Michael moved the view to MF-7 and zoomed into a one mile view. Every device showed up on the satellite view, although they were bunched together due to the fact that they were being viewed from overhead, down one hundred and fifty feet into the complex.

"I'll get in closer." Michael brought the view into a range of fifty feet, right over his room's general area. He chose one of the green dots.

A panel appeared showing all of the relevant information for the LiquiCode reader he chose. It was located at the doorway of the elevator on Level 5.

Parker was not talking, moving or conscious of anything else around him.

"Now, the really disturbing part," Michael warned as he went to a field waiting for an asset name. He typed in his own name, as he did the day before and chose the Sunnyvale individual. The satellite view did not change, as it just superimposed a yellow star, with the name Michael Scott Fields next to it. He clicked on the star. Another panel appeared listing his present pinpointed location within room 521, Level 5, MF-7 and a timestamp of when he arrived. He chose the Asset History Report button and a complete listing of every place he had passed since November 10th, which had a LiquiCode reader installed, scrolled down the screen.

"This sucks," Parker exclaimed as he slumped back in the chair. "How did they read you?" He asked himself. "It must have been the stuff in your wallet. Driver's license probably . . ." He stopped dead. "Take out your wallet and put it on the desk."

Michael reached back and took out the wallet and placed it near the laptop.

"OK, go down to the elevator, ride it up to Level Four and then come back here."

"Alright, but I know how much cash is in the wallet," he joked back.

Michael made his trip up to Level 4 and then came back down to the room. Parker was sitting at the laptop, elbows on the desk, with his hands on either side of his head. "We've got some real trouble here. The system followed you the whole way. That means Bancroft's system has your DP identification in the database and it's receiving information on your movements from all of the readers. He can track your tattoos!"

He stood up and began pacing in an erratic pattern in front of the couch, wringing his hands. "Something is really wrong here. *My* guys can't even access the LiquiCode identification numbers for DP personnel. That stuff is in the Zeus Drive and it's not even on the system. It's a stand-alone server that has to be physically 'plugged in' to be accessed by the top brass."

"I'm sort of following you," Michael was not fully comprehending Parker's anxiety.

"Let's say that I was Bancroft and I wanted to just look at that file in the Zeus Drive. I would have to contact Security, who would verify my voice, then verify my tattoo through the Program-owned computer that I was assigned. Then I would have to set up, with the Zeus Drive Administrator, an encrypted direct link. It would be nearly impossible to download and open the file, as it has software security locks all over it."

"How else could he have taken out information with his system?"

Parker was not listening as he moved back to the chair, "Bring up your movement history, again."

Michael chose his name and then Asset History Report.

"See how far back it goes in tracking you."

Michael began entering dates for the report to display. "It only goes back to November 10th."

Parker sat back in the chair with his hands in his lap, "You know that GMCS keeps Asset Movement records for over a year. On November 10th, Bancroft was already dead."

Michael stared at the computer's screen, "Then Bancroft didn't put the DP personnel files in this system." He turned slowly to Parker, "Who did?"

Parker was looking down at the carpet, "There was only one person at the Bunker during that time period, with that level of Zeus Drive authorization . . . Gus."

They sat in the underground vault, saying nothing, sharing occasional glances at one another. Hopelessness can be shared, but not expressed; other than with a screaming silence.

Parker turned and pointed at Michael, "You know what's going on here? Gus has been Santa Claws, the leader of the terrorist group, since he took over the Bunker on November 6th!"

Michael was ready to throw in some doubts, but the facts were speaking for themselves.

All of the pieces of the puzzle began to float into place as Michael quit staring at Parker's finger and reviewed all of the events that had occurred over the previous few weeks.

"Who helped him in setting up the DP files? He didn't do it by himself. He's nowhere near having the skills of a database administrator."

Parker put his hands on his head, leaned back and looked up at the ceiling. "It had to be someone who knew the whole architecture and how the database presented the information. You know, like a spreadsheet; what column was first and second and so on."

"That would be VJ in my thinking."

Parker stood up, "Mine too. But, Red said the casualty report had him listed as dead." He took out his memory stick, "We need to find out when the list was put together and by whom." He handed the stick to Michael, "OK. Give me a copy of Neal's program. I'll set it up on my personal machine and do some digging too."

"This is going to be tough. We don't want Gus to know that we have an actual working Bancroft system. You know that his people must be monitoring everything going on with the 3938 network."

Something did not feel right about the item listings that the readers around MF-7 were sending.

Michael turned to his computer and accessed all of the RFID readers in and around the complex. There was one on the roof of the Front Door and one over the large east side bay door at the J&K Warehouse.

He clicked on the Front Door reader and requested that it show him all of the RFID tags within a quarter-mile radius.

Nothing showed up. There were no identification tags, of any kind, in the area.

He polled the J&K Warehouse door reader and requested it to show all items in its area. Tags did appear, but their locations were inside the warehouse. There were no tags in the desert. He began to wonder if *anything* was in the desert, above the complex.

He took out a homemade business card from the desk drawer and called the number on the front, as he had done a week before.

"Howdy, Vern here."

"Vern, this is Michael Fields, I rode with you from the parking lot to the Front Door a couple of time and you contacted George when I . . ."

"Sure, I remember you, Mister Fields. You're one of the good ones. Hardly anyone ever talks to me on those runs. Too wrapped up in themselves. What can I do for ya? Need a ride?"

"No, thanks. I just have a question that maybe you can answer."

"Shoot."

"Have you seen, over past few weeks, anyone with metal detectors, walking around the Front Door area?"

The old timer laughed, "I can tell ya' that ain't nobody been walking around that dirt since they finished the Warehouse. Been goin' on almost three years now."

"You sure?"

"Of course I'm sure. I make the run five to ten times a day. Nope, no metal detecting military-types have been there at all."

Michael thought of the unkempt soul on the other end of the call, "Say Vern, are you going to take a couple weeks off over the holidays? I don't think anyone will be needin' a ride during the holidays."

"Shucks, already taken care of. Headin' down to Vegas, like I always do this time of year. I've got a fool proof system to beat the craps tables."

"Good, glad you're gonna get out of town for awhile." He thought for a moment, "You're not going to drive down in the J&K van are you?" *Michael was worried that it wouldn't even make it out of town.*

"Heck no. Drivin' the Porsche down, like I always do."

"Well, have fun and thanks a million for the information."

"See ya in a couple weeks," The once-viewed desert rat replied.

"I hope so, Vern." Michael hung up the phone silently wishing he was going with him.

"What was that all about?" Parker asked.

"There are either no nukes buried around the MFs or no one has been ordered to look for them."

Parker was trying to focus on the new picture. "Then there aren't any?"

"No, there are nukes, just not up there in the dirt," Michael said, pointing to where he and Parker should be; driving away fast.

"Then they're down *here*?"

"That sure appears to be the real story," Michael said.

"Oh, right. Wait a minute. Bancroft's goons just didn't walk in the front door and place nuclear bombs inside each MF."

Michael thought for a moment then slowly turned back to the laptop screen. "Not the *front* door."

Chapter 20

Michael and Parker sat at the laptop for the next four hours. They scoured the bills of laden, receipts and inventory records of each MF warehouse that brought in shipments through the J&K Warehouses at their complexes. They were looking for any irregularity which would suggest a delivery had been made by Bancroft and his associates.

Parker sat back, rubbing his neck, "Well, I can't see anything that raises any red flags. Every MF has nearly the same inventory. I'm beginning to think this whole thing is somebody's vivid imagination."

"Hate to say it, but I'm leaning in that direction also. Let me check my email and see if Neal has come up with anything."

Michael accessed his personal mail box. Only one new message had arrived since he last logged on; it was from Neal with a subject line reading 'Sat Stuff.'

"I think we've got the satellite information." Michael opened the scrambled file.

He copied the coded text and unscrambled it with Neal's Chicken Wire. On the screen was a spreadsheet with twenty-seven items that were controlled by special satellite codes. The codes were listed with corresponding number identifications.

Parker looked at the screen, "Twenty-seven? Is this showing us Bancroft had twenty-seven nukes planted around MF facilities?"

"I think it might be showing the total number of nukes at *all* key December Pact locations," Michael answered as he began printing the document. He closed out the browser and went back to GMCS. The satellite view of the North American continent filled the screen. He pulled the sheet from the printer and handed it to Parker.

He crossed his arms, "OK, how do we find out the locations?"

Parker looked at the page, running his finger down the location column, "Well . . . we will have to find the one that is planted here, get the ID number and work our way back. There must be a sequence here that we can figure out."

Michael's arms went limp, "Great. Well, we now know that there's a bomb, controlled by satellite transmissions, sitting in some room in this complex. It's just so bizarre that something like this could be accomplished without someone finding out until now."

Parker waved the printed sheet, "And George told you that both Hugh and Gus knew all about this?"

Michael nodded and turned to the laptop, "Speaking of Gus, I wonder where he's hiding out? He must be in this system too."

"I have a feeling that I know where he's sitting right now," Parker added.

Michael went to the screen that allowed a detailed search of all Deep Purple personnel and typed in a search for 'Gus'. Only three names came back and none were even close to his name or location.

Michael thought for a moment. "You know what I think? I don't think he ever told anyone his real name. Anyone down in the rank and file anyway."

"How do we find out?"

Michael remembered the lady on the TV wearing the headset. He composed an email to the Video Conferencing Office requesting a conference call with 'Gus'.

Parker watched Michael type in the address, "What's the VCO?"

"It's a secure video conferencing feed that comes in on Channel 121. Only the top guys know about it."

"Then how come *you* know about it?" Parker asked, insinuating that Michael was not up in that club.

"Gus called me on it the other night. I got all the info from the operator. You can request a conference by emailing them. I just did that."

"Think I could use the VCO?" Parker asked.

"I don't see why not. Just send them an email and request it."

A reply from the VCO came back with a spiteful comment about submitting the correct name of the attendee followed by a directory of personnel with a name or nickname of Gus.

There were a hundred and seventy-one names on the list, complete with phone numbers, titles, email addresses and department locations.

"Well, this is why you get the big bucks," Parker commented.

Michael read through the directory, "Now we just need to find something in this information that pertains to Gus."

It was not difficult to pinpoint the name, as Randolph 'Gus' Stoddard was identified as the Program 3938 Director.

They both said the name at the same time, "Randolph?"

There was neither a location nor phone number listed.

Michael accessed the Asset Status screen, "OK, let's turn this thing around and see where ol' Randolph is located right now."

He typed in the Director's name and the satellite view of the earth rotated to the area of Bancroft's bunker in the Yucatan. A yellow star appeared with the text, 'Randolph Stoddard.'

Parker had clasped his hands between his knees and was rocking back and forth in his chair, "This is *so* cool."

"I wouldn't think there would be any readers in the bunker," Michael said, clicking on one of four green dots located in and around the bunker structure. A panel appeared showing a laptop was reading all LiquiCode tags in the area. It was Gus' laptop and he was connected to the GMCS network. Michael chose another green dot and it reported it was an RFID reader, located in an outbuilding being used as a supply warehouse, next to the Bunker.

"Let's see what Gus has in that warehouse." Michael typed in the reader's address and history. A listing of cases and pallets the reader had detected scrolled down the laptop screen.

"It looks like they have enough supplies there to last a year," Michael began reading aloud some of the contents of the boxes as the lines rolled by. Parker had to raise his hands when Michael mentioned 'Baby Formula'.

"Did you just say baby formula?"

"There's a whole pallet of the stuff right there."

"I won't even ask what a pallet of baby formula would be doing in a Mayan Temple outbuilding occupied by heavily-armed soldiers in the middle of the Yucatan jungle."

"Bureaucratic screw ups happen everywhere."

Michael turned in his chair and began talking through a mental collage of facts they had uncovered; "We know that Gus is in the bunker and Bancroft isn't. We know that he has enough supplies to last him for over a year. We know that there are no nukes *around* the MFs, but maybe *in* them."

"And we have the deactivation codes and the ID numbers of all the nukes," Parker added.

Michael held up his finger, "That can only be sent from a Mayan clock enabled computer by the GMCS Device Manager Software module, of which we have, also."

"What don't we know?" Parker questioned, while his eyes squinted in thought.

"We don't know the specifics of the nukes or if they are in *every* MF and December Pact facility, yet," Michael responded in frustration.

Parker picked up the phone.

"Let me call Red and have a meeting in the Level 4 East Mess Hall. We need a plan."

II

11 pm December 9, 2012

Michael and Parker walked into the nearly empty Mess Hall. Only a few customers were sitting at various tables eating. Many were having breakfast as their twelve hour shifts began in an hour. Others had just come off their shift in the warehouses and were having dinner.

Parker pointed the way to a table at the far end of the room where a solitary red-headed man was sitting having coffee. Apparently, 'Red' was a nickname for the 40ish looking, red-haired individual with arms as big as railroad ties.

Michael walked towards the table as the man looked up and put one arm around his food, as a dog guarding his bowl.

Parker's voice called to him, from behind, "Michael, over here."

He turned around to see Parker standing next to a table, where a young woman was sitting with an open laptop. Some papers and a large cup of coffee were placed on the tabletop to her left.

That's Red? He thought. *Oh my God.*

He walked like a zombie, to the table.

"Red, this is Michael Fields." Parker was smiling at Michael's awestruck expression.

"Michael, this is Doctor Elizabeth Redding."

She wrinkled her forehead, "Stop with the doctor stuff, Parker. PhD just stands for Piled Higher and Deeper. It's nice to finally meet you Michael." Her smile grabbed his heart and beat it against his ribcage, like a dog shaking a toy.

Michael slowly took up a seat across from Parker and Red at the long picnic-style metal table, not taking his eyes off the beautiful Shadow.

Parker had known Elizabeth for a number of years and had never seen the anxiety she was now exhibiting. Her eyes were jumping from Michaels face to her keyboard and then to Parker. She was breathing faster and repeatedly brushed back her hair with her left hand. Perhaps it was brought on by too much coffee.

Parker wasted no time in bringing Red up to speed on Gus and the bomb situation. Red nodded occasionally as the situation unfolded before her, continuously glancing at Michael.

Elizabeth put down her coffee cup at the end of the briefing and took a deep breath, "So, somewhere in this place is a nuke that's supposed to go off at the end of some ancient Mayan countdown, eh? And Gus is playing both sides of the chess board. I've been involved in some pretty far-out operations, but I think this one really beats them all."

'Eh? She must be a Canadian', Michael thought, soaking in every move she made. His brain wasn't working up to speed. Actually, it was, but not concentrating on the subject of eminent death by nuclear devastation.

Parker continued, "Michael and I think the bomb is in the Level One warehouse and we need a plan to verify it without anyone getting suspicious. Especially Security, 'cause it will definitely get back to Gus. Who knows? He may have his finger on the button."

"Can't 'cha go over there and just look around? Maybe get a hold of Edwards. I'm sure he would want to know, eh?" She suggested.

"We can't tell anyone in upper management. Don't know who is in this with Gus. And no way should those Security goons find out what we're doing. I have a feeling that they're Gus' personal army," Parker whispered.

Michael's fogged brain cleared, "And we really don't know what we're looking for. We will need to use the mobile Radio Frequency Identification handheld readers, which the warehouse guys have over there, to scan the place and see what 'isn't' supposed to be there."

"So, how can I help?" Red offered.

Parker smiled and leaned closer to lay out his idea, "Well, the warehouse probably has hundreds of pallets in there stacked to the ceiling. It will take two of us to scan the whole place. Also, if we are detected messing around in there, Security will be all over us. And if we're caught the word will get to Gus. We need someone to shut down the cameras for us; until we get in the warehouse, scan the pallets and are back in Michael's room."

"The doors won't open if they don't authorize your tattoos," Red informed them.

Parker thought for a moment, "True, that's gotta be another thing that will have to be done. Think you could operate the doors remotely? Let us in and out?"

Red turned her head and smirked, "You forget who you're talkin' to?"

Parker looked at Michael and pointed at Red with his thumb, "This is the all-time master of breaking into any control system."

Michael added more to the plan, "The handhelds will not tell us what is in the pallets, only the RFID tag number. The association of the tag ID and the actual contents is in the GMCS database. We will need to send the handheld reader data to GMCS and you will have to tell us what the numbers mean."

"Then I better get out my two-way radios." She began to write a 'to-do' list on the tablet to her left.

And she's left-handed. Michael added another of Red's attributes to his growing list of infatuations.

"Will they go that far? I mean, will the signal go all the way from the warehouse down to Level Five?" Parker asked.

"Not really, but I know the guy who runs the Beauty Shoppe on Level One. I'll let him know that we will be using his back room for awhile, when you guys go into the warehouse. The radios will work fine from there. He has a network connection there, too. So there will be no problem getting into the control system administration panel."

"Can you really control all the doors and cameras from there?" Michael was still not convinced that everything was in place for their operation.

"Want to see what fifty million in gold looks like in the Level Six vault?" Red responded, letting out one of her little secrets with a smirk.

"You didn't?" Parker exclaimed, but not that surprised.

"Five months ago, I just had to look." She smiled. "You know me and shiny things. Don't worry; I didn't touch anything, just drooled. Everything you need done to pull off this *excursion* of yours can be done. We have this one nailed."

"How much time do you need to set this up?" Parker asked.

She clicked on the date and time icon, at the lower right corner of her laptop. "Give me a couple days. It's almost the 10th. Let's say Wednesday, the 12th, I should have everything ready to go by then."

Parker stood up, "Great. Have the surveillance system shut off at 11 pm. The place should be pretty deserted by then. Sound good, Michael?"

"I hope you Shadow People can live up to your reputations."

Red stood up, "This is child's play. Did Parker ever tell you about . . ." She stopped mid sentence, "Well, that's up to him."

Michael pointed a finger at Parker and with a confused look on his face, "Hey, couldn't a Shadow Person be considered a Spook?"

Parker thought for a moment, "Boo!"

Chapter 21

Elizabeth Ann Redding was born to John, an electrical contractor and his wife Ruth, a vice president of a mortgage company on August 5, 1979.

Growing up in Iron Mountain, Michigan, she excelled in areas where she often showed up the boys; sports, car repairs and school. She had priorities – as demonstrated on October 6th, 1995, when she neglected to show up at half-time as the elected Homecoming Queen. She was in the basement of a new mall, helping her father program the new security system.

Upon graduation from high school, she was accepted into Stanford University's Electrical Engineering program. Within a month she was pulled into an elite study group, which called themselves *The Circled A's*. It was there she was to meet the most high-strung, rebellious and intelligent person she had ever met; sixteen-year-old Parker.

Even though the young genius had started college at fifteen and was a year ahead of her, they began an inseparable relationship. It was mainly a pissing contest; who could out-do the other in academic achievements, surfing through the gnarly rocks at Santa Cruz and scoring the best time on midnight suicide runs with their highly modified motorcycles, to Santa Rosa and back. What was most surprising was that they never had what one could call a classic love affair. For some bizarre reason Parker was attracted to demure, fragile little blond women who wouldn't know a Quark from a duck. Elizabeth was just his five-foot-six, raven-haired best friend. He loved her as a sister-in-arms rather than a lover.

Parker left Stanford, after getting his Masters, and made the usual rounds of helping get Start-Ups underway. He became one of the Magicians that toured the Silicon Valley IPO circuit like professional Rodeo riders. He was getting burned out and was nearing the end of his roaming ways when Michael

Fields hired him at NexTrÉ. That is where he met Hugh Waterman and was set 'for life'.

Elizabeth continued with her studies, receiving her PhD in 2004. Within two months, the dark-eyed beauty was hired by an organization to manage technology implementations in surveillance operations. Within four years she had her Liqui-Code tattoos and went by only one name -- Red was a Shadow.

Chapter 22

December 11, 2012

Off and on, for nearly the next two days, the three had met in Michael's room converting all of their personal laptops to the new Mayan clock and GMCS configurations.

At 3:30 pm, Michael and Red were scanning Global Visibility satellite maps. Michael pointed at the paper Parker was holding. "Red, as you'll notice on that spreadsheet, there are no Wide Area Network addresses listed for the nukes. Each one is a separate entity that can only be contacted by satellite – with its own code."

He walked over and took the paper from Parker.

"We need to send a deactivation command to every one of these twenty-seven devices scattered around the planet, all at once."

Parker stood up and walked over to look at the GMCS screen. "I see what you are getting at; one satellite can't communicate to all of them. Looks like it would require three or four."

"Or a network of them chained together to transmit and receive as one," Michael suggested.

Parker shrugged, "Well, let's see how many of those baby formula pallets can we turn off with the bird over us." He looked at Red. "OK, do your magic."

Red sat down at the computer and closed out of the GMCS program and went into the network browser. She typed in a secure site address and a user name, followed by a password. The laptop screen turned black and displayed a white wire frame depiction of the earth with all land masses and hundreds of white dots surrounding it. Michael leaned in closer. The smell of her hair was making his concentration on the screen extremely difficult.

"This is a real-time display of all satellites in orbit," Red explained as she moved her cursor over one of the white specks. Text appeared next to it, indicating the name and position. After a few seconds the dots moved slightly, showing their individual movements. A red circle emitted from the dot, depicting the projected orbital path of the device around the globe.

Around the equator, masses of dots appeared, resembling a ring around Saturn. Red pointed at the concentration, "These are the geo-synchronous birds. They're in a fixed geostationary position, moving with the earth's rotation. In essence, they're glued right over a specific location on earth." She typed 'MF-7' in the search field. Fifteen of the dots turned green, twelve turned purple. A single dot turned yellow and text appeared next to it.

"This is one of the satellites the 3938 Program uses. This one is looking at us right now. I'm sure it could communicate with every baby formula crate in North America, including Hawaii and the Virgin Islands. There are a number of these up there that the Program has access to, with footprints covering the earth, depending on what the Program's schedule-of-needs are, at any specific time. I'm sure we can talk to all twenty-seven nukes at once; if they're on the surface. The signal won't go through thirty feet of dirt or stone."

Red looked away from the screen and leaned back. "I'll dig up a procedure for you to get the satellite's attention and get it to you. It should be easy to access the pipes for you to send your commands up and down through, to the nukes."

For the next twenty minutes, Red formulated three possible ways to get the deactivation codes to transmit from four satellites at once with a total footprint that would cover the entire globe. "Of course we will have no way of knowing if the commands got to the devices. If all hell breaks loose, we can assume my thinking was way off." For the first time Michael saw a concerned look on Red's face.

Michael revisited the satellite code Neal had sent him, "It looks like a code generation terminal has generated authorization codes for the entire group of baby formula pallets. I will only need one deactivation command for all of them if I can time-sync with them."

Red turned in her chair, "Hey, we got the Mayan clock on these machines. The nukes should link up with no problem. They're all ticking away in the same time-frame as our laptops."

"Ticking away, that doesn't bring any comfort to the moment," Parker sighed.

At 9 pm they called it a day. Parker and Red walked to the door, "I think we're ready for tomorrow night's nuke hunt," Parker said. Red turned to Michael, "I will kill the cameras and override the door access locks. Won't you need to have the LiquiCode readers turned off too?"

Michael smiled, "No, we'll just be watching TV here in my room, the whole time."

Red cocked her head and squinted at Parker, in total confusion.

"I'll explain it to you on the way up to our floor," Parker responded as they walked into the hallway. Michael shut the door, looking down at the small scar next to his left hand tattoo. "Two places at once."

Chapter 23

11:01 pm, December 12, 2012

"Red, can you read me?" Parker whispered in the radio as he walked with Michael down the deserted Level 1 corridor towards the warehouse.

"Loud and clear."

"Are the cameras down?"

"This whole system is a piece of proverbial cake, my friend! These are some real amateur systems. No doubt built by the lowest bidder. I sent out a notice, a couple of hours ago, that the video systems will be under maintenance and inspection. Security responded that the procedure is allowable for one hour. So . . . you've got one hour."

Parker and Michael both wore their lead shielding wrist supports. They left their 'decoy' vials open in Michael's room. In the virtual wire frame of the world-wide LiquiCode tracking system, they were still in the room. Red's tattoo would indicate that she was in the Beauty Shoppe, so no red flags would be raised to Security, on her location.

"Can you bring up the Device Manager module and inventory files on GMCS?"

"Got it right in front of me."

"OK, open the Level One warehouse door."

The double doors began to swing inward revealing the vast rows of metal shelves crammed with boxes, cases and pallets of miscellaneous material needed to keep the 7,000 inhabitants supplied for three months. As they entered, their footsteps echoed in the immensity of the area.

The warehouse doors slowly closed behind them.

Only a scattering of overhead bulbs were shedding light on the aisles of brown boxes and crates as the environmental lighting controls were emulating the outside world of 11 pm.

They walked the full distance of the two-hundred foot long facility, to the freight elevator shaft.

"Where is everyone?" Michael asked, looking for someone to stop and question them.

"The warehouse crews work in the Food Store warehouses on the other side of the complex, from 9 pm to 5 am. This place is always deserted at night. They park the freight elevator half-way up the shaft."

To the left was the tunnel leading to the garage. A small cubicle, to their right, had been erected by the elevator opening. A sign on the entrance panel stating that the warehouse manager worked within. A desk, equipped with a desktop computer and two handheld RFID readers, was in the enclosure.

Parker used the radio, "Red, get the addresses of the two mobile readers, in the warehouse manager's cube. The cubicle number is 1272. Once you've got them configured, have them send their data to *your* GMCS laptop program. We will use the information you get back from the database to find the pallet."

"Can do," Red replied.

There were two forklifts parked to their left, plugged into battery charging stations. A row of vending machines for drinks and snacks was along the wall to their right.

"I sure hope Red was able to shut down all the cameras," Michael whispered.

"Red's an old hand at this control override stuff. I'm sure the whole video monitoring network has been disabled. Knowing Red, she probably shut down every camera in North America just to have some fun."

"She's pretty amazing, isn't she?" Michael said.

Parker stopped and slowly turned back to Michael, with a 'are you kidding me' look on his face. "Don't tell me that your hormones are bouncing around like peas in a boxcar."

"I just think she's kinda' special. You know . . . in a professional way."

Parker put his hand on his forehead, "Have you ever worked with a woman before? Do you always go whacky when a female enters your life?"

"I've been around a lot of female co-workers. It's just that she really impresses me."

The radio broke into the conversation, "I got the network addresses of the two handheld readers there and configured them to send their data to my laptop."

Michael pointed at the radio, "See?"

Parker shook his head, "Thanks, Red. Me and the Horn-Dog are going out to do our scans."

"What? Didn't get that last transmission . . . or understand it."

"Nothing . . . Michael will explain it later." Parker faked a toothy grin at Michael.

Parker picked up the two mobile readers, which were sitting in their charging cradles, and handed one to Michael. They turned around to face the vast underground warehouse.

There were nine ten-foot wide aisles between the eight 160 foot long double racks stacked with pallets across the 150 foot wide bay.

They began walking down the aisles, remotely scanning all of the RFID labels on the pallets with the handheld readers.

Label identification numbers of the scanned pallets appeared on the handheld displays and were instantly loaded into the memories of the mobile devices. After Michael and Parker walked an aisle they would wirelessly send the results to the Inventory Management application which Red had configured on her laptop to accept the bundles of data.

A listing appeared on Red's monitor identifying the pallets and the contents of the cases and boxes they held by comparing their RFID numbers to the inventory database.

A half an hour passed with repeated confirmation on each pallet's legitimacy.

Parker sent the readings he had just collected on Aisle 8 to Red.

"Parker, I got a read on one of the pallets, but it's not in the database. Either it was never entered or it doesn't belong there."

"Is the label number real?"

"The product code is a real number, but not one that resides in our system. Looks like it might be an illicit clone made up by someone. It's at the bottom of your last scan, in around the last twenty or so. It must be at the end of the aisle, close to where you're standing, I suppose."

Parker called to Michael and they formulated a plan.

"Red, Michael is going to scan the right side, I'll do the left. We'll read about five pallets at a time."

They began their scans, moving slowly. They stopped after five, uploaded the collection to Red, who analyzed the data. They moved to the next set of five pallets. On the third move, Red called to them, "There! It's the next to the last one you scanned."

Parker spoke into the radio, "I'm going to read the barcode, just to make sure."

The number translated to a pallet of baby formula.

Parker slowly looked up from the screen of his reader. "Oh, crap."

Michael stood frozen with a dull aching in his stomach as he recalled the same shipment within the outbuilding of Bancroft's bunker. His eyes moved to the plastic-wrapping around the container. There was the mandated RFID embedded Military Shipping Label stuck onto the middle of the wrapping, plus a large yellow band around the entire crate. A large red label read:

Batteries – Lithium – LB972612 – Qty: 50

Shelf Life Enforced per DR2981C

Do not break seal until January 15, 2013.

Weight: 440 lbs.

They stood for a moment, looking at the shipment. Both began to slowly back away and turned to run like hell.

Michael stopped, "Wait a minute. Where're we gonna go?"

Parker sighed and put his head back, looking at the high ceiling, "Up?"

"You are so right. We need to get this crate to the surface, right now! And as far out into the desert as possible."

"That wasn't the *Up* I was thinking of -- you're plans are better."

Parker looked around the area, "I'll get a forklift and we'll take it up the freight elevator into the J&K Warehouse. There has to be something up there we can load it into and drive it away from here." He picked up the radio, "Red, we found it. Now, you have to override the system to get the freight elevator to work for us. We need to get the pallet up to the J&K Warehouse."

Parker slowly put down the radio and looked at the crate, "What if this isn't it? I mean; what if the pallet was just mislabeled or something?"

Michael tried to reason it out, "We still take it out into the desert and keep running. 'Cause if this ain't it, we're in some serious trouble."

Parker held up his finger, "But if it *is* the nuke and we don't take it up . . . all of the other MFs and December Pact facilities have the same thing in *their* warehouses."

Michael had carried the same thought in his head for the previous few minutes along with George's theory that the nukes may not even be armed. *What if he gets a satellite connection and activates them?*

The Level 1 doorway, leading into the warehouse began to open, knocking all thoughts from his head. Fast moving footsteps of three, perhaps four people were echoing into the warehouse; moving towards the far end of the massive room. A soft, low vibration was felt underfoot just as Michael was pulled into a space between two pallets. Parker let him loose and quickly turned off the radio as the two wedged themselves between the boxes and crates.

The group was passing on the other side of the rack, talking in low whispers and looking behind them for any sign of being followed. There were three men carrying suitcases, moving in nearly a run. A few yards behind were two heavy metal carts, being pushed by an armed security guard and another larger man in casual clothing. The carts were laden with an obviously weighty load as the two men labored to push them at the hurried pace set by the leading three. The material on the carts, were covered with dark green tarpaulins.

The troupe reached the freight elevator. The security guard inserted his card into the door key-slot and the groaning sound of the awakened lift platform filled the room's processed air as it descended. The elevator slowed and stopped before them. The group entered, with the carts, and rose towards the west side of the J & K Warehouse. The grumbling of the lift mechanism ended when the fleeing rats reached the outside world.

Parker climbed out of hiding and turned the radio back on, just as Red was talking.

"Did you guys use the freight elevator? Where are you?"

"We're still in the warehouse. No, we didn't use the elevator; someone else did," Parker answered.

Red called back, "Well, whoever used it -- allowed me to see how to override it. You need it back down now?"

Parker looked at Michael.

Michael sighed in frustration, "No, not now. We need to formulate a real plan. If I'm going out with this thing, I need my laptop and some kind of portable satellite linking kit."

Parker called back to Red, "We aren't going out tonight, but make sure you remember how to access the elevator when we need it in a day or so."

"Roger. By the way, you only have twenty more minutes of surveillance blackout."

"Thanks, we're heading back to you now."

Parker and Michael returned to the Beauty Shoppe without incident and within the remaining fifteen minutes. Red opened the door for them and they moved to the back room, where Red's laptop was connected to the central GMCS datacenter.

"Red, get into the warehouses of all of the other MFs and see if they have baby formula crates also," Parker said as he pulled the folded satellite code spreadsheet from his pocket.

Michael sat in a chair by the door they had entered to the back room, "I don't know if it has dawned on you, yet; there is one of those things in the warehouse, where Gus is sitting."

Parker smiled as he scanned the spreadsheet, "Isn't that great?"

"Yeah, great," Michael responded, trying to make a point. "It means that whomever Bancroft hired to put the nukes in *our* warehouses also put one in *his*."

Parker looked up, "Then Bancroft was being double-crossed. Someone else wants to be the Leader of the World after the big one."

"Sure looks that way."

"If Bancroft, or should I say Gus, is out of the picture, who's gonna be the big Kahuna then?" Parker smirked.

He then got that glazed look in his eyes when the internal light bulb would come on. "Wait a minute, if one of the nukes is in Gus' warehouse, too -- that means someone is not intending on using those things as blackmail tools. They're armed. They're going ahead with the annihilation scenario."

Red shrugged, "Well, that solves the mystery on whether Bancroft was really into the Mayan meaning of the poles shifting. The jerk didn't have a clue. And neither does Gus."

There was silence as Parker ran his finger down the code sheet. He stopped on one of the listings, "Red, do you remember the tag number of the baby formula crate?"

Red turned to her left, "I wrote it down."

"Just give me the last six numbers."

"369273."

"That's it. The numbers match this item that was delivered to MF-7 on September 23rd. You were right, Red. They're all labeled as baby formula, with a cloned tag; so the last numbers in the ID are all the same. This number will show up the same in any language, no matter what is printed on the label."

Parker stood up, "We're heading back down to Michael's room. Open the stairwell doors and leave them unlocked for four minutes. I'll talk to you from there, on the phone."

Red looked at the phone next to her, "The extension number here is 7138."

The two men left the Beauty Shoppe and made their way down the stairwell to Level 5, then over to the door of room 521. Michael took off his wrist supports and the door slid open. He quickly went to the decoy vials and put them back into their lead sleeves.

Parker took off his tattoo shields and called Red at the Beauty Shoppe.

"Red, did you do a search for all items in the system, using those last six numbers we talked about?"

"Twenty-seven items have come up on my screen," Red reported.

"Bingo. We've found them," Parker said, sitting down in the desk chair.

Red's voice took on a gossipy tone, "One more thing, Parker. Just got an email; went to everyone in the complex. Actually it went out to all MFs. It looks like some of our fearless leaders from all of the MFs, are being called 'out of town' for a few days; some big conference or something. It came in from the 3938 Program Office. The Departmental Managers are now in charge."

Parker nodded and looked at Michael, "It looks like the clowns are running the circus. I bet that was Edwards and some of his inner circle, leaving by the freight elevator when we were in the warehouse. So, I guess Gus is getting his buddies out of all of the MFs."

"Wonder how the weather is down in Cancun, eh?" Red sarcastically commented.

"Hope they've got enough baby formula for all of them," Parker responded. "OK, that's it for now, Red. Get out of there. We'll get hold of you tomorrow." He hung up the phone.

Parker turned to Michael, "I think someone has been to the vault."

Chapter 24

Saturday, December 15, 2012

Over the next two days, all three had worked on their assignments. After reviewing their progress, it was decided that the nuke crate could be moved to the surface at 1 am, on the 17th.

Parker had been in Michael's room, for the past twelve hours, trying to pinpoint the exact world-wide locations of the nukes. There were fast-food wrappers and soda cans scattered around the living room – along with two pizza boxes, from the First Level Pizzeria, sitting on the counter top. After four hours of interrogating the global satellite maps and GMCS tracking records of any ID tag with the last six numbers of 369273, he slapped his hands on the desk, "OK, found them all."

"All twenty-seven?" Michael slowly asked, coming out of a nap on the couch.

"Yeah, every one of them." His voice had trailed off, as he crossed his arms and leaned back. There was something he was not saying.

"And?"

"And . . . not every December Pact facility has one."

Michael rubbed his face, "Did Bancroft miss a few?"

"I think he missed a big one and all of their alliances." He reached out and touched the keyboard; the printer came to life. "I'm printing out the spreadsheet of tag ID's, their satellite codes and each location that I just added. And a world map, so that we can outline the ten players."

The documents emerged from the printer and Parker handed them to Michael.

Michael picked up a pen and drew lines around every December Pact nation and their alliance countries, according to the list he had used to send out the email warnings.

They both began to systematically go down the list and put a mark at every location where a pallet of baby formula was delivered.

It confirmed what Parker had assumed.

Michael looked down at the marked-up map, "It looks like ol' Bancroft had formed a pact of his own with another superpower. He really sold out the United States. I guess this was his way of retaliating against not being brought into the 3938 Program."

Parker motioned into the air, "I guess we don't have to worry about turning off nukes on a third of the planet. There aren't any there."

Michael put his hands behind his head, "OK, so now we know who the 'bad guys' might be."

He stood up and went to the desk, "I've been writing down the things that we need before we go back into the warehouse and take it to the surface." He moved aside the small pile of papers that had been accumulating and found his list. "The only missing item is a satellite link kit -- something portable. That could be a show stopper if we don't find one."

Parker went to the kitchen, to heat up some water for a cup of coffee, "Fear not. Red searched the warehouse inventory files and located one on Aisle Two, up on the second shelf. I'm going up there later and borrow it."

Parker's face froze. He stopped the microwave and turned around, "You sent emails to *all* of the December guys, didn't you?"

A chill went up Michael's back, realizing what Parker was leading up to, "Yes."

"That means the word must have gotten back to Gus by now that we're on to him. He knows that we know."

Michael put his arms out, "Well, we're still alive, if that's any consolation. He must not have his finger on the button."

"I wouldn't be too sure of either of those assumptions." Parker turned back to the microwave.

As the clock on the computer turned to 1 pm, a low chime was emitted and the message, 'Connection Lost' appeared on the screen.

Michael crawled under the desk and checked his cables and power. He again tried to connect to the outside network satellite feed to GMCS. There was no response.

The room phone rang; it was Red. "There's something strange going on."

"You lose connection too?" Michael asked.

"*All* communications to the surface just went down, including our Grapes and network lines to all of the other MFs."

Parker could tell by Michael's face that something was wrong. He pushed the speaker phone button as Red continued, "Everything to the outside went out about six minutes ago. The only things working are our own computer network and internal phone lines."

Parker turned on the TV. An announcer was sitting at a news-center-type desk with the MFTV logo behind him explaining the outage. " . . . and everything is being done to restore all communications to the outside. As I mentioned earlier, the Communications Center has assured us it is just some gremlins up to their old high-jinx with some power relays." His idiotic smile confirmed he actually believed the dribble he was handing out.

Parker stood motionless, his eyes transfixed on the idiot on the screen, "Or it just might be the prelude to the destruction of all the MFs, you dumb ass."

He turned to Michael, "You think this is Gus' handiwork?"

"It could be just what the 'dumb ass' on the TV is saying," Michael answered, not believing a word he was saying.

"Hello?" Red was still on the phone.

Parker turned down the TV and walked over to the speakerphone, "Sorry, we were getting the 'official explanation' of the outage according to the liars in the Propaganda Ministry."

Red sounded exasperated, "I heard it. So, you think the outage is coming from outside, eh?"

Parker gestured to the phone, as if Red could actually see him, "What do you think? *They* are shutting us down, one piece at a time."

"And by *They*, I'm assuming you just mean Gus and his cronies?" Red replied, her voice exhibiting the tin-can audio qualities of the speaker phone. Michael thought a moment about her use of 'just Gus'. *Who else would it be?*

Red continued, "Listen, I'll see if I can get into the network and wander around. I might be able to come up with a work-around and get the computers connected to an outside service."

"What about the cell phones? What's the story on those?" Michael asked.

Red demonstrated why she was one of best. "Each level is wired with their own transceivers, tied into a main tower outside. I think the system is still working; it's just that our Grape accounts have been stopped. We can't work around that, because no other phone will work on the system, so we're at the mercy of the service provider."

"Unless we were topside," Parker added.

"True, if we took our personal phones up there, we could make calls. Level One is still too deep to make contact with the cell phone tower."

"OK, if you find out anything, we'll be here."

"Got something else," Red continued.

"Some good news, I hope," Michael said.

"Well, I did some research on what could be in the crates. Parker had told me that the label on the pallet, you guys found, said it weighed around four hundred pounds. It seems that a warhead, like a W87, weighs about that -- including the crate."

"And I assume you mean that a W87 is a nuke device?" Michael asked.

"You got it, Sweetie. It could take out this whole complex."

Parker looked at Michael with a school-boy look and mouthed, 'Sweetie?'

He then spoke aloud to the phone, "OK, thanks. You really cheered us up. Talk in a bit." He pushed the button to end the call and turned to Michael, "Add your personal cell phone to things that are going topside, with the crate. Make sure it's charged up. There will be a lot of calls to make. Did you get the phone numbers of those Administrative Offices of the December Pact you sent the emails to?"

"I have the list on the PC."

"Better print it out and then put everything on your personal laptop. We're not taking the Program's laptop up there. The damn thing will snitch on us."

Parker headed for the door, "I'm going to the Mess Hall and grab something to eat and then run over to check-out that satellite link unit. You should clean up this dump. It looks like someplace I would live in." He went out the door.

Michael hooked up his laptop and began transferring files, building his machine to be part of the new GMCS network. He was nearing the end of an hour's work when a knock on the door brought him back to the physical world.

He closed the cover on the computer and went to the door, "Who is it?"

"Is there a Mister Horn-Dog at home?" It was Red.

Michael opened the door, displaying his flushed face . . . and his embarrassment.

"Look -- that was Parker's comment. I didn't give him reason to . . ."

"Clam down, it's OK," she said, smiling, as she walked into the room. She stopped and looked around the room, "A tornado could go through here and it wouldn't change the way this place looks. You two are slobs. And don't tell me it was all Parker's doing."

Michael stood holding the door, watching her move about the room, shaking her head. Her long black hair hung to the center of her back, and from behind she as just as perfect as the front.

Was Parker right? Did I get goofy around every woman I work with? Michael thought.

He slowly closed the door as she turned to face him. *No. Elizabeth is special,* he assured himself. Her presence felt familiar, more comforting than any other woman he had been around. He had a need to be with her that was driving him from another part of his brain.

"I ran into our buddy, Parker, on his way to scrounge around for some satellite-link stuff. He said that you could use some assistance. What can I help you with?"

Michael felt his collar tightening, even though he was just wearing an MF-7 sweat-shirt. But, what was even stranger was watching Red fumble with her hair and deciding if she should cross her arms or put her hands in her jeans' pockets. It was apparent that she was as uncomfortable with the situation, as he was.

"You OK?" he asked.

"Ah, well, you see . . . ," she looked around the room and moved her left hand to her chin while she motioned in the air with the other. "I wanted to talk with you . . . you know, alone, for a few days now." She dropped both arms and slapped her thighs. "OK, look. I think you are . . . sort of special. There." She walked over to the couch and sat down, drawing her legs up beside her.

Michael finally closed the door, his head swimming and his hand shaking.

She looked at him then down to the floor, "I know . . . this is kind of dumb. This is not like me, you know?"

"You want a soda or something?" Michael heard himself say, while pointing at the kitchen area. His inner-voice began screaming at him, '*A soda or something? What the hell are you doing? Go sit next to her.*'

She shook her head, "No, thanks." Michael could see that the 'all-business' persona of Red had fallen away, leaving a very confused and vulnerable Elizabeth, sitting alone on the couch. "You must think I'm daft or something."

Maybe it's an end-of-the-world 'get close to someone' thing, thought Michael. Although *he* wasn't feeling any need to be close to someone, just because the end was probably near. Or was he?

"Talk to me, Michael. Just don't stand there looking like . . ."

"Sorry, it's just that I'm a bit overwhelmed," his voice cracked. He moved to the couch, threw a pizza crust to the side and sat next to her. "You see, I've been thinking about you more and more, since we meet . . . What? It's only been a week ago? I know I may be way off base, but whenever you're not here, I wish you were. And, when you *are* around me, I'm so distracted that I have trouble concentrating on anything but you."

She smiled and let her expression change from the original look of slight anguish to one of relief and submission. It was a look that Michael had never seen her wear, but was knowledgeable in what it meant.

"You're sweet." She reached for his hand, stopping a few inches from him. He completed the move by folding her fingers into his right palm.

She continued, "There *is* something that's affecting us both. And it is way beyond both of our understanding. I wish I could explain it, but . . . we *need* to be together. Right now."

He blinked and tried to focus on her words and not her eyes, "*Need* to be together?"

Elizabeth took both of his hands in hers, "We only have an hour or so."

They sat for almost a minute, communicating by light squeezes of the hands and occasional long looks into each others eyes. Michael's inner voice was no longer filling his head with 'why and what' questions of this relationship and not waiting for answers. But, he had the answers – he was falling in love with Elizabeth. And she was letting him.

The room, the MF, the whole world evaporated into a physical mist as she leaned towards him and he put his arm around her shoulders. She looked up and closed her eyes. Forty-thousand years of human evolutional instinct took over as he bowed his head and kissed her.

II

Parker had been gone for over two hours, using his Shadow powers to get into the warehouse and check-out the two-way remote satellite unit, complete with an umbrella-like antenna.

Upon returning to Michael's, now clean room, he saw that Red had come down and was typing at the computer. Michael had opened the door for Parker and returned to the couch where he resumed watching Red, like a puppy.

Parker dropped the remote kit on the rug, "OK, cut the grab-ass, we've got to set up this swing set."

"No grab-ass going on in here," Michael informed him.

Red turned her head and winked at Michael, "Not any more." He smiled back.

Parker stood shaking his head, "Oh, crap."

They assembled the equipment and began testing Michael on using it, over and over again. Even though they could not actually connect to a satellite, Red wrote down every step required for Michael to get an uplink when he got to the surface with the pallet, at 3 am on the 17th. They had only one more day to get their plan finely tuned.

Chapter 25

December 16, 2012

Michael had packed his personal computer, satellite uplink instructions and his personal cell phone in his laptop carrying case. He was ready to move the nuke crate to the surface.

At 8 pm, the Grape, which was lying on the desk, began to vibrate. *How could he be getting a call from the outside?* Looking at the screen; an email had just been received. It was from Gus with the subject line reading, 'Channel 121'.

He turned on the television and went to the secure conference channel. *And how could the conference channel still be on, doesn't it originate from MF-1?* He thought.

A different lady, than the one from his first Channel 121 experience, appeared on the screen, wearing the now familiar headset.

"Good evening, Mister Fields. I have a video conference for you. Can you accept?"

"I thought all communications with the outside were down?"

"This channel operates on the 1742 Photon Feed. It does not touch any of the normal communication networks or digital media switches."

"You mean all of the MF higher ups have been communicating on Channel 121?"

"I am not authorized to answer that."

"OK, no matter. Yes, I will accept the video conference."

The operator approved his identity, scanned the room for others and connected the conference call.

The image switched to Gus.

He was in an unusual setting, seated in a prodigious leather chair that was positioned in front of a massive mahogany bookcase. What appeared to be an 18th century French side table, on his left, was cluttered with papers, a folder and a softly glowing tiffany-style cut crystal lamp. He did not fit the surroundings.

"Michael. It's really good to see you again," Gus greeted him with a surprising calmness that he had never heard coming from the man. "The old clock on the wall is showing that it is almost 8:30 pm on December 16th. So you must be well into your alert lock-down now and all must be under control; although, I haven't heard from you in a couple weeks."

"*Our* outside communications have been down," Michael replied.

"Hmm, that's too bad. Wonder what did that?" Gus answered, picking up the folder from the table and slowly rising from the chair. The automatic camera followed him as walked to his left, exposing more of the ornately furnished sitting room with tapestries flowing down the walls and elaborately patterned carpets under his boots. The bookshelves and shaded floor lamps provided an ambiance of peace and intelligence.

"Nice room, Mister Stoddard," Michael said, sarcastically.

Gus stopped in mid-stride and looked to his right, into the camera. "Mister Stoddard? Well, aren't we diligent? Really doing your homework, I see. No one has called me that in years. Almost forgot how authoritative it sounds. Maybe I should insist that I be addressed as such, from now on."

He resumed his steps while raising his hand in a sweeping motion, "You wanted to know about this place. Just a comfortable little underground abode I acquired for conducting my new work. The previous owner didn't need it anymore. You should see the kitchen down on the second floor. I got three chefs in there. Can't speak a word of English, but can cook up a storm."

Gus had walked to the far right side of the room, disclosing a long hallway behind him. In the doorway stood an armed guard wearing full battle dress and holding an automatic weapon to his chest. Gus called out an order to the solider, "Go to Level Three and bring me Mister Carlisle." He motioned for him to leave. The sentry turned around smartly and moved down the hallway as Gus looked back to the camera.

"So, what's on your mind, Michael? You seem a bit out of sorts. Living like a 'shroom not your cup of Joe?"

Michael was feeling even more uneasy with what he was seeing than what he was hearing. Gus was not the Gus he knew, anymore. Maybe he never knew the real man that was strutting in front of the camera.

"What's the truth on Bancroft?"

Gus slowly lowered his hand and shook his head, "Your friend, and mine, Mister Bancroft has moved on to a better place, I am sad to say. It seems that he did not survive the raid." He turned to his left, with his back to Michael. "He met his end right over there, near that gun rack. Trying to grab one of those shotguns, I assume." He paused for a moment looking at the spot he was referring to.

He turned back to the camera, "Michael, I want to get right to the point. I can use your talents, to aid me in my 'new position'."

"And what position would that be?" Michael responded, acting as if he didn't have a clue.

"Some call it the continuation of Itzamna's work."

"Now what would I be doing to aid you in this work? Replacing VJ?"

"Well, now. I *am* impressed! You're one sharp lad. No, there is only one VJ."

"*Was* only one," Michael corrected.

"Ha, got 'cha there. Ol' VJ is still around. One could say that he's a Prisoner of War. Not dead, as reported. You think I could have kept the network operations working without him?"

"By working, I assume you mean knocking out outside communications to all MFs?" Michael was pissed off.

Gus paused for a moment, with a questioning look on his face. He resumed his conversation with a more gentle appeal.

"Michael, you don't have to be one of the sheep. Come join me."

"Doing what?"

"Oh, nothing special," he held out both hands and leaned towards the camera, "Just supervising the sustainment of a new world-wide network of data communications, that's all!"

Michael was not impressed as he set his jaw and put back his shoulders, "You're going to blow up all of the MFs, aren't you?"

Gus put his hands to his chest and put on an innocent look, "Son, *I'm* not going to blow them up. That's all Bancroft's work. I can't change what my predecessor has put into motion; I can only deal with the aftermath. I need to plan on picking up the pieces. I have to put things back together again."

He stood upright and held up his hand, "*I* am now Itzamna; a sort of obligation to the previous holder of this institution. Somehow, I feel that it is my duty." He put his hand down and chuckled. "That Bancroft was one crazy bastard, but I got to hand it to him, he really pulled one over on me." His face took on a glare of a victor after a dirty fight. "Well, almost."

"What about the December Pact nations? Are you going to let them in on what's coming?"

Gus scratched his head and put on an expression of frustration, "I just can't seem to get in contact with them, right now, what with all of the firmware upgrades going on now inside the communications systems and everything."

"So, it's just gonna be you and The Righteous."

Gus looked genuinely surprised, "My goodness, son, you sure do your research!" He held up the thick folder he was carrying, "I was just going over the names of those fortunate people who will be around to perform the duties of running a fresh planet with lots of elbow room." He turned and walked away from the camera with his elbows extending in and out.

Michael raised his voice to Gus' back, "You cannot let this go on; deciding in some saintly manner, who lives and dies; who will be spared to build a new world."

Gus turned around in a defensive posture, took three quick steps towards the camera and dropped the folder on the table, "God! You think I'm playing God?"

"What else would you call it? The lives of countless millions of human beings are in your hands. That's a singularity of power greater than any emperor, dictator or President in the history of Mankind has ever held! Your list there is a condemnation of who is to live and who is to die based on money."

"Let's back up a few steps there, son. This is not *my* list. It's Bancroft's. Although, I do plan on conducting some 'weeding out': when things calm down a bit after the . . . event."

Michael didn't even bother to inform him that *all* of the Righteous on the list would be weeded out, after a few weeks of starvation in the 'facilities' that Bancroft was providing for them to hide in.

Michael needed to get into Gus' head, "And during this 'weeding out' process you have planned, will politics, race or religion carry some weight in the decision process?"

Gus sat back down in the chair and his face softened, "When I was tasked to staff the MFs, it never even entered my mind to make choices based on color or religion. Hell, I never cared if they were black, white, red or green . . . well, not green; we've had too much trouble with those little bastards." He paused for a moment, "Hey, just kiddin' there." It was hard to tell when Gus was actually glazing over secret information or trying to get one over on the listener.

He continued, "I was given parameters on skill sets, age, sex; attributes that would be no different than if I was staffing for a Moon or Mars colony. It was all based on individual criteria that would ensure survivability of the whole."

His face grew stern, "The main reason I called, besides offering you salvation from the upcoming extermination of most of the parasites on this planet, is to confirm that you have *not* found the nuclear devices or how to turn them off."

The confessional staggered Michael as he realized what Gus had been using him for over the past four weeks. He tried to become visually deflated, and slowly responded, "No. I have not found them. And no, I have not discovered how to deactivate them."

Gus leaned back, smiling, "Well, that certainly is good news. I'll pass this information on to my associates; they'll be pleased. They have paid a healthy entry fee, in gold I might add, to be a part of this new beginning. They would hate to have to 'share' the responsibilities with DP people."

"And why would these *associates* now want to follow you?"

"Oh, no, no, no, it's not me, who they think is heading up this operation -- it's Itzamna. From what I've discovered none of them had ever personally met Bancroft to sign up for this, just a representative. It's pretty simple now to keep this whole thing going for the communications that go on between the Elves and the Righteous is all on emails, from Itzamna."

"You've been directing the terrorists ever since you 'took over' Bancroft's role. That's means that you've been altering intelligence reports on Bancroft to make it look like he was still alive. You made everyone believe that he was still hiding out somewhere . . . still planning on ways to bring down the government."

Gus raised his eyebrows, "If Bancroft's alliances knew he was dead, think of what would happen. And can you imagine the repercussions if the truth was known on where Bancroft was getting his support? This December Pact thing would be split right down ethnic and religious lines. It would even spread within the United States."

"Could it be any worse than what is *going* to happen?"

"Of course it is. There would be years of drawn-out conflicts -- billions of dollars would be expended, countless daily battles over meaningless plots of land; even neighborhoods. Every nation on earth would be brought to the edge of desperate poverty. Just think of a whole planet of poor, hungry and ruthless people. You wouldn't even be able to trust your neighbor from slitting your throat in the middle of the night and taking your food. The human race would go full circle; right back to where it was in the Dark Ages."

Gus crossed his legs, exhibiting a warped confidence in his views. "In the upcoming solution, the whole thing will be over in a couple weeks, at the most. It will be swift and absolute. No pussy-footin' around. No one would win -- no matter *who* you prayed to."

"And you think you've safe, down there in the Yucatan?"

"Michael! Who in the hell would attack the Yucatan?"

"But, that's where you're hiding your terrorist friends, right?"

"Friend is not how I would categorize *any* business associate. And Terrorist is a very disturbing word, Michael. No one is terrorizing anyone."

"What about the fifty-thousand people down in the MFs without any outside communication?"

"Technical problems . . . that's probably all it is and that's all they know. They're happy little lambs, with all the comforts of home," Gus said disgustingly.

"But, you just pushed a button and the whole world's communication systems shut down."

Gus put his hand behind his neck . . . he appeared to be distressed. "The whole world? You didn't say anything about the communication outage affecting the whole world. If that's true, how was I able to call you?"

"You don't know?" Michael argued.

"Actually, I don't. I didn't do anything to cause that. As I said, it must be something else. I'm sure it won't last long."

Michael felt he was telling the truth, but was still hiding a great deal.

"What about the nukes? That's pretty terrifying."

Gus pointed at the camera, "Only if you know about them, my ideological friend."

Michael stepped forward, "Maybe someone should tell them and get everyone out of that death trap."

Gus stood up and was visibly irritated, struggling to hold a smile and becoming more animated, "To what end? The bombs will go off anyway." He flung his arms into the air and looked to the ceiling, "It doesn't matter if they're underground or running around on the surface like a bunch of frantic morons . . . the resulting exchanges of missiles from the other superpowers will get them anyway."

His eyes were widening -- his speech became hurried; he was under attack from within to cap the volcano building inside his head. He was struggling to convert an unbeliever. His words were not enough. He held out his arms and slowly spun around, "Michael, look around here. It's all here. This is the center of a new world government; a world where every pioneer will have a purpose – to build and grow. No sheep."

He stood silent – fuming, as his face tightened and his eyes riveted on Michael's face. Two quick steps forward and Gus was pointing directly into the camera lens, "Sheep like you, Fields. Yes, you!" He put both hands in front of him and mocked Michael, "Oh, I want to save my flock. I can't live in a world where I will be an individual. I've gone as far as I can on my own."

Gus turned around and walked away from the camera, fighting the air above him with his fists and yelling, "You make me sick, little man! You're gonna get blown to hell with the rest of them!"

Gus paused and slowly turned around, lowered his arms in frustration. He had instantly transformed back into his old demeanor, "All I can say Michael is that I liked you. You might have gone far, who knows? But, you never had the balls to get out of your second-class status. I thought once that you might possess . . . just an ounce of that pioneer spirit that I admire in some people. Those are the ones I need in the new world. It's too bad there aren't too many of them around anymore"

Gus slowly walked back to the chair he was originally sitting in, and sat down. "I was wrong about you. And due to the fact you do not want to join my team, I'm going to have MF Security place you under house arrest." He shrugged with a smirk on his sweat-covered face. "But don't worry . . . it won't be for too long."

He reached for his remote and was ready to end the meeting.

Michael raised his hand, "Oh, I should let you in on something." He paused, deciding if he should tell Gus that a pallet of baby formula was sitting in his outbuilding, ready to ionize everything within two miles, including Gus.

Gus looked in the camera, "Well, tell me. I've got things to do here."

Michael lowered his arm, "No, let it be a surprise; from us to you."

Gus shook his head, "Good bye, Michael."

Michael waved to the screen, "And good bye to you too, Mister Stoddard."

With a puzzled look, Gus pushed the remote button and the screen went back to the lady in the headset.

"That concludes your conference call, Mister Fields. Is there anything else I can do for you?"

"Where did that call originate? Could you monitor it?"

"The call was connected by a secure photon feed, so monitoring it is quite impossible. The origination of the call can only be traced up to the nearest optical cryptographic router to the originator, which I see is in Oklahoma City."

"If the call originated in the Yucatan, would it still only show up in Oklahoma City?"

"If the caller had a direct feed from the Yucatan to the secure router, yes."

"Can I make a call from here to the other MFs, even though the other media sources are out?"

"As I mentioned, this feed is independent of all other phone and data lines. Yes, you may contact the other MFs." She was getting a bit annoyed.

"OK, thanks. No, there's nothing else you can do for me, right now. I may be making a call in a day or so."

He thought for a moment, "Why don't you take a few weeks off and go visit the Carlsbad Caverns?"

"Sir?"

"Nothing, thank you."

The screen went blank. The red light went off.

Michael felt the tightening of panic within his chest. He had to call Parker before Security started kicking down his door. He picked up the phone and dialed 7432.

"Parker here."

"Parker, it's me. Listen, scrub tonight's mission. Gus has gone insane or something and he's going through with the bombings. He knows that I'm on to him so he's instructed Security to arrest me."

"Alright, keep your head. Red and I will work on a plan to get you out to take care of the nuke. What will you need to turn it off?"

"Ah, my laptop here, that portable satellite-link equipment you took back to your room and about an hour to get the damn thing out of here and up to the surface so I can send it shut-down commands."

He took a deep breath and talked faster.

"Of course, that will depend on whether the satellites are still operational. Gus said that he didn't do anything to cause the communications to go down."

"Wonderful. Maybe GMCS has grown up. We'll get started on another plan. Just be a good 'shroom and don't let the bastards take your spirit. I'll get back to you in a day or so."

"OK, listen; Channel 121 is still working. You guys can get the word out to the other MFs . . . "

The phone went dead.

As he hung up, he heard the television behind him turn on by itself. He turned around and saw the little red light was on, also.

A man, dressed in the uniform of MF Security, was sitting at a console and looking right into the camera. "Michael Fields, I am Officer Mitchell and I have been instructed to inform you that an order has been received from the Program Security Office to place you under house arrest."

"I was expecting you guys to break down my door or something." Michael answered, with a hint of defiance.

"No, there is no need for that. We know where you are . . . at all times. That is one reason that we have no official brig in any MF. Each room can be switched to that configuration."

"So, what am I being charged with? Is there a court thing that I have to go through?"

The officer had not changed his commanding expression from the first moment he appeared on the screen, "No formal charges have been received as of yet. This action is being initiated due to suspicious activities that may be classified as treason against the United States Government."

"And who dreamed up these charges?"

"The orders came from the Program Director's office. It appears you have been contacting unfriendly foreign governments, using your Program email service."

"I had to make them look official," Michael replied with total honesty.

The Officer was not a happy man.

Michael sat down on the couch, "What am I supposed to do? Just sit here?"

"Meals will be sent to your room three times a day. The door to your room has been remotely locked by our Department. The camera that is now on over the television will be on 24 hours a day, but only viewing the area that it is now positioned to monitor. You may still have your privacy in the bedroom area. You will be able to contact this Security Office at any time just by speaking to the camera. We will be monitoring this channel. If there are no further questions, I will sign off."

"No, I have nothing at this time," Michael answered.

The screen went dark, but the little red light stayed on.

Chapter 26

December 20, 2012

Michael had been sitting in his room for four days with no word from the outside, including any communication from Parker, or more importantly, Elizabeth. The only visitors he had seen were the Security personnel who brought him his meals three times a day. They had taken away his Grape and Program laptop, which he had all but erased an hour before they arrived. He still had his personal computer, which he had configured with the new Mayan clock, the satellite codes, Red's connection procedures and Bancroft's GMCS. He had hidden it under the bed and worked on it in the bedroom away from the electronic eyeball in the living room.

It was 11:50 pm and he had been watching the John Wayne movie marathon on the TV. He walked to the kitchen to get a soda.

There was a soft metallic thump and his door flew open, with Parker standing on the other side.

"It's show time!"

Michael could not speak.

Parker waved his hand, "Whoever wants to save the world, follow me!"

Michael looked at the camera over the TV, the red light was out.

"Red is back on the job. All cameras and LiquiCode readers in the complex are down. But, Security did not authorize it this time. We've got to move fast before everything comes back on."

Michael ran to his laptop and shoved it into the case that already contained his personal cell phone and Red's instructions on how to access the satellite and George's clay artifact. Slinging the strap over his shoulder, they both ran into the hallway.

CONTINUANCE

"Red has permanently disabled the stairwell door locks!" Parker called back as he flung open the passage access. They climbed up the stairwell towards the Level 1.

They emerged from the stairs into the top floor hallway and turned left down the corridor at a full run towards the Beauty Shoppe where Red had set up her operations, once again.

Parker spoke into the radio, "We're almost at your door."

The shop door opened just as they stopped in front of it. Red handed Parker the small folded satellite antenna, control box and a bag.

"Good luck, eh?" She leaned forward and kissed Michael. "I'll be here when you get back."

He looked into her shining eyes, "I'll get you out of here." She slowly blinked and smiled softly. She tried to believe him.

She touched Parker's hand, smiled again and closed the door to return to her laptop. Parker pushed Michael, knocking him out of his love-struck daze and the two continued running towards the warehouse door.

Parker called Red on the radio, "Open the doors."

The doors began to swing in, as they ran down the corridor and into the warehouse at full speed. There was no one else in room. The night shift was working at the Food Storage Warehouse, as expected.

Parker sprinted to one of the forklifts parked at the far end and unplugged the charging cable. He put down the antenna and bag and climbed into the seat. He turned it on and raised the forks up a foot off the floor. He called out as he drove past Michael, "Grab that box cutter and follow me."

Parker stopped the forklift ten feet from the nuke pallet and climbed out of the cab just as Michael ran up with the knife.

"That label on the crate has an RFID tag inside of it and possibly printed with LiquiCode. If the readers come on and it is not detected as being still in this warehouse, it may trigger the device. We need to cut off the plastic wrapping and get the label off. We'll leave it here when we take the pallet to the surface."

235

They both moved closer to the wood case sitting on the pallet and examined the wrapping.

"Just don't cut into the label; that will break the printed antenna and send a signal that the tag is being tampered with. That might set the bomb off," Parker warned.

Michael cut down the side of the plastic and they carefully removed it, tossing the wrapping behind some crates in the corner. He cut around the label into the wood case a fraction of an inch and lifted the four inch by six inch sticker away.

"This was NOT in my job description!" Michael blurted out.

"Just put the label into the corner of the plastic on the pallet next to it. It will be facing the same direction and sitting in almost the same location. When the readers come back on, it will show the crate sitting in the same position so Gus won't be alerted that it was moved."

Michael's heart was sending threats to his brain of an upcoming attack if this fondling of a nuclear weapon did not end soon. He carefully slid the label under the adjoining pallet's plastic as Parker climbed back into the seat of the forklift and raised the forks to the height of the hard rubber pallet the crate was sitting on. Michael stepped back, breathing hard as he waved directions to Parker, who guided the heavy metal prongs into position under the pallet. The forks were raised as the crate strained from the change in its weight displacement.

One of the most fragile loads in human history was now resting on the two metal fingers of Parker's vehicle. He slowly backed up, turned left even slower, and lowered the forks to within six inches of the floor.

The trip to the freight elevator was agonizingly slow as time was running out on the camera and reader outage. "Red, bring down the freight elevator. I'm almost at the shaft."

"Coming down," answered Red, as a low rumble immediately filled the shaft. The elevator was descending, very slowly.

Parker stopped the forklift four feet from the lift's opening just as the massive twenty-foot wide platform appeared before him and made a smooth stop precisely level with the warehouse floor. Michael placed his laptop and satellite linking equipment on the back of the forklift and opened one side of the cage. Parker moved forward onto the center of the platform.

"Red, we're on the elevator. Take us up."

"Roger that." The elevator shuttered as it began the thirty-foot ascent. Cool air suddenly began to fill their lungs as they neared the surface and a sense of escape made it impossible not to smile, even while looking at the nuclear bomb that was inches from their faces.

The elevator slowed and stopped at the west end of the J&K Warehouse. Michael pulled back the safety cage and Parker drove their nightmare into the center of the nearly empty building.

There was an older military-style truck parked on the right side of the bay.

Parker lowered the forks to the floor, shut off the forklift and climbed out. "See if they'll let us use that," he said, pointing at the truck.

Michael ran over to the vehicle, jumped up on the running board and opened the door. He called back to Parker, "The keys are in it."

"Start it up, see if it runs and how much gas there is in the tank. If it won't work, we need to run back down to the garage and find something."

Michael climbed into the cab and started the vehicle. He looked at the gas gauge, "It's just about half full," he called back over the noise of the engine.

"Or half empty. Well, put the thing in gear and point it towards the door," Parker called back as he headed to the laden forklift.

Michael pulled the truck into position, put on the parking brake and ran back to open the tailgate. He guided the crate into the bed as Parker eased the volatile load up and forward.

The truck's body barely moved as the pallet was placed upon the bed. Michael closed the tailgate as Parker moved the forklift back five yards and turned it off.

He called to Michael, "OK. That's it. Get the doors open while I put your stuff in the cab and we can get this thing out of here."

Michael ran to the end of the large bay and pushed the button that powered the hangar-like doors of the J&K Warehouse. The groaning of an aging motor vibrated the wooden structure as the doors began to swing open, letting in a rush of the cool night air of the desert. Just as the exit was fully exposed, another and more intense tremor could be felt below their feet.

Red's voice crashed through the radio speaker, filling the depot with her desperate echoing words, "Parker! The blast doors are closing!"

Parker grabbed the radio, "What?"

"Something or someone has commanded the blast doors to close. I can't stop it. They're completely on their own."

"Gus! It's all Gus' doing!" Michael called out as he ran back to the truck. "He's going to seal up the MF so no one can get in or out."

Parker's mind grabbed the global network and infrastructure diagrams that GMCS could access. "It's something more calculating than Gus' little brain causing this."

He spoke into the radio, "Red, are all blast doors closing?"

"Yes. I'm looking at the readout. The one at the front door is almost sealed, 'cause it's only five feet across. It looks like the one between the freight elevator and the Level One warehouse will be completely closed in . . . eight minutes."

Parker slowly lowered the radio as they both stood and looked at each other, knowing what was coming.

"Michael, I'm going back in. Red and I will override the doors, keep the power systems up and establish communications with the other MFs through Channel 121."

Michael's blood froze. He had a sensation of being pulled backwards into a tunnel, watching his life fade into a diminishing spot of precious light at the breach. Two of the most important people in his life were about to be sealed in an impenetrateable crypt, buried in the middle of nowhere.

CONTINUANCE

Parker pointed back at the elevator, "I've got to help get everyone out of here. You just get in the truck, take that *thing* twenty miles north in the middle of nowhere and send out the deactivation codes. And do us all a favor -- don't turn off Gus' baby formula, OK?"

They both knew that this may be the last time they would ever see each other. Parker reached into his pocket and pulled out a handful of solid gold coins and handed them to Michael, "Red thought that you might need these for bargaining later. If the world is going down the toilet, there won't be any ATMs out there."

Michael looked down at the heavy assortment of Canadian, South African and Chinese gold pieces.

"She wasn't completely telling the truth about not grabbing some souvenirs from her vault visit," Parker admitted. "She loves shiny things." He looked to the crate in the back of the truck, then back at Michael, "And crazy guys who drive nukes around the desert -- with the fate of the human race in their hands."

"No pressure . . . eh?" Michael said, raising his eyebrows and imitating Red's quaint punctuation. They both softly laughed, which quickly faded to a thick silence.

With as much confidence as he could muster, Michael buttoned up his coat and motioned to the truck, "Well, I better get that thing out of here."

"You save the world -- I've got to get a cup of coffee. See ya in a couple days." Parker lightly struck Michael's shoulder with his fist, turned and ran for the freight elevator; not looking back.

Michael climbed into the cab of the aged truck and urged it out of the warehouse and into the cold desert night; then onto the paved two-lane road. He took a left and followed the North Star . . . to hopefully catch the last bus to success.

Parker yelled into the radio as he neared the elevator, "Red, take the elevator down!" There was no answer. "Elizabeth!"

The huge platform began to descend with Parker jumping down upon it. As it slowed, reaching the Level 1 warehouse, Parker did not wait for it to come to a complete stop, springing to the concrete floor of the badly lit area. He took a deep breath and began running down the two-hundred foot center aisle, which lead to the entrance of the MFs top floor. As he dashed closer, he could see the two twelve-foot-wide steel doors slowly closing ahead of him. The gap between the panels had closed to a point where only three feet of space remained before they would be locked into place.

He turned sideways and passed between the eight-foot thick sections at a full run, coming to a stumbling stop, fifteen-feet on the other side. He bent over, hands on his knees, breathing hard. The groan of the doors grew louder followed by a deep mechanical sound erupting from around the steel segments as they met each other. Gears began turning within their guts; moving eight massive steel bars into place between the two gigantic partitions . . . four internal explosions brought Parker upright. Explosive bolts had been remotely activated, disabling the latching mechanism.

"What the . . .?" He ran to the door and began to pound with both hands on the cold, black metallic wall. The sounds of his fists beating at the gate of this Hell, echoed in dull strikes throughout the hallway. The rising sounds of running boots behind him indicated that Security had reestablished the surveillance system and they were coming for him. Genuine terror was sweeping over his body. Perhaps they had already pulled Red from her back room hideout . . . or worse. That would explain why she did not answer the last transmission. Maybe she had sent the freight elevator down in the last moments before they broke the door in.

A rifle butt came down on his right shoulder, sending him to the floor in shearing pain as waves of surrealistic images of uniformed sledgehammers flooded his declining consciousness.

Parker had climbed upon a ledge of hope, only to dive back into an abyss of assured death. God did not bless this hole in America.

The bolts had been installed to be detonated as the last step in the final decommissioning of the MF, when it would no longer be required or had out-lived its usefulness. They were permanently fused. The isolated crypt, once known as Mushroom Farm #7, was now sealed for all eternity.

Chapter 27

May 17, 2013

I pray, Dear Reader that this document has provided some insight into the days leading up to December 21st, 2012. And I hope this writing finds you well and surviving, topside, among many nationalities; with the dawning sun and a cool wind upon your face.

I have been walking around this room, imagining someone actually ever reading this document. I decided to write it in the third-person . . .

It has now been almost five months since the Mushroom Farm closed around us. We still have had no communication from any of the other MF complexes, even on Channel 121, or from the surface. I am fearful that disaster has struck them all.

If my friend Michael was not able to send his deactivation command to the December Pact nuke pallets, there must have been a series of devastating nuclear retaliations all over the planet; just as Bancroft and Gus had planned. I have no way of knowing the outcome of Michael's efforts and I am sure at this point, I never will.

As of today, almost a quarter of the original 7,000 inhabitants of MF-7 have gone missing. Perhaps they died due to sickness that has seeped from every molding corner of the complex, or from the 'compliance' delivered by Security rifle butts. I can even accept the more likely scenario -- suicide. Too many have just disappeared. The Waste Management facility can accommodate any type of waste disposal.

Within two months of the blast doors closing this place had become a lawless existence, with everyone for themselves. A month ago a number of factions were formed, basically according to 'service levels', to obtain block allocations of the remaining supplies in the East Stores and provide representation at the Committee for their members. Sadly, by joining a faction, it has allowed us to hang on for a bit longer. If we joined one of these 'gangs' and paid with our food rations and other commodities, it ensured safe passage on the stairwells and continuation of electricity and water to our rooms. The most powerful of the groups is the reorganized MF Security force, which recruited the remaining managers and has evolved into a self-governing, Gestapo-like organization; imposing Marshall Law and regulating all activities within the complex. Not surprising, they established the Committee and control it. There are around 200 of them, against our 5,000, but they have the weapons . . . for now. And I know they're not telling us everything.

The blast doors still remain frozen, although rumors have it that the cutting crews are trying new techniques at getting through. It has been a painful process after the gases ran out on the cutting torches that the Maintenance Department had in their shop. Our attempts at tunneling out are almost laughable as the tools we require to dig up through eight feet of steel reinforced concrete wall and fifty feet of hard clay and stone, are on the other side of the blast doors. The outside air and water supply ducts were also sealed, so escape through those outlets is useless.

Most have all but given up hope of any rescue from the surface, although I cannot understand why an attempt has not occurred. Perhaps Michael was unable to get help or someone up there is stopping it; maybe there is just no one left up there to help us.

I have not discovered who planted the baby formula crates here and at Bancroft's bunker, but I must assume it was the 'bad guys'. I should read the papers more often.

Red has disappeared; which I must assume that Security discovered her in the Beauty Shoppe and dealt with her actions according to some undisclosed procedure. Whatever they did to her, it is apparent she did not divulge our operation, for I have not been approached by The Boots. I miss her.

A couple of things still don't add up, when I think of Gus . . . for that matter, any human operator of the system . . . being able to shut down communications and taking over the entire infrastructure of this place. The doors would not seal with people still inside here. The LiquiCode readers and the countless monitoring sensors would detect that fact and not allow it to occur. Just too many safety factors would have to be systematically over-ridden. And why were the life-support systems still operational if the blast doors were put into a decommission mode?

I have struggled to write this story, almost word for word, as it was told to me by Michael and from my own papers, notes and experience. As Neal would say, it gave me 'something to do' during these long hours of solitude. Few, in this tomb, are associating with others as companionship means nothing any longer. Death is a very personal thing, experienced only by ones' self.

Other things enter my mind also, as I sit here in almost total darkness, breathing stale air that smells of sewage and waiting for my end; maybe the Mayans were right all along. We *might* have been clever enough to divert a nuclear holocaust, but perhaps another unseen cataclysm occurred, right at 11:11 am on December 21st. I think about these things for I have nothing else to think about in these long hours of desperation. There are, no longer, any tears.

You may pass this dialogue on to a friend or disregard it as another bit of propaganda on how great, powerful and intelligent we all had become.

Is it not sad that none of us were?

Ian Thomas Parker

Epilogue to Book One

December 20, 2012

Michael was almost standing on the accelerator of the old truck, giving it as much gas as he could. Even wide-open, the aged vehicle could not hold a steady speed of just over fifty miles-an-hour. He assumed that there must be a governor on the poor thing for he had traveled less than five miles in ten minutes. His ears were ringing from the over-burdened engine noise filling the cab. Exhaust fumes were filling the cab, bleeding in from the rusted-out floor panel and missing driver-side window -- stinging his eyes and strangling his lungs.

Two headlights appeared from the darkness in his side mirror, coming up fast. He looked closer and saw flashing blue lights between the approaching beams. It was Security -- in one of those damned blacked-out SUVs. Michael's watering eyes strained to see the road ahead with the glare of the brutal blinding lights behind him, ricocheting off the mirror.

He pushed and pounded on the steering wheel, perhaps to get another mile-an-hour advantage.

The two bright spots sped up to the back of the truck and then moved to his left -- they were going to move up along side; probably to get a good shot at him and blow his brains out. Time slowed in Michael's brain . . . perhaps he could swerve to the left when they got up along-side. That might cause them to go into the gravel, off the hardtop of the road, and buy him some more time.

A red laser-spot crossed across his windshield. They were getting a bead on him. In the next instant a pinpoint flash of light jumped out of the darkness ahead. The SUV swerved to right, nearly hitting the left rear tire of the truck, spun to the left off the road and tumbled into a shallow ravine. A white-hot ball of fire exploded from the mangled wreckage as Michael began slowing the truck to a stop to look back.

A figure became illuminated by his headlights, standing in the other lane of the road. It was a proud Paiute warrior, wearing a chest shield of blue and white beads, holding a laser-sighted sniper rifle and wearing a Silver Star, attached to a leather braid around his neck. Beside him sat a big old black dog guarding a wooden box. There *were* some heroes left.

George ran over to the passenger door of the truck and lifted Martin up into the cab. He then climbed in, placed the rifle between his knees and put the box containing his Shaman items on the seat between himself and Martin. He looked around the cab, lifted an oily rag off the dash and turned to Michael, "Hope no one sees us in this piece of junk. Me and Martin have an image to maintain, you know."

Michael was so overwhelmed by the events of the past few minutes that he could hardly respond. "What are you . . . two doing here?"

"A couple of my ancestors woke me up, from a great dream I might add, and said you were on your way and needed help." He glanced into the side mirror, "I think Hugh was there." He turned back to Michael. "And the GPS circuitry, that's embedded in that 'ancient artifact' I gave you, was a pretty good indicator that you were headed this way, too." He smiled and nodded, "This is gonna be one great ride."

Michael put the truck in gear and with the biggest smile of his life, followed George's directions to a remote desert valley: where together, they would try to deactivate a prophecy.

CONTINUANCE

BOOK TWO

"They have arrived in ships, larger than any we could ever build. And they possess technology, far beyond our comprehension. They are from a civilization which was built upon a million life spans. They are superior to us and will lead. We are humbled by their knowledge and shall follow. I pray that they do not destroy us."

1) *Aztec Elder; on the Invasion of the Spanish (February, 1519)*

2) *General R.T. Broderick; after his first inspection of an alien Megadrax (July, 1938)*

Foreword

On December 21, 2012, the final milestone was reached and the Mayan – Mu·Suvian Calendar of Preparation had ended. It would be replaced by the Universal Era Calendar when the next wave arrives.

The Human Race had been guided for 6,000 years, to become members of the Community. For the 1900 years leading up 2012, an Earth Government had been established to maintain the goals and ensure that these required milestones were reached. This highly structured organization was only known as The Foundation.

However; The Foundation are in their thirteenth year of an internal civil war. One side fighting to help humanity -- the other: dominate the entire world's population and resources.

The Mushroom Farms (Book One) - the personal journal of Ian Thomas Parker – reflected the misinformation campaign results of the *High Stolists'*. However; the book yielded hidden codes that may decide the outcome for an ultimate establishment of the New World Foundation.

The Government inside all world governments, Time-Dilation Transceivers and the truth about Alien Bases beneath the MFs; all become key components in the world-wide invisible war for the control of the Human Race and possibly the Universe.

Continuance . . . at all costs.

CHAPTER ONE

Sunday - June 16, 2013   13.0.0.0.17

He stunk. Living inside his skin was nauseating, partly because of his demotion from a scientist to a broom-toting janitor; but more to the point, the water rations had been cut back -- again. He hadn't bathed properly in weeks and could hardly stand his own stench. The entire Mushroom Farm #7 complex had degenerated into a vast matrix of disgusting odors. Certain hallways would initiate the gag reflex stronger than others, although all were revolting.

He suspected the two security guards could smell him even before they turned the far corner. They were making their evening rounds about the dimly lit hallways of Level One – South. And they were now about to enter Corridor One, where he was sweeping the floor. He commanded his broom over a badly scuffed patch of the dull grey floor paint, probably created by someone on an electric cart in the distant past. In an effort to ease his anxiety he started to whistle his favorite existential riff from Miles Davis, but the depressing echo made him all too aware of his captivity and deteriorating existence. He stopped his tune, in respect to Mister Davis and the thousands of Deep Purple personnel entombed in the reeking levels below him.

The once honored, forty-year-old scientist was now assigned to janitorial duties in order to earn his keep. It was well publicized within the rumor mills that if you didn't have a purpose, the Committee would arrange another destiny for you.

The constant low frequency murmur of the subterranean generators on Level 3 and the rumbling fans deep within the ducts of the inadequate air circulation system had become intertwined with his own physiology. He was becoming a failing component within the dying machine around him.

A long forgotten and unused quadrant of the floor falsely demanded his immediate attention as the guard approached.

"You missed a spot back there, shit-for-brains!" the more portly of the two Goons spat out from his tinted face shield.

Holding the tattered broom with one hand, he raised the other and displayed his LiquiCode tattoo while bowing swiftly to the spit-polished boots. It was the latest mandate issued by the MF-7 Committee. His black, horn-rimmed glasses slid down the bridge of his nose.

"Yes, sir, I will get right to it." His words barely reflected off the floor he was facing. He listened to them slowing bouncing back into his numbed mind. They were not his words. Or, perhaps, not the words that his soul wanted to hear. They were the words of a man with a broom stooping to thugs with machine guns. They were safe words.

The taller guard held up a small scanner and 'read' the data-holding tattoo on the bowing man's hand. He looked at the small screen and threw an annoying wave back to the pitiful man. The data must have been in order, although the guard really didn't give a damn. Just one more procedure that had to be followed.

New rules and 'resident compliance' orders were being issued daily by the Committee over the closed circuit TV and Public Address systems. The continuous droning of the monotone announcements was ripping away any fabric of individuality and hope from the 'citizens' of the complex.

Announcements, such as; depressing tunneling-crew progress reports, the ever increasing mortuary team assignments and room power and food ration reductions. *Protecting You from Yourselves* -- that was the slogan of the month as ever dwindling movement restrictions were issued hour after hour. The Committee did not want anyone to get hurt; unless *they* ordered it.

A background of dark words filled his head, in a living nightmare; exacerbated by the controlled perpetual twilight in every room and hallway.

Luckily, there were no functioning video monitors on Level One, where the blue jump-suited man swept. Hearing the announcements was torture enough. Being within eyesight of the stone-faced announcer delivering them would have unplugged one more of his failing human senses.

He often dreaded going back to his room, as there was little to keep himself occupied, except watch the television that spewed constant dogma of the Committee, being broadcast from the Level Three studios. "Welcome to MFTV. Your 24-hour entertainment and information source for the entire MF network." Chilling presentations of misinformation and bloated lies -- as occasional, whispered conversations in the mess halls, would eventually reveal.

Only the surveillance cameras were operational, where he swept. Occasionally he would toy with them, moving erratically down the hall; turning back to see the small black boxes desperately attempting to follow his antics. Zooming their lenses and frantically trying to focus on his darting figure.

He would often clean the lenses and dust the boxes, just to keep them 'healthy'.

He was sure that this was the same form of insanity that develops with incarcerated souls who often befriend rats.

The guards continued their synchronized steps, as they passed. They had not stopped to slap him around, as was their propensity, but kept walking. The metallic heal-taps of their boots were sending distressing echoes down the corridor, announcing a pre-curser of abuse to those ahead. The putrid clicks were snapping off the walls and being swallowed in the distance by the all consuming gloom of the passage. Over the past few months, the sounds had penetrated into the hollow souls of the complex's inhabitants. Suicide offered an option out.

CONTINUANCE

He only had five hours left on his twelve-hour night shift; from 6pm to 6am. His day was almost over and soon he could return to his room, after the 'evening meal' down in the Level 2 mess hall. He always looked forward to the meager servings of canned meat, powdered potatoes and something resembling coffee. It was not the food; he needed to sit in the noisy mess hall and watch people. He needed to reassure himself that he was not alone in his suffering. And there were women there, too. Fraternizing with the other sex was prohibited, but looking could not be curtailed. There was one particular girl who worked the serving line . . . even in the rumpled blue jumpsuit her image stayed with him into the dark hours of seclusion in his room.

And his sanity could be maintained, twice a day, in whispered conversations with a few friends he had made in the past six months. They would sit together at the shift's 'morning and evening' meals. However; any lengthy friendship was becoming increasingly rare, as more people were disappearing daily -- with no explanation. And the numbers had been increasing, over the past three months. He hoped that they had just been put on the first shift. It was just a hope.

He often related the situation as himself being a lobster in a big tank at some fancy restaurant, with other lobsters around him. There would be idle talk about the rubber bands around their claws and the crappy water conditions. Maybe even an escape plan or two. Then at any moment, another one of the fellow captives would be gone. He had accepted the analogy. Just deal with it and hope you are not next. Thoughts like this often made him smile. How sad.

To survive an air blast load from an external explosion, government surface structures are generally constructed with reinforced concrete and finished with externally applied three-ply carbon fiber-epoxy laminates. This did not seem to apply to a six-story underground installation. As the scientist-cum-janitor was watching the two guards adjust their automatic weapons on their chests and laughing about some poor bastard they just beat the crap out of, an eight-foot section of the south wall to their right exploded, sending the janitor flying backwards to the floor and the two guards back to hell.

Within 30 seconds, fast moving figures with bandana covered faces began pouring from the dust and smoke-filled opening like angry wasps. All carried weapons and backpacks, and many were talking into microphones attached to headbands.

One of them, his face adorned with two alternate lines of red paint on his cheeks and an unlit stub of a cigar in the corner of his mouth, kneeled next to the janitor. The broom handle was still clasped in the horizontal mans' hand. The broom head itself was not to be seen.

The soldier removed a couple small chunks of cement off the prone man's chest, "You OK? We've come to get you all out of here."

Even though his right ear was bleeding from a ruptured eardrum caused by the blast concussion, the ex-janitor looked up and smiled. "I'm doing fine . . . as long as I don't have to clean up this mess." He held up the handle of his former broom, "I seem to be without a means to do it." He readjusted his glasses which had gone askew on his face. The one lens was cracked along the bottom, probably saving an eye from flying debris.

A small patch, sewn onto the upper arm of the fighter's jacket, depicted a fractured blue pyramid – split into three sections.

The commando spat the remains of his cigar out onto the once-clean floor, "It's going to get a lot messier." He slapped the injured man on his shoulder, shoved a fresh cigar back into his mouth and rose to his feet. "Have a good one."

Signaling to the small squad behind him; he led them further down the hallway.

The invaders appeared to be highly trained and well prepared for the operation. Groups of ten proceeded to strategic locations down the hallway. They took up positions at each intersection before allowing two or three more groups to proceed into the adjoining corridors. The five stairwell exits along the hallway were secured. Shots could be heard coming from the lower levels. In the meantime, commandos continued roaring out of the gaping hole.

An aged big black dog, wearing a red bandana around his neck, appeared from out of the settling cloud of debris. It ambled over to the man, cocked his head and stared at the bloody, dust covered face.

"Martin! Leave that guy alone. Can't you see he's taking a break?" The bellow was from a stocky man with two long silver-white braids flowing from under a weathered cowboy hat. He appeared to be the Leader of the attack; issuing commands into a radio while scanning a map.

Strange sounds could be heard echoing off the walls from the east end of the corridor. Some were definitely gunshots; others resembled sparking tin-foil in a powerful microwave oven.

The leader walked over to the dazed janitor and held out a callused hand. "OK, break's over. Get up."

As the man groaned to his feet, the broom handle was liberated from his hand. He looked to the spot where he had been lying. A patch of painted floor, in the shape of his body, was framed by thick concrete dust and debris. The faint outline of the broom-stick, at the end of his arm, was almost comical. It portrayed a sort of a snow-angel, with a magic wand.

"Who are you?" the Leader demanded.

"My name's Roland. I'm a . . . well, I was, a scientist – Dimensional Transmutations, to be more specific."

"Well, whatever the hell *that* is, you can be it again – if you're willing to fight for it," the Leader said, looking down to the west end of the passage.

Roland slowly responded, "Yes, Sir." He realized that he had to turn his head to the side to hear the man's voice. He put his hand to his ear and brought it back, bloodied, between himself and the man.

The man looked at the bloody palm and turned Roland's head to the side, "You're OK. Not a head wound."

"What?"

"I said walk if off," the man replied louder, handing Roland a ragged handkerchief.

"Alright, Roland, you've just been drafted." He lifted the map he was holding closer to his face and squinted at it in the dim light.

"You know your way around this place?"

"Almost every inch . . . Sir," Roland snorted, clearing his head of concrete dust and holding the tattered rag to his ear.

The rugged man shook his head, "Stop with the Sir stuff, my name's George." He turned at the waist and signed to a small group of soldiers guarding the blast entrance to gather around him. "Alright, Roland – here's the map. We need to find Room 432."

George paused before turning to lead his men further into the four-mile maze of corridors and hallways of Level 1. "Just stay down-wind . . . you stink."

CHAPTER TWO

Level 1 was secured within an hour. There had been limited resistance from the ill-trained MF-7 Security Force. As the invaders moved about the hallways, 90% of the shops, offices and guest quarters were empty. The Accounting and Personnel Offices were in shambles, apparently from being ravaged by individuals needing as much information as possible on all Deep Purple employees encased within the facility. The computers, printers and telephones were missing, also.

The Chapel was ransacked—offering little recognition of a place of worship. The room cried for an exorcism; with overturned pews bowing to a disfigured and broken altar at the front of the room. The animated cobwebs, clinging to every corner of wood and concrete, moved to an unseen breeze. The room could have been mistaken for a storage room, if not for the multi-denominational metal plaque on the doorframe in the hallway.

Crudely printed black and white posters infected nearly every wall. The largest percentage of them, were notifications of new restrictions. Most of the others promoted the Committee and their magnificently fabricated deeds of leadership and compassion.

The video monitors, embedded in the walls and at each hallway intersection, were presenting slide show images of various Committee members and bar charts of water and food consumption levels. The numbers made no sense to the average person and were dubious, to say the least. But they did reflect some very disturbing political philosophy – no doubt adopted by the Committee.

It appeared that all Deep Purple personnel were grouped according to usefulness to the Committee. Some of the charts indicated that individuals whose skills were not directly related to keeping the complex operational were shown with a red line, and were listed to receive only the barest of rations and accommodations. The color scale went up to blue which included Committee members and Security. Water and Air Quality personnel were not too far below that. A graduated system of 'expendability' was visually evident on the charts. As was the disturbing dotted black line which had a caption stating, *Removed*.

The telephone system was still operating, but limited to the lowest floor of the facility; Level 6. That was the domain of the Committee and where the MF-7 Security commanders lived – the main objective of the invasion force.

The commandos quickly took control of the Public Address system and began broadcasting instructions to the enslaved populace as well as surrender demands to the inhabitants of the bottom floor and any Security personnel still providing resistance.

The fight for Level 2, which housed water treatment, air conditioning, air quality and waste disposal, began within minutes of the initial explosion.

The Committee must have foreseen such an assault on the MF. Strategically placed sandbag walls protected fixed automatic weapon positions near the South and North stairwell doors. George's forces were about to face the first of these.

"Eagle One! This is Unit 4. We're pinned down inside the stairwell at door S2-6," the radio blared, as George and his squad stopped in front of the three elevator doors that served the south end of the complex.

"Maintain your position, and keep the bastards occupied for another three minutes," the Leader ordered back.

"Do we use flares now?" the voice called back.

"Negative! Wait for my signal!" George replied.

Four commandos outfitted in rope access gear ran up where George and Roland were standing. An explosive charge was placed on elevator #6 doors and everyone took cover. The door imploded, sending shards of smoking metal cascading down the shaft and onto the roof of the elevator car parked over seventy feet below at Level 6.

CONTINUANCE

"Blow elevator three's door!" George commanded into the radio. Within seconds, an explosion could be heard and felt throughout the hallway.

Roland watched two commandos quickly slam a metal bar, attached to a pulley system with a rope ladder, across the demolished opening. Two other harnessed men attached ropes to their carabineers and moved backwards, into the shaft. The remaining two belayers began to lower their partners into the still smoking depths of the shaft, where they began to rappel down to the Level 2 doors.

Within two minutes, the two were back on Level 1. "All ready down there," one of the returning climbers reported to George.

George paused for a moment, and with great relish, ordered, "Open Level Two!"

A tremendous explosion shook the structure under them. The Level 2 elevator door beneath George and his squad was pulverized by a remote-controlled command. Another was heard in the distance, along with gunfire emitting from the stairwells a level below.

The commandos threw the rope ladder into the shaft, and two teams began climbing down to the new opening in Level 2.

George turned to Roland. "We should have around 80 troops down there in a few minutes, and they should open the way for the 160 waiting in all the stairwells. It's time we headed down to Level Four."

With Martin in close pursuit, George and Roland followed a five-man fire team down the stairwell.

In the mean time, two acetylene torch-cutting units were brought in to begin burning through the frame of the blast door leading to the warehouse. They were working in tandem with another crew that had entered from the other side, down the still operational freight elevator.

The warehouse commando unit wore breathing packs until the halothane/fentanyl gas cocktail, which was delivered into the warehouse down the elevator shaft, dissipated.

The warehouse recovery teams weren't able to begin their entry until the main body secured Level 1, so the Boots wouldn't be alerted that a rescue was underway from the J&K Warehouse on the surface.

Four lifeless security guards were littered about the main warehouse floor when the cutting crews had finally descended. Two more of the armed bastards were discovered lying in the motor pool area.

Not a shot had been fired.

When George and Roland passed the Level 3 entrance, the lighting system was up to full brightness, and they could feel cool air flooding in from the ventilation system. It was apparent that Level 2 was secure and that the facilities' environmental systems were in the hands of the "good guys". Everything seemed to be running at maximum capacity, since there was no need to conserve generator fuel or recycle air any longer.

"If our intelligence is correct, there should be about forty of their Security men per level," George informed his small army. They stopped ten feet above the entrance to Level 4. "That means there should be no more than four or five guarding this door."

"But, there are only seven of us coming out of a small portal, one at a time," Roland said, with a dry mouth.

"Glasses," George called out.

Each of his men pulled out a pair of welding goggles and put them on just above their eyes. The two combatants in the lead reached into their backpacks and took out what appeared to be red sticks of dynamite.

The point man slowly moved to the door and placed a now familiar radio-controlled charge on the metal panel. He quietly moved back up the steel staircase. George turned his back to the door, put his hands over Martin's ears, and nodded over his shoulder to the demolition technician.

The macerated door flew into the hallway in a hundred pieces of searing metal confetti, instantly taking out three of the waiting defenders.

CONTINUANCE

The explosives experts pulled their goggles down, ignited the dynamite-looking sticks and threw them into the smoking hallway. They were magnesium assault flares and shone with the brilliance of the Sun, blinding anyone looking towards the doorway. The fire team bolted into the hallway, immediately killing the two remaining guards.

The flares were kicked away to burn out against the concrete wall, and the "all-clear" was given to George.

The hurried steps of fifteen more of George's force could be heard coming down the stairwell, to join them on Level 4.

Every squad and platoon in the company was reporting "all-clear". The radio and television studios located on Level 3 were fully functional. All surveillance cameras had been turned off, and all security overrides on the six elevators were removed.

Every elevator car was moved up to various floors to await evacuees.

The rescue teams entered the hospital. They were overwhelmed with the number of patients lying in beds, on cots and on the floor. There was only one doctor and two nurses and very few supplies remaining.

"We will evacuate the sick first and then all personnel not required to maintain the complex," George broadcast on his radio. "Take the critically ill out the tunnel, until we can get the blast doors open," he continued, "I want Levels One through Five totally secure in 15 minutes."

Roland looked at George, "What about Level Six?"

"Six is now sealed," he said, stepping over blast debris. "No one goes in; no one comes out."

Roland was disturbed at George's comment. There were at least 200 people in Level 6. True, it was well known that only members of the Committee and MF-7 Security lived there, but to seal them in forever, without a supply of food? He had only known the man for a short time, but from his mannerisms, it did not seem to be his style. Perhaps George meant that they would be starved into submission or incarcerated until the facility could be fully secure and then be brought up for disposition. Or perhaps not.

He looked back at the map as he followed George down the hallway. "Room 432 is the next aisle down. Turn right -- it will be on the left, approximately 52 and a half yards," he called ahead.

"Approximately?" George muttered under his panting breath.

Martin had cautiously moved into the hallway from the stairwell. He spotted George leading the group and took up the chase.

Ten feet before they reached the corner, a security guard suddenly appeared in front of them, weapon raised. Before George could lift his .45, the guard was knocked sideways from his feet by a spray of bullets from an automatic rifle to his left.

Martin had crouched in a defensive stance, growling and was as confused as his two human companions.

"Cool it," ordered George, pistol at the ready. He waited for visual answers to the sight they had just witnessed.

Walking slowly from around the corner appeared a blond Shadow, holding a smoking M16 to his side, taken from another slipshod guard minutes before. He continued to the bullet-riddled body of the former tormenter and looked down. Retribution. Nudging the lifeless lump of black leather, blood and Kevlar with his foot, he turned his head to George, "The name's Parker. Welcome to our toilet."

George lifted his radio, "Eagle One to Hacker . . . we've reached Area 52. All is well."

A voice could be barely heard coming back over the weakened signal of the radio, "Tell him he owes me a beer."

The voice of Michael Fields brought a trembling smile to Parker's gaunt face – the first in six months.

CHAPTER THREE

It took only ten hours for the two cutting teams to get the blast doors open and to begin the mass evacuation of Deep Purple personnel from MF-7. Level 6 elevator access had been cut off and the stairwell exits from the floor were locked tight. Only a single phone line had been left open . . . for negotiations.

George, Parker and the rest of the evacuation teams had been clearing MF-7 of all non-essential personnel level by level. Everyone was tired, but all were driven by a spirit of new hope and adrenalin.

George had been coordinating the evacuation from his temporary Command Center, which was once the MF-7 Administration Office in room 1027. He was writing his report: *'Monday, June 17, 2013. MF-7 Levels 1-5 secured at 1300. Level 6 locked down from above. Main Street still open. Our Black Shirts sustained casualties amounting to 8 dead, 12 wounded. ESA suffered 68 killed, 32 wounded and 21 captured. Tube Doors still secure."*

He paused – too tired to write anymore. But he was able to smile; it was a classic case study in well-trained veteran commandos versus armed street thugs.

He put down his pen and rubbed his eyes. Parker had just walked in to get his fifth cup of real coffee from the jug brought up from the Level 4 East Mess Hall.

George leaned back, "Looks like things are moving along without too much difficulty. What say you and I run into town for a bit?"

Parker still had the M16 he had taken from the unfortunate guard that was walking past his room. He put down his cup, "That sounds great. I sure could use some new scenery."

George stood up and turned to an aide who was typing on a laptop and talking with support personnel on his headset.

"I'm going to the school house. I'll take my radio. Contact the driver that we'll be up in five minutes."

The aide nodded and kept working.

"Come on Martin. Goin' for a ride."

The old dog, who had been dozing in the corner, perked up. He loved rides and was the first one out the door and into the hallway.

"Are we going where Michael is?" Parker asked.

George smiled, "I think he is there."

With Parker, there'd been an instant brotherly connection with Michael -- the moment they'd met in college. He'd never had that same affinity, that kinship, with his own brothers or sister. But then he and his siblings never did fully understand each other. His older brother was a super jock; and his younger brother, Nicky, tended to get in touch primarily when he needed something or was embroiled in yet another mess. As the middle brother, he frequently found himself in a no man's land buffer zone.

It was all good, for it had allowed Parker to develop into the self-surviving, independent 'smart ass' overachiever that had brought him a measure of success within the darker world of Shadow People operations. And it had brought him a close friend . . . Michael.

The three walked down the long hallway and through the now open blast door portal. Parker thought back to the last time he and Michael were in the warehouse. He looked over to the blank spot in the rack that originally housed the crate which contained the nuclear device. He began to walk a bit faster, not wanting to remember, as they made their way to the freight elevator.

The complex-wide public address system was now broadcasting news of the outside world and instructions on how and where to receive new clothing, medical treatment and location of the new 'top-side' communications center. It was just a tent with a short-wave radio, but it was the only way the denizens of the MF might be able to contact their relatives.

As the three ascended in the freight elevator to the surface, Parker remembered the last time he took the ride up . . . and then back down to a living burial. The images would never leave his mind, to the point where he was expecting to wake up at any moment still lying in cell 432.

George's voice cut through the anxiety. "You have anything in your room down there that you want to grab, before we shut the lower levels down for awhile and clean them up?"

"Just my computer, a few clothes and sort of a journal I was keeping," Parker confessed.

George's eyes squinted, "I'll need to see that. Go back down there tomorrow and get it to me." It was an order that came from somewhere deep in the old man's mission.

The intoxicating breeze of the afternoon desert hit Parker halfway up the ascent. Warm sensations of life crawled out of their hiding places in his soul. Images and emotions of the world he had missed began to reappear in his mind, all with a new meaning. He had a transcendent moment and felt that this was the first time he had experienced freedom in its raw form.

But as he and the other rescued inhabitants of MF-7 would soon discover, this was not the world they had left six months ago.

He began to wonder hazily if *he* had changed. Even in the short time he was down there, which his brain had accepted as the rest of eternity, had it affected him in some visual way -- his mannerisms, anxious interactions, trailing speech? He would monitor himself, just in case. However, was it possible for the insane to realize they were insane, when everything they thought and did *seemed* sane to them? And how could he get his bearings on reality, when all around him were the insane leftovers of tyranny and deceit? All of his torment had been caused by individuals who were considered to be the most intelligent, sane people of our own country.

He didn't want to think about it any longer. It was making him crazy. Was that a sign of sanity?

They reached the J&K Warehouse at the top of the ride and walked into the bay. Among the trucks and other vehicles involved with the attack and subsequent evacuation, a faded white van sat idling, waiting for their arrival. Written on the side of the driver's door was the name, *J&K Mushrooms.*

The driver door opened and out climbed a leftover from the days of the 49er Gold Rush. It was Vern, wearing a weather-worn holster at his hip, inhabited by a 1911 Colt .45 caliber pistol.

He waved to them. "George!" He walked over to meet them, arms swinging as if he were trying to keep himself moving in a forward direction. "They said you were on your way up. And Mister Parker . . . Well, I'll be danged. It's really great to see you again." The old timer grabbed Parker's gloved hand with both of his and burst into an ear-to-ear smile.

George opened the side door of the van and the three passengers moved into the back of the vehicle. Vern shut the door and took the driver's seat. After a sound which erupted under their feet that resembled a boxcar tumbling from a high trestle, they rambled out of the warehouse doors and bounced onto the road.

Parker looked out of the grimy windows onto a tent city covering ten acres of desert around the J&K warehouse. Massive mobile power generators spewed black and white smoke into the cloudless sky.

Brown dust clouds followed the evacuation vehicles to the center of the compound, depositing layer upon layer of the desert dirt onto the tepees, wikiups and military style tents.

Long lines of newly rescued souls were waiting outside scores of tents for housing assignments, transportation vouchers, food and new clothing.

Along the west side of the compound were long rows of portable toilets, shower stalls and potable-water trucks. It looked like the grounds of a surrealistic circus. Horses, tents and acrobatic dust devils which were slowly moving all the Nevada desert sand over to Utah.

It was a string of images from a post-war documentary of the past war -- any past war -- in any past time. It was just not supposed to be a war that occurred beneath the sands of the Nevada High Desert – now.

Parker wondered if this scene was being recreated at every other MF, or for that matter, at all of the facilities where a nuke crate was detected.

Martin had moved to the passenger seat, leaning into the wind outside the open window, eyes watering and long black ears flapping in the rush of morning air.

Parker turned back to face George. "Quite an operation out there," he yelled, over the rumbling of the van's tires on the blacktop and failing muffler, while pointing towards the expanding canvas covered desert.

"Watch the road, you old lizard!"

George leaned towards Parker, "Ya' gotta love that crazy bastard." He peered out the window, "It was fortunate that everything went down so well. It's all coming together, considering the overall situation."

George leaned back in the seat as Parker turned to the window. *What overall situation?* He thought.

They traveled another half-mile south when Parker saw an additional large grouping of tents and vehicles.

"What's that all about?"

"That's the entrance to the tunnel we used to get into Level 1. It's an old mine shaft that was used when the MF was first dug out. Vern here remembered it, and we checked it out. It was a great stroke of luck and probably saved us hundred of hours of work and many lives."

Parker lowered his eyebrows, "What does that mean?"

"We've been fighting various factions of mercenaries for about three months now. They hit us, we strike back. They're hired guns of . . . an organization, to patrol the perimeter and keep anyone from taking back the complex. It hasn't been all fun and games up here, either."

"How did you manage to get it done . . . I mean, to get in that cave and dig up to the MF, without the MF Security Forces discovering you?"

"Vern led an eight-man Mucker and Sand Dog crew in there a few nights ago. We left them alone for three days until they finished clearing the tunnel up to the south wall of the MF and setting the explosives. When they got things ready, Vern contacted me and we did the rest."

Vern yelled back over his shoulder, "Old mining buddies of mine from when we worked on Main Street. I told 'em we were going for the *real* Mother Lode."

The van pulled into a large dirt lot and up to an old two-story building standing in the center. It was decorated with a cupola on its crumbling asphalt-tiled roof and four scraggly trees hugging the walls. Ten vehicles -- trucks, vans and motorcycles -- were parked on the hard clay and sand at the north side of the lot. At the far end of the parking area sat a large power generator, its massive cables snaking up to the back wall.

It was evident that the building was once adorned with a fine stucco finish. Wide steps led to a columned archway, and two heavy doors beckoned any young scholar searching for whatever knowledge was allowed to be taken from its halls and well-lit rooms.

The stucco was falling away now. At every corner, sections of the century-old red brick walls were exposed, and layers of bird droppings covered the entryway. Years of graffiti seemed to be holding the building together, as well as the four dead trees propping it up.

Scores of windows were boarded up with brown-painted plywood. A few were open because the wood panels had been removed. There was not a pane of glass to be seen.

There were two sandbag bunkers, one on each side of the building. The barrels of various types of machine guns were protruding from openings in the defensive positions.

As the side door of the van was opened, Vern gestured to the tired building, "This is the old school house. We've been using it as our Command Center for the past few weeks."

Martin jumped out first and began his search for a perfect place to pee. The rest of the group walked up the steps, passed through the door-less entryway and paused in the main vestibule facing the wide wooden staircase to the second floor.

CONTINUANCE

The smell of stale air rushed back into Parker's lungs – but it was a different kind of stale. It was not the recycled air that he had become tolerant of in the MF. It was like air that had never *wanted* to leave the building. A sad air.

Scores of people, some with firearms, others armed with file folders and laptops, moved about the first floor halls and negotiated the staircase.

A figure was walking quickly towards them, coming down the worn hardwood hallway to their left. Parker knew who it was immediately by his gait.

As the form approached, Michael's facial features could be seen fading in and out of the panels of light beaming in through an occasional open window to his right. He stopped in the brilliance of the rising sun that was streaming in from the open, east facing entrance door. His face hurt from smiling.

George turned and walked down the hallway to the right, with Vern and the relieved Martin in tow.

Michael and Parker stood a few feet apart, not knowing how greetings were exchanged in the great beyond – between ghosts.

Michael lifted his hand in a shallow wave. "Hey."

Parker quickly moved forward and wrapped his arms around his friend, pinning both arms to his side and burying his head in Michael's shoulder. He began sobbing.

Michael looked around at the interested few who had stopped to watch the moment, initially feeling embarrassed for his friend and himself. He quickly softened as he focused on the lost soul at his shoulder. He managed to free his arms and slowly raised Parker upright in front of him.

Parker caught his breath and looked Michael up and down. "It appears that . . . you didn't allow anything to blow up lately . . . especially yourself." The words were broken with moments of short composure.

"Nope, nothing blew up," Michael replied, looking closer at Parker's face. "You look like crap."

"Fascism isn't all it's cracked up to be."

"I'm really glad to see you," Michael spoke softly.

"Same here."

Michael tightened his grips on Parker's arms, "Tell me, any word on Red?"

Parker managed to speak, in between spasms in his chest, "Nothing, haven't heard another word from her or about her."

Michael's facial muscles tightened, "I should have gone back in there with you. We should have gotten her out of there, somehow." It was clear that he had been punishing himself over this for months as the words were well rehearsed and painful.

Parker was returning to his uncontrolled crying. A different kind of reality was hitting him all at once – he was alive, but the world he had returned to didn't seem worth living in.

"No, you had to take that crate out and do that voodoo that you do so well."

"Well, I tried. But, nothing happened. Not to the crate, anyway. The whole rest of the world went to pot, but nothing connected with that crate of Baby Formula."

"What did you do with it?"

"George was with me. I'll tell you that story later. Well, after we realized that it wouldn't blow up, or my satellite stuff didn't work, we just pushed the damn thing off the truck and left it there. The satellite hookup stuff is still there, too. Then we just kept driving over to Eagle Lake, in California. It was only about 60 miles but it took us all night. He had some friends there that put us up."

"Were you followed?"

"I was almost caught, but George took care of that. We got to the lake at about 6am, taking all the back roads. That's what took us so long."

"Speaking of taking you so long, why didn't you guys come and get us out sooner?"

"There's some weird stuff happening out there. Everyone's been trying to kill us for the last six months."

"Us? Who us?"

"Well, there is George, me, the People and the Black Shirts. We need you to join us. We need you to get in touch with the Shadows. We've managed to organize a pretty good size force, here on the West Coast. And there are plans in the works to go liberalize MF-6 in Utah."

Parker stepped back, "Black Shirts?"

"That's what George's people call Veterans. He has a whole army full of them. They're awesome."

Parker shook his head, "I just got out of hell -- I don't need to go back. And until I can figure out who in the world we're actually fighting, I'm just gonna be watching from the sidelines. Maybe the crate should have had a nuke in it. What I'm seeing and hearing doesn't sound like it's a world I want to be in anymore. And speaking of nukes . . . why did you even tell me that there was one in that crate to begin with?

Michael slapped his chest, "Me? I didn't say there was a bomb in there. I thought *you* were the one that deduced that one."

Parker held up his hands, "Oh, no . . . it wasn't me."

They both stood for a moment then at nearly the same moment . . . each nodded.

"It was Gus," Michael said.

Vern's voice twanged from down the hallway, "Hey, ya'll. George wants you in here."

Chapter Four

George, Vern and three others were gathered in the 'war room,' at the far end of the north hallway, looking at maps and various documents scattered on the long table in front of them. There were no windows open, only three bright bare light bulbs hanging by hastily strung wire, positioned over the group. Martin was in the corner, on a rug as old and shaggy as himself.

Two radiomen with headphones plugged into high frequency transceivers were sitting at a table placed against the wall, talking with other hams who had managed to get on the air. A single greasy light bulb hung over their heads. Antenna wires ran along the wall and out to the ancient school yard through holes drilled in the plywood windows. The radio operators were typing situation reports on their laptops, as two shortwave scanners sitting at each end of the table, listened for any sporadic transmission from 'out there'.

Each member of the group situated around the center table, had a handheld VHF/UHF transceiver attached to their belts.

The room was alive with voices. Some were from the assemblage in the room, the others coming from the radio speakers.

Occasionally, all activity at the map table would stop to focus on a scratchy voice coming from one of the radios.

George had sent Vern down the hall to get Michael and Parker.

After five minutes, Vern, Parker and Michael entered the room. George closed the door and motioned for all to sit as he stood at the head of the table, holding a compiled report of the attack on MF-7.

"Gentlemen . . . and Ladies. I think everyone knows each other, except Mister Parker. He will be working with us over the next few days. He and Mister Fields are deeply involved with the software that NexTrÉ had produced and both are very familiar with Gus."

All around the table nodded to Parker.

George lifted his hat and scratched his head, "We need to get all this stuff together and move it into the MF. We're gonna set up shop there."

He put his hat back on, picked up a pile of papers from the desk and began shuffling through them, "I would like to formally bring everyone up to speed on the present situation."

He began reading the third page, "The five levels of MF-7, that we needed to secure, are in our hands and 2,731 individuals have been brought up so far. They are being attended to in the temporary tent camp and should be allowed to return to their quarters in a day or so. That is, if they want. All services have been rudimentarily restored and should be up to full operational levels in 24 hours. That means power, water, ventilation . . . everything. The mess halls should be able to start serving meals in that timeframe, also."

He lowered the papers and looked around the table, "Level 6 has been sealed and we are evaluating the situation for further action."

The seated group now nodded to each other as Parker did the math. Seven-thousand went into the complex . . .

George continued, "As most of you know, there were no nuclear devices sitting in the warehouses of the MF's or the other December Pact facilities." He paused for a moment. "That also includes the Yucatan warehouse." He shook his head as he spoke the last line.

Parker slumped in his chair. That meant that Gus must still be out there with his band of Merrie-nuts.

"What we did have, according to Mister Fields, were twenty-seven specific crates, containing . . . the devices. So, we are continually issuing warnings to all December Pact installations to treat them as a bio-threat, at this time. We don't want any of them destroyed. All are being guarded until we can figure out what our next steps should be. We are receiving no leadership from the Council. Apparently, we have to do this on our own.

"What we *do* know is that almost six months ago, at 3:11 in the morning, on December 21st, all electrical grids and telecommunications, all over the planet, went down."

Parker looked over to Michael who just nodded his head.

"Without going down the long list of affected areas, the primary impact was on water treatment, the internet, sewage, transportation and medical services. The world's financial and governing sectors fell apart pretty quickly in the following days and weeks, as you can imagine."

"I bet generator sales hit the roof." Parker tried to bring a spot of light into his own dark picture of the world, as it was being drawn in charcoal by George.

"Only if you had cash," George answered, smiling weakly. "Right now, none of the world's currency seems to be worth the paper it's printed on. No one's sure what the real value of money is."

"Well, what the hell happened?" Parker exclaimed.

"A massive solar flare," Michael answered.

Parker squinted. "Now, wait a minute, I know about Solar Maxima and all that sunspot stuff. We get solar flares all the time. They hit us, affect some of our magnetic fields for a bit and then they fade away . . ." He paused, looking around at the faces. Some were looking down, others had sorrowful expressions. "O.K., so how big was it?"

A middle-aged lady wearing a cowboy hat almost as beat up as George's and sitting near the front of the table, spoke up. "Ever heard of the one in 1958? Probably not, I suspect. There weren't any computers, cell phones, GPS . . . it was a pretty analog world then. That flare was big, but no one really noticed, except for the Northern Lights going crazy. Some reports claim that this one was over 50% stronger with devastating flares that initiated our world-wide radio and digital blackout. It's hard to determine without any working satellites, sensors or computers to report on, it's due to the continuing radiation storms in the upper atmosphere. "

Vern rubbed his stubby face, "Let me add to what Rene is saying." He leaned onto the table and looked over at Parker. "Nearly everything in orbit was whacked. Those were the first things to go. I was down in Vegas; finally hit it big I might add. I knew my Craps system would work, eventually. Nearly busted the house . . . well, anyway, just before 3 am I was watching the off-track screens when, POW! -- all of the monitors went to blue. Then the entire casino went dark for a bit -- until the generators kicked in. When the emergency power came on the monitors stayed blue. No signal comin' in. By the time the slot machines had rebooted, security was gathering everybody up to form lines along the walls and aisles. We knew something big was up when the crowd discovered that none of the cell phones would make a connection. That started the panic."

Michael chimed in, "Cell phones not working provided clues to the immensity of the event's impact on a personal level."

Parker was still not convinced, "So, cell phones wouldn't work. The world started to fall apart 'cause people couldn't use their cell phones. What you're saying is that one solar flare has affected all life on earth?"

Vern leaned back, "Well, let me tell ya the rest of the story and maybe you'll understand a little better."

Parker shrugged, "Sorry. Go on."

Vern looked slowly around the table, like he was going to tell a ghost story around the campfire. Using hand gyrations to emphasize his tale, he began. "So there I was, four in the morning with pockets full of cash, in a town that had just shut down. I made my way to my car I had it parked in the dirt lot across the street. I did that so I didn't have to deal with the parking garages; always have some clown denting your car fenders or doors. Good thing I did, too. Got right on the street and headed up 15 . . . took me an hour to go six miles. Everyone was trying to get someplace else.

"When I finally merged onto 95, I kicked the ol' Porsche in the ass and headed north. And, let me tell ya', it was spooky. I mean, no street lights, no lighted signs – and not even one house had any sign of life in it.

"I got up around Beatty, just before sunrise. And the ol' car was just about running on fumes. I pulled into the gas station, they really only have one, and there was about twenty cars parked in a big jumble. Everyone was standing around in the headlights in groups. I guess they didn't have generators to get the pumps to work, or something. I found out later that the pumps ran on microprocessor chips, so they weren't working. And the credit card readers and cash registers were down for the same reason. Anyway, I didn't wait to find out right then. The crowd looked real nasty; waving arms and yelling at each other. So, I kept going. Figured I could get a bit farther up the road. At least get away from the riot."

"You find a gas station? How did you get back? Michael asked.

"I didn't . . . I buried all the money and died in the desert. Ha! Now wouldn't that have been a real yarn?"

Michael smiled at the old prospector's bizarre sense of humor. George just covered his eyes with his hand and shook his head.

Vern continued, "Well, I drove another ten miles and along to the side of the road sat a tanker truck. So, I pulls up behind him and I see the driver standing in front of the rig, in the headlights. I get out and call to him – you call out first, don't want him to think you're gonna rob him. Those guys are real jumpy.

"Hey, everything OK? Need some help?" I says; not moving forward.

"He calls back to me, "Lost my phone and GPS. The CB is on the blink, too. Who are you?"

"The name's Vern, I'm just trying to get up to the Fallon area. I was in Vegas a few hours back. The whole place is shut down; no power. And everyone's cell phone is out, not just yours. Looks like a massive black-out, or something." I was still keeping my distance.

"Well, I suppose that would explain some things. But, why don't my CB and GPS work? They're radios."

"Got me there, partner. I just thought you were in trouble or something."

"The driver became more at ease and began walking back to where I was. He says, "Naw, just trying to figure out what was going on with my radios. Lost touch with my dispatcher. She's gonna be pissed. She's my wife. Probably thinks I stopped off at one of the whorehouses or something."

"I tried to ease his mind a bit, "She's probably in the dark, too. I think this power outage might be coverin' the whole state . . . maybe farther."

Vern rubbed his stubby beard, "Thinkin' back now, I don't think that really helped him to accept the situation.

"Anyway, I put my hands out, palms up and I says, 'I want to ask you something, and don't get all riled up about it."

"What?"

"You got gasoline in there?"

"About five-thousand gallons of eighty-seven octane," he says. Then I could tell that he got real suspicious and asks why?

"I had to do some fast talkin' then, "None of the gas stations are working. I mean there ain't no gas for probably 400 miles. And there's gonna be a lot of folks comin' up this highway in a bit . . . running on empty."

"He still was eye'n me . . . 'Go on,' he says."

"Well, if I was you, that is . . . seein' how you're already sittin' here . . ., why don't you set up a sort of gas station, right here? Take cash only. Could help out a lot of people. And you would make out pretty good, yourself."

"He thought hard for a minute, and then said that he could use the transfer pump with a smaller nozzle. But, he couldn't make change for anyone.

"I just smiled, patted my stuffed pockets and smiled, "Friend, don't you worry about that."

"I tell you, it was like a pit stop at Indy. We had a couple State Troopers show up and they started directing traffic and controlling the line of cars. They had road flares out there and blinking lights. It was like being in Vegas again. And the cars were coming from both ways. We limited the amount to 12 gallons per vehicle and took cash only. And if they couldn't pay, the Trooper took down their license number and the driver's wife would bill them later. We unloaded that whole truck full of gas. Of course we had to charge a bit more than your average pump price. Not much – and sure didn't do any gouging. The Troopers saw to that."

"Well, I finally got back up here and hunkered down. That is until some of George's people got hold of me. That's when we started the plan to dig into the MF by the old tunnel."

Parker spoke up, "Now. Wait a minute. Did you say that the whole thing started, before 3am?"

Vern thought for a moment, rubbing his chin, "Yeah. 'Cause I remember I was talking to Cindy, the waitress, when the power went out. And she was asking me if I wanted another drink before she got off at 3. She was digging for a tip."

Parker looked over to Michael, "Then the 3:11 am solar flare didn't cause the blackouts."

George stepped in, "Let's just say that the flare was probably a well-timed 'excuse'. Years of careful planning must have been done to take the world into the situation we are now in. The whole collapse was a well orchestrated domino effect. Who did it? I have my suspicions."

The lady spoke up once again, "Reports indicate that more than half the world has been thrown back to living in conditions, technologically no better off than what they were in the early 1800's. What compounds the situation is the fact that there were only one billion people on the planet in 1800. Today, there are close to seven billion. It's not a safe rock to be sitting on right now."

One of the radio operators took off his headset and called to George, "We just got a message from Level 6. They want to talk."

George looked around the table.

Vern shrugged, "Might as well find out what the bastards want. They know we hold the ace."

"I think the sealing of the Tube, three months ago, might have something to do with it, too," George said as he walked over to the radios, "Put me on Jones' personal frequency."

The operator turned a few knobs and handed the headset to George.

"Eagle One to Stogie. Ya hear me Jones?"

"Five by, what 'cha need?"

"Tomorrow morning, about 08:30, send elevator 3 down to 6 – empty. We're gonna bring up some dirt to Level 1. Make sure the cameras are on. If you see weapons, stop the damn thing in between floors. I want your best team waiting for them when they arrive. Put our 'guests' into Conference Room 107. I'll be over there about 9."

"Roger. Stogie out."

George took off the headset and handed it back to the radioman. "Get a message back down to Level 6 that we will let three of them come up, unarmed, to Level 1 – using elevator 3, tomorrow morning at 8:30. Jones will escort them to Conference Room 107."

Parker was still sitting at the table, his mind putting together the information that he had heard minutes before.

He looked around the table. "So, has the whole world gone down the drain?"

"Depends on which part of the world you are referring to," George said, settling into an ancient chair that appeared unsafe for anyone to occupy.

Parker and Michael exchanged questioning glances as Rene pushed what appeared to be a thin newspaper towards Vern, who then passed it to Parker. She pointed at the crude publication, "That's a locally printed newspaper, of sorts. It was done on a manual mimeograph machine. I guess you could call it one of those underground publications. That issue came out a couple months after the flare."

Parker picked up the folded tabloid as the smell of the mimeograph ink took him back to the second grade for a moment. The date on the front page indicated that the news was quite old: Monday - February 12, 2013.

The main story, printed down the left column of the front page, detailed the hardships of the community and various groups that were formed to help with water, sanitation and basic human needs. The high school had been set up to provide temporary housing and rudimentary medical assistance. The cafeteria had become the town's soup kitchen. The rest of the page could have been an account of daily life in the 19th century, not 2013.

Ranchers were shooting rustlers, stores were under armed security and curfews were being enforced with deadly effectiveness. Everyone carried a firearm.

There appeared to be no government, just local factions protecting their own. However, the letters ESA kept cropping up in various stories.

"What's an ESA?" Parker asked anyone.

Rene looked to George for an approving nod and began to speak, "That's the Emergency Services Agency. They just appeared and took over the organization of everything in our area . . . even the police force. They were the only government that was out here. And they were very thorough in their tasks."

Parker lowered the paper, "The ESA. Is that a real government agency? Why didn't the Armed Forces come in and get things in order? What about Executive Order 11490? Isn't that supposed to assure continuity of government, at every level?"

George folded his hands, "The assignments within emergency plans, verses the actual implementation, are two different animals. Especially when the plans are dependant upon instant communications, to be effective. We're in the middle of a situation that's turned our world's technology clock back to almost a pre-electric era. The interesting thing about it was that the ESA knew it was coming, the government didn't."

What Parker had witnessed over the past few hours -- the tent city, the bloodshed, the lack of any infrastructure – this could be the new state of the global human condition.

George looked around the table, "I should add, to everyone here, what is happening with the power, communications and the like, is manmade . . . and it *can* be resolved. This is not a permanent situation."

Rene spoke up again, "Just to add a bit of light for the end of the tunnel; within two or three weeks, after the flare, a number of small municipalities were able to get their power grids up again. It seems that any power distribution network that relied on computer control was totally destroyed.

"Surprisingly, older grids were brought online in a matter of a few weeks. But, not enough output to run large cities. There are a lot of localized areas which rely on their own solar panels, wind and geothermal generators. But again, not enough to get the whole country back up."

George took back the newspaper, "Things have improved, somewhat. Limited power is being distributed, in time-blocks, to about 62% of the country. Enough to keep basic services running. Telecommunications are limited to old relay switching dial phones and short wave radios. Anything involving digital is out. Like TV, internet, cell phones and traffic control. It's like living back in the 50's. I'm sure that's only appealing to anyone into retro. Again, if it has a micro-processor involved, it ain't working."

Michael softly spoke to George, "Did you know about this whole thing before it happened? The flare, the black-outs and the whole damn domino thing?"

"The word was that something big was brewing. Honestly, I didn't know what. I was, and still am, really taken back by the magnitude of it all. And I really *did* think that the crate had something very dangerous in it, if that means anything."

Michael lowered his head, "I believe you. Sorry that I thought you might be involved."

"Oh, but I am. But not in the ways you are thinking. I can't get into it too deep, right now. But everything will be revealed, very shortly. And what you have in your . . . head, and in that laptop of yours, could change everything."

Parker raised his hand, "So, what am I, the hired help?"

George laughed, "No, Parker. You are a Shadow Person. One of the good ones. And we are honored to have you with us. Your time will come. It is written -- just as it is written for me. We all possess everything we need to become great."

"I sure would like to see this writing you go on about."

"It was in all the papers. Didn't you read it?" George joked.

"I'm sure I have a mountain of them in my driveway. I really haven't had the opportunity to pick them up in the last six months."

George could hear the anger in Parker's voice, just under the surface of his sarcasm. He understood the anguish. "Ok people, let's pack up this stuff, set up operations in the MF and get some sleep. The real battle is just beginning."

 **CHAPTER FIVE**

"I have seen these things in my visions – you will be a great warrior, *Tootupe*. The first will occur for your country. The next will be for The Foundation. The last shall be for all Humanity."

George had first heard these words from his grandfather when he was only seven-years-old. The last was as he sat next to his grandfather's death bed; a month before the young Marine was to leave for Viet Nam and fulfill the inevitable first prophecy.

The wisdom of the ancients had always radiated from the old man who had nearly raised George. The great man's words and teachings were etched into his soul and made him both strong and humble.

A particular event occurred on the evening of April 9, 1959.

As George lay on the rug in front of the fireplace, his grandfather lowered the newspaper he had been reading and spoke softly, "The 'wild west' was a reality that existed only in the minds of those who forged the stories. Those stories have taken on realities of their own. The truth was the extermination of indigenous souls for colonization and profit, by lawless *trailblazers*. I hope they do not create a wild west all the way across the Universe."

George remembered the headlines of the newspaper as his grandfather raised it back up, The Mercury Seven *Astronauts* Picked by *NASA*.

The old man's voice emanated from behind the paper wall, "Do not blaze trails, young one. Lead others along the worn paths of ancient wisdom. Give aid and comfort to those you meet along your journey. Leave only your footprints; take only knowledge. And remember this: You will be known past the dream-times by those tracks you leave."

"Did Jesus say that, Grandpa?"

"No, *I* did, Kammu," the old man had replied, leaning forward and lightly tapping the twelve-year-old on the head with the newspaper.

George had responded with a handful of popcorn, "I'm not a jackrabbit! I'm Black Rock! I shall be a warrior for the People. A Strategos of The Foundation just like you."

"And you shall be, on your 23rd birthday. For now . . . you are *my* jackrabbit."

That led to the great popcorn fight of 1959. He had loved his grandfather. His name was Lloyd *Pesape* (Red Ochre) Day.

George *Tootupe* (Black Rock) Day was born on September 14, 1947 as the clock struck one in the morning. Mixed with the newborn's cry were those of a Hawk circling overhead. It was said that the wings reflected the night shadow of the nearby mountain known as Black Butte and blocked out a massive section of the stars overhead – as would a ghostly galleon if sailing the heavens. It was a most unusual and spiritual occurrence. Although, it would all make sense in thirty years.

His emergence into the outside world of bigotry, ignorance and the inanity of the human races' need to dominate began as he entered the gates of the Marine Corps basic training depot.

The most intense cultural shock of the American 'melting pot' can be starkly experienced in any Armed Forces boot camp. Young men and women from every walk of American life -- largely from street-smart urban and close-knit rural communities, they are mashed into a mold which produces the world's most effective fighting machine. The country's next generation of warriors, continuously refined from blueprints originally drawn on cave and tomb walls -- into the time of Caesar and improved over a thousand years of human conflict. We have made a science out of killing our own.

On the day of his graduation, a Major Williams summoned George to his office.

CONTINUANCE

"At ease . . . PFC Day. The reason I have called you here is to first congratulate you on your outstanding performance and receiving Private First Class, right out of boot camp. As a Shoshone myself, I realize how difficult things have been for you; a Native American thrown into a very naive world -- on their views of our cultures and our humanity. I am sure you have been called 'Chief' more times than you care to count.

"The second reason for your summons, is this package that I was instructed to give to you by the commanding general. He received it from your people at home. Go ahead, you can open it. I have a feeling on what it is," he said, smiling.

George tore into the wrapping paper and then slowly opened the cardboard box. It was an Eagle feather, his people's greatest honor and recognition that he was now a true warrior.

The Major walked to his desk and hit his intercom, "Sergeant . . . no one, and I mean *no one* is to enter this room for five minutes." He then picked up an envelope, "As you know, The Foundation and all military organizations, throughout the world, are separated by L'accordo di 1442 (The Agreement of 1442). However, it does allow for training and technology exchanges – that is why you are with us now."

He opened a letter which was embossed with an inverted cross at the top. He read it aloud. "June 23, 1966. Tootupe, you have completed the mandatory boot training, fulfilling the first steps required to perform your birthright duties as The Foundation's Third Level Strategos, as did your grandfather and his before him.

"You now have the option of remaining in the service of the United States Armed Forces for your four full years, from the date of your enlistment, or provide support services to The Foundation until your 23rd birthday. Wherein, you will assume your duties of Strategos for the term of forty-four years as those who have held the post before you. Your answer shall be transmitted to us by the authorized presenter of this reading."

George returned to attention, "Sir, the private wishes to remain in the Corps and serve his country as a Marine, until the end of the stated three years. But, I shall remain a Marine until I die . . . Sir."

The Major folded the paper, "As you wish – Strategos Black Rock. I am transferring you to Non-Commissioned Officers training, as of tomorrow. I wish you the best of luck and am proud to have met you. You will serve our nation and our planet well. I am confident of that."

George stood ridged holding the feather as the Major snapped to attention and saluted the very proud warrior.

For the next two years, George excelled in every aspect of Marine Corps life and duty. Even the heat of the Viet Nam jungles did not bother him, although the humidity was something new.

At 3am, on January 30, 1968, a Viet Cong sapper squad penetrated the wire at the base of the hill where Sergeant George Black Rock and eight other Marines were providing night security. The Bangalore torpedoes blew a huge gap in the razor wire as scores of enemy troops began their assault up the vertical no-mans-land.

Pop-up flares were sent into the clear night, exposing the low-profiled throng of assailants carrying rocket propelled grenades, satchel charges and automatic weapons. The overhead glare of the falling flares made the force appear to be stretched out, all the way up to China.

Overhead illumination is a two-way street in night operations – both sides can see each other.

Sergeant George Black Rock figured the plus and minuses and immediately ordered the radioman to call in heavy artillery illumination and a fire mission from anything flying.

Small arms fire began streaming into the Marine's positions. Two rocket grenades exploded into the side and top of Bunker One, 50 yards away from George and his M60 machine gun position, on top of Bunker Three. 30 yards to his right, at the top of the hill's crest sat Bunker Four and the .50 caliber machine gun 'ma deuce'. There was no return fire coming from Bunker One.

CONTINUANCE

The six defenders began throwing grenades and lead down the hillside.

The VC's objective was the division tactical net radio bunker on the top of the hill. There were four 'off-duty' radio men sleeping in the communications bunker. Three appeared within moments; helmets, rifles and flack jackets thrown over t-shirts. The fourth stayed behind to remove crypto cards, call in reinforcements and stood by to set off incendiary grenades to destroy the radios and codes if overrun. The other three ran to take up positions behind a 6x6 truck parked close by.

It was now ten against the world gone insane.

George had always wondered why Napoleonic tactics were taught in boot camp, as they were devised in the days of cavalry charges, muskets and swords. They would never be employed in 20th century warfare. Wave after wave of human flesh, advancing until the objective was reached, regardless of casualties. He was now seeing it. How do you deal with an enemy with endless waves of flesh and no regard for one's own life?

It was just a fleeting thought as his machine gun cut into the advancing horde.

An explosion, ten yards in front of him, sent him reeling back; dirt embedded in his cheeks and the concussion flattening his chest. He looked to his left to see the 6x6 truck jump into the air in a burst of red and yellow hell. The bed was blown almost vertical as in dropped back to the earth. Two bodies were floating, in slow motion, away from the dying mass of steel and flaming rubber.

The staccato roaring of the .50 caliber, on top of Bunker Four, was causing little damage. It was just adding to the confusion.

The 11th Marine's howitzers were now lobbing illumination high over head. George could see groups of figures moving closer to Bunker One and the flaming truck. The lone Marine, near the burning vehicle, ran to a dirt embankment and began firing into the advancing multitude.

George reached into his knapsack and pulled out the carefully wrapped Eagle feather. He stuck it into the thin strap around his helmet. Grabbing his M16 he turned to the radioman, "Call Bunker Four. Tell them to start laying down fire five yards in front of Bunker One, then continue all the way along the wire in front of us . . . all along our positions. Make a continuous shield. Then feed ammo to Johnson, he's taking over this gun."

Placing three grenades on his jacket, he jumped off the sandbagged roof and began running down the hill to Bunker One.

He could not feel his feet touching the earth . . . it was as if he was being carried. A voice filled his head, "Paatusooba Naka'e. The weakness of your enemy makes your strength."

He thought fast, *What's their weakness?*

He watched the groups huddle below, then move forward a few steps.

They're used to fighting like Woodland tribes! He thought. *They're guerilla fighters, not trained for open area tactics. They're hiding behind each other for cover.*

The whole hillside had been burned clear. There wasn't a tree or bush to hide behind.

He dived next to the survivor of the truck explosion. "Hanson, you OK?"

"OK. Just some burns."

"Come on, we have to appear as many. Hit and run along the ridge. Don't stay anywhere more than a couple seconds."

The .50 caliber was keeping the attackers backing off as the accumulation of overhead flares bloomed brighter.

George threw a grenade at a huddled group and caught a glimpse of a rocket grenade launcher being pointed at Bunker Four. He swiftly took out the soldier aiming it with a couple shots. He then ducked and ran to a pile of dirt, firing again at the closest targets.

Hanson had moved to the corner of Bunker One and let off six shots. He then moved to the other corner and emptied his magazine, taking out four sappers who had made the fatal decision to move forward. He ran to his left and expanded the defensive perimeter while slapping in another magazine.

George took advantage of Hanson's fire and made a dash for the bunker. He dove in, followed by AK47 rounds at his heels.

Hickman was dead and Sedgwick was in shock, eyes staring with bloody streaks running down his face. George moved him aside and picked up the Mk19 grenade launcher. It weighed almost 120 pounds. He struggled to get out of the bunker. He hoped 'ma deuce' had enough ammo to keep laying down fire for a few more moments.

He moved ten yards to the right and set up the tripod. The weapon could deliver a 40mm grenade every second. Each grenade would kill anything within twenty feet. The 48-round can was full. He began peppering the mass below. He shot eight rounds and picked up the weapon to move again.

Hanson had emptied his last magazine and was running to one of the weapons of the truck casualties. He fell, grabbing his leg. He waved to George that he was still breathing, but not able to provide any support.

George moved to his right and dropped the launcher next to a pile of empty sandbags and shot off another ten rounds. Aiming at where the enemy soldiers were heading and not where they were.

The two lead choppers came in low and fast – all four .30 caliber machine guns blazing. The third danced in the air behind the first two, firing all of its 24 -2.75 inch rockets into the scattering VC below.

George felt an aged hand on his shoulder and a far away voice whispering, "We are proud – Tootupe."

The Silver Star citation read 'Gallantry in action against an enemy of the United States'.

It was another lifetime ago -- before he had met Hugh Waterman and before he took his birth-right in The Foundation as the thirteenth Strategos since 1442.

As the, now sixty-six year old man stood in the crumbling and dimly-lit school house, he knew that his grandfather's second prophecy was unfolding around him.

Chapter Six

Thursday morning, at 9am, George and the others walked into Conference Room 107, past the two armed guards who were standing on each side of the open doorway in the hallway. The room had been put back in order and the stench from six months of stale air and sequestered humans had been nearly eliminated.

Seated at the long table were the three representatives from Level 6. Four additional guards were positioned at the corners of the room. Roland recognized the man that had knelt over him after the wall exploded on Level 1. He was seated at the far end of the table, writing on a note pad and chewing on a stubby cigar. He stood up as the group entered. An M9 Beretta 9 mm pistol rested next to the pad of paper.

"Hey, Boss," he called to George.

"Jones, good to see you," George answered, while looking carefully at the three men seated together on the other side of the table. He pulled out a chair across from them.

His attention swiftly focused to the older man, to his left. George nodded to him, without taking his eyes off the pudgy head that rose from the collar of grey suit, "Winslow."

The man looked up, obviously disgusted with the situation and nodded back slowly; his eyes cutting into George's face. "George." He paused to look down and write something on a notepad, "So, it looks like you win this one . . . But it was just a battle, not the war."

George shook his head and looked at the other two, sizing them up.

"Would you two like anything to drink; coffee or something cold?"

The one dressed in the uniform of an ESA officer answered swiftly, "No, not at this time."

A thin man in his late fifties, who was sitting next to the soldier, shook his head while looking down at the table top. He sported a brown corduroy jacket, trimmed grey beard and wire frame glasses.

"OK, suit yourselves," George responded as he sat down and put his own notepad on the table. "Could someone call down to the mess and get me some coffee up here?" He spoke over his shoulder to no one in particular, but to anyone who wanted to help.

He turned back to face the men across from him.

"For those of you who do not know me, my name's George. I'm authorized to talk with you about what we should do with your *associates*, down there in Level Six."

Winslow, still looking down at his notepad, asked, "And what madman gave *you* any authorization to do anything?"

The uniformed man sat up in his chair, "I am Colonel Taylor, the new commander of the MF-7 Security Forces."

Jones interrupted, "The ESA you mean! I didn't see one MF-7 Security person in that whole pile of bodies we hauled out of here."

"The ESA was put in charge of all MF security, after the blast doors closed," the Colonel replied.

"And do you have an explanation on how in the hell they got in here?" Jones yelled back. "Same faces, different name. Same old crap."

George held out his hand to calm Jones and turned his attention to the frail man next to the Colonel.

"And you are . . . ?"

"Reginald Adams. I am, what you could call, a scholar."

"And what sort of things do you . . . study?"

"In short; I am deeply involved in the deciphering of the Tzolk'in and obtaining any artifacts relating to Mu·Suvian intervention within the Mayan and Neolithic civilizations. I am also continuing with various tests relating to the cryptic procedures written in *La Très Sainte Trinosophie*."

George leaned back and looked around the room at the odd expressions on everyone's faces and turned back to Doctor Adams.

"Do they call you Reggie?" George asked the out-of-place captive.

"Some have, when I was a bit younger. I don't mind."

George put his hands together in front of him, "Well, Reggie, excuse us all for our combined reactions to your presence, but in a meeting like this, and with your background, most would not understand why they would send you. Not a choice of skill sets we were expecting. Although, I *am* intrigued and may possibly see the connections. Always glad to meet another resident of the Palace of Sublime Science."

Reggie's face began to beam with excitement, as someone in the room actually knew what in the world he was talking about.

Parker's eyebrows lowered into an inquisitive glance at Michael. Michael returned the look.

The Colonel pointed at the little man to his left, "The MF Committee claims that Doctor Adams may have some information which could aid in your decision about the fate of our people still down below."

It was apparent that the Colonel's presence was aiding in Reginald's self-restraint.

Reggie adjusted his silver wire-frame glasses and looked into George's eyes. When he had mentioned the Tzolk'in, the Sacred Calendar of the Maya, there was an instant reaction of recognition from George. When he spoke of the Mu·Suvians and *La Très Sainte Trinosophie*, it was Winslow's reaction that Jones noticed. It was as if Reggie had just revealed a state secret.

The little man paid no attention to Winslow's glare as he continued to speak directly to George, "May I show you something . . . sir?"

"Please."

The little man reached into his rumpled coat pocket and withdrew a small, flat object. It was about the size of a pack of playing cards, and one side glistened with a polished layer of white crystal. The reverse displayed a painted glyph carved into a smooth deposit of laminated stone.

George took an involuntary short breath and without taking his eyes off the stone, "Colonel . . . Winslow. I would like to speak to Doctor Adams alone for a few minutes, if you don't mind."

Colonel Taylor's chest stuck out, "This is highly irregular . . . I do not think that this is a reciprocal response to our voluntary and well-intended gesture to meet with you . . ."

George again used his hand, patting down the incoming words, "Calm down, Sir. I just want a little one-on-one with him. It might just get your needs met a whole lot faster."

Winslow snorted, "Your side always did want to deal with the 'little people'."

George lowered his head and stared sideways at the beady eyes glaring back, "The 'little people', as you call them, are pretty damn sick of your policies and control and overall crap. And remember, there are more of 'us' than your self-proclaimed *cream of the intelligentsia* maggots. And, pass this around to your bottom-feeders, *we* now have the devices."

"Not *all* of them – nor all of *those*." He pointed at the stone object Reggie was holding.

"It's just a matter of time, Winslow. This first one will lead us to the others."

Without waiting for a response, George cleared the room, sending everyone into the hallway, including the guards.

For the next ten minutes, everyone milled about in the hallway outside of the conference room. Michael walked up and down the corridor talking to himself, as Parker inspected bullet holes in the walls. Colonel Taylor fumed -- pacing back and forth in front of the permanently opened door. He would occasionally glance in to see Reggie's hands swooping over his head and George writing down notes.

CONTINUANCE

Winslow stood between two guards, hands in his pockets, fuming.

At the end of the ten minutes, George stood up and walked to the door. "Parker, would you please come in here for a moment?"

Parker and George met with the anthropologist for another five minutes. Coffee had finally arrived from the mess hall and Taylor, who had given up trying to interrupt George, was sharing the carafe with one of the guards in the hall. Jones was holding the guard's weapon and covering Taylor with his sidearm, loaded with a 15-round magazine. He was hoping for Taylor to make a break and run down the hall. Taylor may have been an arrogant jerk, but he was no fool – he did not make any sudden moves.

George pushed back his chair and turned to the assemblage waiting outside the door. "Would you all please come back in?"

Everyone took up the same positions at the table they had held before and around the room.

Winslow pointed at Reggie, "So, did he give you everything you needed?"

George smiled, "Just a few tidbits of wisdom that you guys deemed too sacred for the unworthy."

Winslow folded his arms and looked to the open doorway, "That's preposterous."

"It's a *new* world order, Winslow – remember?"

Winslow put both hands on the table, "We're closer than you think. And don't think that this little party-crashing episode is going to change it either."

George turned his attention to the Force Commander, "Colonel Taylor, we invite groups of five of your people in Level 6 to come out of the facility to a special area we will set up at the processing center. We will send *you* back down to arrange the evacuation. Again, only five at a time will be permitted up -- unarmed. In two hours, Elevator 3 will be at your disposal – under full guard and surveillance, of course."

Jones had put down his coffee cup and was staring intensely back and forth at George and Taylor. He was so visibly agitated that he had nearly chewed through what was left of his cigar butt.

He could not contain himself any longer, "What? Just gonna let them walk out of here? *'Sorry we imprisoned a few thousand of our own people – killed off a few hundred more - we promise that we won't do it again.'* Come on, George . . . we should be shooting these clowns."

"We were only following orders," Taylor verbally attacked back.

"In how many languages can you say that? 'Cause the world has heard it a thousand times . . . from slicker murderers than you. And I can tell you, we're pretty damn sick of hearing it!" Jones called back.

Taylor was on his feet and Jones was ready to come across the table.

George slapped the solid oak slab, "Both of you, sit down! Those responsible will be dealt with, Mister Jones."

There was a thick pause as if all were waiting for an over inflated balloon to explode.

The Colonel bowed slightly to George and returned to his seat. Jones picked up his pistol, pushed his chair back and walked to the other side of the room. He put his sidearm in the holster and stared at Taylor, keeping his hand on the butt of the weapon.

Winslow spoke up, "We will comply with your evacuation plan. However; They demand to have the Tube reopened. There will be negotiations on that subject." He sat back in his seat, crossed his arms and motioned with his head, "What about Doctor Adams, there?"

"He will remain here and be under my team's supervision," George advised him. "Actually, Mister Parker will be personally in-charge of Reggie."

George paused and turned to Parker, "Who was that science-geek we saved?"

"Roland. He's outside, at the center now," Parker answered.

"Think we could use him . . . after he takes a shower?"

"If you think he's needed?" Parker squinted as he questioned why a scientist was required to help him keep an eye on Reggie. "I will get him back in here. I wonder if Michael should be involved, too?"

"If we wonder enough, the knowledge will arrive, Parker. There shall be no question that Michael should be involved," George said, looking at Michael, who was staring back with a 'deer in the headlight' expression.

Reggie looked at Michael and smiled. It gave Michael a chill. There was something in the smile that delved deep into his past . . . or future.

George turned back to Winslow, "When all your people are out and safe, you and I are going to have a long talk."

Winslow lifted his chin as he slowly uncrossed his arms. "It's about the crates, isn't it?"

George shook his head, "Yes, that -- and also about how and who you're getting your orders from now."

"Are you going to open the Tube?"

George stood up, "I'm still waiting for word from the top on that one."

"Hasn't the Pony Express delivered your orders, yet?"

George put his hands on the table and leaned towards Winslow, "We will get them yesterday."

He shook his head as Winslow was escorted out of the room.

Chapter Seven

Michael sat in a chair within one of the abandoned offices on Level 1. Parker had claimed it as his own and was in the process of bringing in some of the floor's best furniture from other offices.

Across from Michael sat Reggie, hands folded in his lap and looking around the room.

"So, you're a researcher? Must be excit . . . ah, very interesting." Michael had never been a guard before. He wasn't very good at it, he decided.

"It has its rewards," Reggie politely answered. He was visibly quite shaken, as Michael could see by the frail man's large pupils. Or, perhaps the thick glasses he wore just accentuated their diameter – from the outside looking in.

"You still have that flat stone thing that you showed George? It looked pretty old."

"Your Mister George kept it. He said he would give it back after he examined it further. I am not worried about it; he is very knowledgeable as to its' importance. And, yes, it is very old. Over 1,400 years, from all indications."

Michael leaned back, "Whoa. Bet it's worth a fortune."

"Oh, it would be impossible to apply any monetary value to it. It is beyond our world of thinking."

Michael struggled to understand the last comment.

"I have heard of you Michael. I wanted to meet you, but in different circumstances."

"You've heard of me? Why would anyone want to talk about me?"

The professor took out his small notebook and scribbled a couple strange characters on a blank sheet of paper. He held it up for Michael to see. "Do these symbols mean anything to you?"

Michael looked at them, turning his head from side to side. "No. Looks like some kind of pictograph or something."

"I suppose they are, in some way."

"Am I supposed to know what they are?"

"Not really. Just curious if you had ever seen them before."

"Nope. All Greek to me."

Reggie Adams smiled as he put the notepad back in his coat pocket, "Well, way before them. Perhaps in the near future they might mean something to you."

A loud scraping sound erupted through the door, followed by Parker's backside, pulling a sumptuous leather couch in with him.

He turned and collapsed on the cushions, "Check it out, Michael. Wouldn't this look good in my place at the beach?"

"I'm sure that if you're willing to drag it all the way to Santa Cruz, no one would stop you."

Parker sat up, "So, Reggie, you doin' OK?"

"Reggie was just telling me about that rock he showed George."

Taking command of the explanation, Reggie held up his hand, "First, it is not a *rock*; it is one of Twenty Sacred Sign Glyphs of the Mayan Sacred Calendar, known as the Tzolk'in. The Resonator I presented at the meeting was inscribed with the symbol for Death – Cimi."

Parker sat up even farther, "Resonator?"

Reggie shook his head and looked to the floor, "Please, excuse me. I've said too much as it is. I would rather wait for Mister George to be present before I continue."

Parker looked at Michael and mouthed the words "*Mister George?*"

Michael waved him off. "That's OK, Reggie. I can see what you were talking about when you said your work had its moments."

Reggie looked up to Michael. "I said it had its *rewards*. And, yes, the Resonator is one of the biggest anyone in my field of endeavor could ever hope for."

The little man was beginning to appear more comfortable.

A quick series of knocks came from the hallway wall.

An inquisitive voice followed, "Hello?"

Parker turned to see who was wishing to enter his new domain.

"Roland, come on in. Glad you could find the place. I haven't turned on the porch lights, yet."

Parker stood and slapped the visitor on the arm, then turned to Michael.

"Michael Fields, I would like to introduce Roland . . . Roland what?"

"Doctor Roland Jenkins. I'm a scientist, specializing in Dimensional Transmutations and . . . Doctor Reginald Adams!"

Roland quickly walked over to Reggie, who had risen to his feet.

"This is an honor, sir. I had heard that you were brought in from Stanford to work on the Neolithic visits and Tzolk'in connection; I thought I would never get to meet you. I wanted to get on that project so bad. The projected implications of black-hole thermodynamic effects on the earth were clearly defined in those ancient Maya texts."

Michael and Parker shrugged at each other and sat down.

Roland turned back to Parker, "You know who this is?"

"That's Reggie."

"Reggie? Oh, no." He turned back to Doctor Adams, "I'm so sorry . . . they just have no idea. . . "

"Relax, son. It's OK. We're old pals now."

Parker made a flipping gesture with his hand. "Yep, he's just one of the boys, now."

The phone, which Parker had recently *borrowed* from the warehouse, rang on the desk behind him.

He climbed over the back of the couch and picked up the handset, "Parker here."

As he listened to the caller, he motioned for all to sit down.

"OK. No problem. See ya' in three hours." He hung up the phone and flopped back on the couch.

"That was George. We all have to be topside, by the Main Lobby entrance in two hours. We're going to catch a ride over to where we need to meet him. He said that it was alright if we went down to the mess hall for something to eat first. He was sure that you were probably hungry Reg . . . Doctor Adams."

"I could use some food, no question there."

"Alright, everyone to the staircase. George is buying."

Parker walked over to Michael, "George said that you should bring your laptop. Battery charged?"

"Yeah, no problem," Michael answered, very confused.

The celebrated doctor slowly rose to his feet, "Hey Parker. You can call me Reggie." They both smiled and all walked into the hallway.

Chapter Eight

The blast doors leading to the surface from the Main Lobby were opened by the cutting crews within eight hours after the warehouse entry was released.

Parker, Michael, Roland and Reggie walked through the rusty hinged door of the Depression-era clapboard house, which was disguising the North entrance to the MF. The evening air of the desert engulfed them all. Everyone breathed in the arid vastness and reverently remembered better times in their lives.

It had been two hours since Parker had received the phone call from George, who must have been somewhere in the MF at the time. As phone service was still limited to inside the facility. Parker figured that he was probably having that talk with Winslow.

Once again, the J&K Mushroom van was waiting. Vern greeted the group, "Howdy. Ready to take a ride?"

They all climbed into the van and Vern proceeded to drive north.

As they moved down the road, Michael was having the strange feeling that he had done this before. He moved up to kneel between the front seats, next to Vern.

"Hey there, Vern. Are we headed up towards Pyramid Lake?"

"Yep, should be there in twenty minutes."

"And I'm assuming that the lake is not our destination."

"Nope. George told me to go up highway 445 'till we get near High Rock Road. He said you'd know where to go from there."

Michael moved back to his seat and sat down hard. Vern was taking them to the crate.

Roland and Reggie had been talking and writing on notepads since they all went to the mess hall, and they were still at it in the back seat of the van. Only now, they were talking louder over the noise of the vehicle.

Parker sat looking out the window, his chin in his hand, wishing they would shut up.

Michael called to Parker, "Ya' wanna know where we're going?"

"Someplace far out in the desert to drop those two off?"

"To the crate, with the 'whatever' inside of it."

Parker turned to look at Michael's very serious expression.

"So, you're not joking? Why didn't you blow the damn thing up when you had the chance? Or bury it? You could have shipped it to New Jersey. I thought we would never have to see it again."

Michael held out his hand and started touching the palm with his other finger, trying to relate the sequence of events. "When we took it up there last December, I did everything we had planned: set up the satellite uplink, got a connection to the crate's Transceiver, and sent out the codes that we found in the database to the satellite that was flying over. But nothing happened. Either I shut it off or there was nothing in there to shut off."

"Well, you must have done something, 'cause nothing happened . . . if that makes any sense."

Michael held out both hands. "But, something did happen. The solar flare or whatever it was."

Parker shook his head. "But, it had nothing to do with the crate. Unless you tapped into the powers of the Universe, oh mighty Michael, and commanded the Sun to flare. Get real."

He shook his head, "And then you just left it sitting there . . . in the middle of the desert."

"You wanted me to bring it back? Look, I didn't want to take on the responsibility of saving the world to begin with. And look at these damn LiquiCode tattoos!"

Parker leaned forward and put his hand on Michael's shoulder, "No. I'm sorry. Just getting pretty confused. Why are we going back to it? Why are we taking these two with us? And what's George up to anyway?"

They sat back. Parker closed his eyes – he felt as if he had been awake for days.

Michael watched the desert slide by outside the van windows for another 25 miles. The sheer scope, breadth and expanse of the desert were daunting. The mind can play tricks when judging distance in these realms. What looks to be just down the road can turn into a 30-mile trek. It must have been hell on the Pioneers headed west.

Vern's voice took Michael out of his fixed gaze. "Coming up on High Rock. Where to now?"

Michael moved to the front of the van.

"There's a dirt road to the right around this curve. There it is. It's pretty dark out here, so go slow."

Vern pulled the van off the main road and onto the path.

"You'll go down this until you see . . ."

As they rounded a hill a circle of spotlights resembling a football field at night blared into their windshield. At least ten military-type vehicles were parked in an area off the road, just inside a high steel-wire fence.

Vern bounced the van down the hard clay path leading to a gate guarded by three armed soldiers. The uniforms were not familiar to anyone in the back of the van.

This was not the same dark, isolated spot that Michael and George had visited six months before. This was now a high security installation. It was a Forward Operating Base.

In the center of the compound, a large tent was erected, perhaps 40 feet long and 30 feet wide. The four center poles lifted the top to 15 feet above the desert floor. Michael knew what was under that canvas covering.

Vern stopped at the gate and two guards walked to either side of the van and looked in. The one on the driver's side recognized Vern and they talked for a bit. Then the guard gave him instructions on where to park. The gate was opened to let the van enter the compound.

A wide variety of tents and other types of rapid deployment shelters had been erected in two rows along the west side of the secured area. Some were barrack housing structures with floors, insulated walls and lighting. Refrigerated food trailers were parked next to a sprawling fabric dining facility, with seating for 50 or more. Three power generators were softly rumbling at the far end of the compound.

A portable hospital was located near the crate tent, evidenced by a red cross which was painted on the roof.

Michael counted thirty-five uniformed personnel walking about the grounds, ten more in the mess tent and twelve standing guard at various locations around the area.

An area serving as a stable was on the left side of the van as they drove into the camp. Five horses were standing in stalls and being attended to by four 'soldiers'.

After stopping the decrepit bus in the appointed parking spot, Vern and his passengers stepped out and waited for a familiar face.

A young woman dressed in the fatigues of the compound Forces galloped up to them from the right, on a chestnut horse. A rifle was lying across the saddle and she was wearing a headset. A black headband was holding her shoulder-length blonde hair away from her face.

Stopping a couple of yards in front of them, she shouted, "FOB Three welcomes you. George would like you all to proceed to that tent, which you see over there." She pointed to the large canvas structure that Michael was sure was housing the crate. "Please walk along ahead, I will escort you."

Vern called out to his passengers, "I smell food. Think I'll wander over to the mess tent. I'll catch up with you all later. Good to see you again, Captain Summers."

She waved to Vern as the troupe stepped out towards the tent. All except Parker. He was standing in the same spot where he had climbed out of the van, staring up at the girl.

"Is there a problem, sir?" she asked, leaning onto the saddle horn.

"What army are you in?"

"We're the Black Shirts, the *original* homeland security."

"I can see that . . . still riding horses."

"Are you trying to be funny?" She was not amused.

"My name's Parker." He paused. "Ian Parker."

Michael stopped in his tracks, put down his laptop case and looked back. *Had Parker actually told her his first name?*

"Well, Mister Ian Parker, please move along."

He really wasn't listening to the words, just infatuated with the sound of her voice.

"And you are?" he asked.

Her voice wavered as she tried to compose herself, "Please . . . I must *insist* that you join the others."

He didn't budge.

Her hand touched the rifle, "Don't make me shoot you, Mister Parker."

"How many times?"

"What?"

"How many times are you going to shoot me, Annie O? I figure that if you're pissed off and just want to get my attention . . . once. And if you really think I'm such a dangerous guy, maybe twice."

"My name is *not* Annie. And how many times I shoot you will depend greatly on how many bullets I have left *after* the first two."

The horse, as well as everyone listening to this exchange, was getting anxious to move on.

Parker stood his ground.

She pulled back on the reins, "Alright, my name is Tara. Just as you heard Vern say. You want to get moving now?"

Parker began walking towards the others, still looking back at the petite blonde sitting on the tall chestnut stallion. Tara nudged the horse forward to slowly walk behind Parker. A slight smile appeared on her lips.

As they neared the tent, a guard pulled back the flap and motioned for the group to enter.

The interior was illuminated by only one lamp, without a shade, sitting on a table in the corner. At the center sat, not a crate, but a large rectangular metallic frame with a glass globe inside. The object was four feet square and nearly five feet tall. There was a flattened area at the top, denying the object a classification as a perfect orb.

Seated on a rug to the right of the thing was George. His legs were crossed, his familiar hat was off, and he was holding something in his cupped hands.

Martin was lying in the far corner. He slowing raised his head to see who had entered, then back down to his normal resting position. Recognizing Michael, he slowly moved his tail a few times and then closed his eyes again.

At the far end of the tent sat the portable satellite dish and controller box linking kit that Michael had used months earlier, still situated in its original orientation.

George looked to the group he had summoned. "Great to see you all, again. It's been hours. Have a seat." He motioned towards the rug with his forehead.

As Michael and Parker sat down, their eyes were glued to the metal-framed object in front of them.

"So, *this* is what all the fuss was about," Parker mused.

Doctor Adams sat with Roland on the other side of George.

"So, I was correct in my hypothesis. Think we can wake it up?" asked Reggie.

Parker leaned back, "Wake it up?"

"I'm sure we can now," George replied, holding out the Resonator.

Michael looked around at everyone on the rug and asked, "Can anyone tell me what the hell this is?"

Reggie raised his hand, like it was a quiz or something. He then cleared his throat and pointed at the 'thing'. His voice was wavering from some internal volcano, "This is what we would now classify as a type of Mayan Vinculum Transceiver."

Parker spoke up, "A Vi-what?"

"A Vinculum . . . it means a bond or in a chain." Reggie answered.

"When was it built?" Parker asked.

Reggie slowly leaned forward and touched the 6 inch thick round metal bars which formed a square support at the top of the globe. With his quivering hand lightly touching the cold steel, he adjusted his glasses and tilted his head back to get a closer look. "By looking at this protective frame, it was not too long ago . . . perhaps a couple years. Although, the globe is very old indeed; millenniums, I would like to think." He moved his hand to one of the four support columns that connected the top and bottom metal frames, "These vertical shafts seem to be made of a strong glass or porcelain."

He leaned back to a sitting position. "Through our research data, which is based on fragments of ancient Maya texts – most of which was destroyed by the Spanish conquistadors -- the original concept and internal design could be only as old as the Resonator that George is holding. Perhaps Late Pre-Classic; 250 A.D., or close to it. But, again, that is only speculation. I am inclined to think much longer."

Parker did some quick calculations with his finger in the dirt beside the rug, "At that 250 A.D. number you mentioned would make it over 1,700 years!"

"That sounds about right," Reggie nodded.

Michael held up both hands, "OK, hold on. This is getting too damn wacky here. The doc here says that this thing, whatever it is . . ."

"A Transceiver," Reggie spoke up.

"Sure, a Transceiver." Michael shook his head, "Anyway, this Transceiver was thought up a bazillion years ago, someone recently put one together, they stuffed it into a crate and hid it in the MF warehouse. All the while, they were threatening the world with stories that the thing was a nuclear device."

Parker broke in, "Was this *thing* the reason that the MF's were closed up and Security went insane? Over this science fiction story we are hearing? Can anyone tell me that?"

George sighed and put down the Resonator in front of him on the rug, "I had a long *discussion* with Colonel Taylor, earlier. Listening to a liar is like drinking warm water. He *said* that he had no idea what was in the crate. He was ordered to find it and have it removed from the warehouse and brought to the surface. He was also ordered that no one was to leave the MF – at any cost. It seems that Michael and Parker managed to get the crate to the surface for them. However, Michael bringing it up here was not in the good Colonel's plan."

"Why didn't they just come and get it?" Parker asked.

"Within 24 hours, I had the Black Shirts establish this base around it. I must admit I am surprised that they haven't tried. I think they're waiting for something," George said.

Michael turned to Doctor Adams, "So, you knew what was in the crate. Why didn't you tell those nut cases, with the guns?"

"I could only speculate as to what was within the container. To the MF Program people, my reports were just more ramblings of a crazy Ph.D. And as you are realizing, the explanation was really too far out there for anyone to believe in the first place. Even with you all sitting here, actually looking at it, you still don't believe what you are observing. It was a hard sell. But, after the flare event, everyone was coming around to my way of thinking. But you removing it from the MF did not help my efforts in determining what it was. And George's People guarding it out here made it virtually impossible for me to get to it."

George spoke softly, obviously tired, but clear enough for all to hear. "Reggie's story, sorry . . . hypothesis, is not a new one to the ancient peoples. Although, it has always been speculative – being passed down by word of mouth for almost two millennia. Certain details get left out, while other things get added for dramatic effect."

George shook his head slowly. "When Reggie first spoke of the Tzolk'in, I was intrigued. But, when he pulled the Cimi Resonator out of his coat, I nearly pissed my pants. I'm here to tell you that this thing in front of you is probably a form of radio wave transmitter and receiver."

Parker looked at Michael. "Well, good thing you *didn't* blow it up, I suppose. It could be hard to get parts for."

George raised his head far back, looking to the top of the tent. His eyes scanned back and forth, as if looking for something in the folds of the canvas.

"There are 19 more of these, which we must wakeup."

"There were twenty-seven listed in the database," Michael informed the group.

George raised his hand slightly, "Yes, but only twenty of them need a Resonator to start up. We have the first one here."

Michael turned to Reggie, "Did Bancroft, as he was walking around claiming to be Itzamna, have anything to do with this?"

"Well, I guess that in order for him to totally manifest himself into the role of the Mayan God of the Sun, he must of had pretty good knowledge on what ol' Sol was gonna do – flarewise. Itzamna was right up there with Zeus, Odin and Osiris in other cultures."

Michael listened to the tale but needed some down-to-earth facts. "Perhaps I should be more specific; did Bancroft have anything to do with building these things?"

George looked at Reggie, who shrugged, "I suppose someone had to produce these units. And it was not cheap. How he got the globes, I have no idea. Perhaps They helped him. The frame looks like something he might have had made recently. Why were they dispersed all over the world? We are still looking for answers. I think you are going to find some things out, about Bancroft, which may surprise you."

Parker was still skeptical. "And this trans-wham thing here is connected with all that mystical and mythical stuff? And who the hell are They?"

George held his arms in front of him. "Enough – time is running out. Let's turn this thing on."

Everyone on the rug sat looking at the ancient globe.

George turned to Michael, "Go hook up your computer to the satellite uplink."

"What will I try and connect to? Aren't all the satellites dead?"

George reached into his pocket and pulled out a slip of paper. "I got this from Taylor, under some creative threats. According to the Colonel, Program 3938 is still using three birds that will suit our purpose, and they're still flying. They were in low orbit on the other side of the earth when the flare hit. Here are the specs." He handed the paper to Michael and then looked at his watch. "In twenty minutes, an OC bird will be coming over the horizon. You will only have thirteen minutes to send the activation signal up and get it back to the Transceiver on the downlink, before it flies out of range. Roland, why don't you help him?"

Roland, who had been sitting in the shadow of the object, spellbound, quickly rose to his feet. "Anything to help, sir."

"Hey."

"Sorry . . . George."

Michael picked up his laptop as Roland was already moving to the satellite dish.

George held out the Resonator to Reggie. "Would you like to do the honors, Doctor Adams?"

"This is a lifetime's reward, George," the once demeaned man humbly spoke, as he took the crystal and stone token from George's hand.

He stood and carefully leaned upon the Transceiver's cold metal frame and reached over to place the glyph-inscribed amulet upon the flatted top of the glass sphere. The Crystal side was carefully placed to face down.

George kept track of the time, staring intensely at his watch, providing a verbal count-down to Michael.

"Two minutes, twenty seconds, Michael."

Michael had no trouble recreating his configuration with the dish that he had done six months before. He entered the uplink and the separate downlink frequencies of the approaching OC satellite into the required fields on the controller software screen.

The controller came to life. He cut and pasted the 'crate's' address and activation code that he had saved in the original files, into the 'data-to-send' field. He was ready.

"Ten seconds, Michael," George called out.

"All ready here."

A pause, that lasted longer than anyone in the room could remember, was broken by, "Now, Michael."

He hit the Connect command. The laptop's screen displayed a graphic which was intended to indicate the progress of the upload.

Nothing was happening.

"I can't get a connection!" Michael called to George.

"Keep trying, you have time."

Roland leaned over to look at the screen, "It's the ionization in the upper atmosphere. Still there from the flare's effect. It's blocking the signal."

He stood up, obviously anxious, "Keep trying. The ions are in massive magnetic waves, so you have to shoot between them."

Three more attempts were made, all with the same message appearing on his monitor, '*Unable to establish connection.*'

"Four minutes left, Michael," George anxiously announced.

Michael hit the key, one last time.

A micro-satellite, which had been in orbit since 1998 and was just waiting, within its little 16 kilobyte silicon soul, to do one great thing before its maneuvering fuel would be expended and was destined to die as a fiery display over some drifting shrimp boat in the South China Sea, heard Michael's message.

The little satellite, reaching the limit of its window over Michael's position, received the activation code that was sent. It filtered the data and then streamed it back down on the prescribed frequency to the intended address in the message – just missing an approaching ion cloud. It proudly flew over the horizon.

The globe burst into a radiant shower of violet light as the Resonator seemed to float in mid air. The glow moved slowly to the top of the sphere and accumulated into an intense singular beam of swirling purple and blue light; shooting straight up. The photon mass was smashing though the ionosphere like bullets hitting a feather pillow. The tent instantly filled with the smell of ozone, and the tiny hairs on everyone's arms stood to attention.

As the beams' light spun faster, the colors began to disappear. Leaving a column of what appeared to be a disruption in the air; as if looking thru a swirling stream of water.

Michael's computer shut down immediately, as did the satellite uplink controller it was communicating with.

All three generators in the compound yard sputtered and quit, bringing down all of the lights in and around the fenced area. The only illumination within 40 forty miles was the glowing purple tent and the florescent bulbs in the mess hall.

But there was a sound -- a perfect sound. A perfect chord which emanating from the device. Not loud, just present.

Parker was on his feet and waving his hands. "Son of a bitch!" The tattoos on both of his hands felt as if they were on fire. He looked to Michael and Roland. They were flailing their hands also.

Reggie was just looking down at his own deep purple tattoos and smiling.

Parker quickly moved backwards, towards the tent opening. He stopped cold at the sound of drums –- metal drums. It was coming from outside of the tent in some rhythmic pattern older than recorded history.

Michael and Roland had moved along the canvas wall and were standing next to Parker.

All three watched as George stood to the side of the glowing globe, his arms raised to the heavens. He had taken the Eagle feather from his sacred wooden box and had placed it in his hair. He was chanting lines of an ancient poem that was passed to him as a young man, during his shaman education days with his grandfather. The words were never expected to be ever spoken, just passed down. Until this moment - - they were never *required* to be spoken.

The three spectators quickly moved out of the tent and walked to where a silent crowd had formed thirty yards away.

As he looked to the east of the tent, Parker could see where the steady beating was coming from. Eight people were pounding on four large empty oil drums, in the same cadence; while fifteen more had formed a large round circle. They began to sing.

A fire had been lit from the remains of the wooden crate the Thing had arrived in. The blaze was growing larger in the center of the gathering.

Tara pushed her way through the crowd around the tent. "Ian, you OK?"

Parker moved in to face her. "What, you were worried about me?" he said with a smile.

"Ah, no . . . just, concerned . . . about *all* of you," she said.

"I see." He didn't believe her.

She looked around him. "What the hell is going on in there?"

"Where?"

She pointed at the glowing tent behind him. "Right there!"

He looked over his shoulder, "Oh, that. Just a science experiment."

He turned to look at the circled grouping of people, "Can you tell me, what's going on over there?"

"It's an awakening song," she said.

He turned back to face her. "Well, I guess it's working – 'cause something just woke up in that tent."

She looked around and asked "Where's George?"

"He's in there, talking to a big light bulb."

Roland stood to the side of the crowd, his hands covering his face, but still looking at the tent through his open fingers.

Michael put his hand on the scientist's upper arm. "You OK?"

Roland slowly moved his hands off his face, while still pressing his burning palms together, in a prayerful position. He was smiling as he pointed his fingers at the tent.

"It's creating a resonating vortex. Can you see it? Can't you hear it?"

Michael glanced over to the drum-beaters and singers moving about the circle. "I hear a lot of things right now. Do you mean that weird note-song we heard before the banging started?"

"It's still there. You just have to focus on it."

"You think we got zapped when it started up? I mean beta-particles and stuff?" Michael asked, trying to search for the sound that was filling his head minutes before.

"I think the only things that were affected during the startup were electromagnetic fields. I assume that those power generator's electronically controlled fuel-injection systems were saturated. Anything with a microprocessor chip would shut down.

Michael looked over to the Mess Tent, "Why are the lights still on there?"

Roland turned to see the tent with every overhead bulb shinning bright. "I don't know. They couldn't be running on the backup bank of batteries, because the inverter would be out, too. It has a microprocessor in it to control voltage and things."

At that moment, the rumbling of one of the generators shook the ground, followed by the other two coming online, once again flooding the compound with light and shadows.

Roland looked around the compound, "Everything should be OK now. The surge is over."

Michael nodded and smiled. "My laptop and satellite link died, too. Think they're gonna work again?"

"No harm done, I'm sure. How's your watch?"

Michael looked at his battery powered timepiece. "Seems to be running."

Roland showed Michael his own watch. It was an older, windup spring type. Michael's watch was almost five minutes behind.

"At least it came back on," Michael said, shaking his wrist and listening for any sound coming from the timepiece.

"How are your hands?" he asked.

Michael looked at his tattoos. "The burning seems to have subsided."

"It must have been caused during the beams' ramp-up, also. The signal generation passed through the LiquiCode bandwidth. I wouldn't recommend for anyone to stick their hand right into the beam that's shooting out of the top of the thing. It would probably dissolve the entire arm from the inside out."

Roland crossed his arms, "I think a lot of things are going to start coming back on now, if we can find the rest of the Resonators. That's assuming that you know where all twenty-seven crates are located."

"We have their locations," Michael assured him.

Roland rubbed his forehead, "It has been a long six months for the peoples of this planet. I think a couple thousand years of questions are going to be answered, very soon."

They all stood and watched the drum-beaters and singers. There was something in the air almost -- holy.

Chapter Nine

George appeared at the opening of the tent. He was motioning to the three, who had bravely exited when the device had begun to scatter its brilliant violet beams into the night sky.

Tara nudged Parker's arm. "I think George wants you to go back into the tent."

Parker alerted the others and pointed at the tent, "Time to go back in."

He took Tara's hand. "Come on, I may need back-up." She flushed as she felt his fingers intertwine with hers. She followed without dissent.

Four now entered the tent; Roland, Michael and Parker with Tara in tow.

They all sat in a semi-circle, facing George. Resting on the rug was his treasured wooden box. Martin had moved to lie beside George, and Reggie sat to his right.

The interior of the tent was still aglow with the light emitting from the top of the device, but the intensity had diminished. The beam was now a curtain of swirling light.

George still had the feather in his hair, "Well, I think we may have begun a new journey."

"I've been on one for quite a while now," Parker spoke, looking down at the rug, as he reflected back over the past few months.

"I mean the entire human race, Parker."

Reggie held up his hand. "I would just like to say a few words, if I may?" George nodded.

"I believe, and you can correct me if I am wrong, Roland, that this device is *not* a Transceiver."

George looked puzzled and turned his attention to Roland. "Is this true?"

Roland squirmed a bit, as if sitting on a sharp rock. "Well, I was not going to jump right in with that determination, but, yes . . . from everything that I have witnessed, I do believe that Doctor Adams is correct." He pointed at the glowing object. "I can safely say that all of the devices will have this external design, although not all of them will be . . . this."

Michael leaned towards Roland. "What do you mean '*this*'?"

Roland sighed, "This . . . is a Relativistic Electron Beam Generator."

George was the first to speak up after the long pause that followed, which consisted of every non-science person in the fabric room looking around, playing with small stones and scratching their heads.

"What are you talking about?" he asked.

"Doctor Adams was correct in assuming that this might be a Mayan Vinculum Transceiver, as that was what this device *could have been*, by all accounts within the remaining Maya texts. But, there was a chance, as there is in translating any series of ancient documents, that the interpretations of 'the seven powers of light' could mean a lot of things."

"As it is supposed to be a combined *system*, if you will, there should be a relativistic electron Beam Generator activated by an individual Resonator and one Transceiver per system."

He drew a rough diagram in the dirt:

When these two devices are activated, the Vinculum Transceiver will be able to send and receive data out to another Transceiver, in a similar configuration. The beam and Transceiver can be up to 400 miles apart, but shouldn't be any closer than twenty miles."

He drew a second diagram:

"There can also be two Beam Generators and a Transceiver, like this."

"Or, six Beam Generators and a Transceiver; to cover an area of over 3000 miles. Like this one."

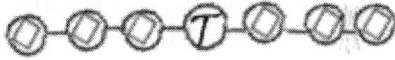

Parker had a look of total confusion, "So the glyph on the Resonator only turns on one of those huge purple beam-shooting things? And when you put one within 400 miles of a Transceiver, it turns it on?

"Not a purple beam thing, it is a relativistic electron Beam Generator," the good doctor corrected. "Yes, that is correct. It will activate the Transceiver."

George turned back to Reggie. "Does it matter which Resonators are used to get the Beam Generator to activate?"

"I don't think it matters." Reggie began touching his left palm with his right fingers, "Remember that the total number of Sacred Sign glyphs is twenty? And each one of the Resonators will be one of these Signs? Each Beam Generator requires a Resonator to activate them – and again, I don't think it matters which Resonator gets plugged into a Generator. The Transceivers do not need a Resonator. They will come on automatically when the closest Beam Generator in its network is turned on; then you can just keep adding more beam devices for more power."

Parker crossed his arms, "This has been real fun, Gentlemen. Now, just exactly what is this 'system' supposed to do?"

Roland looked at Reggie, who nodded. Roland sat up straight. "When a connection is made, data may flow."

Parker slapped his legs and started to stand up. "Well, that solves it for me." Tara held his arm and brought him back down to the rug.

George chuckled, The Nations have a saying, "The higher you climb, the farther you will see. If you can reach the stars, you will see tomorrow -- and yesterday will see you."

Roland nodded his head, "That is *so* much better than the connection thing."

Reggie touched his lower lip, "It is amazing how the ancients knew of such things." He pointed at Michael, "You said that there were twenty-seven crates in the database. Do you know where they are located, exactly?"

Michael stood up, "Let me go over to my laptop. The locations are in there." He walked around the glowing globe and over to where the laptop and satellite uplink equipment were still connected to each other.

George thought about the number of crates that Reggie had spoken of for a moment and the drawings in the dirt. "If we need a Resonator for each Beam Generator and out of the twenty-seven crates . . ."

Reggie pointed at the drawings in the dirt. "To make it work out, there should be seven Mayan Vinculum Transceivers and twenty Beam Generators, which will require a Resonator each."

"We have one Resonator. You have any idea where the other nineteen might be?"

Reggie nodded and smiled, "Things are looking up in that department."

George rubbed his chin, "Well, step one is to verify the location of the crates and get our people to bring them to the surface. Then get them to a central location."

Roland spoke up, "That won't be necessary, George. As long as they are within 400 miles of each other, they can 'talk' to each other."

Parker looked at Reggie, who was smiling. "Wait a minute . . . are you saying that if there was a crate on the surface at each MF, which are less than 400 miles apart, that they would make up a system? That would cover the whole length of the United States."

"Exactly, Mister Parker."

"Then that would mean if MF-6 had a crate with a Transceiver in it, the thing would be operating now?"

Doctor Adams held up his hand, "*If* it was on the surface, and I am confident that it is not. Let's just say that it is within range to receive power from this Beam. However, it would have to be manually turned on first to begin any transmissions."

The vibrations were felt first – they were different from what the generators had created. These were low and pulsating.

George sprang to his feet. "Captain Somers, prepare for incoming!"

Tara had already jumped up and was running to the tent opening. "Yes, sir!"

"Get the civilians to cover!" he yelled after her.

Michael looked up at George. "What is it?"

"Helicopter gun ships -- and they aren't ours."

Parker turned and called to George, who had picked up his hat and was following Martin out of the tent. "Why wouldn't they be ours?"

George stopped, put on his hat and looked back at the stunned group, still sitting on the rug. "We don't *have* any helicopters."

Chapter Ten

The first two rockets hit the motor pool, sending three shattered vehicles tumbling into the fence. The ensuing flames engulfed two trucks and the maintenance tent.

The power generators were immediately shut down and the ceremonial fire was quickly extinguished. The compound was as dark as it could get, considering there was a glowing purple tent illuminating the whole center of the area.

The three former Deep Purple employees were on their hands and knees, moving towards the exit.

"Think we can make it over to Vern's van?" Roland asked.

"I think the van may be flying over to us in a minute," Parker answered, now lying on the dirt floor and peering out of the shelter's opening.

Gunfire could be heard from scores of locations around the compound, mixed with the roar of the gun ships as they passed overhead, returning fire.

"How many helicopters do you see?" Reggie yelled from behind Roland.

"I've counted three so far, could be more – hard to tell," Parker replied, trying to look up into the black sky, without crawling further out into the open.

Roland crawled up to where Parker was lying. "Who are they?" Parker shook his head.

He turned around and called back to Reggie. "Who are they?"

"The ESA."

George and Martin ran up to the three prone figures at the tent entrance. "The tent is lighting up the whole compound. We're sitting ducks!"

Reggie crawled to the front. "They won't attack the device – that's what they want!"

George dropped to both knees. "OK, but can we shut the damn thing down? Turn off the beam somehow?"

Over the sound of a large explosion to their right, Reggie tried to maintain his wits, "We will need something to reach in and remove the Resonator from the glass dome. We can't just reach up there and grab it. And I don't know what will happen if we do try to shut it down."

Another explosion, not over twenty yards away, caused George to drop to his stomach. Martin turned and growled at the flying dirt and shrapnel streaking over their heads. He lowered his head and walked slowly back into the tent.

A straight line of bullets ripped through the top of the tent as the sides were battered by the down draft from another attack helicopter making a strafing run on the camp.

"Shut that down! People are dying out here!" screamed George.

An explosion behind George sent him catapulting into the tent, to lay limp in the purple-tinted light.

Martin was on his feet and running over to George, even before the old man had quit rolling. The warrior raised his hand towards the Beam Generator. "Shut . . . it off." His hand went limp.

Michael had quit scanning for crate locations on his laptop and had crawled backwards to the center of the tent. He stood up and was facing the glowing sphere. At the far end of the room was a spare metal tent pole lying in the dirt.

He ran to the shaft and returned with it to stand a couple of feet from the beam-spewing demon. It was madness.

Squinting from the intense vibration of air and trying to shield his face from the beam that was heating his skin from within, he slowly pushed the metal tube towards the Resonator that was barely visible in the torrent of beams emissions.

Everyone at the entrance had turned around and was watching the end of the pole get closer to the center of the pulsating glass dome. Michael was sure that if he could just hit the Resonator and knock it off the globe, the device would shut down. Everyone else, including the old dog, was hoping for the same.

As the tent pole was within two inches of the crystal glyph, a spiraling finger of violet plasma rushed up the shaft and into Michael's hands. A spectral force surged into his body, causing his head to jerk back suddenly. As a transparent coat of light covered his body he struggled to lean forward and violently shoved the pole at the Resonator. It was a direct hit, causing the amulet to fly straight back off the dome. At the same time the blanket of charged particles, surrounding his body, blew out in all directions throwing him to the hard clay floor. Every nerve in his body seemed to be on fire.

His brain began to spin, flooding his mind with bright flashes and abstract images. The pain was deep in his head, beyond anything resembling a head ache. He opened his eyes and could only see the beam swimming back into the globe. He turned his head to look around the tent . . . it was dark, too dark to make out any figures.

Roland began to crawl towards the nearly unconscious Michael. Parker moved faster and reached his friend first. "Michael, you still here?"

He recognized the voice. "I think so, what happened?"

Roland sat next to Parker, who was helping Michael sit up. "The high frequency, or whatever it was, ran up the outside of pole."

The air was still filled with the sounds of gunfire and attacking helicopters.

"They can see the camp from the fires," Parker called out, still looking out of the tent opening.

Roland looked down at Michael, "Remember what happened when we started this thing up? Remember the electrical coils?"

Michael was still in a fog, "Think it would work on the helicopter engines?"

Roland leaned over and picked up the Resonator.

George looked up, his right side bleeding, "Make 'em pay," he commanded between clinched teeth.

CONTINUANCE

Roland stood up and moved to the front of the Beam Generator and slowly placed the Resonator back onto the dome.

The fabric room turned a vibrant violet as the beam began resonating once again. It did not need to be reconfigured, as the Resonator was now able to start it automatically. It was a key.

Michael, once again, felt the pain in his head. He pressed against his skull with his hands, trying desperately to ease the hurting. And his vision was fading faster. He could no longer see anything and his internal organs were fighting to leave his body.

The beam began to violently swirl, building up resonance as would a vicious spinning top. Powerful vibrations were sent smashing into every electrical device within a half-mile – shutting down Michael's computer instantly.

Like the sound of the wings of great Eagles, huge black machines, spinning out of control, with engines dead, fell out of the night sky. They marked their landings in the dark desert, with thunderous balls of orange and red fire.

George looked up at Martin, who was licking the old man's face. George put his face next to Martin's ear. "We did it. We beat 'em good."

Martin seemed to smile, as he faintly wagged his tail at his best friend in this world, and kept licking.

Chapter Eleven

13.0.0.9.2

It was a very solemn time, for the next three days. It was latent grieving for the combined thousands who had never left the MF and for the dead at the Forward Camp.

The cleanup process went slow. Tents of the dead were burned and their possessions given away. The camp was rebuilt and all top five levels of the MF were inhabitable again. All able personnel gladly helped, although no one seemed to be in much of a hurry. It was a time to rest, reflect and gain strength for the obvious challenges ahead.

George had ceremoniously cleaned his feather, after it had touched the ground and it now rested in his box of sacred items – wrapped in a handkerchief which also covered two wedding rings.

It was 9pm, on the fourth day after the attack on the Forward Base. Parker was lying on the couch in his new office on Level 1, tossing a pillow in the air and catching it; sometimes in his hands, mostly with his face. A large portion of his conversation centered about Tara, whom he had spent most of the last fours days with.

Michael's vision had returned to almost normal, although light was bothering him more than before. He had found some sunglasses and wore them most of the time since they had arrived back to the MF.

The pillow tossing activity and Parker's endless chatter about his newest love was aiding in Michael's frustration with his ailing computer. From the time the laptop had rebooted in the tent, after the beam device had turned off and on, nothing worked correctly. He had been struggling for over an hour to get the screen to display some recognizable text. He had rebooted four times, even using the GMCS master program twice.

The time and date readout, in the lower right corner, was just as scrambled – with lines and circles. The home screen of GMCS looked the same and the keyboard functioned, but he could not type in any recognizable text or access his operating system command panel.

"This thing is so screwed," he sighed, hands moving to his lap. "I might as well throw it away."

Parker momentarily halted his pillow tossing, "Maybe Roland was wrong about the coil saturation thing. The surge from the beam might have whacked your machine for good."

"No, it's still operating. All of the objects; graphics, fields and everything, are OK. Just getting lines and circles when I type and everything jumps around."

"You logged in with no problem, right?"

"Yeah, that's the weird thing. The LiquiCode reader knows it's me. It took the keystrokes as normal, with only the asterisks appearing. Then when the main screen comes up, it just has this junk on it."

Michael turned the screen towards Parker.

He sat up and squinted at the screen, "Looks like the fonts got scrambled," he said, then laid back down to resume the pillow toss. "Want me to get in there and fix it?"

Michael turned the screen back to his position, "It's broke enough, thank you. Why does the cursor always go to the end of the field? I can't type anything like I used to. And these characters seem to . . ." He stopped and leaned into the screen and lifted his sunglasses. His mouth opened as his eyes moved quickly about the display. Darting from the top to the bottom, pausing to focus on a particular spot, then back to the top. He blinked and rubbed his eyes. Parker could see a wave of fear come over his friend's face.

Michael quickly shut the cover on the computer and was breathing heavily.

"You OK?"

Michael started to reply, but could not form any coherent words.

Parker lay back on the couch to resume his catching of the falling pillow, for the three-hundredth time, and looked over at Michael, "Don't let it get you so bummed. It's not like you're going to loose your job or anything over it. You have the whole thing backed up on your flash drive anyway. We'll just reload it later."

Parker stopped tossing the pillow, "I wonder how much back-pay I have coming?"

Michael was still staring at the wall and appeared to not be listening to his friend. The glasses had dropped back down on his nose.

Parker continued to talk, "Remember what I said about the flare, when you first mentioned it?"

Michael blinked a couple times and seemed to be back in the conversation, but was staring down at the closed laptop, "Yeah . . . you said you were some kind of expert, or something."

"Well, not an expert . . . but I do know that what happened with the one we had in December; world power outages and the other crap that's goin' on, is *not* the result of a that flare. It doesn't figure. I mean, to do that much damage, the flare would to have been like a huge microwave oven or something and would have needed to last for days. But then I think back to what George said about it all being man-made. That makes more sense than some solar flare."

Michael swallowed hard . . . his mouth had dried up, "Should I call someone in whatever media that is still operating and have them stop the presses?" He tried hard to get into the conversation, "If I was to *somehow* accomplish that, I'm sure my story about three-thousand year old Resonators turning on some bizarre alien beaming thing would probably move your story to page four."

Parker sat up, "Funny, you're a funny guy. I'm serious about the flare thing. I would just like to put some facts on the table here . . . if you can put down that laptop for a few minutes."

Michael lifted his hands off the laptop cover and turned to face Parker, "OK, you have my full attention."

"You want to take those glasses off? It's like I'm talking to a cop."

Michael lifted the frames.

Parker leaned back and pointed, "Whoa. What's the matter with your eyes?"

"What?"

Parker leaned closer to get a better view, "They're . . . kind of yellowish. Didn't you used to have brown eyes? Are you getting jaundice or something? Did that beam burn your eyeballs?"

Michael took off the glasses and used them as a mirror. It was true. His eye pigment was changing, leaving a soft yellow tint around and about the iris. It was happening to both eyes. The left one appeared to have more brown, but it too was becoming blotchy. He could still focus and there was no pain, aside from the increased sensitivity to light.

"I guess that beam really zapped them." He squinted into the reflection. "This is really strange." He put the glasses back on. "Sorry, the light is still a bit too bright for me."

"Fine . . . whatever. OK, back to what I was saying. Suppose some one or some group had all this planned out, like George alluded to – you know, shutting down the infrastructure right when the flare happened. It would have been a perfect cover. And now they can turn on anything they want, depending on some payment or something. Or keep certain areas, in the dark, as it were."

"Well, that would explain a lot of what we are experiencing, because in order for the digital world to fall apart, it would take an incredible EMF, electromagnetic force - - something on a nuclear bomb level. But, if that had happened, any automobile built after 1980 would be dead. They're loaded with microprocessors. You couldn't even get them started. It looks like any device with a chip in it and is on a *network* or communicates with another device, is dead."

Michael was still looking around the room, with his glasses on, to see if his vision had changed. "That would be a neat trick – but to do something like that on a global scale would take more than a group of people. An effort like that would probably require a world-wide organization. And what could they possible gain from doing it?"

"Like anything else, money and power . . . the same old song. You know, it could be some kind of secret government agency or something," Parker said, with a knowing look.

Michael leaned forward with his forearms on his knees, "Are you suggesting that Program 3938 had anything to do with all this? Frankly, I don't think the Program is all that powerful. From what I've seen, it's mainly for monitoring and administrative operations. I mean something like GMCS would be the only thing that could get into every network in the world."

He stopped as Parker pointed at him, "There. I rest my case."

A knock on the door frame caused them both to look at who wanted their attention. It was George.

"Excuse me for breaking into this very interesting conversation, of which I think you should put a lid on for a while."

"Just kicking around a few ideas, that's all."

George walked in the room with a noticeable lean to his walk. He was favoring his left side which had four stitches closing the shrapnel wound he received in the tent. He stopped to face Parker, "I've read most of your account which you wrote while locked in here. Your *journal*, as you put it."

"It was just some way of passing the time."

Michael looked at Parker, "You wrote a journal?"

George walked over to the couch and sat down slowly, uttering a soft groan, "Oh, yes. It's a tell-all about GMCS and the Mayan connection; Bancroft and his supposed insanity. From what I can get out of it, the theme is mainly about the Mushroom Farms and the Program. I enjoyed the part about Executive Order 11490 – I'm sure you didn't enjoy its fallout, Parker . . . over the past six months."

George turned to face Michael, "It tells quite a lot about *your* activities, Michael, before you joined the Program and everything you guys did before and after you came here to MF-7."

Michael was now embarrassed and a bit upset with Parker, "Why didn't you tell me about this 'account'? Now you're passing it around to everyone before I even got a chance to read it?"

Parker tried to defend himself, "I was going to let you read it, someday. George insisted that he get it first."

Michael turned his attention to George, too upset to look at Parker for the moment, "What does it say about me?"

George held up his hand, "Don't get so excited, Michael. From what I've read, it's just Parker writing down a lot of misinformation."

"What?" Parker was shocked and a bit annoyed at the criticism.

"It's true. And I don't put the blame on you or what Michael had told to you . . ."

"What did I tell you?" asked Michael.

George looked back at Michael, "He tells about how you got involved with Gus, Hugh, the MF's and the crates."

"What kind of misinformation could *I* have passed on to Parker?"

"A tremendous amount of what you both saw and heard was exactly what you were supposed to be exposed to. They made sure of that."

Parker looked at Michael, then George, "*They* made sure? Who are They?"

George smiled, "Although, the parts in there about me are very flattering, thank you."

Michael pushed back, "You said They."

"Oh, I say that a lot -- just one of my little expressions. Call it a quirk."

Michael thought for a moment and looked at Parker, "Did Parker write about Red?"

George raised his eyebrows, "Yes, there's quite a lot in there about her. And he tells of you and her getting together."

Michael was really upset over that last bit of information. He pointed at Parker, "And I suppose if the TV networks were operating, you would broadcast *that* bit of news to the whole world."

"Not the *whole* world. I'm sure most don't care about your love exploits. Hmm . . . Actually, *no one* cares."

George stood up, mainly to keep Michael from flying across the room. He sat down slowly, removed his hat and rubbed his eyes with his fingertips.

"I want you both to calm down and listen to what I have to say. You are going to need this information in order to understand what is going to happen in the next few days – possibly weeks – ahead." His voice had become serious and the aura of a master storyteller was filling the room.

"In our legends, a race of people known as the Hav-Musuvian; or as they preferred to be called, just the Mu·Suvians, came to earth thousands of years ago and constructed vast subterranean metropolises. From the stories passed down, they dressed in robes and sandals, as what was later discovered on neo-Grecian urns and murals. Which is pretty weird, 'cause my people had never even heard of the Greeks.

"Unlike we humans, there wasn't an aggressive bone in their bodies. And it just about cost them their entire civilization. As they had not developed any real weaponry, outside of some 'stun-gun' stuff for whacking wild animals, they were helpless in any kind of major conflict. So, they came here – to *raise* a species of war-loving creatures, physically resembling themselves, that could fight their battles for them; humans. In return, they provided technology and guidance to help our deer-skin covered ancestors from becoming extinct.

"An elite ruling body, for human-to-Mu·Suvian interfacing, was established to funnel this guidance down to the masses. It was an organization comprised from a very privileged selection of the earth's most influential leaders. There were warriors, philosophers, statesmen, theologians, scholars, merchants --

every discipline that was required to build a successful civilization was represented."

"When was this *organization* first formed?" Michael asked.

"Now that's an interesting question. Our legends refer to The Seven Tribes or Lodges. And again, how we knew that there were seven other major civilizations out there could have only come from someone that has been around the world a few times. The roots of this organization seem to appear around 6,000 years ago; 4000 B.C. – the time of the Sumerians.

"As I said, the Sumerians were really first and then out of that experiment had risen the Greeks and Egyptians."

He held up his hands with the fingers extended. He lowered each one as he continued.

"There were the Osirians of the Mediterranean – that lead to the Romans and that whole crowd. On the other side of the planet we had the Rama Empire of India, The Shang Dynasty in China and The Aroi Kingdom; which were the Polynesia, Melanesia and Micronesia people. Back in the Americas were the Mayan - Caral – Olmec – Supe - Moche Civilizations of Central America and Peru. This also was the time when the Nations of North America were really forming. That pretty much covered the major portions of the earth. From these seven the rest of the world 'got civilized'."

Parker's eyes were getting wider as his passion for UFO and alien stories was getting refueled. "So, aliens came down here 6,000 years ago and set up the human race? I knew it! Although, I thought it was 78,000 years ago – and they started the Mu or Lemuria Civilization."

George looked for a long moment at his exuberant listener. He searched for a response that would not make Parker out to be a comic book reader, "I know of the Atlantis stories and all that, but I'm leading up to something here that's a bit more relevant to us all. The only truth to that legend, that I am sure of, is the Mu part."

George looked up at the ceiling and pulled on his right ear, "Now, back to the organization I was talking about. The official name of it is The Foundation. Although, it was only rumored to exist and was given many names by those who wanted it destroyed . . . if it did exist.

"It really came into its own, just after the Dark Ages – after the plaque, Rome falling, Barbarians . . . that whole thing. The first major influence was The Crusades. A number of major splinter Councils were established then, you probably heard about the Templar Knights."

Both Parker and Michael nodded.

"The members of these Councils became powerful and very rich in their own cultures. To a point that they could control every aspect of their subject's lives, just by pulling the strings on those they had put in charge under them. And you must understand that during those times control actually meant life or death. As the world became smaller, through exploration, conquest and communications, it was decided that a single entity, or only one cohesive Foundation should be formed – made up of the most powerful individuals of the initial seven. This happened in 1614. The mandate was that all seven must be represented until a *Realignment of The Foundation* by the College of Minds, was to be called again in 400 years."

Parker was on the edge of the couch, "Let me guess – the Foundation is actually the Illuminati."

"That's a name that some have called it. The Foundation is what *we* call it. Again, it was to be never acknowledged as to actually existing, in the eyes of world."

Michael raised his chin, "I'll bet there were a lot of power struggles back then for membership in this Foundation."

George nodded, "It was a very turbulent time, all the way into the 19th century. Various member groups took over countries, some pushed around their religions and a few succeeded in forming new nations -- as all vied for world dominance to be the leaders of a New Foundation. A New World Order, as it were. The smoke sort of cleared in the 1780's and the final selection of members was completed by the Mu·Suvians."

Parker was eating up every word, "So, the Mu·Suvians made the final choices. How many are in this Foundation?"

SHEER **COVER**®

Thank you for ordering Sheer Cover®.

You may have noticed that you are receiving 3 of our 1.5 grams of **Mineral Foundation** in this shipment, but don't worry we have included even more product than promised. Call Customer Care to order more while supplies last.

We would like take this opportunity to introduce our new Sheer Cover Studio™ **Perfect Shade® Mineral Foundation** - that includes 100% natural minerals now with patented colormatching technology. That means you can get a perfect color match, with no blending, no guesswork and no mistakes. Plus, our Perfect Shade® Mineral Foundation is sweat proof and non-comedogenic, so it won't clog pores!

If you would like to order or customize to try this amazing new foundation please contact our friendly Sheer Cover® Studio Customer Care team 24/7 at 800.506.6281.

Should you have any questions, please contact Customer Care or visit us at sheercover.com.

YB.INP467

Customer Care • 24 hours a day, 7 days a week
US: 800-506-6281 • sheercover.com / Canada: 800-892-5359 • sheercover.ca

"I would place the number at around three thousand or so. They are scattered all over the planet. Every major race and world power is represented."

"Then the Mu·Suvians had the most influence, after The Foundation became into being?" Parker eagerly asked.

"They were, and still are, in charge – let there be no mistake. If you think of a pyramid, the Mu·Suvians were the peak and The Foundation, or Illuminati, as you call it, were the second and third levels. The rest of humanity's civilizations and governments are under that."

Parker moved to the edge of his chair, "How can these Mu·Suvians keep control?"

George held out his hands, "You see, whatever the Mu·Suvians provided to the second level, they could easily take away. Just pull the plug, as it were. In truth, The Foundation as a whole mainly concentrates on the day-to-day survivability of the organization. But very limited on what is to come. The Mu·Suvians knew that if humans were left on their own, the world would fall into . . . well, what it has fallen into now."

"Are you saying that humans have taken over The Foundation?" Michael asked.

"Not completely. Thirteen years ago, a faction of The Foundation controlled by the High Stolist, decided that they no longer needed the help and guidance of the Mu·Suvians. They broke the covenant and began a major effort to take control of, not only all the levels below them, but the one above; at any cost to the human race. The other half of the second level still supports the Mu·Suvians and will continue to help the human race enter the next phase of their development. We have been guided and taught for 6,000 years for what is coming, and walking away from our teachers is not a good idea, right now."

"What is coming?" Michael slowly asked.

George rubbed his face as he searched his mind for an answer. He dropped his hands into his lap. "A ship is on its way. An Ark filled with colonists. The next wave, if you will. The bottom line to all this is that their arrival has been delayed, due to the actions of the High Stolist."

Parker was just staring at George, "Where are they going to land?"

George shrugged, "No one really knows, for security reasons. It has been rumored that the location is only known by The Foundation Level One members."

Michael smiled. "I can guess when the original landing date should have been."

George smiled back, "It was December 21st."

He pointed to Michael's laptop, "The GMCS application, in that computer of yours, holds the key to getting the world back on its feet. And possibly, I'm just guessing now, clearing the way for the Arks' landing."

Michael looked down to his computer case, through his yellowing eyes.

Parker held up his hands, "Well, there ya go. The whole Mayan calendar thing, aliens and Illuminati . . . all wrapped up in a one nice package."

"I don't think it's all that nice, or simple," George said. "Most industrialized nations are in bad shape right now. Things didn't go as planned. And the realignment may never take place."

Parker counted with his fingers, "If this *realignment* was to happen in 400 years . . . that means it will take place next year."

George nodded, "That is why all this is happening now. And the *High Stolist,* who is leading the revolt, is running out of time . . . in more ways than one."

Parker looked over to Michael's concerned face then back to George, "From just hearing a few *legends*, George, you seem to know a lot about this Foundation."

Michael pushed it, "Yeah, George. How is it that you came to know so much about the Mu·Suvians, the Illuminati and the whole world dominance thing?" He smiled at Parker and winked.

George renewed the crease in his hat with his fingers, "The Foundation must be a self sustaining entity; governing, financing and defending itself. Hundreds of generations of elite grandfather-to-grandson positions have been sustained to ensure each arm will be managed effectively and in the mandate of the original seven Tribes. It is told that my family rose from the Sumerian TAK-AN-U, the Heavenly Destroyer. You could say that we were the America's Legion. There were also the Asian, Mediterranean, Polynesian – we kept things pretty much safe for the Mu·Suvians, globally, for the past 6,000 years. It was my legacy to lead the forces of The Foundation against all who oppose or threaten it throughout the Americas."

Both Michael and Parker sat up straight. Parker put his hands on his head, "No way! You're like some kind of general of this Foundation or something?"

Michael was still not buying the story, "I find you in a run-down shack in the middle of the desert, and you say that you control an army or something for the Illuminati?" He leaned back, "Right."

George could tell they didn't believe him. "I have some responsibilities, in a few areas, in a few places."

"Then those troops that invaded the MF and guard the Beam Generator are the forces of the *good* Illuminati?" Parker asked.

George smiled, "I have never heard *good* used in the same sentence with Illuminati."

"Then the whole Foundation, as you call them, are bad guys?" Michael said.

"Only half of them, right now." George said softly.

He put his hat back on, "Well, it really doesn't matter if you believe the story or not, right now. I originally came over here to invite you both to take a little ride with me."

"To where?" asked Parker.

"We've been invited to go down to the basement. At 6am tomorrow morning, be at the Level 5, elevator 3 door. I saw Roland a few minutes ago, going back to his old room to get some personal stuff. I told him to be there, too. Now get some sleep. You're both gonna need it." He cautiously stood up to avoid any stitches breaking loose.

As he turned to leave, "Michael, give me that laptop. I assume that you now know what it all means."

Michael was shocked, "Ah, yes. I think so . . . now."

"Good. Hand it over. We need to have this under constant guard, until we get all of the crates and Resonators."

Michael quickly put the laptop and power supply in his case and handed it to George.

"Don't worry. There will be two armed guards watching it at all times."

As he turned to leave, "I really must meet this Red." He smiled at Michael and left the room. Michael jerked his eyes toward Parker; daggers were shooting out.

"I put some of the juicy stuff that Red told me, in the journal. Don't worry, Casanova, I didn't put it *all* in there. It wasn't meant to be a fairy tale. Now if there were pictures . . ."

Michael picked up one of the pillows that had fallen to the floor and threw it at Parker. Michael then sat back and smiled . . . the pictures were still in his head.

However; what Michael had seen on the screen of his laptop earlier and what George had just told them was too overwhelming. The images of Red making love to him slowly swam to the back of his mind. Not gone, just floating. He stood to walk back to his room. "And George told us to get some sleep . . ."

Chapter Twelve

At 6am, Parker and Michael met Roland at the Level 5, elevator 3 door. None of them had slept much.

Parker looked around, "Well, here *we* are . . . where's everyone else?"

"George and Doctor Adams have already gone down. They took two of George's armed guards with them. They will meet us at Winslow's conference room on Level 6."

Michael pushed the button, calling for a ride down to the next level. The doors opened immediately.

As they entered, Parker touched the panel button labeled Six and faced Michael and Roland as the doors closed. "OK, anyone want to tell me why the Basement is not on the panel? I've never even heard that this place had a basement."

Roland added, "I've examined all of the architectural drawings of this complex and nothing about a basement appears. Even in the classified data bases."

"I bet it's just another section of Level 6 that they might be calling the basement. I wouldn't be surprised if it was just some incredibly long acronym. You know how these guys' minds work."

Parker thought for a moment, "Hmm . . . Black Area Suite, Especially Meant . . . something, something?"

Michael could only shake his head, "Nice try. I think it's an office area where they have all of the secret stuff. I bet the vault is there, too."

His mind went back to Red. She had come down here, to the vault. He held his breath as his heart cried for a moment. He missed her more than he could have ever imagined he would miss anyone.

The doors opened.

Waiting for them stood George, his two armed guards, Reggie and Winslow.

Turning to his right, Winslow led the way as the delegation followed him down two corridors, to a double door labeled Basement. When opened, the portal appeared to be large enough for an electric cart. It did have a LiquiCode access panel, but they had all been disabled throughout the complex. He removed a strange looking metal key from his pocket and inserted it into the lock and pushed the override button under the key. The latching mechanism slammed open from within the wall, accompanied by a small buzzing sound indicating that the doors were released.

The group passed through one side of the heavy double doors, with George taking up the rear. He closed it behind him, with the latching mechanism returning to its locking position. All eyes then fixed on the long hallway ahead of them. It did not resemble any other passage in the entire complex. The walls were painted dark grey. There were no lighting fixtures placed in the ceiling to brighten their way. The only illumination crawled from small scones; the types which adorn the shadowy confines of a theater. They were positioned every fifteen feet on alternating sides of the corridor. The small lights provided a minimal amount of illumination and enhancing the ominous ambiance.

Embedded in the concrete floor were small lamps, placed every five feet in the middle of the entire length of the hallway. The soft blue glows commanded the group's path, as an airport runway would employ. The bulbs quietly appeared from the darkness ahead and faded equally behind the group as they progressed; beckoning them to the end of the passageway.

The air was thick with humidity and as Michael looked around, there were no air ducts visible on the walls, as was the customary design of the MF.

As they approached the end of the concrete channel, Michael could see vague images of the group he was in, being reflected back as they moved closer. It was a massive polished elevator door signaling a dead-end to the hallway. The gleaming barrier spanned the ten-foot width of the wall.

Roland moved to Michael's side, "That elevator is not supposed to be here; according to all of the drawings."

Michael leaned towards him, "I don't think *we* are supposed to be here."

They stopped in front of the metal doors as Winslow placed the key into the control panel. The polished panels slid open revealing a stainless steel chamber; industrialized, sterile and uninviting.

George motioned for Winslow to enter first; the group quietly shuffled behind, filling the confining space of the cabinet with sweating faces and various levels of anxiety.

The doors closed.

There were no buttons to request a floor, nor a panel to indicate the status of the journey. And most important; there was no sensation of any movement.

Parker looked around, "Is this thing broke? Are we moving?"

Winslow turned back to face him, "We are moving, Mister Parker."

"Up, down or sideways?"

Winslow showed a shallow smile, "Interesting question."

Parker shifted his weight to his other leg and tried to feel any sensation of movement. He could not. He leaned against the metal wall, expecting a cooling relief from the increasing humidity and heat. The bulkhead was warm and seemed to be increasing in temperature. "How far are we going?"

Winslow remained facing towards the back of the enclosure. "Some say it travels miles. Don't listen to those rumors." He then raised his hand to gain attention. "Would everyone please face to the rear of the elevator?"

Within seconds, the rear of the chamber opened, revealing a badly-lit tunnel. It was 30 feet wide and cut – or rather melted, from solid rock. A concrete walkway, similar to the one in the hallway they had just left, ran down the center. A small ditch, to channel the water secreting from the walls, hugged both sides of the walkway.

And it was hot.

Along the smooth rock face, to the right of the elevator entrance, hung three coats; spaced along a row of hooks.

Winslow stood ahead of the group and pointed at the coats, "Everyone may remove your jackets, coats, what ever . . . and hang them over there. As you can tell, it's a bit warm down here. It will be more comfortable for you to be in shirtsleeves"

Michael put his coat next to Parkers. George placed his jacket on the far hook, but kept his hat on. His pistol was still resting in the holster, hugging his leg.

Winslow signaled for all to follow as he began walking into the tunnel towards a multi-colored glowing chamber, 50 yards ahead. Moisture covered the walls. As the group moved along the walkway, they passed a number of small streams of water flowing down the rock face. Next to the pathway was a stream running towards the opening ahead.

A red and white sign was impaled onto the stone bulkhead, 'No Unauthorized Admittance. Deadly Force Authorized.' *A harbinger of things to come*, thought Michael.

Winslow stopped a few yards before the end of the tunnel, next to a guard sitting at a table beside a yellow and black striped line painted across the floor. He turned to face the group, "Everyone here will be allowed to pass through the security screen, as you all have tattoos. Except George, that is . . ."

"We're not going any farther without him," Michael spoke up.

"Not to worry, I have a security officer coming to meet us with a LiquiCode Visitor badge," Winslow assured him.

"Is it one of Colonel Taylor's goons?" Parker called out.

Winslow looked around at the faces staring back, "No, in this area, the MF Security Forces have no jurisdiction."

"Is it the government?" asked Michael.

Winslow looked at George, who replied to Michael in a far off murmur, "It's *a* government."

Michael nudged Parker to get his attention. He looked to see what Michael was pointing to above their heads. A sign read, *Level R. 2720' to Surface. 1305' Above Sea Level.* They could only stare.

A crackling sound, which Roland remembered from the battle on Level 1, filled the air. An unarmed security officer, with a smooth shaved head, walked into the tunnel through the security screen. The black-uniformed man stood next to Winslow and crossed his arms. He slowly nodded. "So, Strategos Black Rock, you managed to finally get down here . . . again."

"Play nice or *you'll* never get out of here, Major Lansing," George replied with his eyes squinting.

Lansing sneered, "Always with the threats. I can't wait for the action."

George slowly brought up his hand to his holster.

Lansing quickly pointed to his right, "All weapons must be put on that table. Or your brains will be micro-waved as you pass through the security screen. There will not be any second chances."

"So, *that* is what happened to you. You should be more careful in the future," George spoke over his shoulder as he unbuckled his holster and placed it on the table.

Lansing was not amused, "I want your two 'hired guns' to wait out here."

George turned to his Black Shirt guards that had come down the elevator with the group, "It will be fine. Stay here and intimidate that guy at the table." He looked over to Winslow, who had moved to stand before the yellow and black striped line. It was the notification of the security screen beam area.

Lansing looked at George's hands, "Oh, how unfortunate. You didn't bring your ring. You won't be able to get through the security screen without it, you know. Hate to have you get fried in there." He appeared to be enjoying the moment.

George reached into his pocket and brought out a small lead-lined box. He opened it and took out a man's gold ring. The setting was a lion's head with two blue stones for eyes. He placed it on his right hand ring finger. "If my ring has been deactivated and I get fried in the security screen, my 'hired guns' will shoot anything in uniform," George informed Lansing, the only other person wearing the black outfit, besides the guard at the table.

Parker removed his LiquiCode shielding gloves. This time he *wanted* the reader to see him.

Winslow moved through the invisible screen . . . the rest followed. George adjusted his hat and passed with no ill effects. The guard, at the table, breathed a sigh of relief as George's 'hired guns' lowered their weapons.

The chamber they entered was immense . . . stretching for a half-mile on either side of them, up to the smooth rock walls. Ahead of the stunned group, the cavern reached far in the distance.

"It goes on forever," Parker whispered to Michael.

"I would say a couple miles, at least. You could put a small village in here."

But, it did not contain a village . . . it resembled a military base.

Parker, Roland and Michael stood, with mouths open and eyes widened, not believing the scene in front of them.

Built into the walls, on both sides of the complex, were four levels of solid glass offices.

Electric vehicles of all sorts: trucks, carts and forklifts, moved about the installation. Scores of military personnel were visible in the strong illumination of the cave. Although no devices which would cause the lighting could be seen. It radiated from the very walls of the cavern.

Twenty or more structures were situated in clusters. Multi-story buildings and long warehouses stood along a sweeping avenue, running the entire length of the cave. The design of the buildings was as if they were molded from some gelatinous substance and not constructed of steel and brick. And they were all glassy in appearance – a semi-gloss dark blue, almost black.

CONTINUANCE

It was hot. Perhaps over 90 degrees Fahrenheit -- causing wisps of water vapor to slowly form and suck together a hundred feet overhead. Clouds were forming inside this rock-carved city. It was a self-contained micro-climate, a half-mile under the Nevada desert.

Parker was taking in the view, "I've been to a lot of strange places in my time, but this one tops them all."

Michael looked back to George, "What is this place?"

"It's a maintenance and refueling port. The MF above is the support structure; warehousing, communications, administration; the normal stuff."

Michael and Parker turned around together. Parker shook his head, as if to put some pieces of thought back in place, "Normal stuff?"

George crossed his arms as his eyes panned up the walls around him, "Any support that's required for a Mu·Suvian base; like this -- in times like these."

Roland gasped behind Parker as his knees weakened. Parker quickly reached for him, keeping him from collapsing on the concrete floor. "You OK? What the hell's wrong?"

As he was being helped upright, Roland reached a hand out to Reggie, "Is it? Is it really?"

Reggie took off his glasses and began to wipe off a film of mist and sweat from his forehead with a handkerchief, "Yes, I am afraid it's true. I'm sorry, but I could not speak of it before."

Parker and Michael exchanged worrisome glances as Roland regained his balance. He was sweating, but it was a cold sweat. He motioned for Michael to get closer.

"This is an underground base for . . . "

Winslow quickly broke into the conversation, "It is exactly what George has stated." He pointed to a building a hundred yards to their right, "We will be going to that building. Follow me and please watch for ground vehicles. I don't want anyone to get run over, do we George?" He moved quickly ahead, making sure that Roland and Reggie were with him and away from Michael and Parker.

A small truck sped by Parker, missing him by a couple feet. He nudged Michael's arm, pointing at the receding taillights, "Ground vehicle."

He took two steps and stopped in his tracks. Michael looked back. "What?"

"*Ground* vehicle?"

Michael turned to continue walking with the group ahead, "Just the way these military-types talk."

To his left Michael caught a glimpse of what seemed to be a familiar face. He stopped and waited for Parker to catch up with him, "That guy looks like someone I know or have met. Wait. I remember . . . it's Marco."

"What would that beach-bum be doing down here? And I don't see any resemblance."

"That's because he's walking away. If you could have seen his face, you would know it was him."

"Come on, no one's seen Marco for months. Everyone knows that he was 'eliminated' during the first month. I think I saw his name on the casualty list, too. The heat's getting to you."

George walked up behind them, "Something wrong?"

Parker raised his hands and motioned around him, "Duh."

"Welcome to the Basement." He looked down the long tunnel and pointed, "The Tube doors are a mile southwest of here. Down that way."

Parker smiled, "That's amazing that you can tell directions – even down here."

George smiled, "I use the compass on my watchband, not some ancient skill passed down to me."

They walked a few more steps, "How many times have you been down here, George?"

"Oh . . . maybe ten or twenty times."

Parker stopped walking, "Then you *have* been in the MF before."

"Only from the lobby, to the elevators and then down here; I didn't have access to anything else; like wandering around Level Six. It was due to 'Need to Know' and all that security stuff. Although, I was allowed into the Network Operations Center, but only for some briefings and a few operations we conducted."

"But you are some kind of high-level dude in The Foundation. Seems like you could go wherever you wanted," Parker said.

George laughed, "The President of United States can't even get into the Basement and a few other sites scattered around the country. Depends on what you should know . . . and what you shouldn't know."

Parker's thoughts were churning as George put his hand on his shoulder, "You're OK, Parker. I think you might grow up to be something special. We better catch up with the rest of the group. I have an appointment with something in that building."

Chapter Thirteen

The group assembled in the lobby of the four-story building which hugged the wall of the cavern.

A young lady, in the same style of dark uniform that Lansing was wearing, sat at the reception desk. She greeted Winslow in a very distinctive French accent, "Good morning, Monsieur. I will let the *High Stolist* know that you have arrived."

"So, Leigus is here at MF-7. We are honored. What brought him down from his Château in the Alps?" George commented as he sat in a chair against the wall, directly under the air-conditioning vent. He removed his hat and let the cool air cascade down around him.

Winslow turned and matter-of-factly answered, "He thought the situation here needed his personal attention. So sorry you weren't informed. He has given us all a new avowed purpose and goal. Well, actually, we strived for those goals for a very long time. Now, the purpose is obvious."

George rolled his eyes and crossed his legs.

"What is this place?" Parker whispered to Michael.

'It's the Base Operations Building."

"How do you know that?"

"It's printed on the sign outside the doors," Michael said.

"Oh. I didn't catch that."

Parker furled his eyebrows. He did not see any sign when they entered – and he had searched for one. He slowly began walking around the lobby, looking at the art work on the walls. He made his way to the entry doors and stood looking at the activity outside. Small carts moving along the roadway and uniformed personnel carrying cables and tool boxes. He looked back to see Michael taking a seat on the couch and rummaging through a stack of old magazines on the side table.

Parker stretched his arms, as if bored and looking for something to do. He calmly opened the dark-tinted entry doors and stepped out to look around. Standing for only a few moments, he turned around to go back into the lobby. He needed to look for the sign Michael had mentioned. There was a plaque to the right of the door. It was bronze with a strange logo embossed to the left of some symbols. They were unrecognizable.

This isn't good, he thought to himself. He walked back into the lobby.

Michael looked up as Parker stood and stared at him.

"What?" Michael asked.

Parker moved to a chair and sat down, saying nothing but keeping his eyes on Michael.

The lobby elevator door opened and a man in his mid-fifties, dressed in a business suit, emerged. He had an air of someone who demanded attention. An old-world demeanor – as if he was raised amongst royalty. However, the diamond tie pin and massive jeweled rings on both hands compromised the first impression to that of a casino lounge piano player rather than some kind of supreme executive.

His noble nose was framed by a strong jaw and mirrored sunglasses placed his gaze out of other's reach. He stopped three yards from his 'guests' with heels together and arms at his sides.

"Winslow, it is so good to see you again. It has been a month or so, I believe." They nodded to each other as Winslow motioned to his left, towards George.

The venerable Stolist Leigus looked to the stocky man sporting grey braids, "Well, well . . . if it is not the elusive Foundation Level Three Strategos: George Black Rock Day. I must say that this is a *real* surprise."

"What? Not a pleasure?" George replied.

"No, this is defiantly not a pleasure. Ah, I see you have brought along a few new faces. Doctor Adams; I am familiar with his work, but not the rest of your entourage."

George stood up and adjusted his hat, "I got them all in here on the group rate. The brochure said that if I bring four or more we get a free t-shirt. Can we go to someplace more . . . secure?"

"Are you here to do High Minister Chén's bidding . . . or begging?"

Before George could answer the mellifluous insult, the High Stolist turned to the receptionist, "I will meet with our *visitors* up in Conference Room 410. Pourriez-vous en contact avec quelqu'un de mettre un peu de rafraîchissement dans 410?"

The group moved into the elevator, except for Leigus. He said that he needed to talk with the receptionist. They ascended to the fourth floor. Not a word was spoken.

The car doors slid open. Stepping from the elevator, plush wall-to-wall carpet lifted one gently from the cold concrete slab beneath. The mocha-colored walls, adorned with fine art works, supplied an intellectual background for groupings of antique French settees, delicate side tables and large potted plants.

Winslow took the lead to direct everyone into the meeting room. The room was also luxurious; dark carpeting, walnut paneling and a massive conference table. It belied the fact that they were a half mile under a sagebrush strewn desert.

As they took up positions around the table, a blue jumpsuited aide brought in a rolling cart covered with bottles of water and jugs of coffee.

As he placed the cart in the corner, his eyes met Michael's. It was but for a moment, although it allowed Michael to scan every face he had ever met and stored in his memory. It was Bernie from the Network Operations Center. He cautiously shook his head at Michael and quickly looked back to the cart. He arranged the cups, turned and walked to the door, with his head down.

Michael was struck cold as his eyes followed him out. Parker leaned towards him, "Hey, you alright?"

In a low whisper, Michael answered, "Oh, man. Something is really wrong here. If we ever get out of here, I'll tell you all about it."

Winslow moved to stand at the head of the table. The Stolist walked in and seated himself to the right of Winslow. George was across the table from Leigus.

Winslow began, "I must say, this is quite an interesting group we have here this morning."

Leigus broke in and came right to the point, "Sit down, Winslow. We need to get some things on the table." He was not in an amiable mood. "First; the Tube needs to be opened . . . Now. It's been three months. Get your people to open those portal doors. There are some disturbing reports coming in on a new grouping . . . ten days out. I cannot redirect to the Area any longer. If you don't get the Tube open, we will have to take matters into our own hands and blast the entrance open; along with anyone within two miles of it. Second; No one in the community is very pleased about your adversarial actions upstairs. The Foundation still lives by the *lex talionis*, Strategos."

George picked up the pencil lying on the notepad in front of him and rolled it in his hands. Not looking up, "The planet is not too pleased with your antics, either."

Leigus slapped the table, "So? Screw the masses, they don't have a clue what's going on out there. And we sure are not going to tell them more than their little lives can stand. Things have gone pretty well for the past sixty years here. Actually, it's been on track for centuries. The masses need to be guided, by whatever means necessary. We feed their small minds with hope and hand them bread and trinkets. We *have* been providing guidance . . . the whole Supreme Being thing. The 'don't worry, you will be rewarded when you die' dogma. Well, the time had come to begin the next phase . . . and you people got all teary-eyed about the plan and decided to be on *their* side. We need *logos* to prevail. That is our mission – Ma'at."

"With all respect, Stolist, we too seek order in the universe. But, your agenda has become outdated. Despotic rule is no longer the path. We have reached the Promised Plane and you are breaking L'accordo di 1420," George replied calmly.

Leigus motioned in the air, as if swatting away an insect, "Ah, yes, The Agreement. But, we now have in our possession the means to dissolve any agreements. The universe can now belong to us."

George shook his head, "You do not have everything you need . . . *we* have everything you need."

Leigus pointed at George, "When you started conducting attacks on my people, around the MF perimeter three months ago, we knew you were probably going to close the Tube. And, in doing so, cut off our ability to obtain outside supplies or ship any out to our posts. That is why we brought down half of the MF people from upstairs, shut most of the place down and set up support operations here. And as a consequence, we had to cut back on resources to the remainder still up there."

"You didn't have to lock the place down in the first place!" George answered.

"We *didn't* lock it down. The system did. Some damn intelligence took over in GMCS. It thought it was the end of the world or some crap," Leigus said, his hands going up in frustration.

"Well, I'm sure the software just assumed that when you ordered the shut-down of the world's power grids. That would be a great indication that the end was here," George calmly replied.

Leigus brought his hand down hard on the table, "And we did not do that, either!" With a deep breath he composed himself and began straightening his tie.

A strained crooked smile attempted to make the angry man appear personable as he lifted his head, "OK, all cards on the table. We knew that the Solar Flare would take out half of Program 3938 and Chén's satellites. It would be one final swat, in one swift action. We had attempted to move all of *ours* to the other side of the planet, a few days before. But, they would not respond. So, we lost ten of our birds. We are totally dependant on only two satellites and crude land-based communications."

George shrugged, "If you ask nice, High Minister Chén might let you use some of ours." Leigus was not amused. He turned his attention to the table top.

"Gentlemen, here's the situation. We need our Network Operations Center to be back up, as well as all of the other support functions that the MF performs for this base. We can't keep operating on our auxiliary power generators down here. We need all of the data feeds reinstated from upstairs. We've been getting scattered information from Channel 121 down Main Street and supplies from the Area, but that doesn't give us *both* Program's information we are supposed to be getting from the Communications Center on Level Three."

George responded to the man's attempt at civility, "All this can be done, but not using your slave-labor methods that have been in place for the past six months. This is not your 15th century."

Leigus leaned into the table, "Every economic, financial and military conflict on this planet has been influenced by The Foundation since the 12th century. You, above anyone else in this room, are aware of that fact, George. The Foundation has been totally funded by the perpetuation of human warfare from the beginning."

George shook his head, "You know that is not entirely true. We've made great strides in providing investments and reaping the benefits of the economic growth that technology has brought the world. Why, just in the last century; look at what we've brought to this world."

Leigus waved in air, "Oh, yeah; automobile, airplanes, computers . . . all tinker toys. Well, in the long run I'm glad they haven't gone to complete waste and been put to good use. A few world wars, your Viet Nam thing, the Mid-East . . . at least we made some profit on them."

"I'm talking about medicine, education, communications . . . and now unlimited energy and uninhibited exploration. We are almost there."

Leigus pointed a diamond emblazed finger at George, "We better be controlling those efforts in some pretty creative ways and keep the masses in line, or you can kiss The Foundation good-bye. And you know damn well what will happen then. This planet is going to end up as just a fast-food stop for visitors."

George took off his hat and rubbed his head in frustration. "We have come so far. Why do you people think that by disclosing the real facts, humans will rise up and bring down The Foundation?"

Leigus waved George away, "Those are Chén's 'namby-pamby' ideals. I've seen it all, and humans couldn't deal with that. They need to keep believing in mystical hocus-pocus religions. And they need an incentive to do great things – money is one; but choosing between life and death is the most effective that I have come across."

George turned the facts around, "You're just voicing your side of The Foundation. We're talking about the top level here. We've, somehow, reached the New Era without annihilating ourselves. And they didn't sit around on this rock, holding our hands for six millennia, just to make you a God."

Leigus smiled, "A God? Come now, George. I'm just following in the footsteps of my Foundation Level Two predecessors. How *they* were perceived was only due to ignorance on the part of the masses. And believe me, that was an ignorant bunch. I am just an administrator, who has been blessed with a bit of latitude in my management responsibilities . . . in these more enlightened times. But that will only last as long as the goals are reached. I do not have to remind you of certain consequences if they are not."

Leigus shouted, "And speaking of major issues, what the hell is that maniac, Gus Stoddard, up to? He's managed to get every one of those insane dictator republics to back him. We had those lunatics under control until he stepped in. He's in the Yucatan, isn't he? Wasn't that part of your operations area?"

"It still is," George wanted to hit the bastard. Leigus had not taken over Chén's operation, yet. He maintained his self-control and continued. "We want him out of the picture as bad as you do. But, he has one of the crates. We can't afford him destroying it. He has no idea what it is and we don't intend on letting him know, either," George informed him.

The esteemed Stolist then began speaking in a perfect Paiute dialect to George. They both bantered back and forth for five minutes.

Parker and Michael just sat, with hands folded on the table. Both were trying to appear that they were following the conversation. Neither did. Parker had written on his pad; *60 years? What Plan? Gus is on his own? What's a Stolist?* He showed the notes to Michael, who could only shrug and shake his head.

Roland was sitting next to Reggie, four chairs down from Leigus. He picked up his pencil and began writing on his own pad, then turned it to Reggie. '*Comte Saint-Germain?*'

Reggie looked down and quickly wrote, '*Evil survives.*' He quickly scratched out the writing with his pencil. He pushed the pad back to Roland.

Roland could only stare at the stately man ranting at George. He caught a glimpse of the flailing hands and noticed that Leigus did not have LiquiCode tattoos.

Michael looked at Leigus' right hand and nudged Parker, who had also noticed the same lion's head ring that George had put on at the security screen.

George spoke up, in English, "Yes, but we have: the first Beam Generator, a Resonator, a listing of where the other crates are located . . . and Bancroft's personal GMCS, now able to be operated by a GenZ."

Leigus leaned back in his chair and examined one of the large rings on his left hand, "That is just as we had planned. How else could we get all the basic components together – and those needed to make it all work?" He put his hand down and turned to face Michael. A cold chill ran down Michael's spine as he could see himself in the mirrored reflection of Leigus' glasses.

George broke the tension, "Why are you trying to stop the next landing?"

Leigus looked to the ceiling and sighed, "You really want another ark full of *those things* down here?" He lowered his gaze to George, "We have things under control here."

George gritted his teeth, "I can only imagine on what you consider as under control."

Leigus slowly turned to Winslow. "I think we should bring in our Technical Planning Director and provide our guests with a clearer picture of how they have stepped into something bigger than their imaginations."

Winslow walked to the door and whispered to an attendant who turned and left the room. He then returned to his chair, "The Director will be here in a moment."

Parker whispered to Michael, "Can this get any weirder?"

Leigus stood and straightened his jacket, then his diamond studded cuffs, "I must bid you leave, as there are some very important matters that need immediate attention. We do not have much time. I will leave this meeting in the competent hands of Winslow."

"You can't wake a person who is pretending to be asleep," George muttered.

Leigus softly chuckled, shaking his head as he turned and walked to the door. Just as his hand touched the knob, the entrance opened. He called back to the group still sitting at the table, "May I present our Technical Planning Director . . . Elizabeth Redding."

Michael began to rise, but Parker grabbed his arm to hold him in the chair.

Women have a glow about them -- when they are six-months pregnant.

Chapter Fourteen

Elizabeth 'Red' Redding had been recruited by Leigus' people, just after her graduation from Stanford. The yearly harvesting of the nations' newest geniuses by 'agencies and organizations' was viewed as just where 2 percent of the top disappear, after the sheepskin was put in a drawer.

The Foundation mandated that as many GenZ, as could be 'convinced', were to be gathered for key positions in the next cycle.

Officially assigned to the west coast Shadow organization of Program 3938 where she worked with Parker, her prime service was to Leigus. It involved the finalization of technical operations after the solar flare shut-down. This included the gathering and assembly of the Time-Dilation Systems.

She hated to hide all this from Parker, as they had become soul mates and the closet of friends. But the community she was brought into could not take a single chance. And they had watched her intensely; just as they had watched Michael – his whole life.

Red did not look up as she entered the conference room. Her pastel maternity top, black slacks and soft leather dress pumps were far removed from the blue jumpsuits worn by the majority of people in the building. She passed Leigus and walked straight to the open chair where the Stolist had been sitting and put down the folder she was carrying. It was to be just another briefing for some dignitaries. Emotionless rhetoric, expounded to a faceless audience that would rather be eating pastries.

As she looked up and let her eyes pass around the seated attendees in front of her, she shuttered as the stunned faces of Parker and Michael slapped her soul. The room began to spin as she reached for the edge of the table.

Winslow began to rise, "You alright? Would you like some water?"

She looked down to regain her composure and catch her breath . . . afraid and ashamed to look up. She waved him back into his seat. "I'm OK." She had to keep calm. She knew the consequences, for all three of them, if she could not. "Will this be a briefing on . . . ?"

Winslow put on his best managerial pretense, "You need to fill in our visitors on the importance of getting the Tube open and working jointly to get the systems operational. They seem to think that they have an upper hand in both of those issues."

She took a deep breath and raised her head – looking straight ahead to the far wall, "Gentlemen. The Tube needs to be opened immediately and we need to work jointly on bringing the Time-Dilation Systems online."

She picked up her folder and turned to leave.

Winslow reached out to stop her, "Wait a moment, lady. Is that all you've got to say?"

It was too much. She whirled and raised a trembling hand -- jabbing with her finger at the disgusting lump of administrative garbage, "You bastard! Go to hell!"

She looked to her right – as her pointing finger followed her gaze to Michael and Parker. The unwelcome tears that were welling in her eyes were beginning to overflow down her cheeks. She slowly made a fist and dropped it to her side, "I'm sorry. I'm so sorry." She was out the door before either of them could respond.

George had said nothing while Red was in the room. From what he had read in Parkers' journal, he understood the whole spontaneous relationship that had developed between Red and Michael. He also knew the reason. Michael did not . . . Red did.

George rose up to his feet, pushing the chair back, "Winslow. I think it's time we had a tour. All I have heard is people *telling* me that the Tube needs to be opened. I need you to *show* me why."

Winslow, still taken back by Reds belligerent outburst and departure, blinked to clear his head, "By all means. I think now would be an excellent time to focus our attention on that very subject. I must apologize for Miss Redding's conduct. It's really not like her to . . . "

"It's exactly like her," George smiled knowing that Winslow would be doing *her* bidding, in a very short time.

Roland and Reggie stood, as did Winslow. Michael and Parker remained seated.

George turned to Winslow, "We'll meet you all outside, in the hallway."

Winslow walked to the door and went out, wiping his forehead with a handkerchief. Roland and Reggie followed. George moved over to stand behind Michael and Parker. He put his hands on their shoulders.

"We need to move ahead here. Just keep. Don't respond to anything you have seen or are about to see, in any noticeable way that might jeopardize our safety. Or anyone else's for that matter. Save it for when we go back up."

Parker finally released Michael's arm, "No problem, George. We're right behind you." He stood and nudged Michael, who was lost in his own thoughts and emotions.

George pulled a piece of paper out of his pocket and placed it, face down, on the table in front of Michael, "We shall begin here."

"What's this?" asked Michael.

"I want you to turn it over and tell me what it says."

"Is this some kind of test?" Parker asked.

"It will confirm everything that everyone suspects," George answered, crossing his arms.

Michael slowly reached for the paper and turned it over. There were a series of symbols; all resembling those on the outside building plaque.

Parker looked at the paper then at Michael, whose face was tightening and lips pressing together hard.

"Michael?" George asked softly.

"It says, '*Your question cannot be answered because it depends on incorrect assumptions*'"

Parker could only stare, first at the symbols – then at Michael.

George unfolded his arms, "It is an answer to unanswerable question. The response is called Mu."

Michael put his head in his hands, "What is happening to me?"

"It was the Beam Generator. It released your GenZ side. That which has been dormant in you from your birth."

Parker stood up and moved away from the table. Chilling waves of confusion and fear washed over his reasoning. He began walking around in a small circle, one hand buried deep into his pocket, the other on his head. He stopped, facing the wall and put his hand on it. "Michael. What the hell is going on?"

Michael's head was still in his hands, "I don't know, man! I just don't know!" He began to cry.

He had first become aware of his ability to read the symbols when his laptop had switched to the new font, after the Beam Generator had shut it down in the tent.

George touched Michael's shoulder, again. "When you were struck by the Beam's output frequencies – by the way, that would have killed a normal person – did you not experience a change in your thoughts?"

Parker spun around, "A *normal* person?"

George held his hand up, "Just a moment, Parker." He squeezed Michael's shoulder a little tighter, "Did you feel the change, Michael?"

Michael caught his breath, "I felt something. I saw things, like pieces of a puzzle, all jumbled and falling into a picture. I thought it was what you see just before you die. That thing really zapped me."

He turned in his chair and looked up to George, "What did it all mean?"

George moved the chair out beside Michael and sat down. He motioned for Parker to be seated, also.

"Do you remember your mother, Michael? I know she died when you were very young."

Michael looked into George's eyes. *How did he know about his mother?* Michael thought.

"I believe you were only five when she passed. You were then sent to live with your grandmother in Saint Louis, as your father had some *issues* with your birth."

Michael had never heard of any issues. He was told that his father had died in the jungles of Brazil, searching for plants to aid in the fight to cure cancer.

"What are you getting to? Why are you bringing my mother into this?"

George leaned back, "A Black Project was conducted from January 1, 1974 to December 31, 1978. It was called 'GAIA'. It wasn't an acronym, it was the name. In mythology, Gaia was the primal Greek Goddess who was the personification of the Earth. Basically, the mother of all human life; and a string of some pretty powerful Gods."

Parker, who had taken a seat on the other side of table to sort out his new perception of Michael, leaned forward, "George, I think we've had it up to here with voodoo and hocus-pocus crap. Everything is Secret-this and Secret-that. You're going on about The Foundation and Illuminati. I'm sitting a half-mile down in some bizarro-cave of diamond-studded mega maniacs and whackos. We just found out that Red is alive and pregnant, and has been in some kind of leadership role down here. Michael has gone veggie on me and is now able to communicate with Bigfoot. And you're talking about Greek Gods . . ."

"Michael's and Red's mothers were part of GAIA."

Parker stopped in mid-sentence. Michael stopped breathing.

"Approximately two thousand women were impregnated in laboratories with a, now common process, known as *in-vitro fertilization*. The procedure was not really brought to the mainstream until 1981, so there were risks.

"Three of the woman's eggs were fertilized by an advanced DNA biosynthesis process, outside of her body and implanted back into her. Simply put, the donor's contribution was genetically changed to allow for success. It was a more controlled way of achieving a common goal, and would allow for a greater chance of success . . . and less traumatic than the methods that were being practiced up to then."

Parker was visibly upset, "Now wait a minute, are you saying that we were doing some kind of master race crap? That's a crime against humanity, if I ever heard one. Things really hit the fan in the 40's over that one. I hope a lot of people went to jail."

"It was a black project . . . no one goes to jail," George replied, wishing it was different.

Parker sat up, "Are you talking about a new species of human? 'Cause this is really freaking me out, man."

George spoke softly, "It was not to make some kind of super-human or grow an army of invincible soldiers. It was . . . for something else. Let me explain further."

He struggled to search for the right words, "The project produced perfectly normal children. They just exhibited -- some additional skills. Abilities and tolerances that mainstream society, and most theological sectors, would frown on."

"Like what? Could they walk on water and fly?"

George thought for a moment, "No. Not walk on water."

Parker wanted to interrupt, George kept talking.

"The resulting children were classified as *Generation Zero,* or GenZ for short, and have been monitored their whole lives. A few are Deep Purple personnel."

"A few?" Parker asked, really needing more than just *a few* for an answer.

"The program was conducted across four continents and involved nearly every race on earth."

George paused and looked directly into Michael's eyes, "Due to the changes in their DNA recombination, it was discovered that the children of these women were only able to reproduce among themselves. It's just the total opposite of all known hybrids."

George leaned back in his chair and began to draw a circle on the tabletop with his finger. His eyes lost focus. His voice began soft, "Many did not survive the pregnancy."

Michael remembered the two wedding rings in the bowl on George's fireplace mantel. *Was his wife one of the volunteers?* He thought. He did not want to ask. Perhaps George was just sad for the women that did not survive.

Parker was stuck by the great man's sudden sorrow. "George, you say there were two thousand women? How many children were produced?"

George took a deep breath and raised his head, looking to the far corner of the room, "Well, as I said, genetic engineering was not what is today, even though we had guidance from the Mu·Suvians . . . some things went wrong. Even so, the program resulted in 223 births; 4 were twins. The final numbers showed that there were approximately 400 women a year volunteered and 129 children successfully reached adulthood. Forty-two are living in the U.S."

He looked Michael directly in the eyes, "You were born on July 12, 1976. You shall be celebrating your thirty-seventh birthday in a few weeks. You are a GenZ . . . as is Red."

Parker was now sitting with his hands on his head, elbows on the table. He looked over to Michael, "You owe me *two* beers."

Michael, now trembling, was afraid to ask the next question – fearful of his own being. "Then, that means Elizabeth and I are part Mu·Suvian?"

George stood up and held his hand out to Michael, "Let's meet the others in the hall and head outside for the big tour."

Michael squeezed George's hand, almost holding him back, "Can I see her?"

"That may not be up to either you or Red to decide. GAIA is still ongoing, but under the control of Leigus' people now, in an analytical phase. They are tracking and manipulating the first generation of GenZ to make sure there *is* a second generation.

That is one of our missions handed down from the top. Free Generation Two from Leigus' ultimate plans and make sure that one of Gen-Twos takes his or The High Minister's place. That means your daughter, Michael. Her name will be Inanna."

Parker put both hands on the table, "Is that another one of those *written* things, George?"

"It is *carved*, Parker -- upon the stone tablets of the Sumerians."

Chapter Fifteen

The ships were black. All were resting with their noses pointed into the central taxiway like vampire bats waiting to feed. Each sat upon their own individual support structure, whose massive metal wheels straddled two steel rails that intersected into a single set of tracks which were embedded into the solid rock floor. There were no signs of landing gear on the bottom of the crafts, nor portals or windshields. Hoses and cables were burrowing into open panels on the beasts as technicians in blue jump-suits milled around various pieces of support equipment parked about the mobile platforms.

Along the walls ran a network of ominous metal pipes and rectangular channels to house thick coils of cable. White vapor whips occasionally spurt from ice covered joints along the expanse of the ducts. Water was still evident, moistening the slick rock surfaces.

Parker and Michael sat behind George and Reggie and stared at the smooth surfaces of the varied ship designs that Winslow was pointing out. He was sitting in the front of the seven-passenger cart, next to the driver, conducting the tour of the facility. Roland sat alone in the last bench seat. There were four ships on either side of them as they moved slowly down the center of the taxiway, between the gleaming rails.

Signs, filled with the ever increasing strange symbols, were above and around the parked vehicles. Michael was quietly interpreting them to Parker.

"Those first two on the right are called Mantas. Those four on that side are Manta's, too. That larger one, with the back hatch opened, is called a Nylostra. It looks like some kind of troop transport or supply ship."

Parker tried to get a better look, "You could probably get five or six soldiers in there; or a Jeep or two."

Parker pointed at signs hanging off chains stretched across corridors cut into the far wall and others mounted on various posts. Some were in English, others in French and a few in the symbol characters, "What about those?"

Michael translated the signs, "Warehouse 2, Avenue C, Medical Clinic, Main Street . . . "

"Main Street? That's too much," Parker laughed.

Another sign appeared on their right, over a large closed metal door. The plaque was made of bronze and displayed the symbol characters, along with English; Council.

"Is the Council and the Committee the same thing?" Michael spoke aloud.

George turned around, "No. The Committee is made up of the idiots that governed the MF. The Council is the top bananas of The Foundation. Their main rooms are on the other side of that door. And believe me no one gets in there without The Foundation authorizing it." He turned back to face the front of the cart. "And few come out."

Parker looked to his left and pointed at the black 'aircraft', "You think these things really fly? Or are they just prototype models being built down here for secrecy?"

Michael moved his head around to try and get a better view of the objects, "Fly? They don't have wings, landing gear or cockpits. I think they're just molds for making bodies."

"Or, they might be remote-controlled UAVs; Unmanned Aerial Vehicles," Parker suggested.

Winslow turned in his seat to face George, "Well, Mister Black Rock. Are you getting a clearer picture of our urgency in getting the Tube opened? We need to get these out there -- and soon. We've had them parked down here for over three months."

George leaned forward, "The official title is *Strategos* Black Rock, and I need to see what's really going on -- on this side of the opening, first. The size of those Tube's doors are too big to have been built just for these little things on the left."

Winslow turned back to face the front of the cart, "Oh, you will, *Strategos* Black Rock. We are going to where you have never been allowed to venture before." He motioned for the driver to keep moving towards another cavernous gap in the distance.

The group moved along deeper into the passage, entering what appeared to be a manufacturing area. They rode past small buildings where welding touches were discharging hot arcs of flame and sparks, and side tunnels that stretched beyond the capability of anyone's depth perception. Sounds of heavy machinery echoed off the walls, coming from somewhere deeper in the maze of bored-out passageways.

Bright orange overhead cranes, capable of lifting multi-ton payloads, slowly rumbled above them along 100 foot sections of rails, which were secured into the smooth rock walls with colossal bolts.

There were no other signs indicating where they were or what they were looking at – perhaps visitors were never taken this far into the complex.

The vast expanse of the approaching chamber was intimidating as the cart moved closer. It grew to what appeared to be twice the size of the area which they had entered from the MF elevator.

In the dim bluish light radiating out of the cavity ahead, the silhouette of a darkened five story building manifested itself before them. Its form filled the entire span of the breach in the rock. Reflections bounced off huge circular windows or panels on the side as they moved closer. Other sections of the building seemed to be absorbing any light around it.

The structure took on an isosceles triangle shape, with the widest part facing the cart and the pointed tip somewhere in the distance – perhaps 300 feet into the cavern. It rested on fifteen gigantic gleaming metal pads, spaced every thirty yards. The pads themselves were mounted atop ten-foot diameter steel pillars that rose twenty feet above the grey painted concrete floor.

Second and third story catwalks spanned the chamber around the building, with doors leading into offices cut into the walls. Twenty figures could be seen moving about on the metal walkways.

The driver stopped the cart at a security station, with the ominous yellow and black striped line painted on the floor. It was another security shield. George fidgeted with his Lion's Head ring. The guard looked at everyone in the cart and waved it forward.

After safely passing through the portal, the driver turned the cart to the right and parked. Winslow held out his hands toward the structure. "You think this might be reason that the Tube doors need to be so wide, George?"

Michael and Parker gasped as they got their first view of the awesome thing, stretching out longer than a football field, in front of them. It was not a building – it was a ship. A monstrous craft covered by the darkest blue material they had ever seen.

Metallic groaning noises could be heard around the bay, perhaps expansion and contraction of steel beams. There were more pipes running along the walls, with additional hoses and cables feeding up to open hatches around the ship.

Four stairways, protruding down from large open panels on either side of the bow and stern, were being used by scores of uniformed and blue jump-suited personnel. The stairway, on the starboard side of the bow, was almost too far away to make out how any people were using it.

Michael felt Roland's hands grab his shoulder, "It's a Megadrax 4. Oh my God . . . look at it!"

Parker raised up in his seat, "You sure? It might be a model 2 or 3."

Roland pointed over Michael's shoulder, "It has three elongated thruster panels . . . not four, like in the older models. It *has* to be a model 4."

Winslow raised his head to see Roland, "Very good Doctor Jenkins. I see you have been keeping up with the technology."

"No, not at all; no one has actually . . . I mean, *officially* seen one. There were just fuzzy night videos on the web and tons of UFO rumors,"

Winslow smirked, "Oh, hundreds have seen them over the past few decades. Mainly over water, as it's critical to the internal operation of these . . . ships. We just make those that have claimed to have seen them sound like UFO nuts. We have a network of 'professional skeptics' on the payroll that we reward quite handsomely for their debunking services. They get out stories of *temperature inversion* and *swamp gas*. A little game we play with the 'little people'. Of course, we let bits of info *slip out* every now and then. That keeps the die hard researchers off our back and all over whatever government is in office, at the time."

George had been whispering, back and forth, with Reggie.

Winslow noticed the two talking, "You have any questions? Doctor Adams?"

George straightened up in his seat, "Is this one of theirs, or ours?"

"This one is theirs. There are five all together: one in the UK, one in South Africa; another in Australia and one, somewhere in Asia. Actually, this one is High Minister Chén's that the Mu·Suvians let her cruise around in. The only one that is ours is in the UK. You can tell ours by the lights underneath; military and traffic control regulations. It has a white one at each corner and a red one in the middle. It travels all over the planet; doing surveillance, keep the peace and scaring the hell out of the masses."

George's eyes widened, "Is the Minister here?"

Winslow smirked, "No way. This ship had just come in to drop off some supplies from the east coast distribution center and get some maintenance when *your people* closed the Tube doors. It's been sitting here for over three months. The Minister wouldn't dare come down here. Not with the Stolist visiting."

"What about the crew?" George asked.

"We have quarantined them on the ship. Not allowed past the security screen. That keeps everyone honest."

George wanted to confirm some other suspicions, "Then there are no weapons on these Megadrax?"

"None, they're just for transport. You could call her a freighter. Slow moving in near-earth gravity, but makes the long hauls, out there, in no time."

Parker raised his hands, "How about those small ones back there?"

Winslow looked back, perhaps for effect, as the smaller ships were beyond eyesight. He chuckled with glee, "Oh, those are *all* ours. There's twenty-five all together in the America's Squadron. We have two flights stationed here; those eight birds back there."

George adjusted his hat, "And by your meaning of *Ours*, I assume *they* have weapons."

"Like you have never seen," Winslow said, smiling with pride.

George crossed his arms, "And you wondered why we blocked the Tube doors? You would have sent those things after us, when you realized that we're able to activate the beam, instead of the helicopter gun ships."

Winslow attempted to spin his way out of George's statement, "We did not order those helicopters to attack you. The ESA made that decision -- on their own."

George continued, "The ESA does not make decision on its own. I'm sure Leigus had something to do with it."

He adjusted his hat, "Alright, if we open the Tube doors now, what's going to stop you from sending out those ships? I know you don't have any ground forces, so an air attack is all you have. And your ESA mercenaries wouldn't have a chance in hell on breaking through our defenses. They didn't do too well in the MF."

Winslow stood up and pushed out his chest, "I could request an unprecedented session and bring in the United States Armed Forces."

George held out both hands to the pathetic soul who was throwing out more stomach than chest, "Come on, Winslow! You know the *L'accordo di 1420*. You would be dead before you finished your opening remarks. And must I remind you that they have a pretty good idea on what's happening with the world going to hell and who's causing it? You must feel pretty safe down here."

Winslow pointed at the far end of the cavern, "All the more reason to get those doors open. We need to get this ship out. We need to supply the Outposts."

George paused. "I am very aware of what the Polar Base, and the others, may be dealing with. I am sure they had contingency plans for something like this."

Roland leaned forward, between Parker and Michael, and whispered, "Winslow is lying through his teeth. The Outposts can last years without resupply."

Winslow sat down hard and instructed the driver to go back to the MF entrance.

"What are Outposts?" Michael whispered to Roland.

"Do we have an MF at the South Pole?" Parker added.

"I have a hunch," Roland replied and leaned back in his seat.

Winslow never turned around during the trip back or said a word as the group exited the cart at the passageway leading to the MF elevator. Michael looked to the Operation Building. He strained his eyes to see if he could catch a glimpse of Red . . . perhaps looking out a window. He saw nothing.

At the security screen, Michael stood next to Parker and Roland. George and Winslow stood away from the group and were having some kind of altercation. Winslow was waving his arms, George had his crossed. He would occasionally jab his finger into the little fat mans' chest, for emphasis.

When they had finished, George assembled his group and they gathered their weapons and coats. He silently led them into the elevator for the trip up to Level 5. Michael looked at his watch, it was only noon. There was no perception of time in the cavern. It felt like somewhere between yesterday and tomorrow – in a perpetual twilight. Winslow remained on the other side of the security shield.

The doors closed and the cabin began to rise. George was facing the front, "I want all of you in Conference Room 107, at 10am tomorrow."

Nothing more was said as they exited the elevator at different floors and went their own ways.

Chapter Sixteen

Michael had moved back into his old room, 521, a few days earlier. His Program-issued laptop was still there when he re-entered his former prison cell. He had his backpack stuffed with his only possessions; a couple pairs of jeans, three shirts and some basic essentials, which he had been carrying around various locations for the past six months.

Nothing had been touched. Apparently, after he escaped and had taken the crate, no one had gone back into the room. He had cleaned things up and checked the water and air ventilation to make sure nothing had been cut off – all was in order.

His mind was reeling after the events of the past few hours. He walked alone to his door, from the elevator, in a daze. The LiquiCode access system had been reactivated, mainly for privacy of the tenants and elevator security. Michael held up his hand and could hear the lock disengage. He walked in and turned on the TV. An old western had replaced the continuous dogma of the Committee. He went to the kitchenette to make some coffee.

The almost forgotten sound of the phone ringing nearly caused him to drop the glass coffee pot he was holding under the faucet. It was probably Parker.

He put the pot on the counter and walked over to the phone. Picking up the receiver, he answered, "Hey."

He pressed the earpiece against his head as a low voice answered, "Hi."

It was Red.

Michael's stomach began to twist as his mind went blank. He wanted to tell her a million things, over the past few months . . . now was the time and he could not utter a word.

"You there?" she asked.

"Yes, yes . . . I'm here. Sorry, just a bit shocked. How are you? I mean besides being pregnant and all." *Damn, what's the matter with me?* He thought.

"Well, bet *that* was a shock, eh?" *Damn, what's the matter with me?* She thought.

Michael's mind began to unscramble and the impact of what had happened that morning flooded back in his head. "Why didn't you tell me that you were involved with . . . them? And that we were . . . experiments?"

"You wouldn't even have known what I was talking about." He could hear the frustration in her voice.

"You could have told me about The Foundation and the Basement and . . . everything. I had to hear it all from others. It should have been from you. I mean, we're pretty much in the middle of it all, aren't we?"

"I miss you," the beleaguered voice interrupted. "I'm taking a risk on just calling you. You have *not* heard it all. I really need to see you, in more ways than one. I do miss you, I hope you believe that. I've been worried sick about you. Wondering where you are . . . if you were even still alive." Her voice was breaking. "I can't go through this alone anymore."

Michael could hear her sobs as she talked, "I've missed you more than anything in my life. I was sure you were dead. I need to see you."

She took a deep breath to compose her speech, "I'm taking the Mole down Main Street to the Area, day after tomorrow. I'll get off at Tonopah for a few minutes. Can you meet me there?"

There was a long pause.

"Hello? You still there?" she asked.

Michael struggled to make sense of what she was saying, "Mole? Tonopah? What the hell is that all about? I heard Leigus talk about the Mole."

"See, I told you that you've not heard it all," she informed him. "Look, I can't talk for long. Talk with Doctor Adams; and only him. He will fill you in on where to meet me in Tonopah. I'll leave at 8am day after tomorrow and meet you close to 9."

"OK, I'll get in contact with Reggie." He thought for a moment, "How do you know Doctor Adams?"

"I love you," she whispered. The phone went silent.

Michael stood with the phone still to his ear, staring at the floor. He slowly hung up. "I love you, too."

Should I contact George or go straight to Reggie? He wondered. *No, she said to only talk with Reggie.*

He picked up the phone and dialed the Operator – Reggie was in room 5317. That meant he was three aisles over on the same floor as Michael. He called the room.

"Hello?" The good Doctor answered, with hesitation.

"Reggie, it's me, Michael Fields."

"Michael, what can I do for you?"

Michael was not sure how to begin, "What does Main Street and Tonopah mean to you?"

There was a pause, as Reggie was not sure how to continue, "Did you read that on a sign in the Basement? Why do you want to know?"

"I need to get to Tonopah; be there at 9am, day after tomorrow."

"I see. And how are you planning on getting to Tonopah?"

Michael was becoming more anxious, "I don't know. I just have to be there."

"Why do you want to know about Main Street?"

"Ok, look. Red wants to meet me in Tonopah. She said she will be taking something called the Mole down Main Street. That is all I know. Should I know more? Or do I know too much, already?"

"One can never know too much, Michael. I would rather not talk about this on the phone. Want to meet in the Mess Hall on Level 3? Say, in a half hour?"

"OK. That works for me. See you then." He hung up the phone and looked at his watch, it was 12:50. He finished making some coffee and tried to keep himself occupied until his appointment with Reggie. His mind was on overload . . . both parts of it.

The mess hall was more crowded than he had seen it since the liberation. Michael walked in and stood, scanning the tables. Reggie was sitting at a table, far to the left, against the wall. Michael walked over to the little man who was scribbling on a note pad.

"Doctor Adams. Thanks for meeting with me."

"Stop being so formal, Michael. Sit down. I'm glad you called me. There is so much I want to learn about your recent 'enlightenment'. I'm fascinated about what has happened to you, after the beam was activated."

Michael sat down, "Enlightenment. That's an interesting way of putting it. Tell you what, I'll tell you everything about what has happened to me, if you tell me *why* it's happening to me."

"I will try. I see that you did not invite George or Mister Parker."

"Should I have?"

"No. I mean . . . I don't think that's really necessary, at this time."

Michael noticed that the Doctor's quick rejection seemed a bit out of character. A bit too guarded.

"Red told me to contact you about the Mole and . . . "

Reggie held up his hand and looked around, "We need to be careful on this discussion." He pushed the pad of paper, he had been writing on, in front of Michael. There was a crude hand-drawn map of Nevada with three dots and a line connecting them.

Reggie turned to his left, in the chair, and began talking . . . not looking at Michael. "The first dot, at the top, is this MF. I am sure that you were able to read the sign in the Basement that said Main Street."

Michael took Reggie's mannerism as a need to be secretive. He looked down at the pad and without looking up, "Yes, I saw that sign."

"That was the entrance to the underground rail system, which is called Main Street, which runs from here to the Area . . . that would be the dot at the bottom. The dot in the center is Tonopah."

Michael was looking down, but his mind was elsewhere.

"A subway? All the way down to the Area?"

Reggie nodded, "A high-speed train named the Mole; sort of an express line. It's been in operation for quite a while. Actually, it's just one line in the network."

"Well, how come I can't just go down in the Basement and get on there? Why do I need to go to Tonopah?"

"You are not supposed to know about it. You wouldn't want to get on anyway – Leigus would grab you in a minute. They really want to get their hands on you. You have to be very careful. Want some coffee? I was on my way up to the line when you came in. I'll be right back. Why don't you look at the next page while I'm away?"

"OK, sure," Michael again focused on the drawing as Reggie stood up and walked to the coffee area. He turned the page and the chills on his spine started again.

The paper was filled with the symbols . . . and they all made sense to him. He began to read.

'The ships you saw are all flown by The Foundation's pilots. The Mole stops in Tonopah to allow pilots to get on and off. That is where they are stationed for training and housing in a J&K facility. From there they can be sent on missions from Pyramid Base or the Area.

'For the past three months, since the Tube was sealed by George's people, all supplies had to come from the Area. It has put a strain on the entire network's operations.

'Over three thousand Deep Purple personnel have been taken out of MF-7 to support Pyramid Base operations from the Basement and the Area. They did not die, as recorded on the casualty list, although living in a very controlled environment.

'The ships need massive amounts of fresh water for their operation – whether in ice or liquid form. That is the main reason for Pyramid Base under MF-7.

'Be at the main lobby entrance to the MF, at 5am. Max will be waiting.'

Michael turned the note pad over and stared at the table top.

"Here you are. They said that it was just brewed." Reggie put down two full cups of black liquid caffeine.

Michael looked up slowly, "Is this all true?"

"Yes. And it's very dangerous to be talking about it right now. So, did you want any sugar in that?"

Michael shook his head as he pulled a cup towards him, "You made a couple spelling errors."

Adams shrugged, "I'm not a GenZ. I had to learn the Mu·Suvian language on my own. And Miss Redding has helped me greatly."

Michael sat up with a change of spirit, "How well do you know Red?"

"I've known her, ever since her days at Stanford. I first met her when she took one of my classes in ancient languages. It was like teaching English to Shakespeare. I knew right away that she was a GenZ. When she was recruited by Leigus, it was no surprise to me. She was, also, instrumental in getting me involved with the program when the Resonator situation arose."

"Then you've met Parker before?"

"No, never had that opportunity. She talked about him, but don't worry, he is just one of her best friends. But I must be honest; she has really been worried about *you* for the past few months."

"Why does Leigus want me? Just because I'm a GenZ?"

"Yes, that is part of it . . . and in combination with you knowing GMCS, apparently inside and out. And ever since the program switched to Mu·Suvian mode, after the beam reconfigured it, you are the only one who can actually operate it. I imagine *operate* is the correct terminology."

"How do you know that it switched?" Michael asked slowly. He was becoming a bit paranoid with the amount of knowledge Doctor Adams had about him and GMCS.

"That is what Bancroft and Hugh Waterman had designed it to do. When all the pieces were in place, the change would happen. All of the pieces are now in place . . . it was only logical to presume that it had happened. Did it not?"

"Yes, it did," Michael answered, remembering the moment that his mind snapped into the ability to read the symbols.

"Why don't they just grab the laptop? I'm sure there must be a GenZ out there that could learn to operate it."

"All they need is you and the whole application. I am assuming, again, that you have it backed up on some external drive."

"Yes." Again Michael was becoming suspicious.

"Here is the reason I am prying into the software so much. When the time is right, you will need to load that into another laptop; one for each system that is set up. Once the beams are activated on each system, the attached computer will switch to the Mu·Suvian version of GMCS; just as it did in the tent the other night."

"OK, I understand now, but why is the Mu·Suvian mode so important?"

"It will allow us to communicate – back to ourselves."

Doctor Adams stood up and put the note pad under his arm. "I must be going. I shall contact Max to take you to Tonopah. In the mean time, stay in your room and relax. I will see you at tomorrow mornings' meeting. More surprises await you." He made a slight salute gesture and walked out of the room.

Back to ourselves . . . Is that what Roland was trying to explain to us? He thought.

Michael knew that another sleepless night awaited him.

Chapter Seventeen

There were fifteen seated around the table in the MF-7 conference room on Level One. It was exactly 10am. On the screen was a slide displaying the agenda:

1. Discuss Tube Doors
2. Plan to Find Remaining Resonators
3. Bring all Crates to the Surface
4. Gus – where does his crate belong?
5. Generate Beam Configuration Maps
6. Commandeer a ship
7. Restore – Everything

Michael sat next to Parker and across from Roland. All of the people who were at the meeting in the schoolhouse were there, including Vern and Jones. There were a few others whom Michael did not recognize. In total, the congregation consisted of nine men and six women.

Parker nudged Michael, "It's Sunday. Don't we get a day off, every now and then? He looked up at the screen, "Check out number six."

"I see they finally found something for you do to," Michael joked.

"I don't see anything up there for Alien Kids to do . . ." He stopped and quickly looked at Michael. "I'm sorry. I'm just a dumb ass."

"That's OK. You can't help being a dumb ass." He smiled at his friend. "I've been thinking about it a lot. I just have to get used to being a member of the smallest minority on the planet."

"Hey, you already were; super-nerd."

George walked in and moved to stand at the head of the table. Reggie followed him, carrying a cardboard box. He set the box at the other end of the table and sat down. George held out his hands to gain the attention of the anxious assemblage. He still wore the Lion Head Ring.

"Thank you all for being here this morning. As you can see on the screen, there are a number of items that we need to discuss, as well as, some interesting developments that Doctor Adams would like to talk about."

He turned to the screen and indicated the first item with a laser pointer.

"The Tube Doors . . . they want them opened, we want them closed. As you all know, we began our offensive three months ago. The first objective was to take the hill and the Tube entrance dug into the side of it. That proved very successful as our teams managed to weld a row of massive steel bars across the two 200 foot wide doors, preventing them from opening. And intelligence confirms that it was in the nick of time, as they were preparing to begin a series of strikes against our camps . . . using the Mantas."

There was some mumbling around the table, along with the usual head nodding and shoulder shrugging that follows.

"In the Basement they have one triangle ship; that I learned from Doctor Jenkins is called the Megadrax 4, a small troop transport Nylostra and eight Mantas . . . you know about those fighter airships."

Eyebrows went up as the mumbling increased.

George spoke a bit louder, "I visited with some of their high-level people yesterday, accompanied by a few of you in this room, and the Tube issue seemed to be a very high concern of theirs."

He put both hands on the table and leaned forward, "We agreed that the doors will be opened."

Jones raised his hand, "They'll just come after us with those Manta things!"

"No, they won't. And here's why." George stood upright.

"We will only allow the Megadrax to come and go. There are no weapons on her; just equipment to perform atmospheric, geological and biological studies. It's also used for re-supply operations for the Basement and all of the MFs. If the Council agrees, we will board the Megadrax and be transported to wherever we need to go, in order to set up the beam systems. That would also be to the December Pact facilities as well as the other MFs."

"OK, so what's so damn important about the Megadrax? Why do we need to let it go?"

George looked around the table, "It is High Minister Chén's personal ship."

All muttered together.

Jones again spoke up, "And what prevents them from sneaking out a Manta when the big ship leaves?"

"Your two tons of explosives; which your teams are going to place around the Tube opening. If a Manta's detected, coming up the Tube . . . you blow the whole damn tunnel to hell."

Jones smiled and slowly leaned back in his chair, nodding to those around the table. "And my boys won't hesitate to do it, either."

George turned back to the screen and pointed to the second bullet. "Where are the remaining Resonators?" He turned back to face the group and pointed over to Reggie. "I would like to turn this portion of the meeting over to Doctor Adams. This is his bailiwick."

Reggie stood up with the cardboard box in front of him. He reached in and pulled out another box; highly polished, hand-crafted and ten inches square. He unlatched the hasp and opened it, slowly turning it to the eyes of his audience. Resting on a bed of red velvet was another Resonator. Michael, Parker and Roland all gasped in unison.

"I had been conducting, with the help of our gifted Network Operation Center team, a thorough search of all ancient artifact dealers and collectors, around the world. We looked into every virtual nook and cranny – and under every rock, as it were; looking for the Resonators. That was until the world's internet went down. However, we did hit it big in Phoenix. A certain 'collector' had three in his possession. This is one of them. The other two are in safe keeping."

Parker spoke up, "And did he want a bazillion bucks for them?"

George answered, "He became very 'willing' to part with them."

Parker rubbed the side of his face, "Oh."

George continued, "So, we now have four Resonators. We will intensify our search for the other sixteen. That brings us to the next item on the list; we need to get the six other crates, which will make up the MF beam system, to the surface. As I mentioned earlier, we do have the Megadrax at our disposal – and the full cooperation of Leigus' people, to make this happen."

He turned back to the screen, "However, we know that Gus has a crate. We don't know if it is a Beam Generator or a Transceiver. And we don't know if it is one of our MF seven. We will find that out when all of the crates are brought up. If he does have one of ours . . . there will be another meeting."

He put the laser pointer down, "That is really all I wanted to talk about today. What we need to do right now will keep us all very busy for at least a couple weeks."

Parker raised his hand, "What about 'stealing a ship'? What's that all about?"

George looked at Michael, "I think Michael will be providing us with that information, after his meetings tomorrow."

Michael was dumbstruck. He looked at Reggie, then at George.

George picked up his hat and adjusted it on his head. "Thank you all for coming. I will be in contact with each of you on your tasks."

He turned and walked out of the room. The others began to file out behind him.

Parker looked at Michael, "You're going to steal a ship?"

Michael was still in shock that George had known about his upcoming trip to Tonopah. "No, no . . . I don't think so." He leaned past Parker to look at Reggie, "You told him?"

"It's for your own good, Michael. Everything has been arranged."

Parker was still in wonderment, "You're going to Tonopah to steal a ship?"

"No. Need to meet Red, when she gets off the Mole."

Parker slumped back in the chair, "It *is* getting weirder."

CHAPTER EIGHTEEN

Michael waved to the guard at the security station and said good morning to the receptionist at the desk. Everything appeared to be back to normal in the MF-7 Lobby. As normal as any subterranean installation could be at 4:47am. No one questioned his appearance or leaving out the Hooterville Road exit. Reggie was right; everything had been arranged.

He walked through the decrepit door of the entrance shack and into the early morning, cool desert. It was always a shock to the system to walk from the elegant MF lobby and into the vastness of sand and tumbleweeds above.

Parked in the circular dirt drive was a midnight blue four-door SUV with police lights on the roof and blackout windows. Leaning against the front fender was a uniformed officer with his hands in his paramilitary jacket pockets. He called out, "Morning."

Michael looked around to see if any other vehicles were on their way down the road towards the dirt drive. No headlights, no sounds, no help. He called back, "Good morning."

The man stood upright and walked forward. He was in his mid-forties, clean shaven and wore a 'white-wall' military haircut. His sidearm, strapped low on his thigh, as a wild-west gunfighter would wear it, was very prominent and unnerving. "You must be Michael. I'm Max."

Michael smiled, while shaking his head, "Wow. I sure wasn't expecting a . . ."

"A cop? Actually I'm a security patrol officer." He stopped two yards in front of Michael. With his square chin and shallow cheek bones, the man could have been a very menacing drill instructor in an earlier life or a prize fighter. He did not offer to shake hands -- keeping his tucked in the jacket pockets.

"Since the blackout, anyone with any law enforcement or military training has been drafted to provide security."

"What about the ESA?" Michael asked.

"Who do you think does the drafting?"

"You're an ESA . . . employee?"

"I suppose, if you followed the pay stub."

Michael was very confused. "So, Doctor Adams is working with the ESA?"

"Nope, just me." Max turned back to the vehicle, "Come on, get in. We have a three and a half hour drive ahead of us. Need to get you to Tonopah by 9. We can talk on the way down."

Max got into the driver's seat as Michael opened the passenger side.

"Hey! I'm riding shotgun!" It was Parker, with his M16 between his knees.

Michael stepped back, "What are you doing . . . in there?"

"Got a call from George last night," Parker answered, putting on his seat belt. "He told me to go with you and keep an eye out for any 'bad guys'."

Max called out of the open car door, "Come on. We need to get rolling." He turned the key and starting the engine.

Michael climbed into the back seat and shut the heavy, bullet-proofed door. He put on his sunglasses. Not that is was really necessary, with the blacked-out windows, but he was becoming more self conscious of his eye color. As of recently, he would catch people staring at his eyes when he talked to them, and not paying attention to what he was saying.

Max put the ominous looking vehicle in gear and turned on the headlights. He flipped a switch that activated the blue flashing lights mounted in the front grille and under the taillights. With dirt and dust plumes rising behind the vehicle, he wasted no time in getting onto the paved highway and headed south.

Max turned his head to the right, keeping his eyes on the road, "Doc Adams said that you need to be at the Tonopah stop by 9. It's normally a three and a half hour drive, but with the roads filled with trailers and people trying to get to Walker Lake and Hawthorne, it may be closer to four."

Michael leaned forward to talk between the front seats, "Why are they headed to Walker Lake?"

"Hawthorne's an Army installation and the lake has fresh water, sort of . . . and hundreds of acres to set up refugee camps. The word got out that food rations and water was there, so trailer camps started springing up. Generators were brought in and portable toilets installed. It's a regular mobile city down there.

Parker had been looking at Max, with a very suspicious gaze. "So, I heard you say that you're with the ESA and you're also friends with Reggie – Doctor Adams?"

Max was doing 85 miles per hour as he passed a dirt covered mobile home, being pulled by a rusty truck with Oregon license plates. The two-lane highway stretched far into the distance, dotted with vehicles of every shape and size; all towing trailers and campers. There was only a smattering of traffic coming north.

"Doctor Adams, or Reggie as you call him, is my uncle. He's my mother's brother. I'm Max Rhodes. He called me and said that Michael had to be at the Main Street stop at 9am, in Tonopah. He knew that I could get him there."

Parker continued, "And the ESA part?"

"Everyone needs something to do," Max replied, with a hollow voice accentuated by a nose that had been obviously broken, more than once.

Parker turned his body in his seat and faced Max, "What's the deal with this Main Street?"

Max looked in his side mirror, for no apparent reason, as there was no one within a hundred miles behind him who would be able to catch up and pass. He rubbed his chin, "It's kind of a super train, or subway thing. It runs from Mount Shasta, down to the Area. About 440 miles altogether. There's a few stops on the route: Shasta, as I mentioned – that's the turnaround . . . then there's Herlong, MF-7, Tonopah and the Area. That's the end of the line. There's two rails down there, so a couple trains can be running in both directions. Each train makes two runs a day; one in the morning and one at night. The whole trip takes about four hours. It's a straight shot, the whole way."

"And this thing's been operating for how long?" Michael asked.

"They had the tunnel bored back in the late seventies. I think the first runs were around '85 or '86. No, wait . . . it was in '84. It was when they were going into development fabrication of the stealth program."

Parker leaned back in his seat, "There's been an underground rail system, running from northern California to the full length of Nevada for almost thirty years?"

"It's just one rail route in a larger network. Some go on the surface, some under it." He looked into the mirror at Michael, "Couldn't have done it without your people's technology though. They had equipment that bored through rock like it was butter. I think it actually melted it. They dug out that whole Basement under MF-7, you know that?"

Reggie must have told him that Michael was a GenZ. Michael wanted to scream that they weren't 'his people', but as he began to lean forward, a wave of sudden warmth came over him. He calmly settled back in his seat and stared at the headrest in front of him. The sounds of the tires on the road and the engine whining disappeared. *Was he a Mu·Suvian? Were they his people? Could it be that he actually had a place where he belonged?"*

Parker was looking at Michael and knew something wasn't right but didn't want to bring it out in the car. He kept the conversation going with Max.

"You said they dug out the Basement? When was that?"

"Some say it was about 4,000 years ago – others think it was only 2,500 or so, after they left the Panamint Mountains over by Death Valley. It seems that they couldn't go any deeper in the caverns that were there. And they needed a lot of fresh water, too. Pyramid Lake was perfect for them."

Parker was really getting into the story, "So, is the MF-7 Basement their only – base?"

"They have one under MF-2 up there near Dayton, Ohio. Actually, *that* whole complex is just for research and development of airframes and bioengineering. It's not for refueling or operations like that. They work closely with Wright-Patterson on a lot of projects. You probably heard about Roswell and all that went on with that, right?"

"Oh, yeah . . ." Parker nodded, as the rumors, tall tales and misinformation melted away. He had to find out who Max really was and how he knew so much about . . . everything. "And just what is it that you do? Or, can do?"

Before Max could answer, Michael jumped in, "What do you know about commandeering a ship?"

Max slowly raised his narrowing eyes to the mirror, "What kind of ship?"

Parker glared at Michael. Michael shrugged and let him take over.

Parker sat upright, "What do you know about the Basement?"

"Just about everything I'm allowed to know. Tell me about where you got this 'commandeering a ship' thing."

Parker leaned back and tried to act nonchalant as he looked out his side window, "Didn't really get it from anywhere, just something we heard . . . wondered if you knew anything about it."

"Stealing an Xlitar or a Manta?" Max asked, between clenched teeth.

Parker jerked his head back to see Max looking straight ahead. His hands were gripping the steering wheel – enough to make his knuckles rise and turn white. His brows had dropped down closer to his chiseled granite face. The only movement around his face was the churning muscle in his jaw and a throbbing vein in his forehead. *What thoughts were spinning in his head?* Parker thought, becoming uncomfortable with a possibly insane driver at the wheel.

"I'll grab whatever you need," Max hissed. "Just get me in the Basement."

"Can you fly one of those things?"

Max stared ahead and spoke in slow whisper, "Like I was born with it attached to my ass. That's what I used to do. Yeah . . . flying silent, at two thousand miles an hour, across a dark sky and out flanking a couple of incomings three hundred miles out . . . now I don't." The angry man stopped talking as some past memory took over his thinking. It was as if he had turned into the shadow of himself; a frame out of a grainy film noir in stark contrasts of black and white.

They passed scores of vehicles towing more trailers. All were filled with household items. It was a scene out of the Dustbowl days, with long lines of desperate souls edging their way to someplace better. Most thinking that even a bad place would be better than what they had left behind.

After another fifteen minutes of mostly driving on the wrong side of the road, Max appeared to be calmer and looked into the rear view mirror at Michael, "Reggie said that you're a GenZ. What can you do?"

Michael saw the man's eyes in the mirror, and was taken back by the fact that more people were learning of his origin, "Nothing. I just do programming."

"Come on, all *you people* can do something special. What is it that you can do special – beyond us regular humans?"

Michael could hear guiltless bigotry – and it was directed at him for the first time in his life. The implied sub-human analysis hurt and it made him shirk into a defensive posture. He did not know how to respond. He looked to Parker, who was just as blind-sided by the question. Michael was livid as he held his hand out, "You think we're comic book characters or something? Alright, I can turn into a potato and cause you humans to have a heart attack with just the blink of one of my eyes."

Max knew better as he looked back in the mirror, "Hey, that's funny. I just wondered if you could read the symbols or speak the language. You know . . . the normal things."

Michael lowered his hand. "So, the normal thing for *my kind* is to be able to read and speak Mu·Suvian? How do you know that?"

"Had a friend once who dealt directly with the Mu·Suvians. He died a while back, but used to talk a lot about the GenZ and what kind of things they could do. Stuff like that. His name was Hugh Waterman."

Parker and Michael could not speak, only stare at each other, with wide-eyed 'what the hell?'

Parker turned to Max, "How did you know Hugh? We both knew him, too. Michael used to work with him."

"That must have been when he was doing that software stuff at NexTrÉ. Did you write code for that program he was working on?"

Who is this guy? Parker questioned himself again.

Michael was wondering the same thing, "I did some software engineering with Hugh. Did you work with him, also?

They were passing through Shurz, entering the Walker River area. Max had slowed to 30 and it seemed like they were crawling. Max was visibly agitated with the speed limit. He appeared to be a pretty high-strung individual.

He continued his story, "A couple black projects back in the early eighties, I was a test pilot for awhile on the stealth projects. Then Hugh contacted me to train for the Mu·Suvian ships. He was really up there in the organization and his word carried a lot of weight. Well, actually they weren't their ships, they were ours -- based on their technology. The only ones they have are those big triangular bastards. They fly those. They're like piloting a billboard. Don't handle the gravity too well, hard to maneuver fast close in to earth. They need to be up there, about 30 miles and out. But, the Manta and Xlitar are some real screaming machines."

Parker spoke to Michael, "I guess Reggie got us the right guy. But, why we need to hijack a ship is beyond me."

Michael pointed at Parker, "Well, you're the one who talked to George last. Didn't you ask him?"

Parker turned back to face the front, "Maybe Red has some more information."

Michael leaned back in the overstuffed seat and looked out the tinted side window. His mind went back to seeing Red standing there, pregnant with his child. *I should marry her, as soon as possible.* He thought. *But, maybe she doesn't want to marry me.*

He thought about his unborn daughter, soon to be placed in a world where she will be even a smaller minority than he is now. The daughter of two GenZ. What would they call her? Real bad names, no doubt. Would she be more of a Mu·Suvian than her parents? George had said something about Sumerian stone carvings, or something. As Parker says, 'It's getting weirder'.

No one spoke for another twenty minutes until the sun blasted a brilliant blue off of Walker Lake, as it appeared over the rise. It was an unnatural site – a huge lake in the middle of the desert.

"Holy cow!" Parker exclaimed. "I thought you were talking about a little desert watering hole."

Max pointed ahead, "That's eighteen miles long and seven miles wide and about eighty-five feet deep. Used to be over two-hundred, but the river feeding it got all screwed up with agriculture needs and stuff."

"You live around this area Max?" Parker asked.

"I'm up towards Tahoe. Need the mountains -- the higher the better."

Michael looked out the windshield, then quickly to his left. He rolled down the window. What appeared to be shadowy groups of vegetation or rock formations turned out to be groupings of trailers and camper shells with an occasional stand of motorcycles.

As the SUV drove down the highway, scores of signs and flags were visible at each encampment. The various types and condition of the trailers and campers could be seen segregated into clumps. There appeared to be a class structure, even in desolation.

Humans need to belong. And where they belong must have a name, or a symbol; otherwise it feels like it is not a legitimate thing to belong to. Each camp had a sign; Road Runners, Wild Aces, Dog Patch . . .

"Looks like a Hippie convention," Parker said. He looked ahead and pointed towards hundreds of mounds of dirt, scattered for miles into the distance, "What are those things?"

Max looked to where Parker was gesturing, "Those are ammunition bunkers. Hawthorne is surrounded by those. This whole area is an Army ammunitions depot."

Max began to slow down as he turned his head to Parker, "Reach in the glove compartment and grab that armband that's in there. And put it on." He looked into the mirror at Michael, "Just sit still and don't say anything."

Michael rolled up his window and looked out of the windshield ahead. There was a military roadblock. Max stopped behind a semi tractor-trailer that was being searched. They were next.

The Army guards were looking at some paperwork the truck driver had handed to them and were pointing at the trailer. The driver climbed out of the cab and was making his way back, to open the doors.

Another guard stepped out, from in front of the truck and waved Max to come forward, into the left lane.

As they stopped, two more guards appeared on Parker's side of the vehicle, with weapons at the ready. The guard on Max's side motioned for him to lower the window.

"Good morning. What is your business in Hawthorne?" he asked.

"Just gonna pass through. Need to get down to Tonopah. Escorting a VIP down there," Max replied.

The guard looked at the logo on the door and then at the armband Parker was wearing, "As a rule, we do not allow ESA personnel to enter our perimeter; especially when they are armed." Parker slowly removed his hands from the barrel of his rifle.

Max smiled, "Well, Sergeant . . . things often are not what they appear to be." He turned his hands over on the steering wheel. Two LiquiCode tattoos were plainly visible in the morning light. Michael and Parker were stunned.

The guard nodded, "And you two?"

They both held up their hands to show the Deep Purple identifiers.

The Sergeant waved to a solider in the guard shack, "Bring over a DP Reader."

The private ran up, holding a handheld LiquiCode Reader.

The Sergeant scanned their hands and looked at the display, "We don't get many or you guys around here. Thought you all went back east."

"Michael Fields, Ian Thomas Parker and Captain Maxwell Rhodes; seems to all check out. You all have DoD secret clearances . . . and above." He handed the scanner back to the private. "Well, I'm not going to ask how DP personnel managed to get an ESA vehicle and uniforms. That's *your* war."

Max wrapped his hands back around the steering wheel. "If you don't tell, neither will we."

"Ok, I'll clear you through our perimeter – with an escort. Stay on the highway and everything will be fine. If you leave this road, for any reason, deadly force is authorized. Understand?"

"Loud and clear, Sergeant."

The guard saluted and waved for the gate to be opened. He then pointed at a heavily armed, armored HMMWV. "You will follow that escort, Sir."

"We will be coming back through, perhaps in a few hours. We gonna have any difficulty on the way back up?"

"I will post your travel plan with the South Gate that you will be returning. There should be no problem, Sir."

Max saluted back and pulled forward. The escort began to move slowly down the road with Max close behind. A turret gunner was pointing a machine gun right at their windshield.

Parker was unglued, "You're a DP? Why in the hell didn't you tell us? Why weren't you locked down in the MF, with the rest of us? And why are you working with the ESA?"

Michael leaned forward, "*Captain* Rhodes?"

Max leaned back, "It wouldn't look good, to the gunner up there, if I started slapping you two ladies around. Now sit back and relax. I'll answer your questions, but only one at a time."

They both did as the good Captain commanded.

"Now, first of all; I'm not one of your Program 3938 DP's. I was brought in under Program 2622. I used to fly for them in the Space Wing."

"What Program? A Space Wing?" Parker stuttered.

"Across the United States you've got seven Mushroom Farms. Four of them are serving The Foundation. They're all built 400 miles apart, along north latitude 39 and 38 minutes. There are also four MFs down in Australia, built along south latitude 26 and 22 minutes. The Foundation runs two of those. They're identical to your structures here, but only four levels deep. Two sets of two. The first one starts from Tinbeerwah on the east coast and the other two are out from Hamelin Pool on the west coast."

Michael and Parker said nothing. The scope of what they were involved in the middle of was beyond grasping, without a pitcher of beer in front of them. Michael wondered if Q's was still in business.

"The Space Wing is an attack group that maintains security around our little neighborhood in the Solar System," Max added.

"Now are know you're bullshitting us," Parker said.

"It paid the bills," Max casually answered.

Nothing more was said as they passed through the South Gate roadblock. The escort pulled into the left lane and let them pass. Max, once again, floored it. There were no vehicles ahead of them. It was 6:45. They would cover the next 100 miles in no time, if Max didn't wrap the SUV around a boulder.

Parker had to ask, "We heard, a while back, that there were five Megadrax ships. One was supposedly in South Africa. You know about that?"

Max nodded, "Yep. The South Africa operations are part of Program 2622. They have their three installations on the same latitude as Australia."

Parker was dumbfounded, "What the hell? Are there MFs all over the place?"

"You mean earth? Oh, yeah," Max answered slowly.

Michael thought hard about his answer. He remembered when he was walked through MF-1 by Barney, the HR guy. Michael had said, 'One of these MFs would really be great on the Moon. Instant colonization, just dig a hole and put it in. Think it will ever happen?'

And Barney had replied, 'The Moon . . . or Mars. All it takes is water and money.'

Parker looked back at Michael, "I bet there's a crate in each one – along with our MFs, that makes 16."

Michael was in agreement, but he was still concerned, "We're going to have to get back into the database and look for the 12 missing ones. George has confiscated my laptop, you know."

Max looked over to Parker, "What crates?"

Parker knew that too much information could be passed around in the present situation – perhaps too much already had been. Or maybe a lot of misinformation. Parker looked down at the ESA armband, "Some supply chain stuff we have to account for. I don't need this on anymore do I?"

"Leave it on for awhile. Not sure who's going to be at the stop."

"What about me?" Michael asked.

Max thought for a moment, "If the question comes up, you are our prisoner. We're taking you someplace . . . I'll think of something."

The highway had been clear of any traffic, in either direction. Max would occasionally reach 95 miles per hour on the straight-aways but would always maintain control. No one talked for the next half hour until they reached the Tonopah city limits. It was nearing 8am.

Max rolled down his window as he slowed to the required twenty-five miles per hour speed limit. "We should be out to the Main Street stop in about twenty minutes. It's ten miles east of town. We made good time, considering everything down to and through Hawthorne." He reached down and turned off the blinking lights. "Don't want to be too conspicuous."

Max looked back to Michael, "Never did ask you why you had to get to the stop by 0900."

"Having a meeting," Michael answered, not comfortable about saying any more.

"How long you gonna take? I need to go gas up for the trip back. That station over there is up and running – must be on some generators."

Michael looked to Parker, who only shrugged. "Well, shouldn't be more than a half hour; probably less."

They turned east and within ten minutes were pulling into a dirt lot, next to an old airport hangar. Max stopped, "Here we are."

Michael rolled down his window and looked out. An Air Force van was parked near the rear of the building. There was no other sign of life.

Max turned off the engine and opened his door. "OK, you can take that armband off now. Let's go in."

They walked to a side entrance displaying a sign on the outside wall, 'No Unauthorized Admittance'. Max led them in.

A soldier was sitting at a desk, just inside the hallway entrance. "I'm sorry, ESA personnel are not allowed to be in . . ." Max held up his tattooed hands. Michael and Parker followed suit.

The guard pulled a LiquiCode reader out of the top drawer and scanned the trio. He looked down at the display and back up at Max, "Very good, Sir. Please continue through those doors."

They entered another hallway, with an elevator door to the left. Michael took off his glasses in the dark passage.

Max pointed at the elevator door, "OK, here ya' go. Just hit the down button -- there's only one on the panel. It'll take you down to Main Street. I'll be back in about an hour. Gonna grab something to eat, too. Have fun." He turned and left the building.

Michael pushed the elevator call button. The doors opened immediately. Just as Max had said, there was only one button on the panel. Parker pushed it and they descended.

"How far down do you think this goes?" Michael asked.

"It would have to be at least ten stories or more. We're at a higher altitude here than the MF. I don't know, I'm just rambling."

The car slowed and the doors opened to a brightly lit subway-style stop. White tile covered the walls and the floor was painted a spotless light grey. The temperature was pleasant and the air smelled unusually fresh for a subway. Michael put his sunglasses back on.

Two soldiers were standing by the rails. An Asian woman, whom appeared to be in her late fifties, was seated at a bench. And a young man, in his early twenties, leaned against a pillar . . . he had the look of a barn-storming pilot of ages past. They paid no attention to Parker and Michael.

Parker looked at the clock on the wall, "Hey, look. We made it with minutes to spare."

Michael crossed his arms, "So, what do you think about Max and all that stuff he was saying about another program – 2622? And him being some kind of Space pilot?"

Parker sighed, "Hate to say it, but from everything that Roland, Reggie and George have been saying – and the fact that there is a Megadrax 4 sitting right under us at the MF . . . it doesn't surprise me at all. Don't know the reason behind it all, but it all sounds plausible."

"I think it all has to do with the Mu·Suvians needing to get the beam systems up. And I don't think The Foundation is doing much to help them."

"And why did Reggie have Max brought in? You know George approved it, or we wouldn't be standing here."

"Because he can fly those ships," Michael recapped.

"And why doesn't he fly them anymore?" Parker asked slowly.

The low rumble was coming from the left, deep in the tunnel. The smell of ozone filled the air as the electric train neared the stop. They turned to see a highly polished, blue and white, bullet-nosed engine emerge from the north end burrow – slowing to a stop with six cars behind it.

Michael's heart was pounding in his chest and was sure others could hear it. Parker slung the rifle over his shoulder and took out his comb. He passed it a few times through his hair. "I look OK?"

"Lovely . . . fix your lipstick," Michael mocked.

The doors to the passenger cars slid open. Red stepped out and onto the platform carrying a bag. She looked around and saw Michael and Parker walking towards her. Her hand covered her mouth and she began to cry.

Michael held out his arm to the side and stopped Parker. "Stay here a second." He walked over to Red and without a second thought grabbed her arms, "I love you. Marry me now. We can get the captain of the train to do it, or something."

She began to laugh and cry at the same time. She flung her arms around his neck and buried her forehead in his shoulder. "Oh, God . . . Michael, I've missed you so much. I love you, too."

Michael hugged her tighter, "How are you? Are you OK?" He leaned back and put his hand on her stomach, "Are you both OK?"

She put her hand over his, "We are both just fine. I'm getting great prenatal care from Doctor Samuelson, down in our Medical Clinic. She is great." She pulled him closer. "We both miss you."

Parker walked up behind Michael, "What about me?"

She looked around Michael and held out her hand to grab Parker's, "Shadows can only be seen in the light . . . I've missed you both." She was trying to talk in between sobs. "The train only stops here for five minutes, I need to talk fast and get back on it. They're expecting me at the Area.

She lifted Michael's glasses. "It's happening, isn't it?"

"What?"

"The Synthesis . . . the change. I have heard rumors of this happening to our kind."

"I don't know anything about a synthesis." Michael could not stop holding her, "It's just an allergy or something."

She pushed back, "You are changing, Michael. There are 387 of us and the odds were that at least one of us had the right combination of genes. She reached down into her bag and took out a greeting card. On the envelope it read, 'Happy Birthday, my love'.

She smiled and handed it to him, "May this be the first of many."

Michael took it, "You remembered. But, it won't be for another two weeks." She kissed him then put her cheek close to his and whispered, "I *will* marry you . . . soon. I've needed you so bad. There's a bond that I can't explain – from the first time I saw you. Please be careful. Our daughter needs *us*. Read the card, it will tell you everything that I want to say. Oh, I love you so much."

She let go and stepped back, wiping her eyes. She reached for Parker's hand, "You take care of him, Ian." She looked at Michael, "He's my mate, you know." She picked up her bag, turned and walked back into the passenger car.

The doors slid shut and the train resumed its clandestine journey.

Michael stood holding the envelope and watched the train disappear into the south bound tunnel.

"Can't you two find an easier way to meet?" Parker put his hand on Michael's back, "Come on. Let's get back upstairs."

They walked out of the hangar entrance and into the brilliant high-desert sun. "So, it was nice that she remembered your birthday. And that card is the first of hundreds? You don't even know *twelve* people. And I doubt even two of them would send you a card," Parker said, shading his eyes. "OK, I'll make you one . . . that'll make two."

Michael smiled, "And where are you going to find crayons?"

Michael opened the envelope and removed the card. It was a standard birthday card with an 'I Love You, x' at the bottom. Inside were four, double-sided pages of a letter. They were all written in Mu·Suvian.

"Now that's cool. Love letters that no one can read but you two."

"Not really," Michael slowly answered, as he quickly scanned the pages. He folded them and put them in his pocket. He slid the card back into the envelope. "I'll read it on the way back to the MF."

The sound of heavy tires grinding down on dirt and stone was coming from around the corner of the hangar. It was Max in the SUV. He stopped next to them.

"You guys done already?"

Parker began walking around to the passenger side, "Yep. Got everything we needed."

Michael opened the rear driver-side door, but stood outside the vehicle looking out into the desert. He did not want to go back to the MF. He wanted to go find Red and run. Run into a tomorrow that had nothing to do with tomorrow. He was drowning in layers of deceit, cover ups and misinformation. The whole big picture, as well as the truth, was still in scattered pieces tumbling around in his head.

"Are you coming with us?" Parker called as he settled in the front seat.

Michael held the envelope tighter in his hand and climbed into the seat. He remained in back of the driver's seat so that he could read the pages Red had given him without Max constantly looking at him in the rear view mirror.

Max put the vehicle in gear and they headed north. Back up to MF-7, and inevitably, the Basement.

Chapter Nineteen

Max dropped Michael and Parker off at the Hooterville entrance to the MF at 1:30 pm. It was a less stressful ride back north, as Max was in no hurry to get anywhere. There was only small talk exchanged between Parker and Max. Michael had been busy digesting the pages of Mu·Suvian text that Red had written and placed into the birthday card.

As Parker and Michael began to walk to the entrance of the shack, Max stuck his head out the window, "When you're ready to grab a ship, let Reggie know. He can get in touch with me."

He spun his tires in the dirt, did a donut in the drive and drove out to the pavement.

"He's some cowboy, huh?" Parker choked, as the dust cloud engulfed both of them.

"More like an outlaw," Michael replied, opening the screen door to the entrance.

Walking through the lobby, to catch the elevator down to Level One, Michael kept his gaze to the floor, "Let's go down and get something to eat. I want to talk about the stuff Red wrote in the letter."

Parker held up his hand tattoo to call for the elevator, "Good idea, I'm starved. And really anxious to hear what she had to say. Hope it was good."

"Just more pieces," Michael said softly, stepping through the open doors and into the gleaming cabinet.

They got off the elevator on Level 1 and took elevator 6 down to the mess hall. The lunch crowd was thinning out as they moved quickly through the line. Parker had loaded his tray with enough to feed three people.

Michael found a table and set down his tray and coffee cup. Parker placed his tray across the table, "Be right back. Need to grab a dessert."

Michael, still wearing his sunglasses, was about to pull the pages that Red written out of his pocket, when Parker walked up. Roland and a young woman were with him. She was petite, with naturally curly, jet black hair. She wore a colorful short summer dress and sandals. He had on clean jeans and a wrinkled cotton shirt. At least the jeans were clean.

Parker sat down, with his dessert plate, "Hey, look who I found hiding over in the corner."

Michael smiled, "Roland, good to see you. And who's your friend?"

"Remember when I told you about the girl in the mess hall? This is her, or this is she . . . anyway, this is Brittani. Brittani, this is Michael. You already met Parker."

Michael lifted his hand in a small wave, "No, you never told us about her. But, it's good to meet you."

Brittani smiled, "Roland and I have been, sort of seeing each other, for the past six months."

Roland reached for her hand, "Actually, we would only smile at each other when I came through the serving line. We never actually talked or anything. We weren't allowed to. We finally got together a couple weeks ago."

"So, that's why your skin has cleared up," Parker joked with a mouthful of potatoes.

Brittani blushed and Roland shook his head, "She's returning to her job in the communications center tomorrow and finally getting out of the mess hall. Well, anyway, it's good that I ran into you two. I dug out something in my storage box that you both should look at. Can I get with you guys a bit later?"

Michael looked at his watch, "We should be up in Parker's *office* at around four o'clock. Come on by then."

Roland and Brittani walked out of the hall.

Parker watched them leave, "I've seen her in here quite a lot. Didn't really think about what was under that blue jumpsuit. You just never know what kind of girl is attracted to a nerd." He turned back to face his food tray and pointed at Michael, "Right?"

CONTINUANCE

Michael reached back into his pocket and pulled out the sheets of paper that were in the birthday card from Red. He placed them on the table, next to his tray.

Parker looked over, "So, what did Red have to say in the letter?"

Michael slid the bottom sheet out and turned it over to show a drawing. He was careful that no one else would be able to see it.

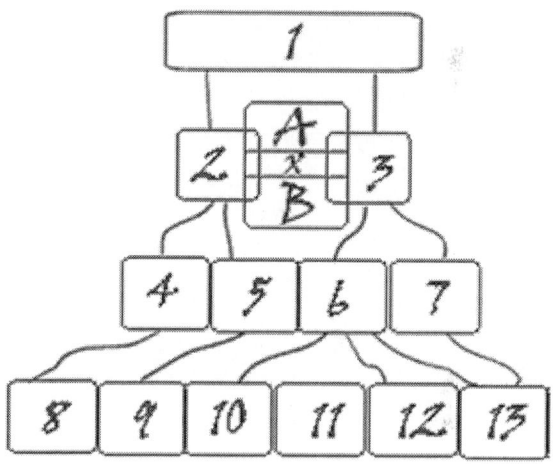

He took out his pen and pointed at the shapes on the page. "She says; 'I have made a diagram of the entire Foundation structure for you to follow. They are numbered so it will mean nothing to anyone who cannot read this text.'"

Parker looked at the drawing, "Man, this is some organizational chart."

Michael began pointing at the boxes as he read the letter, "The top square, number one, are the Mu·Suvians. They are scattered about, with at least a dozen representatives in each of the other boxes below. Their main areas of interest are block numbers 1, A, B, 4, 5 and 11. They trade technology and civilization pathways with the Second Level Foundation leaders

. . . blocks 2 and 3. Leigus is the High Stolist of block 2: High Minister Chén is in command of block 3."

Parker was tracing the lines from each block to another as Michael continued to read.

"Block 4 is government, 5 is financial, 6 is cultural and 7 is defense."

Parker rubbed his chin, "It looks like the Leigus group controls all of the government and financial operations."

Michael used his finger to hold his place in the letter, "Well, listen to this; Blocks 8 and 9 are mostly superpower countries and multinational corporations."

He readjusted his glasses, which were sliding down his nose. "It looks like Leigus' people pull the strings on just about anything that involves politics and money."

Parker pointed at block 3, "What about the ones under Chén?"

"Block 10 is health, welfare and education, 11 is religion, 12 covers agriculture and husbandry and 13 is new technology."

Parker leaned back, "Well, it looks like ol' Stolist Leigus is making the money and Chén is spending it."

Michael raised his pen, "Yes, but remember the old Golden Rule . . . *He who has the gold, makes the rules.*"

Parker leaned back in to the drawing, "At least they got the separation of church and state figured right."

Michael looked at the number 11 block, "Yeah. That one bothers me. I don't even know why that's even on the chart? Neither Leigus nor Chén have a line going to it. Strange."

"What are these A and B?"

Michael returned to the page, "She says that A is Program 3938 and B is Program 2622. All of the MFs are in there, supporting all of the blocks underneath."

Parker was still looking at where the lines connected.

Michael moved down to the bottom of the letter, "Here is the kicker. She says, 'Leigus had formed his own military branch, the ESA, and plans to bring the entire Foundation under his control. This will be done by eliminating High Minister Chén's operations in Blocks 3 and 7. '"

"Isn't George in charge of 7?" Parker asked.

"Sure is," Michael answered.

Parker sat back, "So, Leigus' ESA jumped into action the moment of the flare and blackout."

Michael tapped the table with his pen, "That appears to have been the plan. Then I suppose he would go after the Mu·Suvians; and then have control of everything. And everything includes the entire world."

Parker looked back down at the drawing, "What did The Foundation do before they had the Programs and the MFs?"

"Remember the Pyramids, all over world?" Michael suggested, returning his eyes to the letter.

Parker tapped on the paper with his finger, "You know what Block 2 reminds me of? The Illuminati."

Michael nodded, "I would not be surprised. In fact, looking at the structure and by adding the ESA, I'm pretty sure that is what it is."

Parker leaned back, "So what about that little x, what's that?"

Michael looked up from the page and tapped his nose with his pen, "Red says . . . that x stands for you, me and something called a GenOne."

Michael put down the pen and picked up the papers. Parker was still staring at the spot where the sheets had been lying, his mind racing.

Michael stood up, "Come on. Let's get up to your office."

Parker looked up and pointed at the papers Michael was putting in his pocket, "Why was there a box there for you and me?"

"I really don't know . . . yet. But, I am sure going to find out."

Parker put his hand back on the table and spoke softly, "Michael, I know you must be freaking out, knowing that a part of you is . . ."

"A Mu·Suvian? Listen Ian, a few days ago I was just Michael Fields . . . an orphan with no . . . wait. Maybe I can explain it better."

He sat back down and folded his hands.

"Think back, only a hundred years, where our civilization was and where it was headed. We were just starting to play around with electricity and gasoline engines. We had airplanes that were made of cloth. But, helping us along, step-by-step was a race of people that came here 6,000 years ago from someplace . . . way out there. They didn't give us the answers; they gave us a staircase. And every now and then a gifted individual appeared who could climb the next step and pull the rest of us up."

"Are you talking about Einstein and Tesla?"

"I'm not in a position to even speculate on that. It just seems that when humans needed to reach the next level, the right person always came along. Throughout our evolution; someone discovered fire, invented the wheel, formulated medicines – even music, art and publishing. It's just beyond coincidental or accidental. An idea was flashed into a single mind, all of the components to make it a reality were made clear to them and a lifetime was devoted to make it happen. It became their passion."

Parker squinted, trying to see Michael's eyes through the dark lenses of his glasses, "Did you get zapped with an idea?"

"I don't know. Something happened, I mean, how is it that I can now read Mu·Suvian? And know the things I do about . . . stuff I never knew before? Like the Transceivers and Beams. They're milestones, placed down here, so when our species finally gets to a certain technological level, we will be able to use them."

Parker looked skeptical, "What level would that be?"

"The level we are now. We have the ability to put all the pieces together to activate them."

"We sure have, look what doing that has done to you. Now, I suppose, we need to get to the *next* level and figure out what the hell they're supposed to do."

Michael looked around the room, "I think we are going to find out, real soon." He stood up, "OK, let's go. Roland will be paying us a visit in a little while."

Parker rose to his feet, "You think that if we get all the crates and Resonators, something big is going to happen?"

Michael patted the pages of Red's letter, in his pocket, "Even if Mu·Suvians were only a hundred years ahead of us, think of what they would know? But, it appears to be more like 6,000 years."

"You going to give that diagram to George and tell him what Red said about Leigus?"

Michael adjusted his dark glasses, "I'm not sure, but I think he knows this stuff already. I don't think that we should tell him that we do, too. Not quite yet."

Chapter Twenty

At exactly four o'clock, a knock was heard on the door frame. It was Roland. Parker waved him into the room. The scientist appeared with his own laptop case over his shoulder and a cardboard box. He looked pale as he placed the box on the desk and began to set up the laptop.

Parker and Michael said nothing as Roland began to take items out of the box in a very systematic fashion.

"This is a box of my stuff that was down in the closet of my room." He took out a small box and opened it. "Oh, good, my spare pair of glasses. I didn't think I brought them with me." He took the glasses out of the case and exchanged them on his face. "Well?"

Parker looked at him, "They're the exact same thing as the old ones!"

"No, these aren't cracked," Roland informed him.

After the computer had booted up he removed a large black leather wallet from the carton. "I think it's important for you two to see something."

The wallet had a thick strap attached to the back, running around the ends, locking at the front. He inserted a small key into the mechanism and freed the band. He laid it open on the desk.

Six vinyl sleeves, each holding a single DVD, folded to each side of the opened case. He carefully removed a disk marked *Time Dilation* and placed it into his laptops' drive.

As it began to read the disk, he turned to his two associates, "I didn't think this stuff would ever be relevant to anything, or to anybody I would encounter. I put it together a few years ago after I came across some interesting 'side effects' of Einstein's Relativity Theory. I guess things happen for a reason, for now it seems to be the reason I was brought into the Deep Purple world. And probably the reason they made me a janitor and kept me under watch, after they shut down the MF to the outside world."

He looked closely at Michael, "What happened to your eyes?"

"It's allergies."

"That's very odd. You should see a doctor or something."

The computer screen began displaying animated graphics of folding lines and small spheres moving back and forth across various panels.

Michael leaned closer and pointed at the section that was showing what appeared to be the orbiting planets of our Solar System, with a few extra added. "What's this one all about?"

Roland smiled, as a master would to an astute apprentice, "I see you focused on that one, right away. It is the orbital path of TNOs, more specifically – it is tracking 90482 Orcus."

Parker looked at Roland, "You just make that up -- it's some kind of video game, right?"

"No, it's a real planet. Well, actually, it's a *Trans-Neptunian Object*; just this side of the 50 AU border of the Kuiper Belt."

"Is that where you beamed in from?" Parker was serious.

Roland laughed nervously, knowing the next few minutes would be a hard sell.

Michael motioned for Parker to sit down as he pulled up a chair for himself, "OK, Professor. Fill us in."

Roland took a deep breath and began the most important dissertation of this life.

"When our Solar System was formed, a lot of left over 'stuff' was caught in Neptune's gravitational pull."

"Stuff?" Parker asked.

"Rocks, chucks of ice . . . that kind of stuff." Roland was struggling to put his words into laymen's terms. Stuff may have not been a good choice of words, but Parker seemed to get it.

He continued, "Well, when everything finally came together, forming planets and moons and the like, we had our Solar System. We had the Sun at the center, and everything within its gravitational influence orbiting around it.

"However, there was Neptune. It's located at the very edge of our Solar System and, because of its size, is just barely hanging on to the sun's gravitational pull. If it was any smaller, or any larger, I suspect that it would sail off into space, looking for another sun."

He zoomed in to show Neptune and a number of orbital paths around it.

"It's sixty-times bigger than Earth, so it has its own gravitation influence on that 'stuff' I talked about, flying around at the Solar System's edge."

Parker had crossed his legs and was resting his chin on his hand, "So, Neptune is trying to set up its own system of orbiting planets?"

"I suppose that is a good analogy. It has *captured* a number of objects; those are the Trans-Neptunian Objects I talked about. We call them TNO. There are about 850 of them. But, most are just chunks of rocks. However; there are around six or seven that are large enough to be categorized as small planets – in a way."

Roland bent over and pointed to a sphere moving slowly along a blue line on the screen, "This is showing the orbit of Orcus, around Neptune – moving towards the sun, then back around again. It takes about 245 years to make a complete orbit."

Michael scratched his head, "Does it ever leave our Solar System?"

"That's an interesting question. Because the orbit of Orcus is not in the same plane as the rest of our planets, it resembles the elliptical orbit of Pluto. So, in theory, it does not leave our Solar System because it stays within our 50 Astronomical Unit neighborhood, more or less."

"And an Astronomical Unit is . . . what again?" Parker asked.

Roland stood upright, "Because the distances in space are so vast, we use the AU for those measurements. One AU is the distance from the Earth to the Sun, or about 150 thousand kilometers."

"Only your average Americans here; what's that in miles?"

"93 million miles," Michael broke in.

Parker leaned back, "I'm impressed."

"They teach that in 6th grade. If you would have only stayed in school," Michael mused, slowly shaking his head.

Parker pointed at Michael, "OK, Mister Smart Guy, 50 AU would be . . . ?"

"About 4.7 billion miles," Michael answered in a heartbeat.

Parker turned back to Roland, but still eyeing Michael, "So, Roland, what is the farthest distance this Orcus thing goes to?"

Roland sped up the animated panel, "As you can see; in January, of 2020, it will be 47.5 AUs from Earth -- just crossing into the outer boundaries of our Solar System. Then it will begin another journey around our system."

Parker stopped squinting at the screen and leaned back, "Fun stuff. What does it have to do with everything going on here?"

Roland, trying to hold back from conducting a lengthy lecture, put one hand in his pocket and pointed in the air to his right, "An object, sitting at 47.5 AUs from here, can be reached in 6.6 hours – traveling at the speed of light."

Parker uncrossed his legs and slapped his chest, "Well, I'll get a six-pack; we can crank up the old Ford and do a road trip."

Roland pointed back at the animation with his pencil, "As you can see, Orcus travels the entire length of our Solar System, passing just above it and then below it – at an angle. It has a 'view' of every planet in its 245 year round trip journey."

Michael looked at the little sphere following the line in the animation, "Is it really a planet? Does is have any moons?"

"We aren't sure, but by the way it keeps its' north-south orientation, it probably has at least one moon."

Parker spoke up, "What's it made of?"

Roland moved over to a nearby chair and sat down, "That's another interesting feature. It's mainly ice -- real water ice, not carbon dioxide."

"Why is that so interesting?" Parker questioned.

"Water, my friend, is very important. Remember what Winslow said in the basement? Water is needed for the operation of the Mu·Suvian ships. And I suppose ice is just as good."

Michael had been playing with a pencil during the past few minutes. He now used it as a prop, "Let's get to this speed of light thing. So, if we shot a beam of light at Orcus, it would take about 6.5 hours to get there?"

Roland pushed the center of his heavy glasses back up to the rim of his nose with his finger and moved forward to the edge of his chair, "I'm sure this is where I'm going to lose you."

Parker was going to make a comment; Michael stopped him and motioned for Roland to continue.

"The answer is yes, but only from our time vantage point. If you were riding on the light beam, looking at your own watch, it would only be 3.96 hours. That is a Time-Dilation of 0.6."

"Well, that beats the old Ford," Parker said, holding his hands up.

His brows came down as he slowly lowered his hands. He was having one of his moments. "So, if we were to ride a light beam to Orcus, and then back . . ."

Roland pointed at the animation in the lower right panel of his screen, "The trip would only take us 7.92 hours. But to those, waiting for us on Earth, it would be 13.2 hours – on their clocks."

Michael interrupted, "But, that is if we were riding a light beam. I mean, if our physical bodies were involved, right?"

Roland nodded, "Correct."

Parker looked at Roland, "You really need to get out more. Go marry Brittani and get a life. And lose those dorky glasses."

Roland blushed and laughed it off.

Parker began picturing himself; black helmet, goggles and leather jacket -- straddling a light beam. "Hey, what if I was riding in from Orcus and I passed you guys going the other way? We could throw tomatoes or something at each other. That would be an awesome two-lane highway!"

Roland slowly turned to Michael, whose hair had suddenly sprung up on the back of his neck.

Michael remembered what Roland had said in the tent, and began to repeat it, "If a connection is made . . ."

Roland finished, ". . . Data will flow."

Michael began tapping his hand with the pencil, "Correct me if I'm wrong, Roland, but this highway Parker just mentioned -- it would work going both ways, right? If we were on Orcus and wanted to ride back to Earth . . ." Michael's yellowish eyes were not focused. It appeared that he was not even in the room, until he slowly muttered, "Singular communication."

Roland turned off the animation on the laptop screen and removed the CD. He turned back to face Parker.

Roland took Michaels' pencil, along with his own, and held each one in his two hands, "Let's say, you were riding to Orcus from Earth, on your light beam, and you crossed the road coming from Orcus to Earth. If you threw your tomato at Michael, who was riding in from Orcus and was to arrive at Earth four hours ago . . ." He then crossed the pencils.

Michael nodded, "I would get to Earth with the tomato he threw at me, four hours before Parker even left on his light beam to get to Orcus."

Roland smiled, "Those tomatoes would be data. Some would come back with you to Earth and the rest would keep going to Orcus, with Parker. A relativistic electron beam, like the one in the tent, powering a Vinculum Transceiver, will allow us to do that -- and more. It is a system that permits singularity. That is, as soon as we get a whole system together."

Michael crossed his legs put his hands on his knee, "So, let's get back to this time-travel thing. Imagine that I just heard about a building collapsing and hurt a lot of people. You say that I could send a message, back to me – four hours before it happened. I would then be able to make sure no people were in the building, when it does collapse. Is that what you're getting to here?"

Roland smiled, "Yes. It would be proactive. We could prevent a large number of bad things from happening. Rather than the reactive world we live in today, where we spend a large amount of our lives dealing with the bad things that already *have* happened."

Michael uncrossed his legs and crossed his arms. He was getting very anxious with the thought of changing the future by knowing what was going to happen. And trying to visualize the whole situation was almost beyond human comprehension.

He brought up another mind-bender, "Well, what about the people who were in the building, when it did fall down? If we get them out before it happens . . . would the message, about those people being hurt in the collapse, have even been sent in the first place?"

Roland walked over to the doorway, one hand behind his back, the other on his forehead. He stood a moment and walked back, "What you are suggesting is a parallel universe . . . in sorts. Where there are two, perhaps more, outcomes of every event."

Michael lifted his hand, "That's what *you* are suggesting. You think the human brain can even comprehend such a thing, much less live it . . . everyday?"

Roland put out both hands, "Would it be any different than stopping a child from crossing a four-lane highway? You know what will happen if you allowed it to happen. If the child is killed, we would be moved to live that outcome's existence. If the child was stopped, we would follow another one. And the outcome may have earth changing consequences. Who knows what that child will grow up and become – or would have. The knowledge of 'what if' keeps us on our paths. And that knowledge comes from our past. The entire human race will change when the knowledge begins coming from our future."

Roland sat down, "But, bad things mainly occur when we are not paying attention. If you were not aware that the building was going to fall down, you would not be able to warn yourself or those hurt in the disaster."

Parker began nodding, "This is all cool. But, don't you need one of those beaming things on Orcus, too; in order to make the light-speed highway connect at both ends? I mean . . . to get this future information?"

Roland looked down as he turned to fold his laptop, "I am confident in my assumption that there should be a number of them already there. Perhaps there is one on each side of the globe."

Michael put his hand to his forehead and whispered, "I know that there is." He leaned his head back and looked up at the ceiling, "Why do I know that?"

Parker put his hands behind his head, "Something to do with *our* box on the organizational chart?"

"What chart?" Roland asked.

Michael lowered his gaze to Roland, "This is just the tip of a netherworld iceberg. Once a system is up on earth, *anything* that is broken down to the particle level can be sent back and forth between other systems with the Transceivers. And anything sent out to the Orcus system can be retrieved hours before it was even sent."

Roland sat down. "Now *I* ask you . . . how do you know that?"

Michael suddenly put his head down and held it in his hands, "The crates contain two important technologies. The Beam devices are power generators that, not only provide power to the Transceivers, but each one can be plugged into an existing power grid to supply enough electricity to power an area the size of the entire east coast of the U.S. But they need to be twenty miles apart or the crossing of resonance outputs would be devastating. We need to make sure that there are no other Beam Generators operating within that range."

He bolted upright and held out his hand, "I need a paper and pen!" He was beginning to shake.

Roland took some technical papers out of his box and turned them over to the blank back side. He handed Michael a pen.

Michael began writing and drawing, almost in a trance. Sweat was appearing on his forehead and he was breathing fast.

After five minutes he dropped the pen on the table and leaned back, exhausted.

Parker turned the page Michael had written on to see a series of dots, similar to what Roland had scratched in the dirt inside the tent.

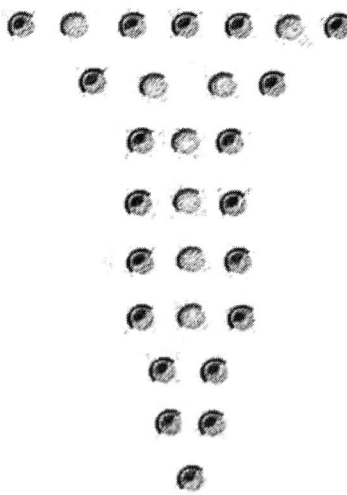

Parker looked at Roland, who was trying to decipher the spots, also. He shrugged and asked Michael, "What are these dots supposed to represent?"

Michael was still leaning back in the chair, his eyes to the ceiling. "That shows what is in each crate and how they are sitting right now, all over the world. The eight white ones are the Vinculum Transceivers, the rest are the Beam Generators, waiting for a Resonator."

He leaned forward and began pointing at the drawing.

"The top row shows the United States Mushroom Farms, numbered from right to left. MF-1 has a Beam Generator; MF-2 has a Transceiver . . . and so on."

He moved closer to the drawing, "The second row is showing the MFs in Australia. The third row: South Africa. The fourth row: The UK. The fifth row: Asia. The sixth row: Moscow. Seventh: Japan. And the eighth row is India."

He returned to leaning back in the chair.

Parker pointed at the last dot, "And what is the single one at the bottom?"

"When we went to the database, back in December, we found twenty-seven crates by searching for the Baby Formula tag identification number. They were only in the database because someone had scanned the pallet label and had entered it. We found the crate in Gus' warehouse by tapping into his LiquiCode reader on his laptop, remember?"

Parker counted the dots. "There are twenty-eight here. Are you saying . . . ?"

"Yes, there are twenty-eight devices out there. That last dot might either be Beam Generator or Transceiver, which is sitting in Gus' warehouse in the Yucatan jungle. We won't know which until we physically examine all of the others. That drawing shows where they all *should* be."

Roland looked at Parker, "How does he know this?"

Parker whispered, "He's a GenZ. I think the Mu·Suvian DNA has finally kicked in . . . just outside of Barstow."

Michael spoke again, "According to that drawing, we just have two Transceivers in the United States MFs. We have four Resonators. One is already on the Beam Generator in the tent, so we only need one more to activate a Beam at MF-3 and turn on the Transceiver at MF-2."

He sat upright, "The other two Resonators must be sent to Program 2622 in Australia, which will allow them to turn on all of their two Transceivers. That will provide a four Transceiver communication footprint with Orcus, 24 hours a day."

Roland had been writing down everything Michael was saying. "OK, do we send them by special delivery? And how do we know who is supposed to get them? Leigus would never go for that."

Parker looked at Michael and smiled, "I think Max needs a ship."

Chapter Twenty-One

The Lorgronson White Paper was not to be made public . . . initially. It was an internal document which was distributed among The Foundation's Second Level members by Doctor Lorgronson, to obtain further funding for his research. The Foundation knew that the final number of survivors would not be a mere eight million, but two billion. He was given the misinformation, which would produce a greater impact. Fear works best when the chances of survival are diminished.

He disappeared within a month of it's publication in a magazine.

It was rumored that the document was submitted for publication by an unnamed source, working under orders from an unnamed agency. Investigations, conducted by a number of political action groups, never turned up enough evidence to prove that the report was a fabrication to attain funding for more black programs. In truth, it did provide enough ground cover to enable the formation of Program 3938, under the guise of Executive Order 11490.

Program 3938 then generated enough fear in the upper intestines of world governments to obtain authorization, and enormous funding, for the construction of seven Mushroom Farms in the US, four in Australia and three in South Africa in 1998.

However; the final 'deal' demanded some transparency and partnerships of the MFs. The final agreement; the US Government was given the authority over MF-1, MF-4 and MF-5 to comply with EO 11490. Australia received the deeds to their MF-1 and MF-4. And South Africa was allowed to operate their own MF-1.

It had not cost The Foundation a cent. It was one of Randolph 'Gus' Stoddard's shining moments of manipulation on the world stage.

He was now in the middle of Act Two.

The only real critics of his current performance were The Foundation. They wanted him dead.

For the past six months, Gus had been initiating his plan to undermine The Foundation so that the Mu·Suvians would choose him as the logical Second Level choice in the *Realignment of The Foundation,* by the College of Minds. His investigations revealed that the College is to be made up of seven members of The Foundation and twelve *representatives* of Level One. He needed to get the seven chosen members of The Foundation on his side, or replace them with his own. What he was able to discover were only four names of the seven that would be on the College.

What concerned Gus the most was a rumor, which was being circulated about the outer regions of The Foundation, stating that many of the representatives of the Mu·Suvians will be GenZ.

He had called upon his connections to get the highly guarded listing of all 129 living GenZs. If he could *persuade* the right ones, he would be a shoe-in at the Realignment. As he read down columns of names and their locations, three of them resulted in one of his maniacal outbursts.

"I *knew* there was another reason Hugh Waterman wanted that Fields kid on the program. He's got the eyes. Damn it! I should have suspected something!" He immediately bolted to his feet, pushing his heavy desk chair over backwards onto the thick carpet. The long-haired black cat, which had wandered into the complex four months earlier and decided to make Gus his own, sprang from the table and dashed for cover at the corner of the bookcase.

Gus stormed around the room while repeatedly looking at the document. He rolled the sheets up and hit his other palm with the tube, "And they're still alive."

Gus walked to the door of his office and yelled at his secretary, sitting at the outer office desk, "Murphy! Set up a meeting with the Righteous. Tell them Itzamna has a proposition."

He had not been this upset since he was informed that half the world was *not* blown into the dark ages on December 21st

by the 'supposed' nuclear devices that were 'supposedly' planted within the MFs.

He up-righted the toppled chair and sat back down at his desk. Mojo, the cat, returned to the desk top and stared at the gruff face as Gus bounced another thought off him, "On the bright side, I now have a list of those mutants. I can find me one to read those chicken-scratchings that Bancroft had in his files. How much do you want to bet; that Michael Fields can read those symbols? And he told me he couldn't. That alien half-breed bastard!"

Murphy appeared at the door, "I have the meeting set up for 1800 hours tomorrow on the optical hookup through Oklahoma. I will contact the Righteous representative to notify the required attendees."

Gus just grunted and waved his hand in the air. He bent to his left and pulled a file out of the bottom drawer. It was labeled 'Mu Network'. He opened it. There were fifteen pages of symbols, dots and lines.

None of it made any sense. However, Gus had reasoned that it must be important for he had found it in the wall safe which had been cut open. He was convinced it had to be connected with the Mu·Suvians.

He looked over to Mojo, "Those alien bastards think they run this whole planet. They had that Bancroft clown wrapped around their antenna, or *whatever* the hell they got." The cat yawned and continued its' life-long goal of achieving the perfect nap.

Gus had never met a Mu·Suvian . . . that he knew of anyway. The truth was; few people had ever met one . . . that *they* knew of. He had often suspected Leigus, whom he had only met once. There was something very weird about him. But, being a Level Three manager working under the Stolist branch of The Foundation, he was never allowed to get close.

Gus woke up Mojo with a slap to the table, "I'm gonna bring that diamond-studded freak down! The College is going to see who can *really* run this show. And if they can't see that, I'll just have to bring them *all* down."

He and his ten Program 3938 cohort managers and directors had absconded with enough gold, from three MF vaults, to set them all up for life. It also continued to pay for a well equipped mercenary force to keep The Foundation off his turf – the well fortified Mayan temple complex above him.

And he controlled the GMCS server farm, buried deep in the ancient tunnels of his compound. Even though the damn thing was broke.

The Righteous contribution of the best computer and network technicians from the US and India had proven fruitless in his attempts to break into the frozen GMCS application servers.

Ever since the program locked down all of the MFs and shut down every microprocessor-enabled device it had uploaded firmware changes to, it was refusing to turn back on. And the Mu·Suvian language, which the software converted to on December 21st, made the task impossible.

Even though Gus would cuss and scream at anyone within bellowing range, claiming Bancroft was a lunatic, he knew better. It had all been carefully planned. Ever since Gus sent Hugh Waterman to supervise the development of GMCS at NexTrÉ, the reports that Hugh was sending back were disturbing. It was true that the final program performed all of the required functions that were in the contract, but Hugh knew something more was being done to the source code . . . after the Program received the final product.

And he was correct, for the results appeared in dramatic fashion. For over a year before the flare/blackout, GMCS had been sending a type of virus to every microprocessor it could 'touch', around the world. Anything that was plugged into a network was infected. The translated command; *Turn off at 11:11am GMT, December 21, 2012 and don't wake up until I tell you to.* The wakeup command would be in digitized Mu·Suvian.

Gus sat back as his thoughts turned to Hugh Waterman. Even though Hugh had worked under High Minister Chén's branch of The Foundation, as did George Black Rock, he was still a good friend. And he was the most respected liaison they had, between the Program and the hosting governments. Gus often regretted how he had used Hugh to get to Bancroft, but all was fair . . . in Gus' mind. He was now in a position to topple Stolist Leigus and, if fate smiled upon him, perhaps High Minister Chén as well.

Gus reached for a sheet of paper and scribbled a quick message, *'Find Michael Fields. Last known location was at MF-7. Bring him to me, alive.'* He called for his secretary, "Murphy! Send this out to Commander Rio. It's urgent."

He handed the note to Murphy, who was turning to leave, "Wait a second." He unrolled the list of the GenZ names and ran his finger down the column. He leaned over the desk and wrote another message, *"Find Elizabeth Redding. Last known location was MF-7 Basement. Kill her."*

Chapter Twenty-Two

At 9am the next morning, Parker, Michael and Roland sat in George's office. They acted as if they had been called in by the Principle.

George was going over some papers, his eyes hidden by his hat brim. He slowly looked up, "The reason I asked you all here, on this fine day, is to go over what Roland had given me last night about Michael's plan to bring up crates, use two Resonators in the US MFs, and send two down to the Australian MFs. He also provided me with the Beam Configuration Map he had drawn up. I needed Roland to explain what all the dots were, but it has opened our eyes to the big picture."

Parker nudged Roland, "You gave that to George? It was just Michael on some mind trip."

George held up his hand, "Not at all. It is the plan we must follow. You must be aware that Michael did not actually come up with all this . . . all on his own."

Parker looked past Roland to Michael, "Is that what you meant by 'getting zapped with an idea'?"

George slowly put his hand down, giving Parker the *look*. Parker turned in his seat to face George, "Sorry."

"This is what we must do. I will arrange a meeting with the Council to get the crates at MF-2, 3 and 6 to the surface. Michael, you and Roland will go to the Beam at MF-3 and activate it with your GMCS laptop, satellite uplink and a Resonator."

He reached down beside the desk and lifted Michael's computer case. He placed it on the desktop.

"Here's your laptop. It's been under guard so nothing has been done to it. When we get a couple more, load and configure them exactly like this one. Then you and Roland will both have one and a spare. Don't let them out of your sights."

Michael and Roland looked at each other and nodded. Michael spoke up, "How soon do we need to go?"

George looked at the papers in front of him, "Prepare to get on the Megadrax in four days, with all your equipment. We will have the Tube open by then and things arranged with Winslow."

Parker raised his hand, "Excuse me. Ah . . ."

George, once again held up his hand, as he picked up the phone. "Yeah, send them in." He returned the handset and smiled at Parker.

Within moments, Reggie walked in the room . . . followed by Max, without his ESA uniform.

"Parker, I think you remember Max. You two are going to steal a Manta and make a delivery of two Resonators to the Australian MFs."

Parker jumped to his feet, "Really? Max and me? How? When?"

George was chuckling, "Please, all of you sit down."

Everyone moved chairs around while Parker slid the settee closer to George's desk and got comfortable. Martin jumped up next to him and found a perfect spot for another nap. When all were finally seated George motioned to Reggie, "Would you like to go first?"

Doctor Adams stood, "As George has probably related to you already, the Tube will be open soon. That will allow the Megadrax to resume its supply missions and other functions it is required to perform. Stolist Leigus has agreed to release the Megadrax transport and take our team to the necessary MFs. Michael and Roland will be a part of that team and will activate the Beam at MF-3 with the Resonator we have in our possession."

Parker spoke up, "We've heard all that, Reggie. What about Max and Me?"

"When the second Beam is activated at MF-3, Michael and Roland will be transported, by the Megadrax, to MF-2 to 'turn on' the Transceiver communications. The power from MF-3's Beam will supply the energy to operate it."

Roland raised his hand, "How long are we going to stay at the MFs?"

"Good question. We have determined that turning on the MF-3 Beam Generator will only take an hour or so. Just unpack it, put in the Resonator and send the activation code up to a satellite. Someone there will supply you with the uplink information and times. Michael and you will be 'on the ground' in Missouri for a very short time. Remember, we have to do all of this at night. That is the only time the Megadrax flies. We don't need any hysterical paranoia running through the masses, at this time. The Megadrax will then travel to MF-6 with Michael to 'turn on' that Transceiver. He will stay there, with another two technicians, to get its stream up and running."

Roland looked at George, then Reggie, "What about me?"

Reggie sat down on the edge of George's desk and pointed at Roland, "You will stay at MF-2, in Ohio, with the second laptop you're going to configure. We will leave you there with support technicians. You will need to operate the data stream on that Transceiver."

He turned to face Michael, "The Beam Generator that's in the tent, north of here, should be now providing the power for its operation. The Megadrax will then return here, allowing the Tube Doors to be opened."

"They're going to leave us at the MFs?" Michael asked, looking at Reggie and then at Roland.

Reggie lifted a finger, "Yes. Not only to operate the data streams, but for your own safety. The Megadrax will then be ordered to return here. That's where Max and Parker come in. Or, rather, go out."

George had to get in on the plan, "Once the Tube doors open, to let the Megadrax back in, Max and Parker will be able fly out."

He looked at Max, "Don't worry, Jones knows the plan, so when he sees you coming, he will not blow the tunnel. And he will make sure no one follows you."

Max nodded, "So, how much time do we have between the Tube doors opening and getting out before we slam, head on, into the oncoming Megadrax?"

"You can get out the doors before they are fully open. The Mantas are not that big. I would say, from the time the doors start to open until they are wide enough to let you out . . . thirty seconds. Now, the time until you slam into the Megadrax, *head on*; sixty seconds."

Parker was sitting on the edge of the couch nodding, "Cool." He then pointed at Max, "But, if he's going to fly the thing, why do you need me?"

George raised his right eyebrow and smiled, "He needs a Weapons Officer in the back seat."

Parker slapped his hands together; "Yeah . . ." Martin woke up and barked once over the sudden intrusion of his slumber.

Max put his hand on Parkers shoulder, "I have a training program on a CD for the Manta. I'm really not supposed to still have it, but it got into my belongings when I left Australia. It's like a flight simulator. It should give Parker a basic understanding and feel for the 'back seat'."

Max lowered his hand and looked around. "I'll need a computer, with a big screen, to put it on."

Parker was beaming. "I can *find* us a computer, no problem. We can set it up in my office."

Reggie sat down as George pointed at Michael and Roland, "You two have four days to get your equipment together and figure out how to get the Transceivers to start communicating. I believe Roland may already have a good idea on how to accomplish that."

Roland looked at Michael and shrugged.

George turned his attention to Max and Parker, "That gives you two five days to work with Reggie and me on getting a plan to commandeer a Manta. Let's aim for the Manta to be flown out at 5 am, on July 1st. We will make sure that the Megadrax will need to be back at the Tube opening then."

"Max, you're going to move into the MF until you and Parker grab the ship. You need to train Parker on the simulator; to keep you two alive if you're intercepted."

"You think we'll meet any resistance?" Max asked.

George pointed at his left palm with right index finger, "The rest of you remember what Winslow said? There are twenty-five Manta and Xlitars in the America's Squadron. With you guys flying away in one of them and seven more stuck in the Basement; that leaves seventeen of those devils that may want to stop you. And I'm sure Leigus will insist on that. The closest base would be the Area, so you won't have much time to outrun them. They're only 250 miles south of here."

Parker turned to Max, "You said that you could out-flank any incoming, 300 miles out."

Max stood slowly to zip his jacket, "Not out, Parker . . . Up."

CHAPTER TWENTY-THREE

The Relativistic Electron Beam Generator, sitting in the tent within the Forward Base, was still glowing as Roland and Michael lifted the flap and walked in. No one had dared to try and turn it off. The smell of ozone filled the interior of the enclosure.

Vern, who had driven them from the MF, followed them in. "So, that's the bugger that all the fuss was about. Sure is an odd looking thing. Kind of like a big paperweight, 'cept for the pumping light inside. So, what's it suppose to do?"

"It's a power source for the Transceiver," Roland answered.

"Where's the Transceiver?"

"Hopefully, sitting in MF-6," Michael said, as he walked towards his satellite uplink equipment on the other side of the tent.

Vern walked towards the globe and examined the shape and size, rubbing his stubby white whiskers, "Don't see no wires. How can it get power all the way to Utah? That's 400 or so miles from here."

Roland stood looking at the device, "I know . . . that's the real puzzle."

Vern looked up to the tent roof, "Must be a shootin' high voltage 'lectricity in the air." He walked completely around the sphere. He held his hand out to within a foot of the glass. "Is it puttin' out any power right now? Don't feel anything."

Michael called out, "You would if you touched it with a metal pole."

Roland walked up beside Vern and held out his hand, "You're right. I don't think it emits any energy until something draws from it."

"Like a dumb ass with a metal pole," Michael added.

Roland pointed at the Resonator, "Don't put your hand over the top, it will burn it off. Even though it's not powering anything right now that we know of it's still emitting some serious energy from around the Resonator."

Vern rubbing his stubby beard, "Well, now, that's a good safety tip." He tried to look through the opaque glass of the globe, "Think that Transceiver thing you talked about, over in Utah, will start runnin' from the 'lectricity this throws out into the air?"

Roland opened his note book and turned to a page, "That is probably the scenario. When this thing started up, the first time, we noticed that the electromagnetic resonance turned off every microprocessor within a couple hundred yards. That's what brought down the attack helicopters and the generators. But, the Mess Hall lights were still on. I did some checking and found out that they are all fluorescent tubes. This Beam Generator puts out high frequency, high voltage. It is definitely transmitting power through the air."

Michael walked back, carrying his uplink equipment, and stood stand well behind Roland. He took no chances on getting too close to the globe. "OK, I'm ready to get out of here."

Vern took his knuckle and tapped on one of the vertical support columns, "Are these made of glass, like the globe?"

"Reggie thinks they might be porcelain." Roland answered.

Vern stood upright, "It is AC or DC?"

Michael looked at Roland, "Well, we hadn't really thought of any electrical output, have we?"

"Well, nothing directly plugged into it . . . just the resonance effect I just told you about," Roland said slowly.

Vern stepped back, "Well, iffin that's a power generator, like you say, then it has to be DC."

"Why is that?" Michael asked.

Vern pointed at the top metallic square, "That metal frame, running around the top of the globe, and the one at the bottom, are separated by those four porcelain insulator columns. That would mean one would be positive and the other negative." He began walking to the tent opening. "And the high voltage coming out of the top would be a kind of AC, in a Tesla sort of way." He started walking towards the tent opening, "I'll be right back. I got a multi-meter in the van. I can check the voltage output of those two metal frames with it."

Michael ran up behind him, "Let me go with you and put this stuff in the van."

Roland took out his notebook and began making a drawing of the Beam Generator, along with Vern's thoughts on the electrical output.

Michael and Vern returned with a digital multi-meter and some jumper cables.

Vern handed Michael the meter as he stretched out the cable on the ground. He laid one end on the rug which was still spread out near the device. He held the other two clamps in his hands. "Make sure the other ends of these things aren't touching each other." Roland kicked the clamps, lying on the rug, two feet apart.

Vern attached one clamp to a 2-inch round bar of steel that held the top metal frame to the insulator column. He kneeled down to attach the other to the bottom. As he moved the clamp to within three feet of the metal, the globe surged in brilliance as a thick bolt of searing plasma jumped from the bottom frame to the clamp, making a loud report.

"Whoa!" shouted Roland, as he began stamping out a fire that had erupted on the rug. The two jumper-cable clamps had been blasted away from one other, with wide melted-copper scars on each.

Vern looked back and smiled, "Well, there ya go. It's DC. I knew it would be." He stood up, "Looks like these two metal frames have to be at least three feet apart. And by the looks of those clamps, it's puttin' out some bodacious amperage."

Roland began writing in his notebook. He paused and looked up, "So, Vern, how are we going to test the voltage levels?"

"We may have a problem there. If this thing puts out as much energy as whatever is plugged into it wants, I'm only gonna get a reading that's the maximum of the ol' meter. But, what it *will* tell us; which one of these frames is plus and which one is minus. But, I betcha' the top is plus. It would only make sense, 'cause the earth makes a pretty good ground. Don't know if we would want the plus to be touchin' that."

He set his meter to DC and touched both frames at once. There were no sparks, no dead Vern.

"Yep, top is plus and bottom is minus. It's like a huge battery. And I was getting about 830 volts on the meter."

Michael wiped his hands on his jeans, after throwing another handful of dirt on the still smoldering rug fire. "Do you think the beam will ever run down, like a regular battery?"

Vern looked at the purple glow, "Looks like its getting recharged from some kind of thing goin' on with the air around it."

"It's probably attracting ions from the atmosphere." Roland said, still writing in his book.

"I bet this doohickey could put out a lot of wattage," Vern speculated.

"I would like to see it just power a light bulb," Michael commented.

Vern thought for a moment, "I bet it could run this whole camp. All we have to do is plug it in, instead of the generators."

A voice came from the outside of the tent, "What's that smell? You guys burning down the tent? That must mean Parker's in there." It was Tara. She appeared at the tent entrance.

Michael smiled, "No, Parker's not here. We just had a little accident with the rug."

"The stink goes all the way down to the stables. We thought it was a pig farm." She walked over to the rug and looked down. "You drop one of your hand-rolled cigarettes on here, Vern?"

"Nope, this gizmo zapped it," he answered.

She looked at the jumper-cables and the melted clamps. "Looks like you guys helped it. So, what are you up to?"

Vern began wrapping up the jumper cables, "Can you get one of your electricians in here with about a hundred feet of power cable? We wanna' hook up this *thing-a-ma-bob* to the power panel."

She looked at Roland, then Michael. "We . . . well, Vern anyway, thinks it can power the whole camp," Michael said.

Tara looked at the rug, "Is this what you call a successful experiment? And now you want to plug it into my whole base camp and burn it down, too?"

Vern picked up his multi-meter and handed the jumper cables to Michael, "The worst that could happen is that we blow a couple fuses in the power box. It's worth a chance."

Before Tara could refuse, Vern waved to Michael, "OK, let's get this stuff back in the van and go help the electrician with the power cables."

Tara lifted her hands, "In spite of what I see on the rug, you do seem to know what you're doing. OK, give it try. But I want my electricians supervising. And if you blow even one fuse, I want it disconnected. Got that?"

Vern was too preoccupied with his connection idea, as he left the tent carrying his jumper cables and meter. She and Michael followed him out of the tent, still trying to get Vern to agree to her conditions. Roland kept writing in his book.

Twenty minutes had passed as Roland was just finishing his report. "Just drop the cable here and we can start stringing it out to the power panel!" It was Vern, just outside the tent entrance.

Michael walked in, through the open tent flap, pulling two thick cable ends. "That's OK, Roland. We got it," he sarcastically called out.

Roland put down the book and ran over to help pull the heavy black lines into the tent.

Vern and three electricians unwound the pile of cable outside of the tent and dragged the other two ends to the battery bank power panel. They attached the cable ends to the battery bank power panel input connection, which normally came from the generators. Vern ran back to the tent.

Once inside he picked up one cable with red tape around the end, "I'm gonna clamp this one to the top frame – it's positive."

There were no sparks.

"Now, the next one . . . you all better step back a bit, ya never know."

He slowly moved the clamp closer, not wanting an arc of searing electrons to jump at him like an angry cobra. The second clamp went on the bottom frame without incident. The globe immediately turned slightly green for three seconds, then back to its normal shade of violet.

"That's it. Seems to be happy," Vern smiled. "Let's go throw the switch and see if we can blow any fuses."

They all went back to the power panel. Nothing had been affected. Vern nodded to the head electrician. The power switch was thrown. A quick shutter reverberated along the sides of the metal case as power surged through the transformers inside the large steel cabinet. A throaty sound could be heard, deep inside the inverter's casing; like an old man emerging from an afternoon nap. It too faded within moments. Vern looked at the grid-tie inverter's dials, which displayed the conversion of the DC voltage from the batteries into AC. "It's putting out a clean voltage to the camp. And the amperage draw is right where it should be. Let's see how long it lasts."

He turned to Roland, who was scribbling faster in his book, "I want you to sit here and monitor those meters. Write down what they say every five minutes or so. If'n anything drops into the red portion of the gauges, come a runnin' and tell me."

The three electricians were standing around nodding and scratching their heads.

Vern walked back to the tent with Michael, "I want to see what happens when everything comes on at dusk. Now, that will be the real test."

Michael looked back at Roland, who had found a chair and was sitting down next to the inverter, "How long do you want Roland to sit there?"

CONTINUANCE

Vern put his hand on Michael's shoulder, "I think that's up to you, Pard'ner. I thought you needed a break from Mister Science."

Chapter Twenty-Four

Hugh Waterman had known that Michael was a GenZ from the deep involvement he had in a number of Black Projects – including the tracking of the children of GAIA. That is why he had insisted that Michael be brought into NexTrÉ to work on G-GIZ and then be folded into Program 3938. Or rather, he was told to.

The fringe world of horizon technology and sacred knowledge has been around since the first caveman found a flaming stick and told everyone he had invented it. Hugh knew that every project he had been connected with were actually back-engineering assignments. Or assembly efforts on plans submitted from minds greater than anyone our species could produce.

So it was when he was placed in charge of overseeing delivery of GMCS at NexTrÉ. The final program was only a compilation of millions of lines code provided by The Foundation. It was funded under the guise of Asset Visibility for the government, but only a small portion of the final application accomplished that function. That premise allowed the entire program to be installed into the computers of the Defenders of the Free World.

As far as Bancroft, he knew what he was given to produce, as the owner of NexTrÉ and a Level 5 member of The Foundation. But the immensity of the final product drove him insane. He thought he should take the role as High Minister in Level 2. The power of reaching the final threshold was all in his head – not in his hands. Another case of too much information can be dangerous.

Hugh knew that Bancroft had ordered additional functionality into the program and was offering it on the open market, before the Mayan Tzolk'in switched to the Mu·Suvian New Era on December 21st, 2012. Hugh had chased him around the world before Gus Stoddard found his location in the Yucatan.

That was the version Gus Stoddard had acquired when he killed Bancroft in the Bunker and passed to Michael on a flash drive.

Fortunately, Bancroft *did* follow instructions on assembling the frames, crating and shipping all of the Beam Generators and Transceivers to their assigned locations before Gus caught up with him. The most amazing fact of the Bancroft involvement was that The Foundation had not been informed of the true functionality of the devices. The Mu·Suvians had gone straight to Bancroft, through a representative, who had delivered the globes and shipping instructions.

Hugh knew of no one in The Foundation who could have produced the original software code that was the backbone of GMCS. And only a few who could understand it when the Mu·Suvian time-shift took over. It, too, had to have come from the Mu·Suvians.

Michael Fields was his only hope to keep it *away* from The Foundation and implement its ultimate objective.

Hugh had met George in the early 80's while conducting some joint insurgent operations in South America. George was The Foundation's high military commander and led his troops against a Landing. It was one of the few times an effort involving both The Foundation and a government's military worked together. A failure would have been disastrous for humanity. They did not lose and George became one of few members of The Foundation that Hugh became true friends with. Conflicts can do that to people.

George had nominated Hugh for membership in The Foundation, after Hugh's wife had died. Hugh had never joined. Being George's friend was as close as he wanted to be to the 'third rail' of the world. He became the unofficial Ambassador of the government to The Foundation. Both sides respected him, both sides mourned his death.

Hugh would miss the Good-Bye Meeting of the 2nd People. He had worked hard to prevent it.

Chapter Twenty-Five

For two days since the meeting in George's office, beneath the hot Northern Nevada high desert, Max had been training Parker on the Manta flight simulator software. George, Reggie and four advisors had been devising a plan to get into the Basement and commandeering a Manta.

Jones and his team of Black Shirt technicians and commandos finished cutting through the welded bars on the Tube, so that the doors could open for the Megadrax. They also planted four high explosive charges around the tunnel's opening with a camera to look into the channel, so that a remote detonation could be set off if a Manta was on its way out.

Vern had returned nightly to the Forward Operations Base to sit next to the Beam Generator; drinking coffee, eating mess hall grub and smoking his hand-rolled cigarettes. The power it was supplying to the camp, through the battery bank, had not failed. He had every fluorescent light disconnected from the camp wiring; as they remained lit 24 hours a day, without needing electricity from the power inverter.

Michael and Roland had found a tent in one of the trucks and had set it up in back of the J&K Warehouse. They loaded a laptop for Roland and a spare backup, which Parker had *found,* with everything that was now on Michael's computer. Both of the new laptops were also displaying only Mu·Suvian symbols and displaying data right to left.

Michael wrote down sequences and symbol combinations for Roland, which were needed to perform the uplink functions in the field.

They had set up the satellite uplink equipment and testing it with occasional links to the few passing satellites, which were not affected by the flare or the firmware virus.

Michael sat back in the canvas chair and looked out of the tent flap at a dust devil spinning thorny tumbleweeds and dark brown dirt 40 feet into the air. "OK, now what?" he asked Roland.

"What do you mean?" Roland wiped his forehead as a light, hot breeze blew into the tent flap – bringing with it more desert dust.

Michael pointed at his laptop, "Both computers work, we can get the satellites to talk to us . . . what are we supposed to do when we get to the Transceivers?" He was hoping Roland had a clue.

Roland leaned on the small wooden table that sat between them, "I've been thinking about this GMCS program. From everything you have shown me, it's got more nooks and crannies than any program I have ever come across. Do you think somewhere, deep in here, there's something that might allow us to link up with the Transceivers? I mean, if it was Bancroft who had the devices built and shipped all of the crates to the MFs, he must have devised a way to communicate with them."

Michael put both hands on his head and looked at the computer screen in front of him. "Well, from what I've been able to figure out; when the Beam Generator turned on, it activated a Private Character file that switched all the fonts to Mu·Suvian and changed key entries from left to right, to right to left. I went into the source code and found twenty or more of these files that are labeled with an 'XZX' extension. I can't open them."

"You think that when the Transceiver is activated, it will turn on one of those files to let you communicate with it?" Roland asked.

"I sure would like to try, before we're dropped off by the Megadrax. I don't even know how we're going to plug into it."

Roland took off his glasses and rubbed his eyes, "Have you checked to see if something has been activated in the program already? I mean, the Beam may have turned those twenty files on." He put his glasses back on, "As Doctor Adams has stated; the Transceiver will have to be turned on somehow. It just won't come to life when we bring it to the surface."

Michael dropped his hands, "That does make sense. OK, let's get deeper into GMCS and see what's there . . . that wasn't before."

Michael went to the Home Screen of the program. He began to chuckle.

"What?" Roland asked, smiling along.

"I didn't catch this before. It's no longer GMCS. It now says *Universal* Monitoring and Control System; UMCS." He leaned over and looked at Roland's screen, "Yep, they both have that."

Roland looked at the time and date on his screen, "Why does this show 13.0.0.9.8?"

"That's today's date in the Mayan, or Mu·Suvian 260 day-count," Michael said.

Roland nodded, "I can see that now. But, I wish it would display Thursday, June 27th, 2013 someplace. This is really messing with my mind."

"Just rely on your wrist watch. It should keep you *relatively* sane." Michael opened his source code file for the once-named program called GMCS. "The firmware virus, sent out to everything GMCS could find, will only recognize the Long Count time. And I'm sure, so will the Transceivers.

Michael went into the system deeper. He pointed at the screen, "And I have no idea what these files ending in XZX are for."

Roland's eyes went out of focus as some heavy-footed neuron activity began stomping around in his head, "Did you say *XZX* extensions?"

Michael thought his tent-mate was having a stroke, "Yeah. You OK?"

Roland started thumping his temple with his finger, "XZX is normally associated with generations. Like in ancestry or harmonics; it's a step in a progression that results in a combination of pairs. Does that make any sense?"

Michael had to think about it for a minute, "So, if I was to use two programs at once, and ask the file to open . . . it would?"

Roland lowered his hand onto the table, "You're the software guru. But it sounds like what Bancroft was looking for. But it would have to be the correct two codes combined. Is that right?" He put his palms together to emphasize his words.

Michael saw something more in Roland's gesture, "*Codes* could be the key." He began looking for anything in his computer which related to LiquiCode. "I sure could use Parker's hacking skills right now. But, this may go deeper than just the software."

A voice came from outside the tent, "Michael Fields?"

"In here!"

One of George's Black Shirts appeared at the tent opening, "George asked me to bring you this note."

Michael took the folded piece of paper and opened it, *'Meet me at elevator six, at 5pm. You and I are going to the Basement.'*

Michael lowered the message and looked at Roland, "I have to go with George, to the Basement."

Roland leaned back in his chair and smiled, "I think you two are going to meet the Council. George said he would set it up."

"Why do I have to go?"

"It would seem that they consider you right up there on George's level," Roland replied.

"But, I'm not even *in* The Foundation. What do I wear?"

"By the look of your eyes, I would say you're deeper in The Foundation than you ever imagined. Don't wear your sunglasses."

Chapter Twenty-Six

George and Michael stood inside the elevator as the doors opened to reveal Winslow and Major Lansing, of the ESA, standing in the hallway of Level Six.

Lansing checked to see that George still had his Lion's Head ring on. His eyes then shifted to Michael as if some sort of magic was going to take place at any moment. Michael was sure that if he just said *Boo*, the man would go for his gun or jump behind Winslow.

Winslow's self-perceived superiority was still intact, "We will take you to the Council Chamber wing. I assume that you still remember the procedures on how we get into the Basement. You will follow me."

The four of them made their way down to the Basement and through the security screen. A cart awaited them and carried the troupe to the metal door labeled Council. Winston removed a large key from his pocket and placed it into one of two locks. Lansing inserted his own version of the same key into the second lock. They turned them together and the door slowly opened inward.

Winslow moved back a couple steps and gestured with a sweeping motion, "There you are." He stood upright with his hands crossed in front of him. "This is a far as Major Lansing and I are allowed to venture. Only Foundation Level Two members are allowed past this point. But, for some insane reason, they have requested that *you* two are to enter."

"Are you a member the Council?" Michael asked.

"I am only a member of the MF Committee. This is where the *big boys* meet," Winslow answered, with more than a little pent up jealousy in his voice.

George smiled, knowing that Winslow had been taken down a peg and was fuming inside, and walked through the open doorway. Michael took off his sunglasses and followed George, glancing at Lansing who was shocked by the sight of his yellow eyes. A simple warning shot over his bow – *be careful of who you bully*.

The door shut behind them as darkness engulfed the hallway. Michael's eyes immediately adjusted to the lack of light and he could see figures walking towards them. "We have a welcoming committee approaching."

George strained to see what Michael was talking about. He could hear light footsteps and quick glimmers of flashing metal off flickering torches on the walls. Within moments, two characters off some Babylonian palace façade appeared before them.

The two armed escorts wore white tunics with long red fringe about the bottom. Their bronze skull caps were etched with representations of feathers and each held a short spear with a triangular silver tip. They wore sandals that were strapped up to where a polished metal shin guard rose to cover the knees.

One of the guards bowed and placed his spear across his chest, in a fashion of salute. "You will follow."

The two sentinels turned and began marching back from where they had emerged, escorting Michael and George through the ominous passageway ahead. The stone conduit was illuminated by burning torches placed into iron brackets bolted into the slick rock walls. The bobbing spear heads flashed a fleeting spectral of reflected firelight about them, adding to the surrealist moment. Michael, increasingly able to see in the ultraviolet and infrared spectrums, noticed that no smoke rose from the flames – gas operated, no doubt.

It appeared that great care had been taken to recreate a millennium-old atmosphere that would instill foreboding apprehension for any Peasantry if they were led down this legacy of untouchable rule. Or, the passage had actually been constructed in a time when Aristocratic privilege was at its apex.

"Whoever designed this place must have really been into Gothic-themed remodeling," Michael whispered to George, attempting to quell his anxiety.

"Don't be surprised if King Arthur himself walked this hall," George replied, not helping with Michael's racing mind. George was not joking.

The hallway ended ahead of them, blocked by two wooden doors.

"What do you think is on the other side?" Michael asked, as they were signaled to halt by the guards in front of the entrance.

"It's the other side of tomorrow," George murmured.

One of the escort guards turned to face George and Michael, holding his spear across his chest. The other deadly usher walked three paces to the right door and used the butt of his ancient weapon to rap upon a metal plate at its center.

The tired door groaned in protest as it was slowly opened from within.

A bearded man, appearing to be as old as the doors, edged into the opened portal and motioned for them to enter. He wore a dark blue robe, encrusted with small crystal particles and a headdress loaned from the ages.

George bowed low, "We are honored, Zhang Guo Lao."

Michael looked at George and quickly bowed; whispering, "Who's that?"

George quietly replied, now looking down at the floor, "The 7th century alchemist, Zhang Guo Lao; one of the Eight Immortals."

Michael quickly turned to look at George, "Are you joking?"

George stood upright, "Well, he sure *thinks* he is, by the look of his outfit. Doubt nothing."

The old man returned the bows and slowly returned the door to its age-old position of obstruction beside its twin companion. It rested with a voluminous dull shutter.

George and Michael stood at the entrance of a mammoth room deserving of a medieval cathedral, but without pews. Sweeping arches, carved from the solid rock, soared above them with intricately engraved vines and roses snaking up their sides. Columns of granite and quartz stood along the walls every ten feet, topped with gargoyles – viciously glaring down upon any evil which may attempt to do harm to residing angels.

Moons, stars and comets, cut in relief, filled the ceiling.

Interweaving vibrations rustled the warm air around them. Just the movement of an arm would change the tones . . . as if one could create music by the correct movement of the body. As they walked forward, Michael smiled as the voices of those protected angels could almost be heard about him.

More torches, some on the walls, others in floor stands, filled the room with yellow light. The marble floor gleamed in all directions. Towards the area where an altar would normally be placed, was an inlaid mosaic of a pyramid, circled by a ring of white quartz. A single chair, expertly carved from a single trunk of ancient oak, was strategically positioned at the center of the pyramidal symbol.

Facing the chair was a twenty-foot long raised bench. Certainly not built and carved for any sermon or requiem to be presented by a holy man. But rather an installation by which a bevy of judges might rein down life altering decisions upon any cowering soul who occupied the seat.

Another chair had been placed twenty feet to the right and rear.

Behind the bench, was a forty-foot square, close representation of Michelangelo's Sistine Chapel centerpiece; *Creation of Adam* – in stained glass. Although, finer examination would reveal that the glass was, in fact, an advanced implementation of nanocrystalline materials – and the masterpiece was created in the 12th century. Four-hundred years before the painting of Adam cautiously reaching for the hand of God.

On either side of the bench, stretching out in semi-circular wings around the mosaic, were two rows of seats – not unlike a gallery or jury boxes. Behind the gallery rows hung vibrant red textiles and century-old tapestries depicting events of some unknown eras. The gallant figures, many mounted on stately steeds and battling creatures of unearthly origins, were not like anything produced in the times of chivalry and knights. The warriors wore flowing robes and headdresses of exotic feathers. And their weapons were not gleaming swords, but short poles adorned with a golden sphere at the end.

A brilliantly colored scene of an atoll comprised of concentric rings, covered with white buildings, temples and sailing ships moving in and out of the blue harbor, draped down at the far left. Michael pointed at it and whispered to George, "Atlantis?"

George leaned in, "Probably made from an aerial photograph."

The most striking, of all the hangings, illustrated a regal horse and a rider adorned in onyx black armor charging past a multi-tiered Japanese castle. It appeared to be from the Samurai-era. In the background, at the top of the piece and in front of billowing clouds, was a Megadrax.

Above each weaving were dark panels of wood, carved with Mu·Suvian symbols. Michael was able to clearly read the text as his 'new' eyes were more functional in darker settings. The engravings were the five Needs: Self Awareness, Self Esteem, Belonging, Physiological and Continuance.

The old man led them to the center chair, "Mister Fields, you will please sit here. Strategos Black Rock, you will sit in that chair beyond. The Council will enter very soon." He bowed again, walked to a door on the far right and disappeared.

George began a sorrowful walk to the far chair as his voice echoed off the finely-cut stone walls, "I don't see why they put me way back here . . . I'm the one who requested this meeting."

Michael lowered himself into the seat of honor, or whatever it was labeled per circumstance.

Michael could hear indistinguishable voices being emitted from behind the Judge's bench. They became more distinctive as the sound of a heavy door closed. There were three individuals, all heard before seen. He sat up straighter in his chair.

The assumed adjudicators all wore dark green hooded robes and identical white masks with no facial features except for eye slits.

They took seats at the bench, side by side, directly in front of Michael.

"We are Dayyani. Are you not the Michael Fields?" one of them spoke; although with masks over their faces he could not determine which one asked. He just sent his answer forward, "Yes. That is correct. I am . . . the Michael Fields."

George, seated in the chair behind Michael, leaned forward to get a better understanding of what was happening.

The questioning continued from another Dayyanum, "And you have been accompanied by Foundation Level Three, Strategos George Black Rock Day. Is this not true?"

Michael turned slightly to his right and pointed to his companion seated twenty feet behind, "Yes, that's him back there."

Another voice, only slightly different from the first, "We have reviewed Strategos Black Rock's request for you, and the five additional technicians listed in the request, to be transported to MF-2 and MF-5 during the first hours of June 30. You must all be assembled at the Megadrax, for departure in fifty-three hours."

Michael sat in the chair, his eyes darting from one masked figure to the next while unconsciously squeezing the hard wood armrests.

A third voice spoke. Nearly identical to the first two, but with a softer manner, "We shall grant Strategos Black Rock's request. This mission, on whom you and your companions will embark, is of the utmost importance to all concerned."

Michael smiled and looked back at George, who just shrugged. Michael's smile faded in confusion as he turned back to face the trio.

The sound of slow shuffling feet was heard to the right. It was the old man who had greeted them at the door. He moved to George and handed him a small wooden box. He bowed and returned to the shadows from which he emerged.

The first voice brought Michael's attention back to the Judges, "We are aware of your plans to take one of the Manta ships on July 2nd at one o'clock in the morning. We will not stop you, nor can we help you . . . except for keeping the

Megadrax out of range for your two pilots to escape. Perhaps High Minister Chén may provide some assistance."

The third voice ended the meeting, "The contents of that box, is all that we *may* be able to offer in your efforts. Go in peace, Michael Fields."

The three stood up and moved back into the darkness behind the bench.

Michael stood up and walked to George, "Alright, we got approval to use the Megadrax."

George remained seated, holding the box in his lap. "What?"

"Those guys, they granted your request . . ." Michael stopped talking. Something was not right.

George slowly stood up. "I didn't hear anything, Michael. It was just you, talking to yourself."

The large wooden door behind them opened, with the old man motioning for them to leave.

They were escorted to the door where Winslow had let them in. The guard rapped on the door with his spear handle. The sound of the locks opening was followed by the door swinging inward. Winslow backed up and let George and Michael pass.

A small crowd had formed, on the other side of the golf cart. Some pointed while others strained to get a view of Michael. The word had spread fast that two 'outsiders' had been called into the High Council Chamber. Many were surprised that George and Michael had even come out alive.

Major Lansing moved forward to disperse the crowd.

Winslow looked down at the box George was holding, "So, did you two get a parting gift?" The comment was that of a jealous school boy.

Michael put on his dark glasses and turned quickly to face Winslow with an iron voice, "We tire of you. We do not want to hear your voice any longer. You will take orders and comply without any of your incessant dribble." He then walked to the cart and sat upright, staring forward. Winslow stood, still holding the door, with his mouth open. George climbed into the cart beside Michael and whispered, "Where did that come from?"

"Where did *what* come from?" Michael asked, puzzled by the question.

George sat back as the cart began to move and said nothing more until they had safely passed through the security shield – which kept people from the surface out and Basement dwellers in.

George pushed the elevator button for Level 5.

The doors closed and the cabinet began to rise to the next floor above. "I think you have crossed a threshold, Michael."

"Me? I'm beginning to wonder about you. You claimed I was talking to myself in the hall and now you're on me about something I don't even know what you're talking about."

"You're becoming . . . like two different people. But in the same body."

Michael gestured with both hands; "I talked to those guys in the masks, and they talked to me. Maybe you couldn't hear them because you were sitting way back in the cheap seats."

"No. I do not doubt the fact that you really heard them. But there were no words spoken. It was all in your head. I'm not saying you're crazy or anything like that; they just made contact with your mind. They had some kind of communication with you that I couldn't hear." George tried to convince him of what transpired. He dared not speak of the dress-down of Winslow. Not yet.

The elevator stopped and the doors opened.

Michael was very worried about what George was telling him. He let the elevator doors close, "Because you didn't hear anything, I'll write down what they told *me* so we can get our plans solidified. We have about 52 hours before the Megadrax leaves."

George nodded, "Good. Let's go to my office and do that. And we can see what they gave us in our *parting gift*."

Michael pushed the button for Level 1 and they resumed their journey, up.

II

The word had also spread rapidly throughout The Foundation and onto Channel 121; 'Michael Fields and George Black Rock were summoned into a High Council Chamber'. The news was especially disturbing to Gus Stoddard, as he read the memo that his communication center had intercepted.

He crushed the paper message in his hand and threw it to the floor, "I can't sit around and let this stuff happen."

He put both hands on the desk and stood up. Five quick paces took him to the bookcase which covered the entire far wall of the office. He kneeled down and pulled out a long drawer, lined on the inside with velvet. Placed vertically into two rows of five slots each were rectangular stone pieces; laminated on one side with crystal and adorned with Mayan symbols on the other. They gleamed in the light of the overhead chandelier.

Gus took one and stood up as the cat rubbed against his boot, "Ya' know, Mojo, I bet The Foundation would like to get their hands on these things . . . whatever they are. I think I have ten, maybe even eleven, aces up my sleeve for some serious career advancement."

Chapter Twenty-Seven

Red sat in a seat by the window of the passenger car as the Mole traveled back north to the MF-7 Basement. It was not because there was anything to look at, except the void of solid rock tunnel wall, but it allowed her to rest her head against the bulkhead. There was one other person in the car; an older Asian women in a smart business suit, sitting at the rear. Red thought she had seen her before, on the previous trip going south.

Red had spent the last two days at the Area, in the Neutral Center, briefing representatives from branches of many services, agencies and nations. Leigus had not attended, as expected, but an arrogant aide from his Los Angeles staff had taken his place. They had brought him in on the underground train from Camp Pendleton. He had said little, as he knew even less. Red carried the meetings and answered as many questions as she could on the power and communication outages and what The Foundation was going to do about it.

As one of the two hundred and thirty-five women ever to be brought into The Foundation and being a GenZ; when she spoke . . . people listened. Unfortunately, all she could say for the past two days was, *be patient, wonderful things are coming.*

She wished that was true.

The scrolling digital banner at the front of the car displayed the train's present speed, current time and which station was coming up. It was 10:23pm and the next stop was Tonopah. She put her head back on the seat and wished Michael was meeting her again there. This time she would run. Run far and fast with Michael . . . and their child. "*To where?*" she thought. She put her forehead against the window and looked at the blackness, "There is nowhere to go."

Her seat jostled. She turned to see a man, about her age, in a grey suit and wearing a dark topcoat sitting next to her. Another, wearing a black Open Road Stetson, had moved to the seat across from them.

"Just sit quietly, Miss Redding. We don't want anyone to get hurt." He had his arms crossed, possibly hiding a weapon under his coat sleeve.

The train began to slow as it entered the Tonopah station.

Red looked back to see if there was anyone she could call out to for help. The woman sitting in the back of the car stood up and began to walk down the aisle toward her. '*I might be able to get her attention,*' she thought. '*We could cause a scene or distraction. They wouldn't dare go after her too.*'

The woman stopped beside the two men and held out her hand, "Come along, Dear. This is our stop."

The two men stood and moved on either side of the woman and waited for Red to gather her bag and move into the aisle way. As the doors opened, the man wearing the hat moved to hold them open as the other man and woman escorted Red off the train and onto the station platform.

The woman was grasping Red's forearm, "Now, watch your step. Don't want you falling down and hurting yourself or the child."

The doors closed on the passenger car and the Mole continued north, without Red.

"Who are you?" Red asked, pulling away from the grip on her arm and looking around at the three faces.

The woman turned her lapel over to display an inverted cross pin. She quickly returned the lapel to its normal lay, "That is all the information we are allowed to disclose, at this time. Please keep moving to the elevator."

The insignia meant nothing to Red.

When they reached the surface, an attack jetcopter was idling near the hangar. It was painted black with no running lights and no markings. The two sets of blades were anxiously slicing through the warm evening air waiting for its passengers to emerge from the depths of the sand. Tumbleweeds bounced away from the swirling turbulence as the four moved to the open door on the side of the craft.

The woman climbed in, followed by Red and the man in the topcoat. The other man, who was holding his hat tightly to his head, ran to the pilot's window, gave the thumbs up and moved back towards the hanger.

Within moments the machine rose to twenty feet, rotated to the left and climbed westward at 200 miles per hour toward the Sierra Nevada Mountains.

II

"Everyone is searching." It was George who brought the news of Red's kidnapping to Michael. "I'm sure she will be used as a bargaining chip. They will not harm her."

These were the only words of comfort George could offer, although he was not entirely sure himself.

CHAPTER TWENTY-EIGHT

The lights had been turned down in George's office. Dimmed to a level not unlike that of a full moon glowing on a cloudless night. The only sound in the room was the incessant low vibration of the ventilation system within the walls, which was felt more than heard.

George sat on the rug he had placed down in front of his desk. Michael was able to remove his dark glasses as he squatted on a pillow from the couch across from the old man. Martin had lain down next to George and was eyeing the strange box they were given by the equally strange Asian fellow in the Council Chamber. It was now placed on the floor between them.

The container's ancient wood had been deeply polished with fragrant oils from some long-ago age; yet continued to provide the scent of spices, smuggler's caravans and long sea journeys.

George opened the lid, stared at the silk-wrapped contents, and looked up at Michael, "There are things in this world that are valuable, and there are things that have no value . . . only worth."

Although, still distraught over Red's kidnapping, Michael attempted to get into the moment, "So, are there some *worthy* things in there?"

George gingerly picked up a scroll, "Beats me." He handed the rolled document to Michael.

He untied the red ribbon that secured the spool and carefully opened the delicate manuscript. Elaborate medieval illuminations, Egyptian-styled etchings and Mayan interpretations of robed Priests and feather-adorned Kings from many eras, cascaded down the left side of the parchment. All were holding globes; perhaps a Beam Generator or maybe a Transceiver.

The one that struck Michael the most was a detailed portrayal of two sandaled men carrying on their shoulders a highly decorated box supported with two poles. Two globes were radiating from the box's interior.

The text, to the right of the graphics, were written in four languages; none of which were English, but one was Mu·Suvian.

"Can you make out what it says?" George asked.

Michael's eyes were rapidly moving across the page, back and forth. "Yes."

"And?"

Michael was almost too excited to talk, "This is what you could call an Operations Manual for the devices. And by the looks of this thing, it wasn't written yesterday."

He warily unrolled the ancient Manual on the floor. It stretched almost ten feet. There were no signs of deterioration or abuse. He pointed at a particular section, "That third set of writings looks like Cuneiform script."

George got on one knee, "Sure does. That was used from the 30th to the 4th century B.C."

Michael felt the parchment-like material, "Sure doesn't feel that old. Of course, I've never touched a book that was 5,000 years old."

George looked at the drawings, "Sure looks like those guys are holding a smaller version of the Beam Generator we have up in the tent. But, without the frame around it."

"Bancroft added the metal frame. It says that both devices were originally just round spheres. The Beam Generator has the flat spot on the top for the Resonator. The Transceiver doesn't."

Michael read some more of the Mu·Suvian writing, "Wow."

"What?" George asked, leaning forward with elevated curiosity.

Michael used his finger to follow the line, "It says that the Generator, they call it the Energy Cell, works best when submerged. '*It gathers energy from the power of the water and gives to the need.'* In this case, I'm guessing that the *need* would be the Transceiver."

George leaned back, "Or anything else that would need energy." He paused, "Such as a Megadrax."

Michael looked up, "That's why water is so important to them. The Generator must use the hydrogen ions somehow." He thought for a moment. "It says it works *best* in water. So, it should work in our regular air but with a lower output. That's why Vern got the thing to power the camp. Imagine how much energy it will put out if we dropped it in water."

George got that look he always gets when he is surprised by something that he shouldn't be surprised about, "So Vern has the device powering the whole camp? Does Captain Summers know about it?"

Michael felt like he just tattled on Vern, "Of course . . . she approved it."

George just nodded, taking a mental note to *speak* to Vern, "What else does the scroll say?"

Michael sheepishly looked back to the writing, "Just stuff we already figured out, like; don't have two Generators closer than a half *gesh* apart when you start them up and don't poke a Generator with a metal pole when it's on. I made that one second one up – I should add it at the bottom."

George smiled, "Gesh?"

Michael put his hand on his forehead, "Oh, sorry. They aren't talking about latitudes and stuff like that. It's going back to some ancient ways of time-distance based on the *gesh* or four minutes. The sun moves across the face of the earth at 175 miles per minute. A whole *gesh* would be 700 miles; so half a gesh is 350 miles. Somehow this stuff makes sense to me. Don't ask me why."

George did understand why, "And what about the Transceiver? How do you operate it?"

Michael moved his finger to half-way down on the Mu·Suvian script and reading right to left, "OK, here it is . . . It's not a Transceiver in here. They refer to it as The Messenger."

George whispered under his breath, "Kwena'a."

"What?"

"The Golden Eagle, *my* People's Messenger."

Michael kept reading, "Oh. OK . . . '*To awaken The Messenger; Sing the Song of Inanna.*'"

Michael sat upright, "What?"

George leaned back on the couch, "Well, another riddle. So, that doesn't mean anything to you . . . in your GenZ being?"

"I can't say that it does, unless the Transceiver responds to audible tones." He thought for long while as George scratched that one spot that caused Martin to melt.

Michael reread the Mu·Suvian text again, looking for something he might have misinterpreted.

George quit making Martin's leg move and turned back to Michael, "You have a speaker on that laptop of yours?"

"Sure. They all do." He smiled. "Ah. So, you think the Song is already in the computers? Bancroft put it in the program?"

George held up his hands, "Hey, I'm just a country boy. But, it would seem that if Bancroft was instructed to develop the software and devices, he would also have been told to put in some way of activating the things."

Michael thought hard. "That's what Roland said when we were in the tent looking for XZX files."

He slowly held up his finger, "You know, I'll bet those files are sequences of tones. And they can only be opened by two individuals with specific LiquiCode numbers that are already in the program. That would explain the whole XZX thing."

George agreed, "That sounds like what might be the answer to the Song thing. And I suspect that you are one of the two LiquiCode numbers that have to be read before your computer can 'sing'."

"Who would the other GenZ be?"

Both of them knew the answer, before Michael even finished the sentence.

Michael nodded and put his head down, "It's Red. We need to find her and take her with us on the Megadrax."

George stood up, "That sure makes sense to me. After all, the Transceivers need to hear the Song of you two's Daughter." He put on his hat and was ready to walk out with Martin.

Michael's head jerked up and he began to speak, "George Black Rock, you must write this down."

George turned quickly. He could see that Michael was in contact with the Mu·Suvians. Martin cowered and moved to sit at the end of the couch and peeked around its corner at Michael. Dogs know.

Grabbing a notepad and pen off the desk, George sat back down on the floor, "I'm ready, go ahead."

Michael's eyes closed and he began to speak, "The original tasks and plan, given to Bancroft by the Mu·Suvians, was to send new firmware to any device that was on any network, in the world. At 11:11 am GMT, on December 21st, 2012, all of those microprocessors would shut down until a restart code was sent by GMCS."

George was writing fast, "OK, I got that . . . continue."

"The outage was to last only three days, until the Beam Generators and Transceivers were configured and could be put 'on-line' after the landing. The black-out would mask the Ark from ground surveillance. It was to be the beginning of the Universal Era for all mankind"

George shook his head, "I thought something wasn't right when everything when to hell. OK, keep going."

"Gus Stoddard had killed Bancroft and had taken over the GMCS server farm in the Yucatan – thus preventing the restart. The lockdown of all the MFs was initiated by Gus Stoddard, hours before the shutdown was to occur. He wanted to keep all Deep Purple and Program 3938 personnel from interfering in his plans to overthrow The Foundation. Of which he stills plans to do. However; when GMCS went into Mu·Suvian mode for the new Era, GMCS could not be operated and the MFs could not be reopened, nor could the world's infected computers be restarted."

George put down his pen, "And that was a perfect time for Leigus to bring in his ESA troops and initiate his own climb to power."

"This is known to us. George Black Rock, until GMCS can be restarted, any system or device which is controlled by a microprocessor is non-functional. This includes virtually every power grid in the world. The only solution is to remove the affected components from the system; either by replacing or bypassing them. If a connection can be made, the restart code is 3745158845447230383241-9. This will suffice until the Beam Generators can be placed into the power grids. This message must be sent to the world immediately."

George's mind was working fast. "We'll get right on it . . . anything else?"

"The Beam Generator, at MF-3, needs to be activated as soon as possible. The two Transceivers, at MF-6 and MF-2, *must* be operational within three days. It is almost too late." He paused. "Strategos Black Rock must retrieve the crate that is in Gus Stoddard's warehouse and take it to Nazca Base within three days. I, also, must be at that location in three days to activate the Beam Generator, which is within the crate."

Michael's head dropped and he quickly looked up, as someone who had just nodded off to sleep in a sitting position.

He stared at George, who was staring at him, "What?"

"Welcome back," George smiled, handing Michael the notepad. "You might want to read what you talk about in your sleep."

Michael cautiously took the pad and read what George had written, "I said this? Wow, didn't know I knew so much."

George took back the paper, "So, it looks like we have a lot to do in the next few days; along with finding Red."

Michael's lips tightened up and his jaw muscles twitched. He looked straight ahead, "I know where she is. Her thoughts are with me. I see the place and how to get there. I will need Max, Parker, a vehicle . . . and guns."

Chapter Twenty-Nine

Within two hours, George's Black Shirts were spreading the instructions Michael had delivered, along with the restart code, on any communication media they could find. They began with shortwave radio and spark-gap Morse code transmitters. Localized power systems began to spring to life. Starting in Fernley, then Reno, then on to Hawthorne where the military took over and rapidly passed the word on their communication networks. Within six hours, most of the West Coast had enough power to establish order and provide more than basic services.

The next morning, not only did George supply Michael with Max and Parker, he detached a small commando squad, under the command of Captain Summers, to go with him and aid in the rescue of Red. There was no way of knowing who was holding her. The scuttlebutt was that Leigus and the ESA were the culprits.

George didn't think so. Somehow Michael *knew* it wasn't so.

George had given Parker a small box before the convoy headed south. "When you are told, give this to Michael. I won't be seeing you all for a while -- perhaps a long while. I need to go to the Basement and have a talk with Winslow."

The small convoy headed south and onto highway 80 where they turned to the west. Using the defunct MF-7 Security SUVs, and Max's *borrowed* ESA vehicle, they moved fast.

Parker was in his customary seat, riding Shotgun with Max. He held his M-16 between his knees. Michael was in the back with Tara. Max was the lead vehicle.

Parker turned around, "So, any idea where we're headed?"

Michael handed the map forward to Parker and pointed at a route, "We need to go down 395 to Coleville; looks like it's only about a hundred miles or so."

Max squared his shoulders, "Hell, we could have *walked* that far for a fight."

"Hopefully there won't be a fight. Sure don't want anyone to get hurt over this," Michael said. "I know she feels threatened, but it doesn't feel like she's deathly afraid. The main thing is that we need to get her up to the MF and onto the Megadrax with me and Roland by tomorrow night."

Parker handed the map to Max and turned back to Michael, "Hey, you should see Max and me do that simulator. We got it down."

Max looked over at Parker, "Remember what I said, it's a whole lot different when there's a couple bad guys on your butt."

Parker smiled and winked at Tara, "He said butt." She smiled back and lightly slapped his arm. She picked up her radio, "I need to let the rest know where we're headed."

As she talked to the troops in the vehicles behind them, Parker leaned towards Michael, "Are you really in contact with Red? I mean that mind-melt thing? That's so cool."

Michael thought about the sensation, "It's not like I can hear her voice, but I know it's her. More like a feeling that directs my thoughts."

"Can you talk, or whatever it is, to her, too?"

"I don't know. Don't think I ever really tried," Michael answered slowly.

"Well, you should let her know that we're on our way," Parker suggested.

Michael leaned back in the seat, closed his eyes and tried to think of Red. He brought back images of anything that would stir a flash of connection; her eyes, hair . . . body. His mind became sidetracked with the last one. He needed to concentrate. He called her name in his mind, over and over. Nothing was happening. He opened his eyes and sat up, "I tried everything that I thought would work, I even . . ." The familiar feeling was loud, "Michael."

He looked around. Parker looked at him, "Hey, you OK?"

"I heard it, or her." He leaned back again and concentrated on the feeling. "Michael. Are you near? I feel you near."

He kept the feeling and answered with his own minds voice, "Yes. We are on the way. We will be there in two hours or less."

"I am with the Elves. Do not harm them. They are us." The feeling faded and Michael sat up.

"Well, did she say to say 'Hi' to me?" Parker asked, in his usual style.

"She's OK. She's with the Elves."

Parker sat back in his seat, "Oh, man. Didn't Gus talk about the Elves? Didn't they help Bancroft?"

Michael thought back, "Yes. We thought that they were the terrorists who were helping him."

Parker rubbed his chin, "From what I remember, I think we were the *only* ones who thought they were terrorists."

Michael looked out the window, "Well, George said that we were fed a lot of misinformation."

"Now wait a minute, what makes you think that they aren't?" Parker asked.

"Red said that they were us. And to me, that means they are GenZ."

"GenZ were helping Gus?"

Michael thought back, "No, remember? Gus said that the communications that went on between the Elves and Itzamna was all on emails. When Gus took on Bancroft's persona of Itzamna, the Elves wouldn't have known the difference. It had to be the Elves that planted the crates in the MFs . . . probably built the Beam Generator and Transceiver frames, too."

Parker sat back in the seat, "Elves, what a stupid name for those guys."

Tara leaned forward, "The ancient word for a God in Mesopotamian Sumer was El, which eventually became Elf in Anglo-Saxon. It's also associated to engel or angel."

Michael thought back to the Gargoyles on the columns in the Council Chamber. They guarded the angels.

Parker turned around to Michael, "Oh, I forgot to mention that my lovely GI Jane also has a minor in anthropology. It's from USC, but I still love her."

Tara leaned back, smiling, "You better."

Max turned on the radio, and a real station was on the air. The announcer was reading off messages for former police and fire personnel to report to their stations. News was being broadcast of water systems being turned on and full electrical services being restored throughout the western and central states. More traffic was appearing, heading north. The trailer camps were breaking up.

It felt like a huge switch was thrown and the human race came back on.

Parker played with the dial and was able to get two FM and three AM stations on the radio. Although two of the AM were in Spanish and were hard to understand with all of the echo chamber effects.

After an hour Max called back to Michael, "We're coming up on the Coleville area; where to now?"

Michael relaxed and waited for an answer. He closed his eyes, "Turn right onto 89 and keep going until it's time to stop." The information was not coming from Red. It felt different.

Max shook his head, "Oh, those are great directions for an invasion force."

The convoy traversed the two-lane road and climbed into the mountains toward Monitor Pass. After another few miles a sharp turn to the right was just ahead. Max slowed to make the curve. A man was standing in the middle of the road, with his hand out to stop the convoy. Max slammed on the brakes, as did the three vehicles behind him.

"You crazy bastard! Get out of the road, I almost killed you!" Max yelled out his window.

Michael sat up, opened his door and climbed out. Tara and Parker jumped out of their side of the vehicle, leveling weapons at the approaching man.

The unarmed man walked towards Michael with his arms swinging at his side. He was smiling as he stopped two yards away, "Welcome, Michael Fields. I am honored to meet you. My name is Andrew Poh. Elizabeth Redding asked me to escort you all to our compound. Please follow me." He turned and walked to a motorcycle that was hidden behind a stand of trees beside the road. He started it and waved to Michael.

Tara, Parker and Michael returned to their seats and Max put the SUV into four-wheel drive. "Hang on everyone. Don't think this path has been used too much." The four vehicles followed Andrew through the trees and up the steep grade toward a sheer outcrop of rock.

They were waved through a gate in a ten-foot tall steel-wire fence, by two men. They were dressed in civilian clothes. Michael looked back to see the gate being closed after the last vehicle passed through. He turned to look ahead. Sitting in a clearing at the base of the cliff were five large log cabins and three smaller storage buildings. Farther to the left was a Helipad with a tarp-covered jetcopter resting upon it.

The convoy pulled up to the first cabin where Red was standing on the porch, with the woman who had taken her off the train. She was wearing a brightly colored summer maternity dress and waving vigorously at Michael.

Before Max put the SUV in Park, Michael jumped out of the car and ran up her, throwing his arms around her and kissing her passionately. She held him even tighter.

Michael held her at arm's length, "I almost didn't recognize you. You look so . . . country."

She giggled, "This dress, my room, just everything I need was waiting for me." She kissed him again, "Except you. And now you're here. So, I guess now I do have everything."

The woman walked down to the bottom step, waving to the rest of the convoy, "Come in . . . come in! Welcome to 'whatever you want to call this place'."

Tara signaled for the twelve commandos, in the other three vehicles, to get out and form a perimeter, a hundred yards out from the houses. She walked up to the woman with as much authority as she could muster.

"I'm Captain Summers of The Foundation's Black Shirts under George Black Rock. We would like an explanation for your abduction of Elizabeth Redding."

The woman held the railing as she carefully maneuvered the last step, carrying a basket of fresh cut flowers in the crook of her other arm. She walked over to Tara, and to the Captain's surprise, took her hand.

With the voice of every grandmother Tara had ever met, "It is *so* good to meet you Tara. I am so happy that George has people like you helping him. Please, just call me Citi."

Tara blinked in surprise at the sound of her first name.

The woman let go of her hand, "Why did we bring Red here? A communication was intercepted from Itzamna, calling for Michael to be abducted and taken to the Yucatan facility and Re*d's extermination*. This was *highly* irregular for any directive coming from Itzamna, so we knew that other powers had been put into play. We had to save Michael, Red and their baby. All three of them are to be very important figures; in *all* our futures."

Citi lowered the basket and held it with both hands. She smiled, "We know this. It is written. Everyone in this complex, are here to serve them. And you should protect them with your life." She turned to walk up the steps, "Would you like a nice cup of green tea, Dear?"

Tara shook her head as she stood stunned. Michael, having overhead Citi's words, turned back to Red, "Is this true? Gus wants you dead?"

"First of all, he wants to get his hands on you, Mister Yellow Eyes. The word is getting around that you're the only one the Mu·Suvians talk to -- besides Leigus." She lifted his sunglasses. "Well, I suppose I can get used to it. But, I hope our daughter's are brown".

Michael was very distraught and pulled his glasses back into place, "Yeah, that will nice, but what about him wanting you dead? What did you do to warrant that? What should you be telling me?"

"I don't think it's so much *me* as it is to eliminate the arrival of Inanna."

"Well, that could be accomplished by killing *you*, right?" He wasn't happy. "And who decided that her name was to be Inanna?"

"It has to be," Red said, her lower lip protruding more than usual.

Michael released her and waved his arms in the air as he turned in a circle, "Why does everyone seem to be so flipped-out about our baby's arrival?" He was facing Red once again. "George was the first one who told me that her name was to be Inanna; something about the Sumerians. They've been gone for thousands of years. Why do they have a say in this? Or do you have a few stashed over in that cabin over there?"

Red laughed, "Of course not. They all live in Omaha and run a convenience store. What's the matter with you, eh?"

"Oh, nothing really. Except that some nut case wants to kill my wife and child."

"Your wife and child? When did that happen? Who is she? Is she prettier than me?" She smiled coyly, repeatedly poking him with her finger.

"You know what I mean."

He took her hand and led her over to a wicker settee on the porch and sat next to her. "I've been going through some awful things in my head. There are voices and images . . . and knowing things that I never learned or experienced, at any time in my life."

Citi walked over to stand in front of Michael and Red. She put the basket on the porch railing. "You are very lucky, Michael. You beat the odds and are moving through the Synthesis. We are very relieved that you both are here and safe."

Michael looked at Red. There was that word again; Synthesis. She was just lovingly smiling back. *It must be a good thing*, he thought. But it wasn't fun being the one it was happening to.

He looked back to Citi, "How many are here?"

"There are forty-seven in this camp now, with two more on the way. Actually, with you three, that makes an even fifty." She turned around to look at Tara and Parker. "Who knows, there may be more, soon."

"Then everyone here is *not* a GenZ?" Red asked.

"No. With you three, that will make twenty-four. The rest of the residents are just regular people, here to work with us, to help us. Most GenZ have had some very bad experiences in the 'outside world'. Many of them were found living in isolation, so they were brought here. Those that are not GenZ go out into the public for them."

Michael adjusted his glasses, "Are you a GenZ? You seem to be . . ."

"A little old to be a GenZ? Yes, Dear, I am. But, I came along many years before any of those here. You might say that I was a result of the Mu·Suvians 'old way' of cross-breeding. My mother was an abductee, as was Leigus'. They needed us to pass on their wishes and information. Sometimes our heads got too big, as you are witnessing now with The Foundation in conflict with itself."

"Do you live here, too?" Red asked.

Citi looked out to the meadow and the mountains climbing beyond, "No. But, it would be a very nice place to call home. The clean air, the flowers . . . no, I have a home a bit farther away. I am just visiting, as it were. Here to help for awhile."

She sighed and picked through the basket of flowers, removing a green beetle that was hitching a ride under a leaf. She held it in her fingers and examined it with her dark eyes, "I remember the old days, when the Mu·Suvians were respected – almost revered by The Foundation. We jumped at the chance to help them. Goodness gracious, The Foundation was formed by them so that humanity could benefit from their knowledge . . . be guided in so many needed ways. I can think of a hundred or more times when they helped us. But, now . . .

Leigus takes their wishes as just that, wishes. As if *he* had all the power in the universe. He just wants to kick them out and run everything himself from now on. Believe me, we may have reached the New Era, but we are far from going it alone."

She carefully placed the bug on the porch rail and watched it run for safety. She slowly turned back and looked very seriously at Michael, "It is now nearing the time that you will be instructed in the old ways. You need to take your place in The Foundation."

Red squeezed Michael's hand as she felt cold run through his body.

He looked at Red and then to Citi, "Now, it seems a bit odd that I'm going to be trained for some new job in The Foundation, when my thirty-eighth birthday is a couple weeks away. Don't you think that they would get someone a little younger for an entry position?"

Citi laughed, while Red tried to hold back laughter. She could not.

"What?" Michael asked.

The woman crossed her arms, "Your age is has nothing to do with it. Everything you need to know is already in your mind. You just need to be trained on how to access the information and use it wisely."

Red placed both hands on Michael's cheeks and looked at him, "You will be trained to take Leigus' place. However, he doesn't know that yet. But I am sure he suspects it. And I am beginning to suspect that Gus Stoddard knows that, too."

Michael could not speak. His eyes darted to Citi, who smiled and slowly nodded.

Red shook his face, "Listen to me. You have been chosen; either by luck of the GAIA odds or some other force we don't know yet. But you are going through the Synthesis – only you."

"So, I won some bizarre DNA contest. And I get some yellow eyes out of the deal. That makes me qualified to take Leigus' place . . . running The Foundation. What the hell is he gonna say? What about High Minister Chén? I bet he's gonna have a cow, too."

Citi laughed, "I wouldn't worry about old Chén, if I were you. Just concentrate on your upcoming training. You will learn to be a true leader. You will learn to balance your soft heart with strength and courage."

"Citi, I don't know if we can stay here. I need to take Red with me. We have to do a very important thing together," Michael said.

Citi smiled, looking at Red's stomach, "I would say you already have."

Michael had no choice but disclose the reason, "We both need to board the Megadrax tomorrow night."

"So we have been told." Citi smiled. "And for you two to go back into the Basement would be disastrous for, not only yourselves, but for all of us."

Michael looked at Red, "So, what are we going to do?"

Citi picked up the basket, "The Mu·Suvians have arranged for the Megadrax to come here to pick you both up. There is a platform, a quarter mile from here, which a few of us have used to board the ship in the past. George has been contacted to have Roland bring all of the equipment you will need for the mission."

Michael cocked his head, "You said that the Mu·Suvians told you."

Citi smiled, "Oh, how silly of me, I forgot to mention that. They talk to me, too." She put her finger to her lips, "But don't you tell anyone. Sure don't want that sick bastard Leigus to know that you've been talking to me." She held out her hand, "Come along Elizabeth. Let's get these flowers in a vase. And I think we both could use a cup of tea."

Chapter Thirty

The sun had set behind the mountains as Michael and Parker sat on the steps of the porch of the cabin. Both were sharing a long promised beer or two. Michael *bought* the first one, Parker the next. Actually, no one bought anything. Max had been saving a case he had *procured* a few weeks earlier and was sitting on the grass in front of the steps, working on his third bottle.

Red and Tara helped a group of women whom were preparing food for them all, including the troops on the perimeter. Although, there seemed to be more food being made than could be consumed in a normal evening. Both women were enjoying being regular people and not soldiers of The Foundation for a few hours. And they laughed and giggled about more than what was happening around them.

Max looked up to Michael in the waning light, "So, how are those night-vision eyes working out for you?"

Michael finally took off the dark glasses and looked upon the vista before him. "Ya' know it's kind of weird. Everything looks like it does on a cloudy day. Or, maybe just before a storm . . . with that strange blue-green tint."

Max looked out to where Michael was viewing, "Well, I can't make out anything worth a damn."

Parker was putting his thumb into the hole of the bottle and pulling it out. It produced a popping sound, over and over; a customary Parker annoyance. He stopped and pointed out to the field, "You think the ESA will try to hit us, up here? Attempt to get Red and then hijack you?"

Max shook his head, "I hope not, we've got seventeen beers to go."

Citi walked out of the cabin door, "Ah, there you all are. Having a Bachelor Party are we?"

CONTINUANCE

Michael looked up to see another woman, about his age, emerge from the cabin. She was followed by Red and Tara. They all had that look . . .

Citi put her arm around the new woman's shoulders, "Michael, this is Reverend Elkins. You can call her Martha. She just stopped by to pay us a visit. Don't you think you should ask Red something, before tomorrow at noon, when we all gather over there in the meadow?"

Michael put down his beer and stood up, swallowing hard. He looked over to Parker, who was smiling like a Hyena. He turned to see Max, holding his beer up in a salute, "Go for it."

Michael walked up to Elizabeth and took her hands. He then led her to the end of the porch. "OK, I suppose this is the right time. I know it is the right place, and every particle of my being knows that you are the right one."

He dropped to one knee. Elizabeth could hardly see him with the tears welling up in her eyes.

"Will you marry me, Elizabeth Redding?"

She dropped slowly to her knees and took his face in her hands, "Yes. Yes. Yes."

They kissed as the small crowd went wild.

Michael and Red walked back to exchange hugs and pats on the back with their well-wishers.

Citi put her hand on Parker's arm, "I think the Best Man has something that he was supposed to give to Michael?"

Parker looked around, "Oh, you mean me." He slapped his pant's pockets and then his jacket. He reached into the inside pocket and pulled out a small box. He handed it to Michael. "George told me to give this to you. But only when I was told to do it. Beats me what it is."

With Red looking on, Michael opened it. Inside, wrapped in a beaded cloth, were the two rings that Michael had first seen on George's fireplace mantel in the squatter's cabin.

The beers held out for another hour. Then some California wine appeared. The feasting and celebration lasted well into the night as decorations were made and a white arbor was built for the meadow. It had been a very long time since anyone in the compound had something to be happy about.

The morning sun brought more activity as Elizabeth and Tara, her Maid of Honor, tried on dresses which the other women in the compound trimmed and sewed.

The men searched for suits for Michael and Parker. An expensive black tux was discovered in a storage closet that fit Michael. Someone had put it away a year earlier, waiting for better times. Parker settled for a peach colored prom jacket, black slacks, and a peach colored matching satin bow tie; all found in a storage bin marked 'dangerous stuff'.

Among the sound of birds and the gentle mountain breezes the wedding vows were spoken. The two rings were exchanged, shifting the profound sadness from which they came, into hope for all mankind.

Before the last phrase was spoken, Elizabeth Fields reached for Michael's right hand and slid on a Lion's Head ring. It was a gift from High Minister Chén, who was just passing on a wish.

As the sun reached its zenith overhead; joyous tears, smiles, dancing and laughter filled the meadow.

The New Era had officially begun.

Chapter Thirty-One

12:20am - June 1st, 2013

There was no sound. No lights. The only indication that something was occurring overhead were the stars. Across the northern horizon, they began to disappear. A few at first; then a triangular void gradually spread amongst them. A gigantic plow was digging a furrow through the heavens; burying celestial bodies in the overturned black æther of the universe. The huge craft came to rest over the small group of GenZ and Tara's soldiers waiting at the platform. A roof of exotic metals had replaced the vast open sky above them and it began to descend.

Parker was looking up, a huge smile on his face, "I bet the UFO watchers are going nuts tonight."

Two rectangular outlines of light burst from the belly of the ship, followed by a flood of white brilliance as the panels began to slide back. As the craft stopped twenty-feet above the group a metal staircase slowly dropped from the front panel and made contact with the wooden platform. The dark form completely covered the area above the entire meadow and camp.

From out of the opening and down the stairs, Roland emerged. He stopped half-way down the steps and looked below at the assemblage. He held up his hand, fingers apart, "Greetings Earthlings! You got a Leader somewhere down there?"

Parker called up, "I could have come up with something more impressive than that!"

Roland shrugged, "OK, *you* can be the alien next time." He lifted his thumb to Michael, "Time to go. These guys are on a tight schedule."

Parker bounded up the wooden steps to the platform and looked up into the opening, "So, who's flying this thing?"

Roland looked up, scanning the bottom of the massive craft, "Don't know. But I'm sure you can guess. The cockpit, or whatever they call it, is way up front and no way to get into it. Never saw anyone go in or come out."

Michael and Red walked up the green painted wooden steps to stand beside Parker. Citi and Tara followed.

"You have any trouble with Winslow or anyone, getting aboard?" Michael asked Roland.

"Nope, George had two of his guards help carry the three laptops and stuff. I guess he had told Winslow that you were already on the road in a car, going over to MF-6. No one questioned it."

Michael turned to face Parker, Tara and Citi. "I, we, want to thank you all for everything you have done for us in the short time we've been here. We will definitely return."

Citi held out her hand to those below, "It was a real pleasure for everyone here. What a joyous time we all shared."

Parker pointed at Michael, "I'll be thinking about you when I'm Down Under. Max and I will be sampling some Aussie beer, walking around the beaches . . ."

Tara punched his arm, "Not without me, you won't."

"You know, it's winter down there." Michael informed him.

Roland headed up the set of steps, "Let's get moving."

Michael picked up Red's bag and they walked up behind him, waving to their friends below. They stopped as Citi stepped up upon the walkway.

Red quickly moved back down to help her, "Are you coming along, too?"

"Why do you think they were scheduled to stop here in the first place? I've been taking this bus longer than I can remember," she said smiling. "Now, let's get on board and get those devices up and running. We need the Transceivers operating as soon as possible."

Michael stood to the side as Citi walked past him and into the ship. Red moved to stand next to him, "I'm beginning to put some strange pieces together here."

Michael followed them up the ramp. He had been putting the pieces together since the night before.

As soon as all were aboard, the stairway began to ascend back into the ship as those on the ground backed away from the platform.

The stairway panel closed as the four travelers stood in the highly-lit entrance chamber, facing a door with an illuminated plate over it. The room lights dimmed as the room was sterilized and pressurized. The plate displayed a set of symbols as the door slid open, revealing a room the size of a ballroom.

"OK, let's go find a seat. Don't lose your boarding passes," Citi said with a soft giggle, walking ahead of the others.

The Megadrax rose silently into the night sky. It slowly rotated to the east, pointing its nose toward MF-3 in Hannibal, Missouri. Without any sensation of gravity force felt by the passengers, it climbed out of sight within seconds, becoming a satellite of earth.

Roland led Michael and Red over to a crescent-shaped couch which hugged a small table in front of it. They sat down as Citi continued to walk to the rear where a young woman, dressed in a uniform that must have been designed for sailing Clipper Ships in the 1800's, greeted her and took her into another room.

Roland leaned over, "Is this wild? I still can't believe it. Inside a Megadrax 4. Think of all the guest appearances I could get on late-night talk shows. Unfortunately, no one would believe me."

Michael gestured to Red, "Roland, this is my wife, Elizabeth. You probably remember her from the meeting we had with Leigus."

Roland shook Red's hand, "Oh, yes. That was really something, the way you really kicked Winslow's butt." He then reached over and picked up Michael's computer case. "Here's your machine, and . . ." He bent down and reached under the table. He brought up the box the Council had given George.

Michael placed it in his lap and opened the lid, "Oh, good. The Scroll, almost forgot about it. There's so much going on right now."

Red touched the ancient wooden container and peered in, "Scroll?"

"The operating instructions for the Transceiver devices we're going to try and turn on."

"Oh. Well, a good thing to bring with you. How could you have forgotten about that?"

Michael leaned over and kissed her, "I suppose I had a few other things on my mind."

Roland coughed to get attention, "The satellite uplink stuff is over there. I'm sure I brought everything we need."

Michael looked around the couch, "Did you bring the Resonator for the Beam Generator at MF-3?"

Roland pulled a velvet cloth out of his pocket. He unfolded the contents, revealing the Mayan glyph on the stone surface.

The young woman, whom had greeted Citi, and an even younger man dressed in the same era uniform as the young woman, walked up to them. "Excuse me, but High Minister Chén would like Elizabeth Fields to join her in her cabin," the woman said.

Michael looked at Elizabeth, "You were right."

Elizabeth gathered her bag, "Now I'm kind of freaked out. Wow. How am I supposed to act? It's like hanging out with a Queen or something," she whispered.

"I think she would like you to act the same way you did back in the cabin. I'll bet she gets the royal treatment way too much," Michael assumed.

"Do I call her Citi?" Elizabeth asked, to anyone that might have and answer.

The young woman leaned towards her and smiled, "I have a feeling that she would like that . . . from you. Please follow me."

The two women walked to the back.

The man in the retro uniform bowed, "I am Carlos. Would you both enjoy a tour around the ship? You may leave your belongings here. Do not worry. They are completely safe."

Michael stood up, "OK. Let's go."

Roland and Michael followed Carlos as he led them along a passageway, towards the back of the craft. They saw ten more 'crew-members' milling about the area. Carlos pointed out guest and crew quarters as they walked. "On longer voyages, there is not a lot to be done. So, we sleep and watch movies." He stopped and smiled, "And eat . . . I will show you the Galley shortly."

"You watch movies?" Michael asked, trying to fathom the thought that the ship was actually nothing more than an intergalactic jetliner, with first-class accommodations.

"Oh yes. The whole vessel is wired for video. We have all the latest movies. And the audio files are huge. There are terabytes of songs available. I upload my favorites occasionally. The High Minister said it was acceptable, as long as I do not play them over the ship-wide system. Many members of the crew do not share *my* taste in music." He stopped at the top of a spiral staircase and waited for another member of the crew to come up, "Watch your step; we are going down to Deck Two."

"Is there any way we can see the engines?" Roland asked.

Carlos put his hand on the staircase railing and smiled, "I thought that would interest you more than the offices and living quarters on this deck. The 'engine' is down here."

They carefully walked in single file, down the precariously winding metal steps. As they descended into the belly of the Megadrax, their eyes were met with a twilight that filled the deep bay.

Standing together on the metallic gird flooring, Carlos pointed to the four large liquid storage tanks spanning the length of the area. "Those are the water tanks that feed the ion converters and cool the Gravity Push Plates and coils. The tanks are made of some kind of metal or something. They are not painted that dark orange color. It's just the natural shade of the material. They're fifteen feet in diameter and over a hundred feet long, each."

"I don't hear any machine sounds, like pumps or engines," Roland said.

"Oh, there are machines, just no moving parts. We need to walk that way," Carlos stated as he began walking toward the tanks.

"Isn't a machine defined by having moving parts that move other things?" Michael asked.

"That is an interesting 20th century reflection. However; this whole ship is a machine, and there are no moving parts to make *it* work," Carlos commented.

"Where are the robots and weird artificial intelligent things that should be wandering around in something like this? I thought there would be some pretty high tech devices doing all the work." Michael asked.

"We are standing in the most intelligent machine ever built. What could top that?" Carlos proudly said.

As they walked down the center of the bay with a water tank on each side of them, Roland whispered to Michael, "Carl Sagan once said that, 'Somewhere, something incredible is waiting to be known.' I think we found a Somewhere."

Below them, through the grating, a solid plate of softly glowing material could be seen. There were large diameter tubes snaking around its surface. It occupied the entire belly of the ship and was bathing it in an eerie blue hue.

Roland pointed down at the object, "What's that thing? Is it radioactive? Should we be wearing protective suits or something?"

"That's the Gravity Push Plate on Deck Three. You can see the cooling pipes attached to it. And, no, it is not radioactive. It's just vibrating so fast that the material glows. Pretty cool, huh?"

Michael looked down, "Vibrating? I don't hear anything."

Carlos stopped and joined them in looking through the metal mesh they were standing on, "I'm not an engineer or anything. They just tell me that it vibrates, or something like that. And it is so fast that it begins to weigh more than the earth can hold in one spot. So it goes up and takes the ship with it." He stood up, "You can get more information from one of the engineers in the back."

Roland stood upright and looked at Michael, "I think I know what is going on here. The material is being resonated so violently, or *loud* if you will, that it appears like a massive body of single element matter. Perhaps it is emulating a body ten-thousand miles wide or something. Way too large for the earth to pull down in a concentrated area. This ship just makes the Earth think it's another moon. The louder it *sounds*, the less gravitational pull the earth, or any celestial body, will have on it."

Michael shook his head, "So, if they want to take off, they turn up the volume, and to land they turn it down."

Roland smiled, "Turn, as you say *the volume*, to a point where they could orbit, or just get attracted by another body out there – like the moon. By doing that they would be able to slingshot around the galaxy."

Michael turned to Carlos, "What about just going forward? We're flying to Missouri, how do they do that?"

Carlos shrugged, "We just go up to where the pilot thinks it's safe, and they turn on some kind of thruster."

Roland pointed his finger, "I bet it is the same technology that is down there. They must have Gravity Push Plates in the rear of this thing."

Carlos nodded, "Well, actually, there are three big panels on the stern; two on either side of the bow and two on both sides, aft. That might be the steering."

Roland put his hands in his pockets, "That's the three elongated panels we saw on the back end when we were down in the Basement. That is so awesome."

They continued to walk towards the stern of the ship again.

Michael was still looking down at the glowing plate beneath them, "So, where do they get all the power to run this . . . Gravity Push system?"

Carlos stopped, causing Michael to look up. In a giant, clear-glass chamber before them, sat a Beam Generator. It was almost totally immersed in water and was radiating the familiar violet glow that they had witnessed in the tent.

"Gentlemen, our source of power," Carlos said, pointing at the globe. It did not have the metal frame around it, as did the one which was in the crate.

Michael and Roland quickly walked up to the chamber. Roland nudged Michael while pointing at the top of the Generator. There was a crystal Resonator resting on the flat portion of the globe that was not covered in water.

"Well, old Vern was right. The thing does work better in water," Michael stated.

"I think I can see why water is so important to the Mu·Suvians now," Roland said, still in awe of the Generator resting in the chamber.

"And a good reason as to why they are on earth," Michael added.

Roland backed up, "Well, earth and Orcus."

Michael stood back from the chamber, "Imagine if we had cars and planes that had this technology."

Roland held up both hands and stretched out his arms, "We *do* have the technology. What, or who, is stopping us from using it?"

Michael knew the answer, "I don't think it is Citi Chén and her side of The Foundation. So that kind of narrows it down."

Roland nodded and then smiled, "I bet the Manta ships have the same technology; that's why they didn't have any landing gear. I wonder if Parker knows that."

Michael smiled back, "And I wonder if he knows that those things can fly to the moon? He's going to be so physced."

Carlos broke in, "We need to keep moving, not much time left to give you the whole tour. The ship should be over MF-3 in a half hour."

They continued their tour through the engineering section, where one of the technicians confirmed Roland's idea on the properties of the Gravity Push. They walked through a few labs that were analyzing soil and water samples.

The Deck One tour ended in front of a large door at the very back of the ship.

Carlos placed his ID card in front of the door sensor. The dual ten-foot tall door slid open. In the center of the room sat two Mantas.

"Holy Toledo!" Roland exclaimed.

The small ships were resting three feet off the deck, without any landing gear or supports. They were glued in mid-air, with their cockpits open and hoses running into various panels on the skin. Their noses were pointed to the Starboard bulkhead, where an outline crease of a large door could be seen. The Fighters could be launched from this room.

Roland began to move forward.

Carlos put his arm out, "We are not allowed in there. Only the maintenance and flight crews can go beyond this point. When the outside doors are opened, there is no atmosphere in there. It's for everyone's safety."

"This is a Mother Ship!" Roland could hardly contain himself.

"What do you mean by, *no atmosphere*?" Michael asked.

"They are only used for self-defense. Not really configured for near-earth operations," Carlos explained.

Roland nodded, "So, they are only flown, out there."

"That is correct. They are launched at about 100 miles up."

"Then you must have human pilots aboard who can fly them?" Michael wondered.

"Not that I know of; we are not scheduled to leave on any *long trips* for awhile."

"OK. Then tell me why you would need these Fighters on a 'long trip'?" Michael asked.

Carlos' mood switched to becoming very serious and a bit agitated. He had his ID card scanned again. The door slid back into position. He turned back to Michael, "For defense, as I have stated."

An alarm began to sound.

Carlos motioned with his hand towards another spiral staircase, "We must get back up to Deck Two and prepare to dock at MF-3."

II

There was no sensation of descending, as the ship dropped towards the MF-3 landing site. Michael and Roland gathered their equipment as Elizabeth walked towards them.

"You guys have everything you need?" she asked.

Michael adjusted his laptop case on his shoulder, "I've got you. What more could a man ask for?"

She patted her stomach, "You got *us*, Big Boy. Maybe *more* than you could ask for." She smiled and kissed his cheek. "We will wait here for you. Be careful and don't be long."

Roland gave her a small wave, "I hope to see you soon, too."

Carlos hung up the inner-ship phone, and walked over to the couch, "We will be opening the gangway doors in a few minutes. You both need to move into the access room, please."

Michael and Roland stood silently in the decompression room. The panel light blinked and the stairway panel began. With butter-smooth actuation the staircase telescoped out and dropped.

Below them were five figures surrounding the platform; similar to the one they had used at the GenZ camp. Michael removed his dark glasses and could see that they were armed. He followed Roland down the steps and they were greeted by a man in a Black Shirt uniform.

He saluted, "Welcome to MF-3. I am Captain Daly. Strategos Black Rock has instructed me on what aid you will be requiring to complete the startup of the device." He turned and pointed to a small stand of trees. "The crate has been moved into a tent by those trees. I have a three technicians waiting to assist you." He reached into his pocket and pulled out a sheet of paper. "This is the satellite uplink information that you will be using. The bird is due in thirty-seven minutes."

As they walked to the tent, the staircase retracted behind them and the panel closed on the ship. Within moments it was rising straight up.

The team carefully uncrated the Beam Generator and positioned the satellite uplink equipment. Michael set up his laptop and loaded the satellite codes into the program. He looked into his database and found the activation code for the Beam Generator, according to its presumed location at MF-3. Roland carefully took the Resonator out of the velvet cloth and placed it onto the globe.

Michael turned to Captain Daly, "Tell everyone to leave the area and turn off all electronic equipment. And keep an eye out for any intruders."

The Captain did not move for a moment, as it was the first time he clearly saw Michael's eyes. He quickly saluted and walked out of the tent, still looking back over his shoulder.

Roland sat on the grass floor. "Well, I think you freaked out the Captain. So, think it will come on?"

"We did everything exactly as we did with the first one. It just depends on whether the right crate was delivered to MF-3. *And*, if this satellite information they gave us is correct. How much time do we have?"

Roland looked at his watch, "According to what's written on the paper that Captain 'Pooped Pants' gave us . . . four minutes and counting."

Michael waited as Roland called out the time.

Roland turned his head towards Michael with a worried look, "You remember what the scroll said about the Beams needing to be twenty miles apart? What about the one that's in the Megadrax?"

Michael thought about it for a second, "I have a feeling that the ship is either twenty miles away or up by now. Plus, I think the chamber and the water it is sitting in will protect it. When they come back down will be the real test."

"What about us?" Roland asked.

"Well then, see you in the next life. I'll be the one with the yellow eyes. You can't miss me."

Roland looked at his watch, "Stand by . . . three, two, one; Now!"

Michael made the connection. He anxiously hit the Send key and waited for the code to be transmitted up to the satellite.

Within seconds the Beam Generator came to life, radiating intense purple light throughout the tent. Michael had forgotten about his LiquiCode tattoos as the stinging pain returned. The radiance began to swirl around the generator and turn transparent . . . to Roland. Michael could still see the ultraviolet colors and beyond. And as before, Michael's computer shut down.

Captain Daly came back into the tent, shading his eyes, "Was it successful?"

"All is A-OK," Roland informed him.

Michael stood up, "We need to pack up all this equipment and get back on the ship."

The Captain called for some of his men to help. Roland supervised the break-down.

Michael walked over to Daly.

"Captain, you need to put up a fence and secure this whole area. I will need a company of your best troops here to make sure this unit stays on."

The Captain jerked to attention and saluted, "It shall be done, *Stolist Fields*." He turned and left the tent.

Roland stood a few feet away, with his mouth agape. Michael could hardly believe it either. They looked at each other. "The word is out, I guess," Roland muttered.

Michael shook his head, "This could be very dangerous. There can't be two Stolists, at the same time. Can there?"

A soldier walked into the tent, "Sir, the ship has returned. It awaits your presence."

Roland looked at his hands, "Well, the damn pain has stopped. *And* we are still alive . . . even with two generators side by side."

Michael thought about that for a minute. "I bet they didn't want them within twenty miles during a *start-up*. Or in case one of them had to be restarted. That would make sense. These things put out some serious frequencies. You should see them."

"I will take your word for it, *High Stolist.*" Roland smiled and Michael could see that it was spoken out of respect.

"I don't know how Brittney puts up with your butt-kissing ways," Michael joked.

"It's gotten me this far, where ever I am now," Roland said, looking around.

"All of your gear is at the platform, sir." A young Black Shirt informed them.

Michael picked up his laptop case, "Well then, time to go. It's on to MF-2. We've earned our pay on this one."

Chapter Thirty-Two

Twenty minutes later, the Megadrax dropped to a static position, two-thousand feet over MF-2.

Elizabeth walked out from Citi's room and joined Michael and Roland on the couch.

From down the hallway Carlos came running. He was out of breath as he stopped next to Michael, "We received a radio message from below. They won't let us land. They said that they will shoot us down."

Michael stood up, "Who are *they*?"

Carlos was wringing his hands, "It might be High Stolist Leigus' people. They still control MF-2. Who else would know the radio frequency of this ship?"

Appearing from the same hallway Carlos had just run down, was Citi. And she was not happy. "Michael! We need to talk."

Michael was dumbfounded, "About what? What can I do?"

"Not you and I . . . *we* need to get in contact with the Mu·Suvians and talk with them."

Roland spoke up, "What about the pilots? Aren't they Mu·Suvians?"

Citi sat on the couch, "Yes, but they are just pilots. We need to contact the High Council." She thought for a moment, "Or maybe not. Those people down there are *not* Leigus' soldiers." She turned to Carlos and patted his hand, "Now don't you worry. They can't shoot this ship down. We would be 200 miles up before any missile could ever think of locking on to us." She stood up, "Michael, come with me."

Michael stood up and followed Citi to a small room which was down the far corridor. Carlos quickly followed, eventually getting in front to open the door with a quick bow.

What a Brownnoser. Is this what I'm in for as Stolist; a bunch of those 'yes men' always hanging around? Michael thought.

Citi walked to a table and picked up a remote control device. She pointed it at the wall and an infrared image of the ground, below the ship, appeared. She panned the camera until the grouping of seven figures, standing around the platform, filled the screen. They were not in any recognizable uniforms, and all held weapons.

"I suspect they are hired guns sent by Gus Stoddard. They know you and Elizabeth are aboard. They could kill two birds with one stone, as it were." She nodded slowly, "So, we will let them have you . . . and the ship."

She smiled as she picked up the phone. Michael looked at the screen, then at Citi. "What?"

She used her hand to quiet him as she began speaking in Mu·Suvian. She then hung up the phone and faced Michael, "I talked with the pilots. I told them to land." She then walked to the screen, "On the ground."

It happened in an instant, without much of a bump.

The High Minister shook her head, "Hired guns. Gus should have hired brains." She walked to the door. "We have fifteen armed 'technicians' on-board who will accompany you, Elizabeth and Roland to the crate. They will provide security as long as the device is operating. It is under a tent, fifty yards to the north."

Michael followed her back to the couch where Elizabeth and Roland were anxiously waiting.

"Carlos was correct when he said that MF-2 was still in the hands of Leigus' ESA people. We will not be getting any support from them, nor will they try and take the Transceiver. The Foundation, as well as the Mu·Suvians, need it up and running."

"We will do our best, High Minister," Michael said.

Citi lightly slapped his arm, "Stop it. You and Elizabeth call me Citi. We are nearly Family you know."

"And me?" Roland asked coyly.

She turned and smiled at him, "Only *after* you marry Brittani. I don't want any single men getting fresh with me."

They all laughed.

Citi led them to an access room on the Port side of the spacious area. "You will have to use this side door to leave the ship. There seems to be some *debris* blocking the belly ramp."

The armed technicians arrived at the tent first. The hired mercenaries had killed four Black Shirts who had been uncrating the Transceiver. Their bodies laid about the dirt floor. None were holding weapons. An officer was found outside, wounded. Michael and Elizabeth ran up to him and knelt down, "I'm Michael Fields. Where are you hit?"

The young officer looked up and smiled, "Lieutenant O'Connor, sir. They caught us by surprise. We weren't expecting any resistance. My side and leg . . . brought me down."

One of Citi's men brought over a medical kit and began working on the officer.

He quickly examined the fallen man, "He'll be OK, sir. But, we need to get him to the Infirmary in the ship." Stretcher teams showed up and took O'Connor and the four dead Black Shirts to the Megadrax.

When the last stretcher was inside the vessel, the side access door closed and all watched the massive triangle rise straight up, into the night. Somehow Michael knew that Citi Chén would know when it was time to come back down and get him and Elizabeth.

Roland and the support technicians had finished unpacking the Transceiver and were setting up Roland's laptop. It had been configured to duplicate Michael's computer. The globe was radiating a soft blue aura. It was getting power from the Beam Generator at MF-3, just as predicted. The device appeared to be exactly like the others; glass globe in a metal frame. The only difference was no flat spot on the top for a Resonator to be placed.

The remaining armed personnel from the ship (Chén's personal guard), had formed a large circle around the tent.

CONTINUANCE

Michael and Elizabeth walked in and sat in two folding chairs, next to the table where the laptop was placed. Michael took the scroll out of the box and opened it on the table. He scanned it quickly and then started the computer. After the laptop had fully booted, he navigated to the file named *XZX_startup*. It was written in Mu·Suvian.

Two panels appeared, requesting code input. Michael looked at Roland, who nodded. He then placed his LiquiCode tattoo over the laptops' built-in scanner. The first panel displayed a long string of numbers. Michael smiled at Elizabeth, "OK, ma' lady. Let's see if you're the chosen one."

She held her right hand over the scanner and the second panel displayed another long string of numbers, which looked very similar to Michaels'. Michael touched the Enter key.

The screen turned neon red and a sequence of tones began to blast from the computer's speaker. Long notes, short notes, clicks and thumps.

Michael turned to Elizabeth, "The Song of Inanna. I guess you really are *the one*."

The 'song' went on for twenty seconds; then . . . the Transceiver turned the same neon red as the screen. The computer screen faded to black, showing four small grey panels on the side of the screen with Mu·Suvian characters next to them. There were two large white panels taking up the center portion of the display; one at the top and one at the bottom.

Michael typed in some data in each of the small panels.

Roland leaned over, "Is the microphone on?"

Michael checked the Audio Properties icon, "Yep."

"And how about the Transceiver's power output; what did you set it for?"

"Thirty seconds," Michael answered.

Elizabeth leaned over and kissed Michael, then stood up and kissed Roland on the cheek, "The two most brilliant geeks I know; what ever it was that you just did."

Roland blushed and kneeled beside Michael's chair, looking up at Elizabeth, "You ain't seen nothing, yet."

They sat looking at the bottom panel. Within moments, the Transceiver played a short series of tones and the words 'Message from: 84A6: 'Hello GenZ World' appeared.

Elizabeth looked at the screen, then at the two grinning monkeys next to her. "And? What is that, eh?" she asked.

Michael actually giggled and then typed; 'Hello GenZ World.' He hit the Enter key.

Surrounded by the crimson glow of the tent, the small computer's speaker played the tones that matched the letters in the Mu·Suvian character sequence.

Elizabeth crossed her arms, looked back at the glowing sphere and sat back in the chair, "You want to tell me what's going on? I don't see anything so great here."

The Transceiver began 'playing' again and the bottom panel displayed, 'Message from: 84A6: 'I love you, Elizabeth Fields.'

She sat upright and blinked . . . then looked at Michael with a scared look on her face.

He shook his head, laughing as he typed into the top panel, 'I love you, Elizabeth Fields.' He hit Enter and the laptop played tones.

Elizabeth slowly sat back, looking at the computer screen. "You are getting the message . . . even before you type it."

Roland pointed at the small panel on the display, "Thirty seconds before. We can set it up to . . . maybe four hours or more."

"How is that possible?" she asked, not believing a word of it.

"We are dumping into a particle stream that is already coming this way. If that makes any sense," Michael explained.

"OK. And where is this 'particle stream' coming from?" She asked, expecting some two-hour explanation.

"90482 Orcus," replied Roland.

"Is that a zip code or something?"

"No . . . just the designation of a Trans-Neptunian Object. We just call it Orcus for short," Roland informed her.

Elizabeth just nodded and looked at both of them, while thinking of ways to escape and calling the funny-farm people to come get them.

Michael reached for her hand, "Really, we aren't making this up. There is a Transceiver on Orcus, that the Mu·Suvians put there, to allow us to send information back to ourselves. We don't know the reason, yet. But, it's awesome."

She grasped his left hand with both of hers, "OK, I guess I have to believe you. Your little demonstration was quite impressive and very effective. I must admit; it really freaked me out." She looked around the tent, "Now what?"

Michael was trying to make a sketch of the screen and the various panels, with his other hand. He wrote what each one stood for and what needed to be typed into each one. He handed it to Roland, "OK. This should keep you experimenting until I get the other Transceiver up and running at MF-6. Then we can try to communicate with one another and test other stuff. I'm sure that this unit is number 84A6, because the messages that came in were from this Transceiver. I will send stuff to you at that 'address'. When you see my first message, put my Transceiver's number in the third small box on the left. We should have direct communication then. And we can see what this thing can really do."

Roland looked at the paper, "OK. So, I just sit here for the next couple of months? What's the plan?"

One of Citi's men walked into the tent, "Sir, the ship is returning."

Michael stood up, "I think we're going to find out, real soon."

All three walked into the night air and watched the gigantic shadowy triangle slowly descend.

It did not touch the ground, as before. The crushed bodies of Gus' mercenaries had been carried away and the belly panel opened. The staircase slowly dropped to the grassy field. A rear panel opened and another gangway telescoped out and down. Ten uniformed members of the crew then emerged, carrying equipment down the metal ramp. Tents, boxes of food, pallets of water and various piles of camping gear were placed on the ground.

"What are they doing?" Elizabeth asked.

"You and I get back on the ship and Roland stays here."

Michael put his hand on Roland's shoulder, "I think you're going to be roughing it for a few days, by the look of what Citi is dropping off."

A crewmember walked up to Roland and handed him a box, "I was told to give this to you. It's an inverter. It will take the output of whatever is powering *that* thing in there and turn it into AC for your laptop and lights."

Roland took the box and looked at Michael, "You know what this means? Those Beam Generators can power just about anything, without wires. You just need to have one of these things to plug your electrical stuff into."

Michael looked at the box, "Well, I think there might be a limit on amperage, but you're right. We may still have to connect the Beam Generators to the Power Grid for running a whole city, but these boxes could be put into cars and all sorts of mobile things. Oh, boy. Things are really going to change fast on this old planet."

Another crewperson ran up to Michael, "We are ready to depart, sir." She held her little pillbox hat on her head and ran back to the ship.

Michael looked down at his watch, "It's 2:51 Pacific time. I should be connecting with you, from MF-6, at about 4 am." Michael slapped Roland on the back, "Talk to you in a bit. I hope."

"In bits and bytes, I'll be ready. See you . . . whenever," Roland waved as Michael and Elizabeth walked across the field to climb the staircase.

The Megadrax secured its panels and again rose into the Ohio sky. Turning its nose west, the craft silently climbed within seconds, to mingle with the stars.

Roland put his hands in his pockets and slowly walked back to the tent. The sounds of crickets and the movement of surrounding tree branches in the breeze filled the summer darkness. It was a personal peace – as only peace should be.

He stopped and looked up; straining his eyes to perhaps catch a parting glimpse of the magnificent Megadrax and those aboard, "No wonder the ancients thought they were gods."

Chapter Thirty-Three

The call came in on Channel 121 at 4:45 am Central Time.

An operator appeared on the monitor. She was wearing a headset, a four-in-the-morning smile and spoke in a too-cheery flight attendant voice, "Good morning, Mister Stoddard. I have a video conference for you. Will you accept?"

Gus flopped down in front of the monitor in an over-stuffed chair. Mojo immediately jumped into his lap. The Texan was attired in a robe, boots and his hat. He was not as cordial back to the operator, "Yeah, sure. Who the hell is it? Better be important . . . calling me in the middle of the night." He pushed the button on the remote to activate his camera. The red light, above the TV monitor, glowed red.

The screen switched to an image of a black dog, looking straight into the caller's camera. His large brown eyes darted from the camera to the image of Gus on its own screen.

Mojo looked up, arched his back and hissed. He then jumped off Gus' lap to find a more un-intimidating location. A man was standing behind the dog, with his back to the camera. Gus did not have to guess who the call was now coming from. The braids of grey hair flowing from under the cowboy hat provided the signature. It was George.

Gus quickly stood up and put his hands on his hips, "I'll be damned. If it isn't ol' Black Rock himself, coming down off his high horse to talk with little ol' me. And you're still wearing that road-kill hat, I see."

George turned around, "Stoddard, you have crossed the line. I have been ordered to put some things right."

"And who told you to make such a bold move? It sure wasn't Chén, that milk toast. The High Minister doesn't have the guts to take on anything that involves violence. And I know Leigus hates your guts . . . "

"Actually, it *was* Leigus. And here's a news flash, he hates *yours*. It could be that you both have the same insane plan to try and take over The Foundation," George replied, moving to a chair. "For thirteen years, it's been Leigus and his power hungry crowd against Chén and the Mu·Suvian Council. We almost had semi-peace in The Foundation restored, until you decided to go mental and kill Bancroft and take over GMCS. You screwed up the infrastructure of every nation on the planet."

Gus rubbed his eye, "Boo-Hoo, I'm all broken up. It seems that I'm losing friends left and right." He walked towards the camera and pointed at George, "Look, I just took over the system. I didn't make it shut down the world. It did that on its own." He walked back to the chair and sat down.

George shook his head, "But, you killed the guy that could have stopped it."

Gus waved his hand, "OK, let's cut the crap, what do you want?"

George leaned back in his chair, "I'm coming down there, tomorrow night. I think you have some items that belonged to Bancroft which The Foundation needs. I was thinking that we could come up with some kind of exchange or arrangement."

Gus put his hand to his chin scratched the stubble of his unshaven face, "An exchange? Let me think about that. And you said possibly an *arrangement*?" He was getting the feeling that his plan for moving up in The Foundation may be underway.

George folded his hands in his lap, "I can't promise anything, but The Foundation is pretty desperate. I think I can get them to agree to a *limited* number of requests that you may have in mind."

Gus slapped his leg, "Well, shoot! I'm a reasonable som-a-bitch as you're gonna find anywhere. I think we might be able to do some horse tradin'." He leaned towards the camera, "And I'm assuming we're both talkin' about them ten rock and crystal pieces, with the glyphs on 'em. Right?"

George had struck gold. He was hoping Bancroft had taken possession of the Resonators before he went to the Yucatan. George maintained his calm, "Those are the items."

Gus reached over to his right and picked up the box containing the Resonators and opened it for George to see. ""Well, come on down. I got 'em right here. As you can see, I'm not pulling your leg."

George nodded, "Very good. I'll be arriving at Airstrip UX7 at 2200 hours, tomorrow night, your time. We'll be coming down in a Nylostra, unescorted. I have some things to arrange tonight and let The Foundation know you are willing to make a deal. I am sure that there will be a representative from the top, coming along, also. After I have that box, and all ten Resonators, we can discuss an arrangement."

Gus put the box back onto the table, "I'll meet you there. It's only a half hour from here. I'll bring a list of 'items' that I will expect in return."

George folded his hands in his lap, "Then our meeting should prove most beneficial. I shall talk with you tomorrow night."

Gus waved his right hand, "I'll see ya' then, Ol' Buddy. And no guns, right?"

George nodded, "We will be unarmed."

The screen went dark.

Gus stood up and went to his desk. A communication, from his informer at MF-2, was lying on the top of a stack of papers that he needed to sign. It had arrived minutes before the call from George came in. He picked it up and quickly scanned it. He grew more distressed as he rubbed the sleep from his eyes and carefully read it over again. His mercenaries had not disposed of Red or captured Michael Fields. It also indicated that the Megadrax had landed and crushed Commander Rio and his crack troops, flatter than armadillos in the road; killing all seven of them.

The final line of the communiqué mentioned a red glowing object, inside a tent which was surrounded by soldiers.

He pointed at the message and spoke to Mojo, now sitting on the desk, "That should be something I should look in to."

George turned off his screen and walked to the phone. He dialed and waited.

"Winslow. We're going for a ride tomorrow night. I need a meeting with you and Colonel Taylor right now. I'm coming down to the Basement."

Chapter Thirty-Four

At 3:07 am, the Megadrax passed high over Highway 15 and dropped to sit three-thousand feet over Champlin Peak in Utah. It rotated 90 degrees to the north and slowly descended into a barren valley.

A familiar wooden platform, painted a camouflaged brown and green, offered itself up to the lowering metal staircase.

Inside the ship; Citi, Carlos and the young woman aide walked from Citi's room. Elizabeth and Michael were lightly dozing on the couch.

Citi jostled Michael's shoulder, "Come along now. We are over MF-6, time to get your belongings together. They have to have this ship back to MF-7 by 4:30 am. Some things have changed back there. There are some new plans brewing."

The young woman was carrying Citi's bag.

Elizabeth sat up, "You're not going with us, are you Citi?"

"Yes, I am. I don't dare return to MF-7. Not yet, anyway. I should stay here for a while anyway. I will be needed," she answered.

Michael began to speak, but the High Minister held up her hand, "Not to worry. George's Black Shirts have secured MF-6 and set up a Forward Base around the Transceiver crate. I will be perfectly safe here."

Michael finally spoke, "What about any ESA troops in the area?"

Citi instructed Carlos to pick up Michael's satellite link-up equipment and they began walking towards the Access Room, "There are none of *those* people within hundreds of miles of MF-6. The Black Shirts have taken care of that."

Elizabeth, Michael and the two attendants joined her in the air-lock room and waited for the stairway to descend to the platform below.

CONTINUANCE

As they walked down, two rows of George's troops were standing at attention at the foot of the wooden structure, weapons raised in a salute. An officer waited for the arriving delegation to stand on the desert sand.

He saluted, "MF-6 welcomes you, Stolist Fields."

Michael attempted to return the salute while looking at Citi. She smiled and leaned towards him, "They don't know who I am. This is *your* party."

The officer pointed to a large fabric structure that had already been surrounded by a high wire fence. "The crate has been brought to the surface and is enclosed in that tent." Six other tents were also within the confines of the barrier. Perhaps thirty armed soldiers had been placed outside the wire, creating a very serious obstacle for any would-be intruder to penetrate.

Citi, Michael and Elizabeth walked behind the officer, between the two rows of soldiers, toward the gate in the fence. They reached the tent with the crate inside. There were three 'technicians' waiting for them, with hammers and crowbars in hand.

Michael pointed at the crate, "No hammers, just use the crowbars. Let's get the wood removed." They began 'unwrapping' the device.

Citi's female attendant arrived with her bag and stood at the tent opening. Carlos continued into the tent, struggling with the arm-load of satellite equipment.

Michael pointed to a spot in the corner, "Just put that stuff over there, Carlos. We won't be needing it for this device."

Carlos' mouth dropped. "But, I carried it all the way from the ship . . ."

"Just put it over there, for now." Michael looked over to Citi who was smiling. She had a bit of mischief in her, it seemed.

Michael instructed set up his laptop.

Elizabeth and Citi took chairs on the other side of the room and were served tea and cookies by Black Shirt personnel. "This is exciting, don't you think?" Citi whispered to Elizabeth.

"This is just creepy," she said, under her breath.

As the crate was removed Michael was relieved to see that the globe was radiating a soft blue light. It was in the same 'stand-by mode' as he had witnessed in Ohio. He no longer needed the scroll. He knew what to do. He turned and motioned for Elizabeth to join him.

As she sat in the folding chair next to him, "Think this one will work, too?" she asked.

Michael started the 'Song of Inanna' and the tent filled with a series of notes, not heard for nearly a millennium.

The brilliant crimson red glow began radiating off the globe. Citi moved to the edge of her chair, "My word. Isn't that something?"

Elizabeth turned to face her, "You ain't seen nothing, yet."

The red XZX program log-in screen appeared on the laptop. The first panel showed Michael's LiquiCode number, then Elizabeth's as they passed their tattoos over the laptop's scanner.

He pressed the Enter key.

The main communication screen, with its black background framing the white and grey panels faded into view. Michael set the three option panels to the same numbers he had used with the MF-2 Transceiver. He then entered 84A6 in the fourth.

"OK, let's see if Roland is awake."

He typed in, *'Mr. Watson, come here, I need you.'*

Within eight seconds, the bottom panel displayed, *'Message from: 84A6: Awake. Sorry for the delay. I had to type in your number: 73D5.'*

Michael wrote down both Transceiver address numbers on a sheet of paper, smiled and leaned back, "I have a feeling that mankind may now posses a new form of instantaneous communications; no wires, no delay, no radio waves and a range of hundreds or thousands . . . maybe even millions of miles apart."

"I was thinking even farther than that. I'm guessing to the stars . . . and back again," Elizabeth added, smiling.

Michael leaned forward and typed to Roland, *'It appears that if we don't put in a number for the Transceiver we want to talk to, the message will just come back to the same computer that sent it. And the time it appears back, before we sent it, is set by the power output. Just like we figured.'* He sent the message.

Roland wrote back, *''Message from: 84A6: That is correct. Now can I get some sleep?'*

Michael responded, *'Good night, Mr. Watson.'*

The lower panel displayed, *'Message from: 84A6: Good night, Mr. Bell.'*

"See how this works? All of the instructions are on this scroll." Michael wanted to make sure that Elizabeth understood how everything functioned.

She nodded, "Really a piece of cake, eh?"

Michael turned to see Citi standing in back of his chair. She was staring at the screen and then at the Transceiver. "It is all true. After 6,000 years, all of the milestones have been met. We are nearly officially members of the universe. It is all up to you two, and a few friends, to keep us going."

Michael and Elizabeth looked at each other, in hopes that the other would explain what she was talking about. Citi motioned for a chair. Of course Carlos was the first to bring one. She slowly sat down.

She began, "We, the human race, have had these devices given to us before, over the many ages we have managed to somehow survive. Although, they were not as large as this one. You may have seen them depicted in ancient tomb carvings or on the walls of temples . . . small ones, always being held by some king or priest. Or they were being carried around inside an arc or displayed on some holy platform. Those holy men could make the Beam Generators come on with sacred Resonating crystals and do amazing feats of magic with the power the devices produced. Scared the hell out of the ignorant masses they wanted to control.

"They could even make the Transceivers respond by singing the right series of tones for 'The Song of Inanna', but they didn't have anything to power up, like light bulbs or electric razors. Nor did they have any means to communicate with the

Transceivers. True, there were a few that could get messages back and forth by interpreting the tone sequences – those sacred prayers they sang. But nothing that would impress the Mu·Suvians like the technology we have in front of us now."

Elizabeth had been squeezing Michaels hand throughout the whole time Citi was talking . . . tighter and tighter. He shook her loose. "Sorry," she said. She folded her hands across her stomach as Citi continued.

"These devices have been given to us as milestones, to see how far we have progressed. Once we had evolved far enough in manufacturing, social development, economics . . . and had developed all of the technology required to make them operate, the Mu·Suvians would allow us everything we could ever imagine in taking the next step."

"The next step?" Elizabeth asked.

Citi smiled, "Take our place in the universe. Colonize, explore, travel to the stars, acquire advanced sciences, agriculture and medicines . . . the list of the amazing things that await our species is very long. That is, if we do not exterminate ourselves in the next year or so."

"Well, what about the Mayan Calendar thing and December 21st, 2012? What was the significance of that?" Michael asked.

"That was the date that the Mu·Suvians were going to bring us the teachers. If we allow that to happen, then the New Ear will begin. As you have witnessed, human greed and the struggle for power with The Foundation has almost ruined our chances for bringing the teachers."

"Almost?" asked Elizabeth.

"The High Council was ready to 'shut us down' when Leigus made his move to topple Level One. Through some delicate negotiations, members of the Seven Tribes and myself, managed to get a short reprieve. Actually, it was all based on the realization that Michael will surely become the next High Stolist. So . . . getting the Beam Generators and Transceivers working is a big plus in your corner if you can do it."

Citi was handed another cup of tea. "Oh, and I should mention, the fact that Elizabeth is your wife, and pregnant for

Inanna . . . there are a lot of smiling faces in the Mu·Suvian community over that. OK, I don't think they can smile. But, a new hope has risen among them."

Elizabeth raised her hand slightly, "If the Mu·Suvians wanted us to reach this level of civilization you are talking about, why didn't they just step in and demand things of us? Like no more wars, and focus on education and things like that?"

Citi shook her head, "They tried. During the early days with the Greeks, Sumerians and other advanced cultures. But, they all fell apart when other 'beliefs' around them invaded and destroyed any advancement that had been accomplished. You see, the Mu·Suvians had met with every civilization on the planet, at one time or another. But, because of the primitive cultures they encountered, most thought they were gods. So, a number of power-hungry individuals crawled out from under their rocks and proclaimed themselves as holy men and were able to talk with the gods. They then proclaimed themselves as leaders of some religion that they had devised and took control of the tribes. Leaving them uneducated and in servitude, for the gain of more power and wealth for the religious leaders."

Elizabeth was confused, "Why didn't the Mu·Suvians step in and do something about that? It must have been obvious that these civilizations were degrading themselves."

Citi sighed, "The Mu·Suvians do not understand the concept of religion. They understand and live by order. At the time, religion appeared to be a form of order which humans needed. So, they went along with it. Too bad, huh?"

"Is that why there is no religious sector in The Foundation now?" Michael asked.

"Exactly," answered Citi. "They learned that when religion is the main criteria for filling human positions of power; it always leads to the same end – keep the masses ignorant and kill everyone that doesn't believe what you do. The Foundation is in constant conflict with a number of major religions around the world. We try to advance our species . . . the religious sectors want . . . well, you know."

Citi put down her cup, "Let us not talk of this until later. I need to show you both something before we continue."

She bent forward, placing her hand under her right eye. She raised back up to face them. A dark-colored contact had been removed, revealing a yellow iris.

Michael leaned back as Elizabeth grabbed his arm.

"Don't be alarmed. It is true. I am the same as you, Michael. Or should I say, you are the same as me . . . and Leigus. Yes, he wears these damn contacts, also. We will get you fitted for a pair, shortly. It's less intimidating to those around you. And they are tinted, so you will not need to wear sunglasses outside any longer. Although; Leigus still wears mirrored ones, to keep anyone from watching his shifty eyes."

She slowly looked around the room, then back at her audience of two. "I am three-hundred and eighty-two years old . . . or will be in October, on the 12th actually. I am expecting you three to come to the party," she smiled. "You will bring little Inanna of course?"

Elizabeth nodded, "Of course." She struggled to answer, "Where ever that will be."

Citi looked upward, to some loving memory far away in her mind, "At my little house; about sixty-five miles southwest of Haikou. It's near Nada on the island of Hainan. You can't miss it; red door, some potted plants on the porch." She smiled, "It's been a while since I have been home. There will be just a few close friends invited, nothing special."

She picked up her tea cup. "The good thing is, I'm younger than that *Elitist* Leigus. He is just about ready to hit the wall. He will be turning the big 'four-hundred' and is becoming more irrational by the day. That is why he is acting more than his usual tyrannical self right now and trying to take over everything before the Realignment of The Foundation. The place and time for that will be announced in a few weeks. I am sure that all this stuff that is happening to the world right now is Leigus' one last grasp at infamy."

Michael's brain was on overload as he leaned forward, "I know of the importance of the College of Minds meeting, but what's so significant about Leigus hitting four-hundred years?"

Citi sighed deeply, "That is as long as *we* live, Michael. It's almost to the day. That is unless we happen to go before then, by accident or other means. We are not immortal, just a longer life-span than most."

Elizabeth's nails dug into Michael's arm, as she spoke up, almost frantic, "Are you saying, a GenZ who has *those* eyes will live to be four-hundred years old? I thought the eye thing was just something that happens to a few of us. I heard GenZs call it the Synthesis. It's some weird reaction or something . . ." She was near tears.

Citi shook her head, looking at Michael. "No, it's a result of the DNA roulette wheel. One, sometimes two come along every fourth century to head The Foundation."

Elizabeth put her hands on her stomach, afraid to ask the next question as her lower lip trembled, "Two?"

Citi smiled softly, "Yes, my dear. Inanna will also have yellow eyes."

The High Minister stood up, "Michael, you have one more task to perform. It should only be for a short time. Don't worry about Elizabeth. I will watch out for her while you are away."

Carlos quickly moved forward and held her arm as she slowly walked towards the tent opening. Stopping a few steps before the exit she turned back to face Michael and Elizabeth.

"Oh, just for future reference, I will reach four-hundred when Inanna is eighteen."

She turned and left the tent.

Elizabeth turned her anguished face to Michael as she put her arms tightly around him and pressed her check against his chest. Unstoppable tears flooded her eyes.

It was for all of them she wept.

Chapter Thirty-Five

4:32 am July 3rd, 2013

Reggie, Max and Parker stood outside of the former ESA vehicle looking up at the Megadrax as it slowly moved overhead and stopped. Martin was looking down at a varmint hole. Reggie was taking care of him while George was away. Martin didn't mind, as long as he got some good food out of the deal.

The four of them had travelled to the front gate of the Forward Base, where the Beam Generator was still operating, inside the tent

The ship began to descend two hundred yards to the east, as the stairway panel began to open. Reggie turned to Max and handed him a small, velvet covered object, "Here's the Resonator that you will need for your mission. There's a Manta in the launch bay of the Megadrax, all set to go. You boys ready?"

Parker looked at the monstrous, gravity-defying vehicle, silently moving down, "Hey, Reggie. Tell me again why we didn't go with Michael and Red from the GenZ camp?"

"George said that he can't trust anyone. We were tipped off that Winslow and the ESA would be waiting for you two if you tried to steal a Manta from the Basement. So, we kept you on the ground, in plain sight. We wanted them to know that you were still in MF-7 and not in the Megadrax. The LiquiCode readers have been tracking you throughout the complex, giving them your whereabouts. It was a good diversion. All their attention is focused on stopping you two from getting into the Basement right now. We're sure that Winslow doesn't know that this ship has its own Manta."

Parker raised his gloved hand, "Well, I know they think I'm still in my room in the MF. I left my LiquiCode decoy there."

Max held up his hands, now covered with a pair of Parker's lead-lined gloves. "And they don't have a clue on where I am; certainly not standing here."

Max looked to his right and watched the staircase deploy, "Why don't we just take the Megadrax to Australia and deliver the Resonator?"

Reggie took of his glasses and began cleaning the desert dust off the lenses, "Leigus would have it shot down over Open Ocean in an instant if it ever leaves the Americas. He wouldn't want to take a chance on it falling to the ground. It would compromise his plans. Both The Foundation and the Mu·Suvians sure don't need another Roswell incident. Plus, he knows High Minister Chén could be on-board. That would not look good at the *Realignment of The Foundation.* As long as the Megadrax appears to be conducting supply runs within the boundaries of the Lower 48 and up to the Outposts, Leigus will stay away."

The ship stopped above the sand with the staircase fully deployed. Two crew members walked down to stand on either side of the first step.

Reggie put his hand on Parker's shoulder, "Give 'em hell, Ian."

Parker smiled, "I forgot my passport. Think they'll let me into Australia?"

Max shook Reggie's hand and then picked up his flight case, which now contained the Resonator, "We'll be talkin' to ya."

Parker and Max moved to the staircase and walked up the metal stairs, followed by the crewmen.

The ramp retracted and the colossal ship began to rise. Within moments it was out of sight in the cloud covered sky.

When the air-lock door was opened, Max and Parker were met by an officer of the crew. On the left side of his dark blue turtleneck sweater was a gold triangular emblem resting inside a silver circle. Each of his leather shoulder straps were adorned with two round-cut diamonds.

Max stood to attention and saluted, "Captain Maxwell Rhodes, permission to come aboard."

The Commander saluted back, "I'm Commander Orlando Merritt; Flight Control Officer of the *Second Moon*. She welcomes you both."

Parker looked around the large room, "I'm just a passenger. The name's Parker." He attempted a salute, which Merritt did not return. He lowered his arm, "You can just call me . . . Parker. So, this ship has a name; The Second Moon. This is so cool."

Merritt raised an eyebrow and turned. He waved for them to follow, "I will take you to the Briefing Room where we can introduce you to your ship."

Parker moved next to Max, "Introduce us . . .?"

Max leaned towards Parker, "The simulator was one thing, this is reality. The Manta needs to communicate and interface with us."

"And how do we do that?" Parker asked.

Max shifted his flight case to his other hand, "Like anyone else; we talk to it."

They were led into a large room with rows of theater-type seating, situated in front of a thirty-foot-wide screen.

Max and Parker sat down in the front row as Commander Merritt walked to the front, to stand beside the screen. A graphic appeared, showing an animation of a Megadrax rising above the earth.

"We will shortly move into Low Earth Orbit, about 150 miles up. The Second Moon will remain there until your launch at Midnight, MF-7 time. We will maintain a geosynchronous position and remain relatively out of sight until then. You two will have the next eighteen hours to prepare for your mission, get further trained on the Manta and rest up."

Max raised his hand, "Has the ship been programmed for the mission to Australia?"

CONTINUANCE

Merritt looked around the room, then at Max. "That is the reason that you will need further planning and training. There will be no flight to Australia."

Parker slowly looked at Max who was staring at the commander. "If the mission is not to Australia, then why are we here?"

"The story that you were going to fly to Australia tonight, in support of Program 2622, is only a cover. We received intelligence which indicated that the mission was leaked to Leigus, who now has ordered his fighters, stationed at QX17, to intercept you off the coast of Hawaii. It is exactly what we wanted him to do."

Max put both hands in the air and looked at Parker, "Well, I guess I'm officially a Mushroom. 'Been kept in the dark and fed bullshit."

Parker raised his hand, "Excuse me, but if we aren't going Down Under, where *are* we going?"

Merritt straightened his tie and read off a sheet of paper he was holding, "The Foundation has issued the following coordinates for the delivery of the Resonator: 14 degrees, 42 seconds south, 75 degrees, and 10 seconds west." Merritt lowed the paper, "That is all I can tell you."

Parker looked slowly at Max, "You recognize that street address?"

Max nodded slightly, as his disturbed expression indicated he knew it well, "Earth Base One."

Merritt continued, "Every aspect of the flight has been put into the Manta's memory banks, including the mission objective. Mainly; the reason why that Resonator needs to get to your destination and what you may encounter on the way and when you get there. Namely those who do *not* want you to succeed."

"It needs to know all that?" Parker whispered to Max.

Merritt heard the question, "The Manta is almost as intelligent as The Second Moon, in an artificial sense. We never refer to the ships as only machines. They are an autonomous life form. They are very dangerous beasts and will do anything to protect their Alpha, or human occupant, as long as there is mutual respect. Think of the Second Moon as an elephant and the Manta as a Pit Bull; it might make the picture a bit clearer on what you are dealing with. They will take any measure to instinctively survive, but without a human presence, there is no reason. In other words, when the Alpha dies, so does the Manta; usually through their own actions."

Max shook his head, "What does that mean, in our language?"

"They have a digital instinct . . . humans have intuition. Combined, it equals reason. Humans can make decisions based on emotional and personality traits. Autonomous machines can not make moral judgments that are in line with human judgment. They have limited ability to perceive alternative means of self-preservation. When the human presence is dead . . . the Manta's only instinct is to take on the entire attacking force. Kill everything before the threat kills them. They will always loose." He struggled with the next line, "Death is viewed differently in the virtual world. It is an 'off' that can persist for eternity, until the next 'on'."

Max put his hands behind his head, "Sounds like a silicon-based religion to me."

The Commander slowly nodded and looked down at his watch, "It is now 05:17. You can go over to the mess hall and get some breakfast and then check into your rooms to get some sleep. After your evening meal, we will start the mission briefing and further training; back in this room, at 1800 hours."

Parker raised his hand, "So, if the Australian mission was just a story, won't Leigus' people figure it out in a few hours and start looking for us and The Second Moon?"

"We will launch Dolly as a decoy, at 2100 hours."

Parker leaned forward, "Dolly?"

"Dolly is the name of the second Manta in the launch bay," Merritt explained, putting both hands behind his back.

"She has been programmed to appear to be flying straight to the Australian MF-2. At an altitude of twenty miles and a ground speed of 2,000 knots, it will look as if she would arrive there in 3.5 hours. Of course, she will be detected and fighters will be sent out to destroy her. Dolly will then drop and hide in a cave on Ka'ula, Hawaii before Leigus' interceptors can reach her."

He turned to face the animation on the screen, "This is the whole plan. You can think about it at breakfast. Your ship will be launched at 2400 hours. You will reach your destination around three hours after that. I say *around*, for there may be some obstacles to overcome on your flight down there. When you leave the docking bay, you will be traveling at 17,000 mile per hour in relation to ground speed. That will match the earth's rotation. But, because the ship is Gravity Push, all you need to do is lower yourself down -- incrementally. There will be no reentry speed or heat to worry about. Again, Captain Rhodes knows the entry maneuver; as does Elvis."

Parker looked around the room and then up at the Commander, "Elvis? Who's Elvis?"

"That's *your* ship's name."

Parker stared at Merritt; then slowly turned to Max, "Our ship is named *Elvis*."

"Aren't ships supposed to have female names?" Max asked.

"Not always," the Commander replied. "We tried to call it Betty or something, but *it* refused to comply. It wanted Elvis. The High Minister thinks it's cute – so. Elvis it is."

Parker leaned towards Max, "*It* wants to be called Elvis?"

Merritt turned back to the screen, "The Second Moon will be maintaining a static position over MF-7 when you are launched; that means you will need to travel 4,600 nautical miles to reach your destination. You will stay in LEO and drop to your flight altitude of 140,000 feet, 2,500 miles south of here. You will be right over the Pacific Ocean; off the coast of Nicaragua. The only land you will pass directly over, before you reach Peru, will be Isla Guy Fawkes, in the Galapagos. They may pick you up on their tracking system, but they won't send out an alarm for falling space debris – you would be moving too slow for that. You're just another UFO that no one will report for fear of ridicule."

Parker again leaned over to Max, "No one wants to report an Elvis sighting either."

Merritt turned off the screen, "You will reach the coastline of Lima, at 03:30 Peru time. We expect Leigus will have fighters there to meet you, as he will have discovered our decoy operation by then."

Parker smiled and nudged Max.

Max spoke up, "So, what do we do when we get there? Who's supposed to get this Resonator?"

"Elvis knows what to do. That information is beyond my security level. Now, go get some grub and some sleep. I will see you back here at 1800 hours." He walked them to the door and turned them over to a yeoman, to get them settled in.

The yeoman led them down a long passageway as scores of crew members passed them. Parker looked over to Max, "So, you want to tell me about this Earth Base One?"

"It's down in Peru, near a place called Nazca. Scattered around on the Pampa Colorada are a bunch of drawings and lines that the Nazca Indians etched into the dirt at around 200 BC to about 600 AD. You've probably seen them on TV; a huge spider, hummingbird, monkey . . . images like that. But, the most important things are the lines."

"Lines?"

"They drew lines; incredibly long and straight. A few theories stated that they were 'landing strips' for aliens. Well, in a way they are, but not in the way *we* think of landing strips."

"Is that why they call it Earth Base One?"

"It's Base One actually. There are two important lines there, which intersect, forming a cross. If you follow the one pointing north, it goes straight up to MF-7. The one pointing east will fall right on Ilha de Orango, an island off the coast of Guinea-Bissau. So, if you draw a line from Mf-7 to de Orango, it creates the Northern Ley Line of 3938. Looking at it on a globe map, it's one of seven sectors that the earth is divided into. It has something to do with the seven original Tribes or Councils. They talked about it in one of my classes when I first got into the Program. That stuff is beyond me. It's all mumbo-jumbo, as far as I'm concerned."

Parker tried to envision a globe map, with the seven sectors Max had mentioned. He stopped.

Max looked back, "Hey, what's up?"

"Mumbo-jumbo? Look around you. We're in low earth orbit, in an alien Megadrax, training for a mission to fight anti-gravity robot ships of the Illuminati. And you don't believe in the seven Tribes?"

Max turned and began walking, "Seven Tribes or Eight Reindeer . . . I don't have to believe. As long as they don't shoot at me, we'll all get along nicely."

II

After a tour of the ship and some sleep, they walked back into the briefing room and sat down.

Commander Merritt picked up two helmets off the table and handed them to Max and Parker. "Please put these on."

Max put his helmet on, with a familiarity that only comes from professional repetition. Parker fumbled with his, getting his ears folded over and his cheeks sticking out from the misaligned padding. Max helped him get it right.

Parker could not hear a thing; as a soft white noise filled his head, masking any auditory impulses from his ears. Max dropped the visor and the entire Weapons Control console appeared in front of Parker's eyes. It looked the same as what he had been practicing on with the flight simulator.

"Good morning, Ian Thomas Parker." The voice was everywhere inside the helmet. He turned his head and was looking at a blank wall inside of some large bay area. He looked up and saw a ceiling; a metal grid floor was beneath him.

"What's going on here?" he called out.

Max lifted the visor, "You're the ship's weapons. You see what Elvis perceives, in all directions. I see the same thing, except my console is the pilot's panel."

"OK, I can deal with that . . . but what about the voice?" Parker asked.

"That's Elvis," Commander Merritt answered. "Introduce yourself. He knows all about you, already."

Max dropped Parker's visor.

"Hello?" Parker asked cautiously.

"Hello," Elvis responded.

"I've got to tell you, this is very unnerving for me," Parker said.

"I am a bit anxious, also, Ian."

"Please, just call me Parker. All my friends do."

"Very well . . . Parker. I am sure we shall become fast friends during our upcoming time together."

Parker was feeling very uncomfortable.

Elvis continued, in a voice that could not be distinguished from a real person, "Would you mind if I interfaced so that we could prepare for our missions?"

Parker was *really* feeling uncomfortable now. "Interface? Well, I suppose so . . ."

His head was involuntarily thrown back and his hands grasped the arms on the chair. There was no pain, just a rush of sound and light flooding his brain. It was over in moments.

He sat upright, knuckles turning white. He blinked to clear his vision.

"Please look at the console, Parker," Elvis asked.

Parker looked down to see the familiar readouts and buttons.

"Now, turn on the exahertz scanner."

"How? It's just a display on my visor."

"Just put your hand out and touch it."

Parker reached out for the three-dimensional image that appeared to be two feet away. He could see his arm and hand in his visor – but it was not his real hand. It was a hologram matching his movements. He was able to turn on the scanner in the virtual world in front of him, with his virtual finger.

He wiggled his fingers, "How did you do that? I'm not wearing a glove or anything that connects me to the helmet."

"You are connected to *me* – we are interfaced. In a short time, you will learn to operate the console without even moving your arm. I am your hands. Your brain impulses now work with me. It is the same with Captain Max."

"Well, answer me this, if I take this helmet off, will I need to go through that interface thing again when I put it back on?"

"No, we are one now."

Max's voice filled the helmet, "Parker, everything OK in there?"

"Hey, Max. Yeah. All is just . . . fine."

Max continued, "The ship, *Elvis*, has got me all set up and I'm going over the pre-flight check. If you ask me, they should go back to humans flying these things, not letting some dumbass computer, or whatever it is, take over. You can take off your helmet now. Commander Merritt will take you to the launch bay."

"Is that where you are now?"

"No, I'm in the Pilot Room. They're getting me hooked up in The Chair."

Parker took off the helmet and saw Merritt standing in front of him. "What's a Pilot Room and The Chair?"

"That's where Max will be flying Elvis from."

Parker slumped back in the chair, "He's not going with me?"

Merritt took Parker's helmet and helped him to his feet, "Oh, he will be with you; just not physically."

Parker rubbed his helmet-hair with both hands, "Now this really sucks. I'm going to be in that thing all alone?"

"You won't be alone." The voice came from the back of the room. It was Michael, carrying a helmet, with the third Mu·Suvian configured laptop hanging from his shoulder.

Chapter Thirty-Six

George sat next to Winslow, at the rear of the Nylostra transport ship, in the MF-7 Basement. Colonel Taylor and Jones sat in the seats across from them, in the ten foot wide compartment. It was 6 pm Pacific time. With the slow moving craft they were in, they would meet Gus Stoddard in two hours, 10 pm Central time; just as George had promised.

Winslow was wringing his hands, "You say Stoddard is going to meet us at Airstrip UX7? Are you positive that he will turn over the Resonators to us?"

George leaned back and crossed his arms, "As long as you present him with an acceptable arrangement that will let us all play nice, and approved by Leigus."

Winslow hugged his briefcase, "I have the documents in here. The Stolist will agree to let Mister Stoddard go his way, if he turns over the Resonators and the GMCS control center to us."

George unfolded his arms, "By *us*, I'm assuming you mean The Foundation in general, and not to just Leigus."

"Yes . . . of course," Winslow stuttered.

"I just want Stoddard dead," Taylor spat out.

"My list is longer," Jones added, looking at Winslow, then Taylor.

The lights dimmed and a voice filled the ship, "Uplift in two minutes: Fasten all restraints and standby for pressurization."

There was no sensation of movement as the craft rose off its stanchions and floated down the Basement's stone taxiway, towards the Tube shaft. Within moments, it was streaking through the evening dusk to reach a safe altitude of thirty miles above the desert below. The temperature outside the ship dropped to -130 Fahrenheit as the unseen pilot turned the nose of the Nylostra to a heading of 118 degrees. They silently slid upon the roof of the stratosphere for the next ninety minutes.

Winslow and Jones both took out books from their cases and began reading in the diminished light. Colonel Taylor had leaned back to get some sleep. George opened his notepad and began catching up on his reports.

After an hour, Jones put down his book and looked at George, "I always wanted to ask you this; how far back does your lineage go in The Foundation?"

George put his pen away in his pocket and leaned forward, "Well, my family's association with it began in 1486 with the second Strategos of The Foundation. He was the Aztec leader Ahuitzotl; the greatest known military leader of Pre-Columbian Mesoamerica."

Jones shook his head, "Now *that* is impressive. Most people might be able to dig up stuff on their great-grandparents . . . sometimes."

Winslow had closed his book and began to listen. Taylor pretended to be asleep.

George continued, "I say the second, 'cause the first Strategos was chosen in 1442. The legend still floats around, that is was the Holy Roman Emperor Frederick III. Of course, he wasn't even a close relative. But, *after* him, it was decided that a constantly changing religious influence on the military security of The Foundation would be disastrous; so a warrior-ancestry was to be followed. However; we lost the honor for three centuries, in 1520, when Ahuitzotl died. The Foundation decided that a military leader, trained in 'modern warfare' would be more effective in those times of expansion.

"You must be talking about the Europeans coming over here," Jones said.

George lifted his hat and smoothed his hair back, "Actually, I'm talking about them going everywhere. They called it the New World Conquest. The whole period, from 1520 to 1880, was a disaster for most Native Peoples. It was the fall of the Aztecs and the Spanish kept going north and took over California. Three-quarters of the indigenous population there 'disappeared'. Along with the Expansionist's weapons of destruction they also brought along Old World diseases."

He looked up and held his finger in the air, "I'm sure that's when The Foundation was run by the Leigus-types. They just wanted the land and riches. The United States was established in that period, and there are lots of rumors on who set *that* all up. Plus, the War Between the States and the so-called 'Indian Wars' occurred then, too."

Jones pulled out a cigar from his pocket and unwrapped it, "So, when did your family take over the Strategos position again?"

George leaned back and crossed his legs, "In 1882 the position was handed back to the 'rightful' holders. I'm sure that the High Minister took over control at that point. Things seemed to become more stable. For the record, I am the 13th Strategos of The Foundation. My grandfather was the 12th and his grandfather was the 11th."

"How long do you hold the position? Is there a limit?" Winslow asked, now very much engrossed in the story.

"We take on the position on our 23rd birthday, and hand it to our grandson on our 67th. It's forty-four years, to the day."

Taylor slowly opened his eyes, "You're just about there, old man. Any plans for retirement?" He said with a sly grin.

George smiled back, "I plan on going out in a hail of gunfire. Care to join me?"

Taylor held out his finger, as if it were a gun, and pretended to shoot.

The lights slowly brightened around them as an ethereal voice interrupted the conversation, "We are in final approach to Airstrip UX7. Please remain seated until the departure ramp has been fully deployed." The lights went completely out.

A slight jarring of the compartment, as if they had hit a pothole in the road, signaled their landing. Fresh, humid and hot air flooded the ship as the bulkhead behind them began to open and lower. Taylor was the first to stand and walk down the ramp into the darkness. Jones followed.

George adjusted his hat, "Come on Winslow, time to earn your keep."

He stepped into the night and looked around for any sign of Gus. The Texan's voice came from the right of the ramp. "George! Hey, ol' Buddy. Glad to see you made it in one piece. Who ya' got with you?"

George strained to see into the darkness, "I've brought Colonel Taylor of the ESA, Captain Jones of the Black Shirts and Leigus' representative, a Mister Winslow."

Spotlights burst the calm of the night, flooding the ship and the four passengers with thousands of watts of light. George shaded his eyes and looked around to see the grassy landing area and two military trucks parked fifty yards away. Jungle vegetation outlined the circular clearing. There was no landing strip; it was made for helicopters and Gravity Push craft.

The distorted outline of a man wearing a Stetson cast a long shadow on the grass. It was Gus walking towards the ramp. Three other figures followed him. As they moved closer, George could see that one carried the box which Gus had showed him, containing the Resonators. The other two were armed with machine guns.

George pointed at the oncoming men, "You said 'no weapons'!"

Gus raised his hand, "What kind of host would I be if I didn't provide security for you all? Never know who or what is lurking in these jungles."

"Or what scum comes out of it," Jones whispered to George.

Gus stopped at the foot of the ramp, "So, you got some paperwork for me, such as an agreement between *my* organization and The Foundation?"

Winslow fumbled with his briefcase and pulled out a two-page document. He handed it to George who scanned the contents.

"It appears, Mister Stoddard, that The Foundation would like to offer you a Level Three Director position, in charge of your own operation, to be designated as Global Data Management. This is in exchange for the ten Resonators you are holding and Level Two representation within your organization."

He handed the papers to Gus.

Gus did not look at them; just held the documents to his side.

"Who came up with this pile of manure, Leigus and his crowd? And just who would be these Level Two representatives, Colonel Taylor there and The ESA?"

He lifted the papers and slapped them with his other hand, "And I'm supposed to be jumping around all excited, like a fart in a frying pan, about being a Level Three flunky?" He dropped the documents to the ground. "I think I need to present my case a bit stronger." He signaled to the armed escorts, who pointed their weapons at the four visitors.

"OK, now it seems that I have more bargaining power with Leigus and The Foundation. This is turning out better than I expected. Would you all follow me to your new accommodations?"

.Taylor pointed at Gus, "Just how stupid do you think we are, Stoddard?"

Within two seconds, four Mantas dropped from the darkness overhead and became riveted to the air, 200 feet above Gus and his men. Weapon panels opened. The two guards, with their mouths gapping, lowered their rifles.

Gus grabbed the Resonator case and turned around, "This is bullshit!" He began stomping back to his vehicle, cursing everyone he had ever met.

"Put down the box!" George called to him. "We won't attack if you put down the box!"

Gus dropped the box to the grass and gave it a kick. "Take the damn thing! And get the hell out of here before I order my ground-to-air missiles to blow your asses away!"

"Go get it Jones, we have you covered," George ordered.

Jones reached into his coat and pulled an automatic pistol from the shoulder holster, "No problem."

"How did you get that past the Security Screen in the Basement?" Taylor asked.

"You got the wrong people checking packages coming in from Main Street," Jones replied as he ran to pick up the box.

George called to Gus, "Stay right where you are until we lift off. We will call off the Mantas then."

Jones returned with the box and all four of them moved back into the Nylostra. The ramp closed quickly and the ship rose to 10,000 feet.

"Move to the secondary objective," George called out.

Within moments the ship was hovering over Gus Stoddard's ancient pyramid complex where the GMCS center was housed and the warehouse containing the Beam Generator crate was located.

George looked over at Taylor, "Those weren't Leigus' Mantas, were they?"

Taylor smiled, "A few things have changed, since our talk last night. I know where The Foundation is headed and being connected with Leigus is not the safest position to be in when the Ark arrives."

Two of Taylor's Mantas, that were guarding Gus, appeared from the darkness and lowered to 1,000 feet over the complex. The other two were still on station, weapons trained on Gus and his escorts.

Alarms sounded around the stone fortress as spotlights were turned skyward to illuminate the two ships overhead. Ground fire erupted with tracers streaking towards the hovering intruders.

The undetected Nylostra silently floated to the ground, landing beside the warehouse, with the ramp already deployed as it was descending.

George, Taylor and Jones ran out the back of the ship and straight into the warehouse. Winslow stayed inside the protective hull, hugging the Resonator box.

A guard, standing inside the warehouse entrance, was caught by surprise and was taken out by Jones before he could lift his rifle. Taylor grabbed the weapon.

"Everyone take an aisle; the crate has a yellow band around it – and a red label that says, Lithium Batteries," George called out.

Outside the warehouse was carnage. The Mantas were killing anything that moved and sending cannon fire and rockets into the outbuildings and caves. The GMCS center took a direct hit.

"Over here!" Jones yelled.

George and Taylor ran to where Jones was standing – in front of the yellow-banded wooden crate.

"Now what'll we do?" Taylor asked. "How do we get it out of here?"

George looked around, "Beats me, I didn't think we would even get this far."

Jones pointed down to the back of the warehouse, "A pallet jack!" He ran to get it.

Two rifle shots caused George to drop down in a crouch. He looked behind him to see another guard fall to the floor. Taylor still had his rifle at his shoulder, smoke oozing from the barrel.

"Got a weapon for you now." He ran over and picked up the fallen man's machine gun. He walked back and handed it to George. "Do I have to show you how to use this?"

George smiled, "Which end do I point at the bad guys?"

Taylor smiled back. It was true; your enemy's enemy is your friend.

Jones returned, pulling the pallet jack behind him. The three men loaded the crate onto it and rolled it to the warehouse entrance.

Armed soldiers began pouring out of a cave entrance, fifty yards away. They spotted the Nylostra and the three men stealing one of their crates. Bullets began hitting the stone walls of the warehouse.

"Jones, get the crate to the ship. We'll cover you!" George commanded.

Jones handed his pistol to George, and with a final push, the three got the crate rolling. Jones pulled it out of the warehouse. Winslow ran out to help and the two of them rolled the crate up the ramp and into the Nylostra.

George reached down and grabbed a handful of wet dirt. He smeared two fingers across his face, leaving wavy lines of the black mud. He turned to Taylor and placed his whole hand on the side of the Colonel's face. The imprint of his muddied palm and fingers had instantly transformed the former foe into a trusted ally.

George and Taylor kneeled beside some stone bollards, on either side of the warehouse entrance, and waited for the throng of oncoming soldiers. George reached into his inside coat pocket and took out his feather. He put it into the leather band of his hat. They both began to return fire upon the advancing defenders.

"You may get your death wish, old man," Taylor yelled over to George.

"That's only because you shoot like an old woman!" George called back.

A grenade exploded a few yards to their right. Another erupted near the ramp of the ship.

George turned to face Jones, "Get out of here! Take it to Nazca! We'll meet you there!"

Jones paused for a moment, looking George straight in the eye. He saluted and called out behind him, "Take this ship up!"

The craft began to rise as the ramp swiftly closed. In a final horrify glimpse through the smoke, Jones watched George fall backwards; his feathered hat and weapon tumbling into the dirt. In five seconds the ship was out of sight, into the darkness above.

Chapter Thirty-Seven
The Miracle at Nazca – July 5, 2013

Michael sat up front, Parker behind him, in the two-seater fighter. They watched the glass canopy close around them, which added to their anxiety of waiting for the launch door to open and being thrust into the vacuum of space.

The holographic control panel glowed in front of Parker's eyes, even brighter, as the lights in the launch bay dimmed.

"Well, Parker. This is exciting. I feel very confident that this mission will be highly successful." The voice was Elvis, coming from inside their helmets.

Parker spoke up, "Max, you out there? I sure hope *you* know what you're doing. Elvis is beginning to freak me out."

"Right here, Parker. Everything is fine. I see what you and Michael can see and all of the ship's systems are functioning perfectly."

Michael spoke next, "You have the Resonator back there, Parker?"

"Right here, next to a picture of my motorcycle."

"What about a picture of Tara?" Michael asked.

"Well, I have that, too, but I can't look at it, 'cause Max says he sees what I see. It's a great picture I took the other night, if you know what I mean?"

"Pervert," Michael laughed.

"Stand by Manta Charlie-four." The voice belonged to Commander Merritt at Flight Control. "You have clearance for launch. The long-range scan reports that no debris or other aircraft will enter your vector, for the first leg of your flight path. Good luck."

"Manta Charlie-four, rolling," Elvis replied.

The launch bay lights went out completely as the door opened in front of the ship. The clearest night sky, that Michael had ever seen, appeared before them. The Manta moved forward and out of the Megadrax, as if it was pushed, like a toy boat in bathtub. It floated into 'nothing', thirty miles above the earth.

"Can I have this ship when we're done? This is so cool," Parker whispered.

The nose began to turn, until they were parallel with the Megadrax, only facing to the rear of the huge mother-ship. They began to drop.

"Ok, boys. Course set to 139.8. We're off to Peru," Max informed them.

"Do you consider me 'one of the boys', Max?" Elvis asked.

"Sure . . . what ever. Parker, are you picking up anything on the exahertz scanner?"

"Nope, looks like what Merritt said, clear path ahead. And there's nothing coming in from the West. I don't think Leigus' boys have discovered that Dolly is a decoy, yet."

"OK, we're gonna stay at thirty miles up for about two hours, so you might as well get comfortable. We'll just appear as space junk from the ground tracking stations. When we drop for final approach, over Lima, that's where the fun may begin."

Parker adjusted his seat harness, "Say, Max. Why did you leave Program 2622 anyway? It seems like that would need a man of your skills. Being a Manta pilot and all."

There was a long pause.

"I was going to 'go public' on all this UFO cover-up stuff. Tell the truth on what was really going on . . . our ships, their ships, the Space Force; the whole thing. After I sat around and talked to Reggie, I realized that it was getting too close to the New Era. I was having some real philosophical problems with that. You know, what's going to happen to the average person when all this is dumped on them, all at once. I thought by putting out a little bit of truth, up front, the rest would not be so mind-blowing, as it were."

"I can clearly see your point, Max," Elvis replied.

"I wasn't talking to you, robot. So, anyway, the grownups got a hold of me and gave me a choice: work with the ESA and never say another word, or be sent to an 'outpost'. I suppose there was a third, but I didn't press it."

Parker spoke up, "Man, I would probably do the same thing. I mean, if we ever get out of this mess, I may go on the lecture circuit. Tell everything."

Michael broke in, "After we complete this mission, the whole world will know anyway, Parker. The time for dishing out small bits of information is over. It's gonna be a huge awaking, for all mankind."

"And it should be very enlightening and comforting to all," Elvis added.

"Have you ever been assigned to a refuse detail on the dark side of the moon, Elvis?" Max asked.

"No, Max. That would be very depressing. There would be no one to talk to."

"Well, we would appreciate that your comments be related to mission reports only. No editorials."

"Elvis, this is Michael. Is there a device, which was installed within your communications area, which you have never used?"

"Yes, Michael. It is a particle transceiver. It was part of the equipment which the Mu·Suvians provided to my builders. But, it has never been activated. I think of it, the same way you relate to your appendix. The real function is unknown, but there was no reason to take it out . . . unless it attempts to terminate me."

Michael reached down for the laptop. "Well, we are going to get it functioning. And don't worry, it will not 'terminate' you."

Within ten minutes, Michael had the activation program showing on his computer.

"Elvis, I am going to play some audio, off my laptop. I want you to listen to it and pipe it into the particle transceiver. Understood?"

"Yes, Michael, I am ready."

Michael started the 'Song of Inanna' program. The tones filled the ship as a small red indicator light appeared on his visor.

"I believe the device has been activated, Michael," Elvis informed him.

Michael filled in the boxes on the laptop display. He entered 73D5 and typed *'I Love you. I am with Parker and we are fine.'* He hit the enter key.

He waited.

The bottom panel displayed, *'Message from: 73D5: I miss you so much! Citi and I are glad you both are OK. All is well here. Come back soon. Happy 4th of July. I Love you, too.'*

Michael sat back and read the message again, "Hey, Parker. You know it's the 4th of July?"

"Wasn't there a movie or something about that, a while ago, with aliens and stuff?" Parker asked.

"Welcome to reality, my friend," Max answered.

Michael put in address 84A6 and typed, 'Roland, got a new address, write it down. Everything OK there?' He sent the message.

He waited again.

The bottom panel again displayed a response, *'Message from: 84A6: All is well. FYI your address is 16F4. Raining here again . . . I miss the desert.'*

Michael smiled and spoke to Parker, "Remember when we talked about parallel universe stuff?"

"You mean telling yourself something that has happened, before it happens? Yeah, I do. And my brain still hurts from thinking about it."

"Well, we may experience it, first hand, in a couple hours. Max, when I tell you to perform a maneuver, do not question it. Understand?"

"Yes, sir," Max replied.

"That goes the same for you, Elvis."

"I will comply, Stolist Fields."

"What about me, your Most Greatness?" Parker asked.

"You just keep us safe, in both universes."

The next hour passed swiftly, as Michael and Parker were awed at the sights around and below them. They floated along, pointing out landmarks to each other and seeing more stars than either thought existed.

Max had been silent the whole time . . . until his voice indicated that they were going down, "Keep your eyes peeled, Parker. We're dropping down to ten miles over Lima, Peru, where we'll adjust to a heading of 132.4. We'll be vulnerable for attack from now on."

"I'm on it, Max."

Michael opened his laptop cover and entered a thirty second time dilation. The bottom panel immediately displayed: '*Message from: 16F4: Testing.*'

He type *Testing* in the panel and sent it to himself. All was set.

The Manta dropped swiftly, as planned, and maintained a ground speed of 2,000 mile per hour. They had 230 miles to go.

Parker's panel began blinking as three dots appeared; 166 miles away at 35.6 degrees. They were moving in at 1,200 miles per hour.

"We got company, Max!" Parker reported.

Michael looked down at his laptop screen and waited.

The panel displayed: '*Message from: 16F4: Heading 117 – 20 miles up.*'

Michael called out the commands, "Heading 117, go up to twenty miles."

The ship immediately shot upward. There was no G-force experienced, due to the Push Gravity of the craft.

"Can you get a lock on them, Parker?" Max asked.

"No, they're moving around too fast. I mean . . . it's impossible."

The panel displayed: '*Message from: 16F4: Heading 134 – drop to 10,000 feet and stop.*'

Michael repeated the message out loud and watched the ground come rushing up. They stood in the air as Michael waited for the next message.

Parker reported again, "Still the same thing, I can't lock on 'em."

The panel displayed: '*Message from: 16F4: We are hit – on fire - going down - from 231 . . . use Elvis*'

Michael read the message in horror. "Parker! Look to 231!"

Parker turned his head to the heading Michael had called out. Another Manta had been sitting on the ground and was just rising over the ridge – it fired a missile.

"Incoming!" Parker called out.

"Take over Elvis!" Michael ordered.

Instantly, the voice of the ship became lower, "Lock and load, Parker." The craft rose straight up -- five miles in two seconds. It then made a 90 degree turn to the right for two miles and stopped in mid-air.

The missile had given up trying to track the ship and sped off over the ocean.

Parker had *his* missiles locked onto three of the human-piloted aggressors who had also stopped in mid-air to try and find Elvis. Parker launched three missiles.

Elvis instantly dropped to a few yards off the ground and waited for prey. "Catch me, if you can . . . humans."

The billon dollar fireballs, from the three destroyed Mantas, filled the dim sky as no other 4th of July fireworks display could ever match.

Parker's eyes moved quickly across the scanner screen.

"Talk to me Parker," Elvis said.

"Hang on, I can't find . . . OK, got 'em. But, he's too far out to hit and moving north."

"Don't let him get away!" Max broke in. "He'll bring back more."

"Too late!" Parker reported. "Three more blips coming in from 338 . . ." He stopped. "Wait a minute!"

"I am receiving transponder codes from the incoming ships," Elvis said. "They are attached to Colonel Taylor's Wing from MF-7. There are two Mantas and a Nylostra. They are bringing the crate."

A fireball could be seen, far off in the northern sky.

"They got him," Parker said slowly.

Parker leaned back in his seat, "Well, what do you think of that?"

Elvis again spoke up, "Oh, I just wanted to say sorry about the 'human' thing."

Max replied, "And I want to apologize for my *dumb-ass computer* remark . . . Elvis. You're now officially -- *one of the boys*."

Parker blinked to clear his thinking, "Hey, Michael. Weren't we killed a few minutes ago?"

"In that other universe, Parker."

"Well, didn't you send yourself those messages?"

"I would have, if it were *this* Michael Fields. But, the Michael Fields sending me the messages was dead before I got them. So, I didn't send out anything to the present me."

"Oh, crap. My head hurts again," Parker replied.

"Take us to the landing spot, Max. You have the controls," Michael ordered.

They followed the Nylostra to a five by six mile flat plane of sandy desert, which had been inscribed with two, four mile long, straight lines. One placed to point straight up to MF-7, the other pointing east; to Ilha de Orango in Guinea-Bissau. All four ships landed at the intersection of the cross.

Michael and Parker quickly climbed out of Elvis and ran over to the Nylostra, as the ramp was being lowered. Jones walked down to meet them.

"You got the crate from Gus? Did he complain much?" Michael asked, all out of breath.

Jones shook his head, "He didn't know what hit him."

Parker looked into the compartment, "Who's with you?"

Jones turned around and pointed, "Winslow."

"That's it?" asked Michael. "George didn't come with you?"

Jones looked down, "We had to leave him at Gus' warehouse. He and Colonel Taylor were holding off Stoddard's men so we could get away with the crate."

Michael and Parker looked at each other, nether could say anything.

"I don't think you have to worry about Gus, the GMCS control center or any more of Leigus' troops getting in the way again." He walked up the ramp. "So, where do you want this thing?"

Michael pointed at the intersection, still reeling at the thought of George being left behind, "Somewhere over there, I suppose."

Parker went up the ramp to help pull out the crate, which was still sitting on the pallet jack. The two Manta pilots walked up to Michael and saluted, "Lieutenants Morris and Rico, Sir. Anything we can do, Stolist?"

Michael turned around, "You two have done enough for now. Thanks for taking out that last Manta and escorting the Nylostra down here."

"Just following Colonel Taylor's orders. It seems that his support had shifted to you and away from Leigus, for some reason." Lieutenant Rico pulled a sheet of paper from his flight jacket.

"I was told to give this to you, Sir; if we ever managed to all meet up. Each of the pilots in Colonel Taylors's squadron, are carrying the same paper, just to make sure you would receive it."

It was a listing of all the satellites and their access codes, which were to pass over Nazca Base One, in the next ninety-six hours. Michael looked at his watch. "What time is it here?"

Lieutenant Rico looked at his own watch, "It's now 04:45. It is the same as Eastern in the U.S. Two hours ahead of MF-7."

Michael scanned the satellite data on the paper with his finger. "There's one coming over in twenty-eight minutes. We need to get this set up."

The Beam Generator was positioned in the middle of the cross and everyone helped to remove the wooden crate that contained it. Michael unloaded the satellite uplink equipment from Elvis, which he had used to start up the last generator. Parker helped him set it up. He then connected his laptop to the controller.

Michael sat on the ground, accessing the Generators code from his list of crates. "I think we're ready. We have nine minutes to go. Put in the Resonator, Parker. Crystal side down."

Parker placed the stone onto the flat portion of the globes top.

A loud siren echoed across the valley floor.

"What did I do?" Parker exclaimed, running back to Michael.

"You didn't do anything. The sound's coming from Elvis."

They all hurried over to the small attack ship

"What's with the siren?" Parker asked.

"There are seven of Leigus' attack fighters on their way here from the Area. I picked them up on Parker's long range scanner. I think three of them are Mantas. The other four are jet aircraft. I have notified Max. He is standing by," Elvis reported.

"Time to scramble, boys," Parker commanded, as he began climbing back into Elvis. The two other pilots ran back to their ships.

"Where are *you* going?" Michael said, grabbing Parkers arm.

Parker looked back, "Hey, you get that generator thing going. Jones and Winslow can help you. Max, Elvis and I have to cover your butt." He pulled away from Michael's grip and seated himself in the back seat.

Michael leaned into the cockpit, "Have you gone completely insane? Seven against three . . . it's suicide!"

Parker put on his helmet and lifted the visor, "Ya gotta love them odds. Guess I've been hanging around George too long."

The canopy closed as he brought down his visor. With a 'thumbs up' he rose into the sky on his robotic war pony.

Michael stood on the hard ground and watched his best friend ascend. He prayed that he would see him again. But he knew the odds. His heart was sinking as he looked at his watch . . . five minutes until the Beam activation satellite would be within range.

Jones ran up to Michael, "What do you want us to do, Boss?"

"Tell the Nylostra pilot to head south; at least twenty miles. Winslow can go with it, as far as I'm concerned. I'll need you to sit beside me and call out the time. You have any LiquiCode tattoos?"

Jones held up his hands, "Nope, they didn't want me in their club."

"Good, then you won't have any discomfort when the Beam turns on. Now, get that ship out of here."

Jones rushed to the ship. Within moments, the ramp was being raised as the Nylostra left the cold, barren ground. It streaked off to the south, in an instant.

Jones joined Michael at the laptop and uplink equipment.

"Now what?" he asked, sitting down on the grey dirt.

"We wait. Let me know when it's 5:13, exactly."

High over head, and fifty miles north, Parker, Elvis and the two other Mantas sat suspended in the Peruvian sky . . . waiting for Leigus' fighters.

Michael and Jones sat on the cold desert sand in front of the laptop. Idle talk kept their minds off of the air battle that was happening far behind them.

"Do you think George and Taylor held out?" Michael asked.

"I'm not sure. I saw George go down. Taylor was still fighting. It didn't look good," Jones replied, checking the time on his watch.

"If George dies, who will take his place? I mean, he didn't have any children, much less a grandson to pass The Strategos position on to," Michael wondered.

"I suppose the High Council will determine that," Jones guessed.

The soft glow of the display showed that Michael's finger was positioned over the 'Send' key. Jones began to call out the time.

"Twenty seconds. Ten seconds. Now!"

Michael closed his eyes and sent the activation codes into space, hoping all the streaming data was correct.

The Beam Generator sprang to life; its swirling radiant colors ripped out of the globes center and were sent dancing across the arid plateau. The intensity grew as the swelling spectrum twisted into itself, turning the grayscale valley into a surrealistic landscape of florescent violet.

Michael's tattoos burned as never before as he watched the laptop screen turn black and shut down. Jones had both of his hands pressed to his face, covering his eyes.

In a final burst of unheard resonance, the energy phased into a single vector beam and shot into the night sky.

All was quiet for five seconds; before grains of sand and gravel around Michael and Jones began to vibrate, as would drops of water on a hot greasy skillet.

A small mound of dirt, resembling an emerging gopher, appeared twenty yards in front of them. Then another pushed up to their right, thirty yards away. Out of the first appeared a red glowing tube, sliding up to three feet above the hard valley surface. The crimson light provided an astonishing view around them. More tubes were appearing, perhaps thirty in all, forming the outline of a rectangle over a half-mile long and four-hundred feet wide.

They both stood up and turned in circles, watching the tubes perform a variety of sequential patterns, not unlike a theater marquee.

"What in the hell's going on?" Jones asked.

"The generator has activated these things. I bet they've been buried here for centuries, waiting to 'wake up'," Michael guessed.

"Waiting for what?"

Michael slowly looked up, "I think we're about to find out."

It was a cylindrical-shaped object. And it appeared to be made of a silvery metal, not like the Megadrax black covering. It began to descend directly over the intersection of the lines carved into the desert floor. It slowly aligned perfectly with the glowing tubes below it. The craft was as long as the half-mile stretch of 'landing lights' which were guided it down.

From out of the northern blackness appeared three of Leigus' fighters, cannons blazing at the colossal ship. Michael's stomach tightened up. They must have escaped from Parker and the others. *Was Parker still alive?*

Jones grabbed Michael's arm and pulled him along, away from the Beam Generator and the glaring red tubes, "Get out of the light."

"There's no place to take cover, what's the difference?" Michael responded, pulling his arm free from Jones' grip.

The fighters were making strafing runs above the ship so that it could not ascend. The metal skin was not showing any sign of damage, but a fighter colliding with it would be disastrous. The Ark stopped its decent at 2,000 feet and was turning for an escape.

Michael strained to make mental contact with whom or whatever was on the ship. His mind was blank.

One of the fighters moved to the east, passing directly over Michael and Jones. It was a Manta. The other two were conventional jets, slow moving and taking longer to make their turns.

"It spotted us," Jones said, falling flat to the ground.

Michael looked around, "We can't turn the generator off and on to bring it down. It would affect that ship, too."

"Then we're toast," Jones called up from the ground. His ever present cigar stub was now lying in the sand, a foot away.

The Manta was rotating towards them.

A blinding streak filled the night sky from the east. Another came in from the north. Two missiles, two kills. The Manta above Michael disintegrated in mid-air. One of the jet fighters 'augured in' with its' tail pipe flaming, at the edge of the valley to the south. There was no parachute.

Two Mantas appeared from the east, three more from the north. The remaining jet veered to the west and went to super-sonic. One of incoming ships from the east followed the retreating Leigus jet. A fireball was visible over the western ridge. The Manta returned. The jet did not.

The Ark returned to its original landing orientation and continued its' decent.

Jones got to his feet as the five ships lowered to the valley floor. He reached down and picked up his cigar butt and shoved it back into the corner of his mouth. Michael watched the gigantic cylindrical craft finish its decent, stopping six-feet off the ground. Three staircases began to deploy from the front, back and middle of the Extraterrestrial Ark.

Canopies began to open on each of the small fighters that had landed.

A familiar voice emanated from the nearest one, "Hey, now you owe me a whole *case* of beer!" It was Parker, removing his helmet.

"Hell, I'll buy you a whole bar!" Michael called back, trembling over the events of past few minutes, and at seeing Parker still breathing.

Jones looked over to see Colonel Taylor rising from the back seat of the second ship. He jogged over to him, "Man, I hate to say this, but I am *really* glad to see you."

Taylor looked at him, "Got another cigar?"

Jones smiled and reached into his coat. He pulled one out and handed it up to him.

"You might want to think about trading in that uniform for one of ours," Jones said, gesturing at the ESA jacket Taylor was wearing.

"Same work, different clothes," Taylor replied, biting off the end of the cigar.

Taylor pointed it at the furthest parked Manta, "We all need to get over to that ship." Jones helped him out and waved to Michael to follow.

The canopy finished opening all the way on the farthest Manta as everyone crowded around it.

"George!" Michael exclaimed, looking into the cockpit and seeing the old man's hands gripping the sides of the seat.

Jones and Michael took the helmet off George and helped him out of the enclosure. There was blood all over the seat and Michaels' coat. George had been wounded in two spots, from what they could see in the eerier red light that surrounded them; upper right leg and left shoulder.

Parker ran up to the old man lying on the ground, "He was yelling into the radio, a while back; calling out orders like he always does. He commanded the whole battle. Is he gonna make it?" He looked down at the prone man, "George! Are you alive?"

George opened his eyes, "For crying out loud, Parker, you don't have to shout. I'm only a couple feet away. You want me to get a headache, too?" He smiled at the faces looking down at him.

Taylor moved in and knelt down. He had brought a first-aid kit from his ship. "You're supposed to *dodge* the bullets, not catch them."

George reached up with his right hand and put it on Taylor's shoulder, "They were only aiming at the important one." The two warriors exchanged a look and smile, which only old soldiers could understand.

Michael jolted upright as a voice filled his head, *"Stolist Fields. We are pleased that you have managed to bring in the*

New Era. Your companions deserve the highest tributes we can bestow for providing for our safety."

Michael began talking, "We welcome you. Our planet has longed for your arrival. The Fifth World can now begin. Please let me know if there is anything we can do for you."

The voice continued, *"It is our turn to help you."*

Michael turned to see five uniformed figures running towards them, from the silver ship. One of them carried a stretcher. As they moved closer, their masked faces could be seen in the red glow of the landing lights. They wore the same masks that Michael had seen on the Council members.

The group around George stepped back as the white-gloved crewmen lifted the wounded warrior onto the stretcher and quickly carried back him to the ship. As they passed, Parker placed George's hat on his chest. His feather was still in the hat band.

"Strategos Black Rock shall recover. His wounds are not a threat to his life. We now invite you and your companions, to come aboard. There is much to discuss."

"We shall be honored," Michael replied.

Parker was standing next to Jones and put his hand on Michael's shoulder, "Have you finally gone over the edge? Who are you talking to; me or Jones?"

"To them," he pointed at the ship.

He stood and looked at the faces in front of him: Parker, Colonel Taylor, Lieutenants Morris and Rico and the two pilots that had flown down from Gus' place with George and Taylor.

"OK, everyone on your best behavior; we have been invited into their ship."

"What about me?" a voice called from behind.

Michael looked behind him, "Is that you, Elvis?"

"Yes, Michael. I hope I have satisfied all of the mission requirements."

"Hey, Robo-jock, don't hog *all* the credit." It was Max on the intercom.

CONTINUANCE

Michael spoke up, "You both will receive the highest recommendations of The Foundation. It was a job well done."

Michael turned to his team with his eyes now glowing a full yellow, "Well, gentlemen. Let's get this civilization back on track, shall we?"

They walked to the mammoth transport ship which had now safely brought the next wave of Mu·Suvians to aid in the next phase of human development; the teachers, the physicians and the scientists.

The group walked between two rows of masked crew members; all smartly dressed in their best white uniforms and all standing at attention. As Parker reached the top of the staircase, he turned back to see Elvis. The tiny ship blinked its lights twice as Parker *finally* performed a perfect salute.

Chapter Thirty-Eight
The New Era

The next three months were the most exciting weeks the peoples of earth that had experienced in over 6,000 years.

The world-wide announcement of the Mu·Suvians' return, and the full disclosure of the truth about the existence of extraterrestrial life, did not overwhelm the inhabitants of earth as was prophesized. The truth was always suspected and yearned for. We were not alone.

Of course, a lot of carefully worded amendments were added to a few select books, which a number of religious organizations had been distributing around for a few centuries.

Plans were provided by the Mu·Suvians and construction began on 1,500 massive Beam Generation stations. Each one capable of providing twelve megawatt hours of clean electrical power, per year, to every one of the 207 nations on earth.

Nor did the offerings, from the Mu·Suvians end there. Cures for a multitude of cancers and most major diseases were introduced to the medical world. Advanced technologies and programs to improve agriculture, transportation, financial and resource management were generously provided.

And the most treasured gift of all, for an over-populated, stagnant earth; a joint venture into the colonization and re-generation of Mars was initiated. Not only would this provide work for half the world's population, in building the components and constant supplies required for the 200 year project, it fulfilled the human need for exploration, discovery and taming of new frontiers.

Wars still raged, between a number of quarreling governments and weapons were still being produced. But, the Mu·Suvians only took it in stride. It is just the way we are – humans will never change. At least earth would not be allowed to blow itself into oblivion now. The New Foundation would see to that.

Leigus had been driven out of The Foundation within two weeks of the Mu·Suvian landing at Nazca. He had been exiled to his home in the Alps and was under house arrest. His health was failing and he had no visitors. No one cared.

Michael had 'unofficially' taken over the role of *Stolist of The Foundation*. He and Elizabeth were now living in a house, overlooking Santa Cruz. On a clear day they could see far below to Parker's pastel-colored beach bungalow. He and Tara now lived there; after they flew down in Elvis to elope in Vega. It was reported that Vern had bought an entire casino and the couple were given the whole top floor for their honeymoon and ensuing parties. Every Shadow was invited. No doubt the insurance covered the damages.

The Mushroom Farms were reactivated, some to serve as training facilities for the Mars colonization project – as the environments were identical. This was proven by the success of the moon-based Mushroom Farm . . . (this outpost is *still* a secret).

Reggie and Roland took up permanent residence in MF-7, taking over the Level 3 Science Lab.

Max was promoted to major and was serving as Wing Commander with General Taylor's Space Security Command.

Jones was promoted to a Black Shirt Colonel, taking over security at every Mushroom Farm on the planet and eliminating any remnants of the ESA which still remained.

George and Martin returned to the Squatters cabin, where the old warrior recovered from his wounds. A day did not go by where there was not a house full of visitors; cleaning, cooking and papering. They both were getting used to the 'good life'.

Inanna took her place in the universe, aboard The Second Moon, on September 12, 2013. The ship was resting at 118,837 mile above the Earth, exactly half-way to the Moon. Both heavenly bodies smiled onto each side of the ship as she took her first breath.

Her godmother, Citi Chén, began spoiling her within two weeks.

A new path for the human race to follow had been created; to once again, take on their roles of explorers, farmers and settlers of new lands.

The human race had become the official Guardians of the Mu·Suvians. For one of the first times, in the history of Mankind's evolution, all the peoples of the world felt as one. They were the new neighbors in the Universe, down a lonely side street in The Milky Way. Their home is a brilliant blue with white clouds adorning the roof. And the mailbox now proudly displays – *The Family of Man*.

EPILOGUE

Realignment of The Foundation
College of Minds – Edinburgh, UK
October 14, 2013

Over two-thousand people, representing every race of humanity, filled the ancient hall. Nineteen hooded figures sat behind a long, sweeping bench which formed a raised crescent against the far curtained wall. Nine wore blue robes, six were draped in red and three wore white. It was known, by the assemblage, that seven of the presiding 'judges' were members of The Foundation. The other twelve, who were wearing masks, were *representatives* of Level One.

The only purple-robed judge, a mask-less man with a silver white beard, slowly rose from the chair which sat at the center of the long bench. He looked around at the two-thousand faces in front of him. The other robed figures remained seated; nine on either side of him. He picked up a gavel and struck it twice on a thick flat stone. As the echo faded, it became the only sound present in the vast room.

He picked up a heavy leather-bound book off the bench top and opened it to a page that was marked with a red satin ribbon. After adjusting his glasses and stoking the beard, he began to speak in a commanding voice that carried to the back of the room.

"Be it known, throughout The Foundation, a GenZ has been chosen to perform the duties of Stolist of Level Two. Michael Scott Fields, come forward from the secrets of darkness and be seen."

Michael stood, looking straight ahead.

"Be it known, throughout The Foundation, a warrior has been chosen to apprentice under The Strategos of The Americas, George 'Black Rock' Day, to provide stability for *both* branches of Level Two in that region; for generations to come. Ian Thomas Parker, come forward from the secrets of darkness and be seen."

Parker stood, but looked around the room, pointing at familiar faces and smiling like a talk-show host.

"The existing Strategos, of the six other Tribes and Lodges present today, will continue in their established lines of succession."

The old judge closed the book and placed it on the bench. He took off his glasses and spoke in a softer, kindly voice.

"Be it known, throughout The Foundation, a GenOne has been chosen to apprentice under The High Minister of Level Two, Citi Chén, to *eventually* perform the duties of The High Minister of Level Two; for generations to come. Inanna Redding Fields, come forward from the secrets of darkness and be seen."

Elizabeth stood, holding the one-month-old Inanna.

Together, they walked to the platform in front of the bench. They turned to face the assemblage.

The purple-robed judge raised both his hands and called out to the far reaches of the realms, "The Realignment of the New Foundation has been completed. We are adjourned."

He stuck the stone with the gavel once more. All nineteen judges stood and began to slowly file out of the room.

The first to rise in the audience and applaud was George, who was seated in the front row with Martin sitting upright at his feet. Citi then rose and begin to applaud, slowly at first, then as fast as her frail hands could move. Next to stand were Tara, Max, Reggie, Vern, Roland, Jones and General Taylor. They were followed by the roar of applause and cheers from the two-thousand members of The Foundation in the room . . . then silently, the Universe held its breath for what was to come.

END

CONTINUANCE

"There are a lot of smiling faces in the Mu·Suvian community over that. OK, I don't think they can smile. But, a new hope has risen among them."

High Minister Citi Chén (July, 2013)

About The Author

j. Newcombe Hodges has been writing 'probable fiction' for over fifteen years, under the names of A.J. Fuller and Hamilton Greysun; developed over seventeen audio books and produced *The Radio Theater Hour*. He has now delved deep into his vast experience and contacts, to bring out his fifth and most revealing novel: CONTINUANCE.

As one of the foremost leaders in the development and integration of new technology and innovations for decades, he has become a pioneer in the world of Automatic Identification and Horizon Technologies.

Mr. Hodges speaks monthly at industry conferences around the U.S. and appears frequently on radio and television programs; focusing on present and future technology's impact upon the world's future.

Hodges is a Senior Scientist of Advanced Technologies, working closely with the U.S. Department of Defense, implementing cutting-edge technology.

Proof

Made in the USA